Also by Cathy Perkins

The Professor

Honor Code

Cypher

So About the Money

the Money

CATHY PERKINS

ISBN - 10: 1-942003-03-X
ISBN – 13: 978-1-942003-03-8

Edited by Nina Bruhns
Cover by Gwen Phifer Campbell Cook

Red Mountain Publishing

Dedication

Beth -
This one is for you.

So About the Money

When Holly Price trips over a friend's dead body while hiking, her life takes a nosedive into a world of intrigue and danger. The verdict is murder—and Holly is the prime suspect. Of course, it doesn't help matters that the infinitely sexy—and very pissed off—cop threatening to arrest her is JC Dimitrak, her jilted ex-fiancé.

To protect her future, her business...and her heart...the intrepid forensic accountant must use all her considerable investigative skills to follow the money through an intricate web of shadow companies, while staying one step ahead of her ex-fiancé. She better solve the case before the real killer decides CPA stands for Certified Pain in the Ass...and the next dead body found beside the river is Holly's.

Cathy Perkins is one of those authors whose talent you spot immediately and latch onto as she becomes one of your must-reads. Her Holly and JC are fun (and hot) in *So About the Money* and you'll not only laugh and enjoy the ride, you'll be looking Perkins up to see what else she has out right now.

~ Toni McGee Causey, bestselling author of the Bobbie Faye series

"...an entertaining read, filled with funny snappy dialogue."
~ RT Review

CPA Holly Price juggles dodgy clients, flakey parent, ex-lovers and a murdered friend before she gets to the bottom line in this fast and fun read.

~ Patricia Smiley, bestselling author of Cool Cache

So About
the Money

CATHY PERKINS

Chapter One

Big Flats, eastern Washington

Holly Price picked the wrong moment to admire the Snake River. She managed a quick glimpse of blue water rushing between barren black cliffs before she tripped and staggered off the narrow trail.

Alex Montoya glanced back. "You okay?"

"Yeah." Her hiking boot caught another of the rocks littering the sagebrush-studded plateau. Arms windmilling, she fought to stay on her feet. *Don't face plant. Do. Not. Face plant.*

She stumbled through a clump of tall grass and a pheasant burst out the other side.

"Rooster!" Alex snapped his shotgun against his shoulder, pivoting to track the bird.

The pheasant struggled into the air with a flurry of feathers. A handful of pellets dropped as it made a break for freedom. Who knew "scare the crap out of you" could be literal, was Holly's next thought—and probably the bird's last.

Two seconds later, a head-rocking blast hit Holly's ears and the pheasant tumbled from the sky.

"Damn."

"Did you miss?" She tried to suppress the hopeful note.

CATHY PERKINS

"I winged him. Find him, Duke."

The German shorthair raced ahead, intent on the falling bird.

"It's alive?" She gave the rocky field a dubious inspection—not many places for an injured bird to hide.

"Don't worry." Her date tossed the words over his shoulder. He jogged to the edge of the cliff. "Duke'll find him."

Holly's shoulders sagged. "Great."

She followed Alex, but stopped a cautious two feet from the dropoff. Below her, Alex scrambled toward the mushiest patch of ground she'd seen since moving back to godforsaken eastern Washington. "Why are we going down there?"

"That's where the bird went." His teeth gleamed against his tanned skin. "Stay close."

Feet sliding on the rocky soil, he charged after his bird dog and vanished into the tangled foliage lining the Snake River.

Well, damn.

When he'd invited her to Big Flats, she'd heard "hike," while he meant "hunt." Given the glorious fall day—sunshine and a blue sky that went on forever—she'd expected another picnic. Two weeks ago, Alex had taken her to a mountain meadow. A sandwich and a bottle of wine later, they'd kissed like teenagers and she'd thought about throwing both caution and her clothes to the wind.

Today, he'd morphed into some kind of Neanderthal maniac—me mighty hunter, you Jane. It was a mixed metaphor, but a slow burn started in her belly. She'd tried to be a good sport, but this was ridiculous.

She checked the land behind her—a dry plain dotted with stunted sagebrush, cheatgrass, and jumbled rocks—as if a giant "exit here" sign might appear.

No such luck.

She could probably find the parking lot.

Maybe.

Ditching Alex held a huge appeal, but the thought of quitting chaffed as badly as the grit in her boot.

Alrighty.

Hands spread for balance, she eased down the goat trail to the boggy tract. She dodged some blackberry canes and stepped onto a line of broken reeds that marked the path through the underbrush.

Alex had been so proud of the first rooster he'd shot that morning. He'd held it out, expecting praise the way her mother's cat, Fonzie, did when he laid something brown, furry, and dead at her feet. All Holly had seen was the beauty of the mottled breast feathers, the brilliant bands of neck color, and the lifeless flop of the pheasant's head.

She sighed, resigned. Chasing birds and shooting at them didn't even register on her Fun Things To Do list. She and Alex really didn't have much in common. Maybe she shouldn't keep dating him.

Even if he was fun.

When he wasn't playing with guns.

She shoved further into the thicket and followed the faint trail of bent stalks. Getting lost was so not on her agenda. She never had trouble with directions in the city, but out here she couldn't tell one bush from another.

The trail split, the narrow ribbons churned to muck by hunters' boots. She glanced behind her. She didn't have any breadcrumbs to mark the way back to the cliff.

"Alex?"

Only vague thrashing sounds answered her.

Okay, she could figure this out. The left-hand side looked slightly more trampled, so she pushed past the leaning cattails. Willows, canes, and some kind of bushes towered overhead, crowding the boggy track. Soft mud sucked at her boots. The air stank of rotting vegetation and gulls squabbled in the distance. A dozen yards later, the trail divided again.

She peered forward and behind. "Alex," she called, louder this time. "Where are you?"

She might be the commitment-phobe in this relationship, but surely Alex wouldn't leave her out here. Everywhere she looked, dangling leaves and dried canes blocked her path. The sharp staccato of a dog's excited bark broke the silence. Duke—ahead and to the right. The dog must have found the wounded pheasant.

She edged past a mushy spot. A harsher tang that reminded her of the dead fish they'd passed earlier grew stronger with each step. Nose covered with her hand, she rehearsed choice phrases to unleash on Alex when she finally found him, starting with a sarcastic, "Thanks for your concern," before descending rapidly to "asshole."

Something big rustled in the dense undergrowth behind her. Heart pounding, she spun around and peered into the thicket. They had coyotes out here. And drug grower/dealer guys. The only person they'd seen between the gravel parking area and this jungle was an Aryan Nation skinhead dude. Her heart stutter stepped. Oh, crap. What if this was his territory?

The noise from something plunging through the brush grew louder, closer. Blindly, she turned and crashed through the tangled foliage.

The rushes ended at a mound of dirt. She staggered into the clearing, her gaze zeroing in on Alex. Leaning over something on the ground, he tugged at Duke's collar. The dog struggled, twisting his body in a muscular objection.

"Alex. Thank God." Her knees felt weaker than she wanted to admit. "I heard something in the bushes back there."

"Probably a deer. Stay back." He wrestled the dog to the side. His brusque tone shattered her mini-panic.

Well, don't I feel silly.

A quick glance around registered the details. A drooping cottonwood canopied the clearing. Sunlit water lapped at the muddy shore. Gulls whirled overhead in a protesting flurry, lingering in a swirling complaint of dirty white feathers. The clearing looked like a teenagers' party spot. Tattered food wrappers and empty beer bottles littered the ground. Filthy, torn clothing formed a soggy heap at the water's edge.

The wind gusted off the inlet, carrying a stench across the clearing.

"Phew." As bad as it smelled, she wondered if a dead fish was caught in the trash. A few birds remained near the river, their wings raised high, voices screeching defiance.

The pile of clothes had female-shaped contours. Eyes narrowed, Holly gave it a closer look. A pale, mud-streaked foot extended toward her. "Is that a woman?"

She moved closer, curiosity overriding her earlier fear. "Is she drunk?"

"Don't come over here." Alex clipped a short leash to Duke's collar.

Harsh, abrupt. He'd never spoken to her like that before. A hint of unease coiled around her chest. She took in his grim expression. "What's wrong?"

One of the gulls lunged. It stabbed through the matted hair screening the woman's face and pecked at a glittering object.

"Stop it." Holly rushed forward, flinging out her arms. "Leave her alone!"

The birds scrambled away.

Alex grabbed her arm. "Don't."

Tugging against his restraint, she took another step, then gagged as the condition of the woman's body registered. Unnatural stillness. Carrion birds. Waterlogged, rotting skin.

Missing parts.

Not drunk.

Dead.

"Oh my God." She backed away. Bile crept up her throat.

Focus on something, anything except the body.

Unable to look away, the golden shape at the woman's throat caught Holly's attention—a pair of hearts, a large diamond at the juncture. Recognition rippled a chill through her that had nothing to do with the wind. She immediately rejected the possibility— dozens of people could own a necklace like that.

The breeze ruffled the corpse's dark hair and revealed more of the ravaged face. Memory replaced the dead woman's missing features. Laughing eyes filled empty sockets. Rosebud lips covered gaping teeth.

Holly's head acknowledged what her heart already knew. The necklace was a custom piece—and she'd seen it a dozen times.

"It's Marcy."

A roaring started in her ears and her breakfast splattered her boots.

~$~

Cars, people, and a confusion of lights and sounds crowded the potholed parking lot. Holly stared at the groups of men and let the swamp of radio chatter, static, car engines, and voices form a protective barrier against too much reality. The men's uniforms varied—she identified sheriff's deputies, game wardens, search and rescue, highway patrol, and emergency medical techs—but the super-charged testosterone was everywhere. The murder of a young woman, especially a beautiful young woman like Marcy, had brought law enforcement out in droves.

Holly closed her eyes and hitched the blanket around her

shoulders. If she wasn't so freaked out about Marcy, being around this many cops would make her skin crawl. The small hairs on her neck kept lifting, as if they were little antennae, searching for a threat.

Stop it. Not all cops were like Frank Phalen.

Rubbing first her neck and then her temples, she hoped to somehow escape the whole nightmare. Instead, her thoughts returned to the twined hearts, the winking stone.

The empty eye sockets.

Dear God, Marcy's dead.

"Ms. Price?"

"Holly?" Alex's voice—the tone said it wasn't the first time he'd called her name.

"Think she's in shock?" Alex asked the deputy.

She straightened her spine and transferred her attention to the brown-uniformed man who was studying her with equal measures of concern and irritation. Just because she'd thrown up and cried while she and Alex were waiting for the police—including Officer Brown Uniform—to show up, there was no reason to treat her like she was made of glass.

"I'm fine."

A gust of wind swirled off the river. She pulled the blanket closer and shivered.

Brown Uniform tugged his hat lower on his head. "Let's give her a few more minutes."

He turned back to Alex. "How is it you were so deep into that bog?"

Alex pushed his hands into his pockets. "Normally, I wouldn't go back there. You know how it is. Can't get a clear shot if you flush something, and it's a bitch to find anything if you do. I clipped a rooster. It ran. I didn't want to leave it wounded, so when Duke caught a line on it, I followed him. It never occurred to me

7

to tell Holly to wait up top."

Both men turned a look on her that said she wasn't very bright.

"You told me to stay with you," she said, irritated at their discussing her as if she were an inanimate object. Alex's possessive tone and Brown Uniform's speculative expression made her madder.

They ignored her.

"Tell me one more time, how'd you find that body?" The deputy drew Alex away.

His words unleashed the memory of the bloated, bird-pecked corpse. Holly's stomach cramped. *How could this happen to you, Marcy?*

Part of her kept playing the dumb what-if game. What if she hadn't tripped and spooked the bird? What if the pheasant hadn't tried to fly away? The circular thoughts were pointless. She and Alex might not have found the body, but Marcy would still be dead.

Desperate for distraction, she focused on the activity around her. Men and dogs trailed across the causeway. They straggled through a field in the direction of the bluff and the bog beyond it. Others clumped in twos and threes, doing whatever men did.

Another man, one who wasn't wearing a uniform, strolled across the parking lot and stopped beside her. She stifled a groan. For the past two hours, assorted law enforcement types had asked her numerous questions—the same questions.

The game warden introduced himself. "Now, Ms. Price." His voice was as raspy and weather-roughened as his face. "I'm mostly out here checking on hunters, making sure they're using the right ammunition, keeping the poachers honest, that sort of thing, but seeing as how this young woman's body showed up in my game management area, I have a few questions."

The shrewd expression in his eyes said he was smarter than he sounded. The deference the other cops showed him made her wary of the good ol' boy routine.

He hitched his Carhartts, resettled his gear, and then pulled out a small leather notebook and pen. "Tell me, how well did you know this young woman?"

"Is it really Marcy?"

"I heard tell you said it was Ms. Ramirez. Now why would you think a thing like that?"

"I think it is. I mean, she's missing—she's been missing since Tuesday—and she always wore a double-heart necklace..."

"That necklace the victim's wearing, I heard you recognized it."

"Marcy wore one like that. I thought it was beautiful." A flash of Marcy fingering the hearts, a dreamy expression on her face, shot through Holly's mind and tears again filled her eyes.

If the warden noticed, he didn't mention her reaction. "Seems like a spendy piece of jewelry, not a trinket you'd pick up at the department store. You know where she got it?"

Holly blinked back the tears and shook her head.

"A gift?" he asked.

"Maybe. If it was, I don't know who gave it to her."

He tapped his pen against his pad. "You say she was missing. How'd you know she didn't just go off with her boyfriend?"

Holly raised her hands in an I-don't-know gesture. "Her sister reported it on Wednesday. I figured they were in a position to know."

Another Blazer with a set of rooftop lights rattled past the news vehicles on the state highway and continued down the narrow road into the crowded parking lot. The men parted, then repositioned themselves in its wake.

The game warden glanced at the vehicle. "That's the Franklin

County detective who'll be handling this investigation for me. I need to speak with him. Now you just hold still a minute."

He crossed the parking lot toward the Blazer.

The driver's door opened and a tall, dark-haired man emerged. The street clothes set him apart from the assorted cops, but the aura of authority surrounding him was already turning heads.

"Oh, crap," Holly muttered.

And she'd thought this day couldn't get any worse.

A detective's shield winked in the sunlight as the newcomer reached into his truck and pulled out a heavy coat. Uniformed men converged on him. The deputies shuffled around, reorienting themselves in some obscure male pecking order, undoubtedly ready to update him on the investigation.

It was official. This was the worst day of her life.

Marcy was dead.

She and Alex were apparently suspects.

And her ex-fiancé was the lead investigator.

Chapter Two

No, no, no, echoed through Holly's head.

Her ex-fiancé, JC Dimitrak, hitched the coat over his shoulders and turned his attention to the surrounding officers.

Alex moved next to her. "Another one?"

She edged around Alex, positioning him between JC and her. At least the detective hadn't seen her yet. She couldn't deal with JC right now. She'd hoped to *never* deal with him again.

She'd managed to avoid him the entire five months she'd been back in Richland—something that had taken more effort than she'd expected in a town of fifty thousand. Why did he have to be in charge of this investigation?

Alex dropped an arm around her. "How're you holding up?"

She had enough in her head with Marcy. Thank God Alex didn't know about JC. The only thing worse than dealing with them separately was handling them together. "I've had better days."

"You and me both. This isn't exactly our normal routine." Alex gestured at the crowded parking lot and then looked in the direction of the hidden bog.

"Are they sure it's Marcy?" Her dead friend might not be her first choice for conversation topics, but talking about Marcy beat obsessing about JC and whatever he was planning, thinking, or saying. Holly scrubbed her hands over her face. That sounded horrible, but JC's presence screwed up her ability to think straight about *anything.*

"They haven't told me jack." Discouragement flattened Alex's voice. "They just keep asking questions."

"I know the feeling. Think they're nearly finished?"

"God, I hope so. I don't know how many more times and ways I can say, 'I don't know who killed her.' "

"Can we leave?" The other police officers had her information. Maybe talking to JC wasn't *really* necessary.

Alex shrugged. "They have their processes. Cops never struck me as particularly flexible people."

A gust of wind eddied around them and she shivered.

"You cold?" He tightened his arm.

"I'm freezing." She scooted closer to Alex. He definitely had redeeming qualities. Right now, they included shoulders wide enough to block both the wind and JC's line of sight.

"I'll be glad when they're done." The strain of the past hours showed in the gray tinge under his olive complexion. Lines pinched the corners of his eyes and mouth, and the bleak expression was one she'd never seen before. He'd known Marcy longer than she had, so her death would hit him hard. And clearly the officers had hammered him with tougher questions than the ones they'd asked her.

Men's voices carried across the narrow parking lot. Mostly she caught words and phrases, but after all this time she could still pick out JC's deep, rumbly voice.

Finally the cops' conversation seemed to wind down. "The couple who found the body is right over here," the game warden said.

Here it comes. She resisted the urge to peek around Alex's shoulder.

12

"Alejandro Montoya and Holly Price," the warden continued.

"Who?" JC asked.

She braced herself and stepped forward. Hands clenched, she met the detective's hard-eyed scowl.

"So they found the body?" JC spoke to the game warden but his eyes never left hers. "Anyone check to see if it still had a heart?"

"Real mature." Heat flooded her cheeks as the insult slapped her. "You had to say something. You couldn't just let it go."

Six years vanished and all the hurt and anger of their last confrontation lay between them. Everyone froze, as if wondering how to back away without losing a body part. Then a couple of officers stepped forward.

Looking to protect JC or her?

"I take it you two have met."

Alex's voice. She startled. Intent on JC, she'd forgotten Alex was there.

Damn. Think he picked up on that little detail?

Eyes narrowed, Alex's gaze swung from her to JC.

She struggled to keep the turmoil twisting her stomach out of her words. "That's JC Dimitrak. I *thought* I knew him, once upon a time. I found out the hard way I didn't."

JC held his ground, studying her. After a beat, his attention transferred to Alex and she saw the same cool scrutiny in his expression. She'd have given a lot to know what he was thinking.

She examined the hard planes of his face. Then again, maybe she didn't want to know.

"This is hardly the place to discuss ancient history." JC's voice was as frigid as his little black heart.

You started it, she wanted to sputter. But she wasn't going to act like a two-year-old. Or like she cared what JC thought. Or...or...

"You're the last person I expected to see out here," he said.

His comment covered multiple levels. He hadn't expected to see her at a murder scene. At a game management area. In Richland, at all.

She lifted her chin and hoped her voice matched his icy tone. "How would *you* know where I'd be or what I like to do?"

His gaze drifted down her body, his expression considering, with a trace of smug.

Her face grew warmer. Okay. There were things he'd known she liked.

She crossed her arms. "My being here's a temporary arrangement."

Alex's face grew stonier with each barbed exchange. "Are we under arrest?" he asked the detective.

"No."

"Then we're leaving. You know how to find us."

"Not so fast there, young fella," the game warden spoke up. "I need to finish interviewing Ms. Price."

He crooked a finger, calling her to join JC and him.

Alex glared. She wasn't far from the same degree of irritation. People did not summon her like she was their...their...bird dog.

The game warden signaled again, a bigger sweep of his hand. Reluctantly, she joined the two men.

"Let's see." The older man tapped his pen against his notebook, a gesture that was starting to irritate her. "Now, what is it you do for a living?"

She looked from the warden to JC. Who was actually in charge?

JC smiled—a grim one—at her confusion. "This is federal land. The warden's in charge until he releases the scene."

Great.

She turned to the game warden. At least business was easier

14

to talk about than emotions. "My regular job is with the Mergers and Acquisitions Group in Seattle, but right now I'm working for Desert Accounting."

From the corner of her eye, she saw JC's smile widen to a grin. Clearly, he was enjoying the squirm factor of her being back in Richland, working at a place she'd sworn she never would.

"That's a big change for a single woman like you. We get a lot of young people moving to eastern Washington, wanting to raise a family in a more wholesome environment."

She refrained from reminding the warden they were at a murder scene that was far from wholesome.

"What made you decide to move across the Cascades and work for a local accountant?" he asked.

"My parents own the accounting firm. My mother needed some help."

"Your mother needed help, hmm? What about your father? He didn't need help?"

She sneaked another glance at JC. Like she wanted to bring up infidelity in front of him. "They separated. I really don't see how any of that's relevant to who murdered my friend."

The game warden's face and voice hardened. "We decide what's relevant. You just answer the questions."

His words kicked over a dozen memories, none of them good. The Seattle cops had dismissed her concerns about Frank. Overlooked the stalking, the growing threats. Refused initially to enforce the restraining order against one of their own.

You can't trust cops.

The game warden's insistent voice intruded. "A lot of couples separate over infidelity. I heard the victim was a pretty little gal. Worked in the office right across the hall. From you. Your dad... So where is your dad these days?"

She slammed the door on the past. This guy was not going to

build a conspiracy theory about Marcy having an affair with her father. The blasted yoga instructor, yes, but not Marcy. "He moved to Arizona. Last I heard he was living in a sweat lodge. And he certainly isn't the only man I know who can't keep his pants zipped."

The smile left JC's face.

Stop it. Ignore JC. Just give them the facts. They don't need the details.

"Hmm." The warden scribbled something, then waited a beat—tapping his pen—as if he wanted to see if she'd say anything else. "The only shotgun and hunting license I've seen today belongs to Mr. Montoya. So why's a young woman like you out here?"

After another twenty minutes of answering the same questions she'd answered when the first policemen arrived, she was ready to go home and crawl in bed. To wake up and find it was all a bad dream. That Marcy was just fine.

"That young man worked with the victim, didn't he?" The warden nodded in Alex's direction.

Alex glared at her—or rather the three of them. The way things were going, he ought to watch his own back. "If the body really is, was, Marcy, she didn't work for Alex."

The warden flipped a few pages in his notebook. "Says here Mr. Montoya and his family own a restaurant. Marcy Ramirez didn't work for him?"

"Marcy worked for Tim Stevens." The officer knew that— he'd accused her father of having an affair with the pretty "gal" across the hall. Alex was Tim's business partner in the real estate development company, but she didn't think he needed to have that pointed out, especially with the cops already all over Alex's possible involvement. All the officers had asked too many questions about both Alex's and her relationship with Marcy.

The warden gave her an assessing look. "You know Mr.

Stevens?"

"He's a client. I met Marcy through him."

"Interesting the way you four are mixed up together," JC said.

She gave him a narrow-eyed glare. He was loving watching her squirm. "None of us had any reason to hurt Marcy. She's our friend." She left unspoken, *So why can't we wrap this up and you guys go find the killer?*

The game warden made another note on his pad. "Now, we got over 800 acres out here. How is it you two managed to find the body when it was all tangled up in the bushes?"

"We just followed the dog." She shuddered and shook off the memory of the body in the clearing.

"Okay, I got it straight now. Mr. Montoya led you to the body."

Fresh adrenaline shot through her system. "No, of course not. Alex didn't lead me—"

"Then how did you know the body was in the bog?" the officer interrupted.

"We didn't know the body was there. We just found her. We didn't kill her."

He asked a few more questions, then slid his notebook into his jacket pocket. "I think that's it for now. Detective Dimitrak, she's all yours."

Not just no, but *hell* no. Never in a million years.

JC's lips twitched, as if he'd also caught the double entendre. "I have more questions."

Of course he did.

She looked into JC's cold eyes and remembered a time when his gaze was hot with desire and filled with love. The memory oozed through cracks in her emotional control. It seeped like hot acid, burning with fresh betrayal instead of lying dormant as ancient history. Her throat tightened and tears pricked her eyes.

She couldn't handle this. Not now.

Hands fisted, she struggled to keep the tears from falling. "Can we do this later?"

JC's face tightened, as if he planned to automatically turn her down.

She swallowed her pride. "Please?"

A silent moment stretched, then he gave a curt nod. "Okay."

The tears, the tremble in her voice, or the memory of what they'd once meant to each other—she wasn't sure what made him change his mind. Whatever it was, she could guarantee he'd make her pay for it later, but for now, gratitude sliced through the pain.

"Don't get any thoughts about leaving town. Plug some time into your calendar for us to chat, because I have questions. Lots and lots of them."

Oh, goody.

Wouldn't that be fun.

Chapter Three

An hour later, Holly leaned her forehead against the tile wall of her shower. Warm water pounded her shoulders. Tears streamed down her cheeks. Marcy had been one of the first people who reached out to her when she moved back to Richland.

And now the woman was dead.

The pipes shuddered. The hot water ran out.

"Argh!" Holly dodged the freezing water and reached for the taps. Add a water heater to the list of Things To Replace.

She dried off and hung up the towels. A glance at the mirror drew a disgusted snort. *Oh, let's just make this day a full and complete disaster.*

She looked like crap. Not that looks had ever been her strong point. At twenty-eight, she was still the tall, blond, scrawny kid she'd been during college.

Not that it mattered. She straightened her shoulders. A woman's worth wasn't defined by the outside package.

Her inner teenager whined, *The next time I saw JC, I wanted to look amazing.*

She told the idiot to shut up.

She'd managed to not think about JC Dimitrak for nearly six years. There was no reason to change anything today.

Except now she looked like a murder suspect. She didn't have a choice whether or not to talk to him.

But jeez—who'd have thought JC "Just Crazy" Dimitrak would end up in law enforcement?

Still, it was done. Seventh layer of hell, between the reunion with JC and Marcy's horrible death, but she'd survived. Running away, selling Desert Accounting at a bargain-basement price, sounded amazingly attractive. She could move back to civilization on the west side of the Cascade Mountains and never have to deal with any of it again.

Too bad it was a fantasy. She couldn't run out on her mother.

She wandered into the living room, or as her friends had dubbed it, the construction disaster area. For a moment, she imagined a soft leather sofa in front of the fireplace, books piled on shelves, a cashmere throw, and nothing to do on a Sunday afternoon except slip away into a good story.

Another fantasy.

Alex peeled himself off the floor.

She started and covered the flinch. "You're still here." She'd hoped Alex had acted on her subtle suggestion. *Go home.*

"Thought you might need me." He stretched, a long muscular display.

Tell me you did not just pose.

He wrapped an arm around her shoulders. "Sorry you had to see Marcy like that."

An image of the shattered corpse they'd found in the bog pounced and Holly's stomach cramped.

"How're you doing?" Alex asked.

"I'm weirded out. It still doesn't seem real." Too restless to be confined, she twitched a shoulder, dislodged his arm, and moved toward the windows. "Did I ever tell you about the first time I met Marcy?"

He shook his head.

"I'd gone over to Stevens Ventures to talk to Tim about quarterly taxes. I was walking down the hall when I heard this lilting voice coming from his office, crooning, 'Where are you, you little bugger?' "

She smiled at the memory. "For a minute I wondered what was going on, but curiosity got the better of me. I peeked in Tim's office and saw Marcy's butt wagging in the air. She was crawling out backward from under the desk, holding a metal knob like a trophy."

Holly raised her hand in remembered imitation. "She sat back on her heels, going, 'Now I have to figure out how it fits back together.' And she laughed. It was pure happiness, the kind of laugh you can't help joining, when you're just glad to be alive."

Her echoing laughter escaped as a muffled sob. "Except now she's dead."

Alex crossed the room and pulled her close. "It's okay. Marcy was a sweet kid. I remember when she started working for Tim. She was like a puppy, wanting to please so bad she about quivered."

Holly frowned and moved back, not sure she liked the analogy. "She always struck me as confident and outgoing."

"She is now. I mean, she was. I mean, she opened up after she'd been working there for a while."

"I can't get my head around the reality—she's dead."

Alex dropped his hands onto her waist. His tone moved into the husky range. "But we're alive."

Oh, no. He couldn't mean that affirmation-of-life-through-sex thing. It was *so* not the time for an intimate moment. And then there was the whole was-he-the-right-guy? issue.

"Alex? I'm not ready for this." Their relationship hadn't reached that level, and she wasn't sure it ever would. Today's events had convinced her Alex was someone fun to do stuff with, period.

Definitely better than watching Friday night movies alone, but not anyone she wanted as a close, long-term addition in her life. "All I can see right now is those birds and a mangled body. I haven't even started to process the fact that Marcy won't be in the office tomorrow."

Sex was *so* not happening.

Still, she didn't want to be a complete bitch. "I do appreciate your staying."

He got the rest of the message and dropped his hands. "I wanted to make sure you weren't too freaked out." His expression disgruntled, he stepped over to her painting supplies, picked up the masking tape, and spun it around his fingers.

From a purely selfish perspective, having him in the house would be good. Someone to talk to. Someone to keep the images of Marcy's body away.

He tossed the tape back onto the pile. It rolled across the floor, gathering dust and cat hair. He shoved his hands into his jeans pockets. "I should head out. Check on the restaurant. I still have to open it tonight."

Oh, since he wasn't getting any, it was time to bail? Nice.

She retrieved the tape and brushed at the debris. *Thanks a bunch.* "Your family can handle the restaurant if you're upset about Marcy."

"My mother knows Mrs. Ramirez." He gave a small shrug. "She'll worry."

About Marcy, Mrs. Ramirez, or Alex? Not that it mattered—Alex's mother micromanaged both his life and his restaurant. "She'll have heard about Marcy. She'll want to know you're okay," she said, giving him an out.

He's upset about Marcy too, she reminded herself. And guys never know what to do with their emotions.

"Mama gets bossy when she's worried. If she runs off any

more staff, I'll have to start recruiting my cousins to work as busboys."

The irritating *brittz* of the doorbell—another item on her long list of Things To Replace—interrupted.

"You expecting somebody?" Alex asked.

"I hope it isn't a reporter." Shaking her head, she crossed the room. "If my mom heard about this…"

She pushed the curtain aside, peeked through the long sidelight window and recoiled.

No reporter.

No mother.

JC Dimitrak stood on her doorstep.

She didn't know why she was surprised. She'd known he'd show up eventually, but *now?* This soon?

He dipped his head in greeting. Even tired and grim-faced, he still looked better than sex on a stick.

Where did *that* come from? She scrambled to pull her thoughts together and opened the door.

Wait a minute, her inner teenager shrieked. *I'm not ready.*

"May I come in?"

"What are you doing here? I mean, at my house?"

"Remember the 'Can we do this later?' part?"

Stepping back, she widened the opening. JC wore the same dark slacks and heavy coat he'd had on at the game management area. He unbuttoned his overcoat, revealing the huge pistol clamped to his belt beside his badge. This man—this *stranger*, she reminded herself, because she didn't know him anymore—was definitely a leader. He had the commanding presence, backed by more than a hint of sex appeal.

He'd always had it.

Only now he was armed. And undoubtedly dangerous.

"I take it this is an official visit," she said.

He ignored the observation, and instead gave her yoga pants, T-shirt, and wet hair a slow inspection. The twitch of his eyebrow and assessing glance told her he knew she wasn't wearing a bra.

Alex moved into the foyer. "Why are you here?"

JC glanced at Alex. Sex assumptions hung like a cartoon balloon over his head. For a moment, something that might've been anger or jealousy tightened his face. Then it vanished. "Did I catch you at a bad time?"

She said, "No" at the same time Alex said, "Yes."

"Glad we cleared that up." JC's smile didn't reach his eyes. "I need to get your statement, Holly. Before you take off again."

She propped her fist on her hip. "You know, the way I remember things, *you* walked out."

"Don't go there, Holly. You don't know the first thing about me."

"I know everything that matters."

Alex stepped up. "We've both done everything we can to cooperate, but quit hiding behind your badge. If you have a problem with Holly, you should bow out of the investigation."

JC gave him a cool examination. "I need to talk to each of you. Alone. We can do that at the station, if you'd prefer."

"No way. I'm not going to the police station without a lawyer," Alex said.

"You can leave."

Wow. She *really* hadn't thought the day could get any worse. "Guys. Break." She jammed her fingers into a time-out "T."

"Maybe we should call Phil Brewer." Alex folded his arms across his chest in universal male posturing position.

While he got points for trying to defend her, she rejected his choice with, "Phil does corporate work."

Alex glared at the detective. "He'd still know how to make this guy quit harassing you."

JC didn't say a word, but behind his stiff face he seemed to be enjoying stirring the pot.

"Stop. He isn't harassing me." Weirding her out, yes. Harassing, no. She knew what that felt like. Right now, JC might be doing the über-cop routine, but if the tension got any hotter, they could roast marshmallows. And nobody was going to sing "Kumbaya."

"Alex." She touched his arm, finally moving his attention off the detective. "I'm tired. I'd rather get this over with. Go on to the restaurant. I'll be okay."

For one long moment, she was afraid he was going to push the issue.

With a sharp snort of irritation, he turned, strode across the room, and grabbed his jacket. Thrusting his arms into the sleeves, he headed for the door. He made a move like he intended to kiss her.

She froze. The oh-God-not-in-front-of-my-mother cringe warred with the in-your-face-JC snub.

And from the half-smile on JC's face, he'd caught her hesitation, even if Alex didn't seem to notice.

"I'll call you in a little while." *To make sure JC's gone*, bristled from his scowl. Alex brushed his lips across hers and vanished through the front door.

Alrighty.

JC Dimitrak.

She drew in a deep breath. "What do you want to know?"

He crossed the foyer. His hard soles rapped against the bare subfloor. "Love what you've done with the place."

Silently counting to ten, she decided to interpret the comment as a compliment, although he clearly hadn't intended it that way. "I'm working on it. The guy who used to own the house opened up the interior. I don't know what they were thinking back in the

70s, but the original house completely ignored the view, which is its best feature. It had those narrow, clerestory windows that kinda remind me of bunker openings."

She stared at the living room's new, oversized panes and forced her mouth to close. Babbling wasn't going to keep them from talking about Marcy.

Talking about Marcy's dead body would make her murder so much more real.

"What'd he do? Get in over his head?"

"The guy who owned it? Yeah. The bank foreclosed."

JC gestured at the buckets and painting supplies. "Weekend project?"

"I planned to paint." She wasn't sure what to make of his tone or the question. Was he assuming she was a cold-hearted bitch for planning to paint *today*, the day she'd found a friend's body?

Well, she already knew where he stood on the bitch-meter, but he could've at least asked *when* she set out the paint instead of figuring she was breaking out the roller *today*.

She planned to paint because it was normal. Because it was what normal people did. Normal people whose friends weren't dead.

No way was she admitting any of that.

"The carpet installer's scheduled for next week. He recommended I paint before he replaces the rug."

They both glanced at the hideous shag carpet.

"Good idea." A grin tugged at JC's mouth.

She bit her lip to keep from smiling—the shag was truly awful—but the tension in the room dropped by ten degrees.

He looked at her, studying her expression. "Actually, I'm impressed you took on the renovation."

She raised an eyebrow.

"I thought you said you'd never live in Richland again."

"You heard what you wanted to hear." One of the reasons they'd broken up was he'd wanted a stay-at-home wife, stuck behind a picket fence. She'd had no interest in playing the Stepford Wife role. Any chance they'd had of creating *any* kind of home crashed and burned when she came home from college after one of their arguments—about her being in Seattle and her plans to stay there after graduation—and found him with another woman.

But here she was, in Richland.

With a house.

An empty house.

Whatever.

"The house is an investment. Most of my friends think I'm nuts for renovating it myself."

His lips tightened around a smile.

If she didn't know him, she'd have missed it. One of the things he'd loved about her—*said* he'd loved—was her tendency to throw herself into projects other people thought were crazy. She always pulled them off, though.

"This place *is* butt-ugly on the outside, but you have to admit the view is stunning." *Keep him focused on the externals.* The last thing she wanted was for him to look at her too closely. To see inside her the way he used to.

JC didn't need to know she loved the ugly little house. Everything about the house and the renovation was tangible. Did she fix the water heater or not? Get the room painted or not? There were none of the murky gray areas like there were in the rest of her life, where maybe she succeeded—or maybe she didn't.

He moved past her to the window, then turned and leaned against the wall. "I heard you were back."

She gave him an *and-your-point-is?* look. What had he expected? That she'd call him? Show up on *his* cheating, black-hearted doorstep?

"Why'd you move back to Richland?"

She wasn't going to tell him her father had suffered a midlife brain fart and taken off with his yoga instructor, or that she'd made a deal with her mother to bail out the family accounting business, a decision she regretted on practically a daily basis. And at a deeper level, his question pissed her off because he knew damn well *exactly* why she was there. She'd seen the cop powwow information exchange out at Big Flats, where the deputies had brought JC up to speed. All he was doing now was digging for personal information.

She crossed her arms and ignored the way her body heated up just because he was in the room. Stupid body. If it heated up, it was because she was mad. Period. "You know why I moved. And if you were really interested, it would take you about two seconds to find out when I changed the address on my driver's license from Seattle to Richland."

He smiled and two dimples appeared.

She caught her breath. Oh, man. How could she have forgotten about his dimples?

It didn't matter how many times she told herself they were just a simple indentation of flesh. Dimples made serious, grown-up men look like they still had a mischievous little boy inside. The kind who sledded down the forbidden steepest slopes, dyed the dog green for St. Patty's Day, or knew how to be especially devilish in bed.

And she personally knew every one of those items applied to JC.

In spite of her irritation, she smiled at him and his grin widened. His shoulders relaxed and his eyes grew a shade warmer. "You never could pass up a chance to jerk my chain."

"You set yourself up often enough."

Why was he making nice? She did the mental head-slap. *What was she thinking?* JC stood for "Just Cool" as often as it did "Just Crazy."

"Is this your loosen-up-the-idiot routine, so I'll say something stupid like, 'I killed Marcy'?"

His face immediately closed off, but before he could make another comment, she pulled on the composed shell she used at the negotiating table. "Look. At least for tonight, let's declare a truce. You quit taking jabs at me and I won't take any swipes at you. I'll tell you everything I know about Marcy."

He pushed away from the wall and nodded. "Sounds good to me."

"If we're going to talk about her, I need coffee." She headed toward the kitchen.

JC followed her into the large area beyond the vacant living room. "Nice."

There was no snark in his tone this time.

She surveyed the renovated space with pride. A tile-topped peninsula—she'd set every one of those suckers—separated the kitchen from the dining area. Cherry cabinets lined the interior walls and surrounded the Bosch appliances. City lights sparkled through the oversized windows at night, but right now she could see eighty miles to the Blue Mountains.

"Have a seat." She pulled out coffee and filled the machine. "With all that activity at Big Flats, I'm surprised you're here. Shouldn't you be following leads or something?"

From the safety of distance, she gave him a closer examination. His hair was shorter. No big surprise there, he *was* a policeman. His face was tanned; apparently he still spent time outdoors. The lines at the corners of his eyes were new. He'd filled out, not that he'd been a wimp when she knew him. She checked out the broad chest and shoulders tapering to slim hips and

29

remembered why hormones had fried her brain when she was in college.

Good thing she was too smart for that now.

All his assets still didn't outweigh the big ol' blot in his liability column, a.k.a. infidelity.

He dropped his coat on a counter stool, but claimed the chair at the head of the table. "You looked like you were nearly out on your feet earlier, so I let you go home." A lazy smile, the kind that used to set her heart racing, warmed his expression. "You still look good, though."

"Hmm." Telling her pulse and her traitorous hormones to go take another cold shower, she gave her ratty yoga pants and T-shirt an appraising glance. She didn't have to see her hair to know it had already dried in the desert air without benefit of blow-dryer, styling gel, or flatiron. "What do you want, JC?"

He laughed.

It was the belly-deep, I'm-an-idiot-and-you-called-me-on-it combined with I-don't-take-myself-too-seriously chuckle she remembered. One of the protective barriers holding in her anger and hurt creaked a little, as though it was rusty and maybe she didn't need it anymore.

No, no, no. He was *not* getting under her skin.

The coffee machine made steamy brewing noises behind her. Deliberately turning her back on him and his smile, she picked up his coat and headed toward the closet. As she draped the garment over a wooden hanger, her nose caught floral perfume wafting from the wool. Definitely not JC's cologne.

Her stomach knotted. She should've known there'd be a woman in his life.

Anger knifed through any remaining illusions. She knew better than to trust anything he said or did. But what did he think he was doing, giving her that *c'mon* look?

She slapped the hanger onto the closet rod. He wasn't wearing a ring. Was he still married to what's-her-face? Like being married stopped anybody. Look at Dad. If he fell off the rails, why should she expect JC to be different?

She already *knew* JC wasn't different.

She returned to the kitchen and slammed around a few coffee mugs. She wasn't sure if she was mad at her father, JC, or herself for still being even the tiniest little bit attracted to him.

Damn him.

He had a notepad open on the table. "I have some questions."

"Well, we can keep this short and I'll start painting. Here are all the answers." She ticked them off on her fingers. "I thought we were going hiking. I had no idea it was opening weekend for pheasant hunting. I had no idea Marcy's body was in that swampy area. And no, I didn't kill her. Would you like your coffee in a to-go cup?"

All business now, he leveled a stare at her she figured was supposed to be intimidating, but the assorted investment bankers, venture capitalists, and arrogant attorneys she'd dealt with in Seattle had made her immune to that kind of nonsense. JC was an amateur compared to them.

"Don't be a bitch, Holly. It doesn't suit you."

She pressed her hands onto the counter and managed to keep her expression neutral. She wished she could control the warmth climbing her cheeks. She'd known those dimpled signals were just a crappy ploy. Nobody turned it off and on like that if it was real. "Dammit JC, quit jerking me around. I'll do whatever I can to help you find Marcy's killer, but I don't know what I can say that'll make any difference."

"You knew Ms. Ramirez. What can you tell me about her? What was she like?"

Holly pulled in a deep breath. *Do it for Marcy.*

"So the body is definitely Marcy's?"

He nodded, but didn't elaborate.

"Damn. I'd hoped…" The tiny spark of hope she'd harbored vanished and left the world a little darker.

With a sigh, she leaned against the counter and thought about the woman who'd become her friend. "Marcy works—worked—across the hall at Stevens Ventures. She was fun, outgoing. We did lunch, happy hour at Bookwalter, that kind of thing. We had different backgrounds, but we just clicked, you know?"

The coffeemaker sputtered behind her.

"I liked her. I wish I'd gotten a chance to know her better." She stared at the floor before raising her gaze to meet his. "I can't believe she's dead. Who would want to kill her? Why?"

"That's what I'm trying to figure out. Do you know who Ms. Ramirez was dating?"

"I wish I could be more help, but I don't know much about her personal life."

"I thought you were friends."

"We are…were." Holly lifted a shoulder. "She never talked about a boyfriend. I think she was seeing someone, but like I said…"

"Do you know anybody who'd want to hurt her?"

"I can't think of anybody. She was so…nice." Holly chewed her lower lip, frustrated with her explanation. "I'm not doing a very good job telling you about her. What she was like, as a person. Marcy…loved pretty clothes. And she loved to dance. You should've seen her. She could move like the music came from inside her, and if she was dancing with somebody—"

"She dance with anybody in particular?"

Holly blinked. The memory of the dance floor where she'd admired Marcy's footwork vanished, and she returned to a grim-faced cop who wanted to know if one of her friends had killed the woman. No way was she going to say Alex and Marcy should've auditioned for that dance show together. Alex had been her date when they went dancing, not Marcy's. "Nobody in particular."

"So no known enemies?"

"Not that I know of." She removed a spoon from a drawer. "Do you think this was a random violence thing? You know, wrong time, wrong place?"

"It's possible."

"How'd she end up out at the Snake River?"

"We seem to have this backward—I ask the questions and you answer them."

"Then ask a question I know the answer to." She thought about Marcy's body ending up at Big Flats while she returned to the coffeemaker and filled the mugs. "If she knew her killer, she might've gone out to the river to meet him. Or maybe the bad guy took her there."

"And you don't know anybody she'd meet out there."

"No."

She left her coffee black, but reached into the refrigerator for milk. She added some to JC's mug along with a healthy scoop of sugar.

"Sorry, no cream." She placed the drink in front of him.

JC stared at the mug, then cocked his head to look at her. "You remember how I like my coffee." His eyes were warm and friendly. Gold flecks lightened the brown depths.

He had beautiful eyes. She'd gotten lost in them once.

Her breathing hitched. There more in his eyes than warmth.

Longing.

Regret.

A shiny sphere swelled, as delicate and gossamer as a child's blown bubble. Hope? Happiness?

Love?

Time rewound and they were six years younger, madly in love, and spending every possible minute together. Memories of times and places she'd brought him coffee surged through her. Seattle's Best, study breaks. Her dorm, his apartment, tangled sheets. Hot coffee, hotter kisses.

She slammed the gate on memory lane. He'd made his choice. "It's only coffee. I thought all cops like coffee."

He blinked at her flat tone. His gaze dropped to the notebook. "You stated you went to lunch with Ms. Ramirez. Who else went with you? What did you talk about?"

It was his official voice, cool and impersonal. *Good. Let's keep this purely professional.*

She pulled out a chair and sat down. "Marcy's sister, Yessica, went with us. Occasionally, someone else from the office came."

Sipping coffee for fortification, she told him the basics, the people they ran around with, the places they went. "One thing I *do* know. Marcy hated the Great Outdoors. She would never, ever have been near Big Flats by her own choice."

JC scribbled notes. "Where were you last Tuesday?"

She nearly spewed coffee. "Do you actually think I killed my friend?"

His face was expressionless. "Answer the question."

Stunned he'd even *remotely* consider her a possible murderer, her hands rose and fell in an incredulous gesture. "At work. At meetings."

"Can you be more specific?"

"I don't remember exactly, but it'll be on my work calendar."

"I'll need a copy of your schedule. Ms. Ramirez disappeared on Tuesday, according to her sister. The ME estimated time of death as Tuesday evening. I need to know where you were during that time period."

Her jaw dropped. "You're serious."

His eyes didn't waver. "I wouldn't have asked if I weren't."

"Do I need an attorney?"

He jotted a note on his paper. "Anything different happen last week? Before her sisters reported her missing?"

Holly stalled by taking another sip of coffee. Should she call a lawyer? She eyed JC over the rim of her mug. In spite of the way things ended between them, she still believed he'd play fair. And she hadn't said anything he could twist around—except some personal innuendo he couldn't use against her.

With a sigh, she placed her mug on a coaster and hoped she was being helpful and not naïve. "At first, we thought Yessica was overreacting. Marcy hadn't been gone a day and her sister was acting like Bigfoot had stomped out of the Cascades and dragged her home to his cave."

Warmth again flooded her face. "I didn't mean that the way it sounded. Obviously, she was right to be worried. It's just that Marcy had taken off before, so the rest of us weren't really concerned."

"When? Any idea where she went?"

"Marcy took off earlier this fall, said she wanted to be by herself. She made it real clear she didn't want to talk about it." Holly shrugged. "When she took off this time, our receptionist talked to the Stevens Ventures receptionist. Marcy had told her she was going away with her boyfriend. And no, I don't know who she meant."

"Nothing like firsthand information." JC lifted a derisive eyebrow. "I never knew you to listen to gossip."

"Hey, you asked. You're the frikkin' detective. You go figure out who killed her. Just be damned sure you put in your report it wasn't me."

For a long moment, JC stared at her. Then he closed the folio, laid his pen on the table, and folded his arms across his chest. Eyes narrowed, his expression reflected a mental debate. Knowing him, mostly likely it was whether to treat her like a suspect, a witness, or an ex-girlfriend. "I expected more cooperation from you."

She mimicked his body language—stiff back, squared shoulders, minus the glare. "I *am* cooperating. I answered every one of your questions."

"The whole time I've been here, you've said a lot of words, but everything you've told me adds up to a big fat zero." His tone was level, coolly devoid of emotion. "I have to ask myself, why is she being so evasive?"

"Wha..?" She sputtered with outrage, but he cut her off with a slashing hand motion.

"Tell me, Holly. What am I supposed to think? You and your boyfriend *just happen* to find the murdered body of a woman who is your friend and his partner's employee. Interesting coincidence?"

Chapter Four

JC's suspicions lay on the table between them.

Holly stared at him and hung onto her incredulity and her temper. "It may be a coincidence, but it's only an issue if you make it one. This interview is over."

"You said you'd help." Disapproval frosted his voice.

She crossed her arms in a defensive move. This wasn't about JC and the antagonism between them, her frustration with Desert Accounting, or her life in exile. "I said I'll help you find Marcy's killer. All you have to do is ask about her. Quit pushing me on the other stuff. I didn't kill her, and you know it."

His gaze dropped to his notepad. Rather than reopen it, he drummed his fingers across the cover.

Dammit, was he admitting he was being an ass about their past or did he actually need her help? How was she supposed to help when she didn't know anything?

The muscles across his shoulders relaxed, and his voice warmed from deep freeze to room temperature. "I need to understand Ms. Ramirez's regular routine. Then we can retrace her steps and figure out when and where she disappeared. Fill me in on the details of her day."

Holly softened her posture and reached for her coffee mug. "You should talk to Tim Stevens or one of the Stevens Ventures office staff. They can tell you more than I can."

"I have that covered. An outside opinion can be helpful."

She fiddled with the mug, stalling. What did that mean? Had he already talked to people at Stevens Ventures? Did he think Tim was lying?

Did he think *she* was?

JC's expression didn't give her any hints about his thoughts.

"As near as I could tell, Marcy did a little of everything." Her hand swirled in a vague, encompassing gesture. "Bookkeeper, project manager. She even filled in occasionally as the receptionist."

"A key employee."

Holly sipped coffee, then placed the mug on the table. "Marcy was smart and she caught on fast. Tim talked about promoting her to full-time project manager. When she didn't come in Wednesday, people assumed she'd gone up the Valley to check on one of the sites. At the time—until her sister said Marcy was missing—everybody figured she was working out of the Yakima office."

JC scribbled on his note pad. "What does that mean? Work out of Yakima? Check on the sites?"

"Inspections, checking on contractors."

"This was at buildings Stevens leases out?"

"No. The property managers handle the occupied buildings—rents, maintenance, that kind of thing. Marcy occasionally did an inspection for the managers, but she handled properties under renovation. She was working on several projects, but the Yakima one was the largest."

He rocked his pen between his fingers, his expression a thoughtful frown. "She could've vanished from any of those places."

"Marcy never mentioned trouble with the workmen." Holly

combed her fingers through her hair, trying to remember anything else Marcy had said about her trips around the Valley. At an almost subconscious level, she noticed JC's gaze tracking her movement. *Yikes*. Not preening.

She dropped her hand. "But you can see why we weren't too concerned about her whereabouts."

Whereabouts? Did she really just use that word in a sentence?

His dimples flashed, as if he knew exactly what she was thinking. "No signs of duress?"

"Duress?" A blush warmed her cheeks and she cursed her fair complexion.

"No one saw or knew anything indicating she didn't leave voluntarily."

"Oh. Right." *Brilliant.*

Hoping to blow past the faux pas, she said, "I talked to Brea—the Stevens Ventures receptionist."

He raised an eyebrow, asking how this was relevant.

"Last week, when we thought Marcy was missing"—*instead of dead*—"Brea said Marcy had mentioned a guy named Lee, said he might come by their office, but I don't know if that's who Marcy took off with."

JC sat up a lot straighter. "Ms. Ramirez's ex was in town?"

"Marcy has an ex? I mean, *had* an ex?" JC seemed to already know about the guy, whoever he was. "Why didn't she tell people about him? You think he's the one?"

"How long have you been dating Alejandro Montoya?"

Holly blinked. "I thought we agreed you'd just ask about Marcy."

"Answer the question." The hard-ass cop was back in charge.

Was Alex still a suspect? Or was JC using the investigation as an excuse to pry into her current relationship? "Why?"

"Holly." His glare was part threat and part exasperation.

"Fine." She threw up her hands. "Not that it's any of your *official* business. Not long, a month or so."

His lips tightened when she emphasized *official*. "How well do you know him?"

She wasn't sure how to answer. Well enough to go out. Well enough to at least *think* about sex.

Yeah, like that was a good idea.

Not.

None of that was an answer she wanted to give, especially to JC. She shrugged. "I'm getting to know him."

JC draped an ankle over his knee. "I need background information. Where does he work?"

"He owns a restaurant in Pasco. He told the cops about it this morning."

The detective lifted an eyebrow, clearly expecting more.

"What?" She lifted her hands, palm up. She and Alex might not be headed for a happily ever after, but he wasn't a murderer.

"I understand he's Tim Stevens' business partner."

Alex and Tim invested together, but as far as she knew, they weren't criminal masterminds. "I believe we've established that fact. Is there something specific you want to know?"

"Tell me about Ms. Ramirez and Tim Stevens' relationship."

"Tim is Marcy's boss, not her boyfriend."

"I know she worked for him. Did Ms. Ramirez get along with him?"

So now Tim was a suspect? "Everybody gets along with Tim. Tim and his wife Nicole treat everybody—employees, clients—like friends. They asked me to their Labor Day party."

"And?" he asked. "Relevance?"

"Wait a minute." She crossed to the alcove she used as a home office, rummaged through the drawer, and found a picture. "This was taken at their party. Tim gave all of us a copy."

JC squinted at the photo. "Is that Ms. Ramirez?"

Holly smoothed the creases from the surface. The picture showed half a dozen people clustered in a tight pack. Holly stood to one side, sandwiched between Alex and a property manager. Thankfully, the photo had been taken early in the day and she still wore a cute cover-up over her bathing suit.

She focused her attention on Marcy. Even with her dark, lustrous hair scraped back in a wind-blown ponytail, wearing a ridiculous John Deere baseball cap, Marcy looked adorable. Her dark eyes glittered with laughter and her grin was wall-to-wall. This was how Holly wanted to remember her, not as the horrible corpse they'd found.

Her finger traced the gold necklace at Marcy's throat and lingered on the intertwined hearts. Who'd have thought the ornament would one day help identify her body?

"May I?" JC extended his hand and she surrendered the picture. He studied Marcy's image. "The necklace."

"Marcy started wearing it a couple of months ago. That party was on Labor Day, so I guess she got it around then. She wore it all the time."

"Do you know where she got it? Who gave it to her?"

"She never said."

He continued to stare at the picture. "I wasn't aware you were so tight with that group. I see Alejandro Montoya was at the party, too."

Why did he insist on using Alex's full, Hispanic name? "Tim's a client. As you pointed out, Alex is his business partner."

"Do you hang out with all your clients in a bathing suit?"

She stiffened. "What business is that of yours?"

Their past history was still complicating this...whatever it was—meeting, interview, interrogation.

JC placed the photo where she could see Marcy's smile.

Holly glanced from the picture to the detective. She didn't need his less than subtle reminder about his reason for being there. Except this wasn't about Marcy anymore.

She pushed back from the table and rose. She crossed the empty living room—a walk rather than a stomp—and pulled his coat from the closet.

He remained seated at the table, watching her.

"When you decide to actually investigate Marcy's death, we'll talk. For now, you're leaving. We're done."

He shook his head. "We're just getting started."

"Then I better start my own investigation, because this isn't getting anywhere."

Chapter Five

Sunday, late afternoon

Holly cruised Howard Amon Park's small parking lot. She scanned the rows for her best friend's car, hoping she was in the right place. Laurie Gordon's Prius was tiny, but distinctive.

The park ran for miles along the west bank of the Columbia River, from somewhere below the Blue Bridge in Kennewick all the way to the Hanford Nuclear Site. It widened periodically into named areas, but she always had trouble remembering what the different segments were called. She should've just told Laurie to meet her at the Fingernail. The bandshell's pale blue top poked through the trees like the index finger it resembled.

She parked, climbed from the car, and tugged the zipper on her jacket higher. She'd changed into jeans and a fleece top, but the wind off the river carried a bite. Rather than pace, she leaned against her Beemer's fender and watched other people enjoy the autumn sunshine. Teenagers, families. Ordinary people living ordinary lives.

The sun felt good on her face. Eyes closed, she tilted her head. Children's voices, the teenagers' music, and an occasional car rumbling through the parking lot receded into a background drone. White noise for relaxation.

"Holly?"

The male voice jolted her to attention. Heart thumping, she pivoted toward the sound.

Never let your guard down. Especially not in public. That was one lesson she'd learned from Frank.

"Sorry," the middle-aged man said. "I didn't mean to startle you."

Hand pressed to her chest, she managed a weak smile when she recognized him as a client.

"I wanted to introduce my wife." He gestured to a brunette who held a leash connected to something small, fluffy, and cute.

They chatted and petted the dog, while Holly told her overactive imagination to get a grip. A few minutes later, the couple headed for the wide, riverside path.

A Prius purred into the lot and parked. The sun caught the bright blue streaks in Laurie's dark hair as she emerged. Before Holly could wonder how the hospital administration reacted to the hair enhancement, Laurie closed the gap between them, wrapped arms around her, and squeezed.

"I can't believe Marcy's dead." Holly leaned against her friend, worn out by too many emotional slams. For a while, they hugged in shared grief. Finally, she sniffed and dabbed a knuckle under her eyes. "I thought I was all cried out."

"That takes a while." Laurie pulled tissues from her pocket and handed her one.

They wiped their eyes and blew their noses. Without making a conscious decision, they strolled toward the paved walking path.

Laurie scuffed through the fallen leaves. "You didn't have to drive over here. I could've come by your house."

Holly threaded an arm through Laurie's. "You had to work and I needed to get out of the house. Being alone with my thoughts was driving me nuts."

"Some cops in the ER were talking about Marcy. I swear, news ran through the hospital faster than the flu." Laurie worked on the hospital's administrative side and heard every rumor swirling around the medical center.

"Big surprise the cops were gossiping," Holly muttered.

Within minutes, they left Howard Amon Park. Movement gave Holly's restless, mixed-up emotions an outlet. Slowly, her shoulders loosened and her stomach unclenched.

The path followed the riverbank to another unnamed pocket park where a couple played with a toddler in the heaps of leaves. Holly smiled at the innocent happiness.

Laurie broke the silence. "I can't believe it. Marcy. Dead. It doesn't make sense."

And the day's disasters crashed back over Holly.

"Having to answer nine thousand questions about Marcy and my alleged involvement made it way too real."

"What?" Shock mingled with outrage in Laurie's tone.

"Yeah, I'm a Person of Interest."

Laurie sputtered, but Holly said, "All those cops out at the game management area, most of them were just doing their job. I get that. I mean, it did piss me off they obviously suspected Alex and me, but mostly they were polite. Professional. But I swear, they all asked the same questions. I seriously wanted to ask, don't you people *talk* to each other?"

"Maybe you should've busted out and used sign language." Laurie waved her hands in a lousy imitation of the *hello* gesture.

"Maybe if I'd used sign language in the first place, they'd have let me go home sooner." Holly grimaced. "The question that keeps running through my head is *why?* Marcy was so nice, and in so many ways, she's just like us. She had a job, a family. She paid her bills. Went to church on Sunday."

"I can't imagine her mixed up in anything that could turn

around and get her murdered."

"Do you think she stumbled into something? I saw this Aryan Nation guy out there who scared the crap out of me. The skinheads and the Mexican bandits grow dope around here. Maybe Marcy wandered into one of their 'grows' and they shot her."

"Did you see any plants or signs someone was camping out?"

"There was a lot of trash—food wrappers and stuff—where we found her."

Laurie shook her head. "That's probably where people were fishing and too lazy to pack their trash out. And you know as well as I do that Marcy wouldn't have been poking around out there."

"I'm running out of possibilities. Could it have been someone else who screwed up? Someone she was involved with?"

Instead of brushing off the comment, Laurie pursed her lips, clearly thinking about it. "Marcy never talked about guys—anybody she was dating or guys in general. That's not normal. Women talk about their men."

Holly sidestepped the piles of poop the park geese had left on the paved path. The geese had ignored them when they didn't offer food. "That always bothered me, too. Friends talk about their love lives. Or complain about the lack of one."

"I hate saying anything bad about Marcy, but it always felt like she was hiding something."

Holly gave Laurie an incredulous look. "We all have things we don't want to talk about. It doesn't mean she was doing anything wrong."

"I didn't say that. It's just, at times, I wondered if she was seeing a married man."

Her mouth fell open and she sputtered, "Really? Why'd you think that?"

Laurie shrugged. "Sometimes I got that happy, I-have-a-secret vibe from her."

"A married man?"

"Sorry, it's just a feeling. I guess that's a sore subject for you, your dad and all."

"Let's don't add my father to today's disasters." Holly waved a hand, dismissing the topic and the apology. "Did Marcy ever tell you where she got that diamond necklace?"

"I wondered if it was a gift. I don't know how much Tim's paying her, but it looked more expensive than any jewelry I can afford."

A pair of seagulls swooped off the river. They hovered overhead, coarse voices screeching. Holly recoiled. Her hands flew out and covered her head. "Get away from me!"

Memory reran the scene from the clearing. The gulls. The body. The ravished face.

Holly's whole body tightened. Adrenaline—and fear—spiked through her system. She yanked off her hat and swatted at the birds. "Go away."

With a final cry of defiance, the gulls tilted their wings and headed upriver.

"Come on. They're gone." Laurie grabbed her arm and pulled.

Eyes averted from the river and the birds, Holly stumbled after her. They retreated to a bench where the trees protected them from the wind. "Sorry."

"The hat dance was a riot, but what was that about?" Laurie pushed back Holly's hair and lifted her chin. "Jeez, you're shaking."

Warmth climbed her cheeks. She swallowed the enormous lump in her throat. "I forgot there'd be seagulls here. Seeing Marcy's body…those horrible birds. I'll never be able to look at seagulls the same way."

A shudder crawled across her shoulders and down her spine. She told Laurie about finding the body, ending with a quick description of Marcy's face. "They *ate* her."

"Oh my God. That's horrible." Laurie pulled her into a sympathetic hug. "I'd have totally freaked if I found her."

"I pretty much did." She looked at the concern in her friend's eyes and again felt tears well.

Blinking back the tears, she concentrated on the foliage of the closest tree. The leaves danced in the breeze, shifting bands of color. By the time the first leaf floated away from the branch, she was fairly certain her voice would be level. "I keep hoping it's a bad dream. That Marcy will show up, shouting, 'Surprise!'"

"People our age are not supposed to die." Laurie rubbed her chin. "It's so weird that you and Alex found her. I mean, it's spooky how connected you are. You and Alex knew Marcy. She worked for Tim. Tim's your client."

Holly rolled her eyes. "You sound like JC."

"JC? You mean JC Dimitrak? I haven't heard that name in a long time. What's he got to do with anything?"

Holly rose and headed for the path. "On top of everything else in my screwed-up life, guess who's the detective on the case?"

Laurie knew her too well. Horrified disbelief colored her tone. "No."

"Yes."

"Oh. My God. I know he's a cop. He was there? What did you do?"

" 'Awkward' didn't begin to describe it. I was already in shock. We found this horrible body and it was *Marcy*. Alex and I were being questioned by all these cops, and then JC showed up." She wanted to bang her head against the nearest tree. "All that crap from six years ago was like it happened six minutes ago. First words out of his mouth were a huge personal hit. Of course, Alex noticed. After that, he and JC did everything but pee on the ground, marking their territory."

"Hmm." Laurie lips curved in a three-pointed smile. "So is it pheromones or do you two still have things to resolve?"

Holly made a rude noise.

"What are you going to do about it?"

She jammed her hands in her pockets and blew out a frustrated breath. "JC? Nothing."

"Nothing?"

"What would be the point? I'm going back to Seattle. Living there was never in the Life Rules According To JC Dimitrak." She flashed a wry smile at her friend. "No offense. I know you like it here."

Laurie was quiet for so long, Holly turned to stare at her. "What?"

"Is that really fair? You don't know what JC's like now."

"Excuse me? We're supposed to be talking about Marcy. Besides, whose side are you on?"

"Why does there have to be sides? Look, I know what JC did was despicable—"

"Ya think?"

Laurie ignored the sarcasm. "Did you ever consider maybe it wasn't completely black and white?"

Holly gave a fallen limb a savage kick. "I was there. There were no shades of gray."

"I've changed since college. You've changed. Why do you think he hasn't? It sounds to me like you're still attracted to each other. Why not see where it goes?"

They'd almost reached the parking lot before Holly heaved a long sigh and said, "JC and I want different things. Fundamentally different. He never accepted that I want a career, much less that my career is as important as what he does. I don't see that changing."

"He's taken his lumps like the rest of us. Did you know he's divorced?"

Part of her wanted to snark, *Oh, the little woman at home, ironing his shirts and minding the babies didn't work out?* But the rest of her didn't want to be immature. Laurie had a point. JC had lived his own life while she was gone. Holly didn't know anything about him except he still made her knees weak and other parts melt. She shook her head, rejecting those thoughts.

"The marriage didn't last long."

Laurie had apparently interpreted her headshake as an answer to her question about JC's divorce. Holly wasn't interested in talking about JC and she sure wasn't interested in discussing the woman he'd married mere months after they broke up. From the corner of her eye, she saw her friend studying her and wondered what was behind all the comments. "Now what?"

Laurie turned away. "Well, if JC's out of the picture, want to run across the river and let Alex feed us?"

"Not just no, but hell, no."

"Tell me how you really feel."

"His family will be there and after the day I've had, I don't want to put up with his mother."

"Too bad," Laurie said. "The boy can cook."

"I don't know what's going to happen with Alex. I thought we were having fun, but can you believe he tried to use Marcy's death as an excuse to jump into bed? Talk about bad timing."

Laurie burst out laughing. "Gotta give him points for trying."

"It did *not* earn him any points. It just made him pissier when JC showed up to ask another million questions."

"Wait. JC came by your house? I thought you meant he was at the game refuge, place, thing."

"That wasn't enough for him. He had to come take a few digs at my house."

"That seems weird. Maybe he thought he was doing you a

favor by not making you go to the police station."

"If we'd gone to the station, it would've been more professional. Or official. Instead, there were some seriously strange vibes. He'd make a personal remark and then slam me with, *Did you kill Marcy?* It felt like..." Holly hesitated, wondering if she should say this, even to Laurie.

"Like what?"

She blew out a breath. "Revenge. That he's treating me like a suspect so he can harass me. Coming by my house—he can't actually believe I'd hurt Marcy."

"JC's playing it by the book, questioning anyone who was there. The cops can't really think you were involved."

"You should've heard the questions they asked. Seen the way they looked at Alex and me."

"Huh." A twitch of concern flitted across Laurie's face.

"Seriously. With them looking at me as a suspect, I guess I better figure out what's really going on."

Chapter Six

Monday morning

Holly strode through the office building's atrium. She glanced at the Stevens Ventures office as she passed it. She'd have to look at the place every time she entered or left Desert Accounting—one more reminder Marcy was dead.

Juggling her briefcase, purse, and a bag of Spudnuts, she crossed the lobby at Desert Accounting and made her way to the corner office. She'd inherited the space along with her father's traditional furniture and his role as the accounting practice rainmaker.

She dropped the Spudnut bag on the massive wooden desk and licked maple nut glaze off her thumb. The desk divided the office in two. Behind the desk were her swivel chair, file cabinets, and a window overlooking the road, while visitor chairs stood on the side closest to the door.

Right now, she'd love to exchange all of it for her sleek modern desk in downtown Seattle.

She dipped into the greasy bag and fished out another puffed potato doughnut. She *would* miss the Spudnuts when she moved back to Seattle, though.

Her packed calendar and the mountain of file folders on the

credenza beside the desk mocked her. Slouching into her chair, she chewed the pastry and studied the pile. The clients would understand if she rescheduled, but when could she squeeze them in?

She was supposed to bring in new business so her mother could sell the practice to a larger firm. Talk about a vicious cycle—success meant more work for everybody, including her.

Especially her.

Lately, her mother also expected her to manage the projects—and use the foot-in-the-door opportunity to up-sell more of their services.

Get with the program, the pragmatist in her head ordered. *You have work to do.*

Instead of opening a client folder, she drummed her fingers against the armrest and stared through the window at the traffic on Grandridge. Her brain was stuck in a disbelieving loop—Marcy was dead. Life was short and unpredictable.

Occasionally, another thought slipped in. *Was she focusing her life on the right things?*

And if she was being honest, at least with herself, she'd wasted more than a little time last night tossing and turning, trying not to think about JC.

Add the "I'm-a-suspect" angle and the loop was complete.

The desk phone rang.

She caught herself before automatically answering. News of her involvement had her cell and landline ringing nonstop. A reporter from the *Tri-City Courier* had called repeatedly—murders were big news, he'd said at one point. The stories were carrying his byline, he'd added, so she should talk only to him.

Translation—the coverage could get him noticed by a larger newspaper.

Marcy was not a package to sell for his personal promotion.

His article this morning had stated she and Alex were "Persons of Interest," a.k.a. the prime suspects. That combination had earned him a place on her personal Do Not Call list. But between dodging the press, updating clients, and reassuring her friends, she hadn't accomplished a thing this morning.

Instead of answering the phone, she closed the Spudnut bag, wiped her hands, and grabbed the uppermost folder on the pile. Silverstone Dairies. Ugh.

Her mother had to pass the frickin' CPA exam and get licensed. When her father bailed on them, he'd screwed over his wife professionally as well as personally. Without Holly's CPA license—if she hadn't agreed to come back to Richland—her mother would've been forced to close the accounting practice.

Which meant Holly had to take crash courses in things like cow accounting.

She opened the file. For one long, rebellious moment she wondered if her mother was putting off taking the exam so Holly would have to stick around.

She stared at the spreadsheet, but the numbers and notes refused to tell their story. Her mind was stuck in the Marcy gear. She'd told Laurie she wanted to figure out why Marcy died, but she didn't have a clue where to begin.

Her gaze drifted over the files and landed on the Steven Ventures folder. Tim Stevens. She should start her investigation by questioning Marcy's boss. He'd know about her daily routine and whether there'd been any recent changes.

Holly picked up the phone and pressed the button for an outside line.

"Where're the Spudnuts?" JC's voice ambushed her.

Stifling a shriek, she dropped the phone. "Jeez. Don't sneak up on me."

Detective JC Dimitrak, who clearly wasn't there to inquire

about her feelings, ideas, or business success, leaned against the doorframe.

"Didn't your mother teach you not to take the Lord's name in vain?" He ran a hand over his already smooth hair. "'Course, being that jumpy could be interpreted as feeling guilty."

She gave him an *Oh, please* look, and didn't dignify his commit with a response. Instead, she returned his assessing gaze with one of her own. His clean-shaven skin seemed tight, the strain around his eyes more pronounced than it had been the previous day. Whatever he normally did on the job, he wasn't immune to the stress of brutal crime. She caught herself before she could feel sorry for him, but she did like him a little better for caring what happened to Marcy.

"Didn't we do this already?" she asked.

"I'm being thorough." JC stepped into her office like he owned the place.

" 'Bulldog' is a better description."

He picked up the bakery bag and inspected the contents. "Maple nut are my favorite."

She thought about grabbing the bag away from him, just because he was JC. "You can have *one*," she said grudgingly.

Much as she wanted Marcy's killer caught, she didn't have time for round two—or was it three?—with him that morning. "You thoroughly interrogated me yesterday. Today, you're just being a pain."

"Yesterday was my warm-up." Without asking permission, JC claimed a seat in the visitor chair. He crossed an ankle over his knee, spreading out, taking up too much room. He popped a Spudnut into his mouth. A blissful expression crossed his face.

She scowled. "Don't get too comfortable. You keep showing up here"—*and that reporter keeps implying I'm dirty*—"and I won't have a business left to run."

She turned her back on him and selected the files she'd need for her meeting later that morning. She stacked them in the center of her desk. Flashing subliminal—*I'm busy.*

With a cool look over her shoulder, she reached for her briefcase. "You can't possibly have more questions."

"I always have questions." His eyes gleamed. "The subject is what varies."

She froze mid-reach and did a double-take. Last night he'd sorta played with the *we-used-to-be-intimate* card. Apparently, today it was going to be *we're-best-buds.* She straightened, the briefcase clasped loosely in her hand. "I assume your subject is still Marcy."

"Of course. And you hold the Most Helpful Witness slot."

"I'm not your prime suspect anymore?"

His eyes crinkled at the corners, like he really wanted to make a smartass remark. "I had to grill you yesterday. You found the body in the middle of a swamp, in the middle of nowhere."

"Technically, the dog found the body. Since when is getting lost a crime?"

"You know I had to question everybody at the scene."

"You did that already. So let me rephrase it for you. Why are you here?"

What *was* happening here? JC kept throwing off mixed signals, but hadn't she made it infinitely clear she wasn't interested in him?

Says who? Her inner teenager checked out the hunk sitting on the other side of the desk.

"Occasionally you have some useful insights," he said.

"Newsflash. I worked about thirty acquisitions last year. People pay big bucks for my insights."

"For corporate stuff." His derisive tone said exactly what he thought of her job, which pissed her off all over again. He'd never made any effort to understand what she did or why she enjoyed the challenge. "Not exactly the same as police work."

"Seems a lot alike to me. Ask a bunch of questions. Wade through a ton of paperwork. Write up reports. Same thing."

Except for the whole "dead" part.

"What is it you'd like my insights about *this* time?" Her tone was saccharine sweet.

His good cop, charm-the-idiots-into-implicating-themselves persona vanished. His tone and eyes hardened. "Do you ever stop asking questions and just answer them?"

She gave him an exasperated glare. "Ignoring the little detail about you treating me like a suspect, unless you plan to share what you've learned about Marcy, I told you what I knew yesterday. I have a job and responsibilities too." She pointed at the crowded schedule visible on Outlook.

He ignored her computer. "I have questions. Questions about the victim."

With a resigned sigh, she stuffed the files into her briefcase and dropped it beside her desk.

He shifted in his seat. In spite of the hard, uncomfortable chair, he looked completely at home.

Damn, he was like a dog, practically marking whatever territory he occupied. "What do you want to know?" she asked impatiently. "That I haven't already told you. Twice."

He pulled his pen from his jacket pocket and gave her another assessing glance. He opened his folio, made a notation at the top of the page. "I checked. You moved here nearly five months ago."

You never looked me up hung in the air unspoken.

"And your point is?"

His features settled into hard planes. He thumbed through the pages of his notebook.

JC didn't need her for his investigation. Clearly she didn't know enough about Marcy's personal life to point him toward a suspect. During her sleepless night, she'd realized nothing had changed. JC was still making the rules—trying to, anyway—and bending them for his own purposes. Letting her go home, and then showing up at her house. Coming to her office, and acting...how? Almost as though he wanted to start something again. But then he'd zing her, or go into cop mode, which made her wonder if it was all a ploy. If he still suspected her of being involved—allegedly involved—in Marcy's death.

She rubbed her temples. The whole mess was giving her a massive headache.

"This is pointless." In one smooth move, she rose from her desk, slung her purse over her shoulder, and grabbed her briefcase.

"What are you doing? I'm not finished."

"Then walk and talk. I have a meeting."

His foot hit the floor with a responding *thud*. "I have an investigation."

"And I have responsibilities to other people. I've already told you everything I know about Marcy." She stepped around the end of her desk. "So either arrest me, or start walking."

JC stood, blocking her escape route. "I want to know about Tim Stevens' business."

"You know damned well I can't discuss client business." She glared at him. "The basics of Tim's company are in the public domain. Go look them up yourself."

"You could give me that insight you're so famous for."

With a snort of impatience, she shifted the briefcase to her other hand. "Tim's a developer. He contracts some projects, builds them for other people. He owns and leases other ones, like the office complex he's building near Southridge."

She sidestepped JC while he scribbled a note.

He followed her into the hallway. "I need a list of the

properties he owns and financial information on each one. And the latest statements for Alejandro Montoya's restaurant."

Her jaw dropped. "Are you crazy? I can't give you that."

"Why not?" He returned her incredulous stare. "You're not a lawyer. It's not privileged information."

"You and I *both* know it's privileged. The ethics requirements of my license are very clear. No unauthorized disclosure of financial information."

He opened his mouth, but she cut him off. "I work corporate mergers and acquisitions in Seattle. Breathing a word about a transaction won't just bring the deal to a screeching halt, it could bring the Securities and Exchange Commission down on me like the proverbial ton of bricks."

She waved her free hand, indicating the entire office. "The same rules apply at Desert Accounting. And in case you missed the point, that means don't bother asking anyone else here because they won't tell you, either."

"I'm trying to catch a murderer, not coddle a—" He bit off the remaining words.

She slammed a fist onto her hip. "A what? A bean counter?"

"Most people want to help the police." Every line of his body reflected frustration. "I thought you wanted to find Marcy's killer."

"Wait a minute." She punctuated her words with a pointed finger. "Are you saying Tim and Alex are officially suspects now? That's insane."

"If you think they're so innocent, you shouldn't mind giving me the financial information. If it clears them, I can move on."

Everything JC did—showing up, the Spudnuts, playing nice—had just been a ploy to soften her up and get her talking, so he could slide in questions about Tim and Alex. Damn, but the man was infuriating. "How is their financial information remotely related to Marcy's murder?"

"I need the information." JC sounded impatient.

She turned and stalked toward the lobby. "You can move on to another suspect. Alex and Tim didn't have anything to do with Marcy's death."

JC trailed her down the hallway. "What makes you so sure?"

"What makes *you* so sure they were involved?"

"What are you hiding?"

She glared at him over her shoulder. "Give me a freaking break. Tim and Alex aren't like that. They couldn't have killed her."

"Not even to save their own asses?"

Shocked, she studied his face, but he'd gone to complete cop mode. His hard expression revealed nothing. "From what? As far as I know, the only laws Tim and Alex have ever broken involve speeding tickets."

"At this stage of an investigation, the more innocent someone seems, the more suspicious I am."

"First honest statement I've heard from you. Does that blanket condemnation include me?"

He didn't move an eyelash.

Raising her chin, she kept her tone and gaze level, rigid self-control containing the seething inside her. "If you have evidence they're involved in Marcy's murder and have a financial motive, you'll have no problem getting a judge to sign a warrant."

Chapter Seven

Holly stormed into Desert Accounting's lobby with JC right on her heels. The tension between them was as thick and impenetrable as the walls of Fort Knox. She made it three steps into the reception area before she patted her jacket pocket and stopped in her tracks.

He did a quick sidestep around her. "What are you doing now?"

"Damn it, JC. You made me forget my phone."

Before he could say another word, she marched back to her office. She snatched up her cell and turned, ready to stomp back into the lobby.

Her common sense kicked in. *Whoa. Chill out. Get your act together.*

She took a deep breath and braced her palms against the desk. Letting JC see how much he upset her would be a major strategic error.

In his current mood, he'd probably interpret it as a guilty conscience.

For whatever reason, he seemed determined to pin Marcy's murder on her, Tim, or Alex. And even if he wasn't doing something that ridiculous, as far as she could tell, he was headed down the wrong path.

Clearly, he wasn't going to tell her anything about the investigation, so she'd have to figure out herself what he knew— or thought he knew. Which meant talking to the people he *should've* talked to. And since Tim Stevens was her client—as JC kept harping on—she had every reason in the world to stop in and talk to him.

So there, Mr. Super Sleuth Junior Cluemaster Detective.

Once she had some answers, she could redirect JC's investigation.

She felt better already.

The detective in question was doing his charming guy impression when she returned to the lobby. He leaned against the reception desk, flashing those damned dimples at Tracey. Normally the receptionist was the office mom—appointment-taker and excuse-maker. Tracey remembered the client's names— and those of their spouses, children, grandchildren, and favorite hunting dog. Right now, she looked as if she'd climb over the counter separating her desk from the waiting area if JC merely crooked his finger in her direction. Phones were ringing, all the lines lit up, but Tracey looked like she'd never heard the phrase, *Answer the phone.*

JC's body tightened enough for Holly to know he'd noticed her, but Tracey was still gazing longingly at the man, eating up the attention like she was seventeen instead of forty-seven.

Holly's gaze drifted to JC's long, lean body. What had six years' experience done for him? He'd been her first love, but she wasn't a kid any longer. Had it all been hormones and young lust? Before she could wonder what he looked like without the tailored shirt, she sent her drooling inner teenager to her room and locked the door.

"If I can interrupt?" she asked.

JC's lips twitched at her ironic tone.

Tracey blinked. "What? Oh, Holly, are you leaving now?"

What gave her away? The briefcase or the coat? She nodded, ignoring JC. Slim hips resting against Tracey's desk, he was giving Holly a slow inspection that seemed to remove her clothing piece by piece.

He was just doing it because he knew it irritated her.

"Have you seen my mother this morning?" she asked Tracey.

"Donna's still at the Chamber of Commerce breakfast."

JC's dimples reappeared. "I can't believe you're back in Richland, working for your mom."

Something she'd sworn she'd never do. She gave him a withering look. "A temporary arrangement."

She hadn't asked about his mother, a woman she'd adored during their college years, because it seemed hypocritical to mention Antheia when she was no longer involved with her son.

No, that wasn't right. She wasn't going to talk about Antheia because JC was using *her* mother as a putdown and she refused to use *his* mother that way.

The front door opened, saving Holly from round four with JC. Nicole Stevens entered and flashed a thousand-watt smile. "G'morning."

"Hello, Nicole." Tracey turned her attention from the detective to the swing-top floating around the petite blonde's killer body. "That's a darling outfit."

"You like it? It's a Lilly P." Nicole beamed with pleasure. From her Manolo Blahnik shoes to her diamond-studded ears, Tim's wife always projected an image of leisure and wealth. Extravagance seemed to be Nicole's middle name. Holly was relieved *she* didn't have to pay off the woman's charge cards.

Nicole executed a model-worthy pivot on her stiletto heels, and set the blouse's fabric in motion. "What do you think, Holly? Does it make me look big?"

Holly took in the innocent face Nicole presented. The comment felt like another of the woman's subtle digs. Her size four, perfectly proportioned body made Holly feel like an awkward giant. "You look lovely."

Nicole focused on the purse hanging from Holly's shoulder. "Is that a Borgedorf?"

She instantly forgave Nicole for the "big" comment and swiveled the zebra-striped hobo so all three women could appreciate the details. "Isn't it great? I found it last weekend."

She left out the half-price detail.

"It's modern and retro at the same time," Tracey said approvingly.

JC rolled his eyes.

What did a guy know?

Finger tapping her tiny, pointed chin, Nicole studied the bag. "Isn't that *last* year's design?"

Way to kill the moment.

Nicole turned back to Tracey. Usually, Nicole looked like she belonged at a 1950s Junior League function, but from the current expression on her face, *Desperate Housewives* might be more appropriate. "Is Tim here?"

"I haven't seen him," Tracey said.

Strange. Tim's Mercedes was in their shared parking lot. "Isn't he in his office?" Holly asked.

Nicole's glow dimmed. "I can't find him anywhere."

From the corner of her eye, Holly saw JC lock onto Tim Stevens' wife like Alex's bird dog after a pheasant.

Good.

She wasn't exactly throwing the woman under the bus, but if JC focused on Nicole, he might get off Holly's back about providing client financial information. As a bonus, talking to JC would keep Nicole out of the Stevens Ventures office long enough for Holly to talk to Tim—or at least to ask Brea where he was today.

"I'm headed over to Tri-Ag," Holly told Tracey. "I probably won't make it back before my two o'clock meeting. Please ask my mother to call me."

JC coughed, as though covering a laugh. He pushed away from Tracey's desk. "Could I have a word with you, Mrs. Stevens?"

Holly kept the smile off her face. Could she call them or what?

Most likely Nicole didn't know enough about Tim's business to tell JC anything, but he could have fun trying.

Of course, he *ought* to be out looking for the real killer.

Chapter Eight

Holly pushed through Desert Accounting's front door, crossed the atrium, and entered the Stevens Ventures office. The Western men's club decorating motif Tim had chosen always annoyed her, as if he'd missed the last forty years of women's achievements. Masculine, desert-hued colors, leather and heavy oak furniture—it was all part of the über-conservative, wife-belongs-at-home nonsense she constantly battled on the east side of the Cascades.

The reception desk, which blocked access to the office interior, sat vacant. A light blinked on the phone console, but the office was strangely quiet.

"Brea?"

No answer.

She tapped her toe for thirty seconds, then decided the sensible thing to do was bypass reception and head straight to Tim's office. High heels muffled by the thick carpet, she strode down the hall. She rounded the corner and ran smack into Lillian.

The payroll clerk rocked backward. Short, curly brown hair framed an expressive face, which quickly transformed from surprise to recognition. Lillian's left hand extended, palm up. She brushed bent fingertips across the palm, saying, "Excuse me" in sign language.

"Sorry." Holly brought her palm to her chest, moved it in small circles.

"I didn't hear you," Lillian signed. A smile smoothed the remaining tension from her face.

Holly rolled her eyes at the pun. "I'm glad I ran into you."

Since Lillian shared an office with Marcy, she might actually be a better person to start the investigation with than Tim. Even if she couldn't hear, Lillian was bound to know about Marcy's routine. Holly signed, "Do you have time to talk about Marcy?"

The brunette stiffened, then subtly leaned away, as if distancing herself from the question.

The renewed tension surprised Holly. She thought the two women had gotten along. Before she could ask what was wrong, Lillian gestured at her watch and signed, "I have an appointment. We can talk later."

She watched the payroll clerk walk away, shrugged, and entered Tim's office. Drawn blinds left the room shadowed. The conversation area and conference table were vacant, but a man leaned against the massive desk. Clothes disheveled, hair wild, he turned when she flicked on the lights.

"Ugh." He closed his eyes in a tight squint, stumbling to remain upright.

"Tim?" *What the hell?*

His hands rose and pushed through his already spiky hair.

A dozen possible business disasters cycled through her head. "What's wrong?"

"Holly? What...?" His voice trailed off in a confusion of whiskey fumes. He splayed a hand on the desk and peered around the room, checking its contents. "Is this...your office?"

"It's yours, Tim." She dumped her briefcase on the closest chair. "Did something happen with Southridge?"

He collapsed against the desk, rattling a whiskey bottle against the wooden surface. He tilted so badly the furniture barely held him upright. "I can't believe she's dead."

"Marcy?" Holly studied his ravaged face. He looked worse than she felt, and she'd seen the body. "I know you worked together, but I didn't realize you were that close."

An unwanted thought intruded. *How close were they?* More than friends?

No way. Tim gave every indication he was happily married. Even if Nicole played the bitch-in-helpless-waif-clothing routine, Tim doted on her. Still, his reaction seemed out of proportion for someone who was only an employee.

"She was a friend—a good friend." He scrubbed a hand over his face. "She listened. Nobody does that. She deserved more than the crap Alders put her through. More than..."

"Who's Alders? What crap?"

"God, I hate that guy." Tim jerked upright. His hands closed into fists.

He stopped as abruptly as he'd moved. Wavering on unsteady feet, his lower lip trembled and his jaw worked.

Still trying to catch up, Holly watched his emotional crumbling. Good grief. When was the last time she'd seen a guy cry? Besides over a stupid football game?

"She's dead." He lunged forward and enveloped Holly is a sweaty hug. Booze seeped through his pores, mingled with stale perspiration.

Yuck.

Wracking sobs shook his body. She didn't know whether to be concerned, horrified, or embarrassed. Instinct took over and she patted his shoulder as if he were a child. "It'll be okay."

He clenched her tighter and blubbered loudly against her neck.

Oh, jeez.

She turned her head, wrinkling her nose at the stench, and glanced at the door. Where was Brea when she needed her? "Shhh..."

Renewed sobs answered her.

Confused snippets of their conversation rotated through her mind, but she kept coming back to, *Why is he drunk? Why is he so upset?*

Finally, his tears subsided to shuddering breaths, and she wondered what to say that wouldn't embarrass both of them. She eased him away from her chest. "Nicole's in my office. Why don't you let her take you home?"

A look close to panic slid across his face. "Hell, no. She flips out if I have a drink."

A drink? She eyed the bottle on his desk. How about the whole friggin' bottle?

"Okay. What if I ask Brea to get some coffee?" She couldn't leave him like this, but she had to get moving or she really would be late for her meeting.

Maybe she should take him with her.

She resisted the urge to glance at her watch. "C'mon. Caffeine. How about a quick run to the Bikini Barista?"

"I can't." He wiped his nose against his sleeve. "Southridge financing closes next week. Gotta do stuff."

His tone reminded Holly of a petulant teenager. *Who are you and what have you done with my charming, confident client?*

She didn't want to set the guy off again, but maybe she could offer loan staff—from somewhere—to help him. "I guess Marcy...not being here...leaves you short-handed."

"I can handle it." A look that said *oh shit* slid across his face, but he slouched against his desk. He took a deep breath and seemed to pull himself together. "What's up?"

Okay, here goes. Tim had been drinking, but it wasn't like she

69

was looking for courtroom evidence. "I'm trying to understand what was going on in Marcy's life. She worked for you and—"

Tim reared back and lost his balance. A sweaty smear trailed his hand across the polished wood. "You think *I* did something to her?"

"No." She backpedaled hard. "I just thought, I mean, she did spend most of her time here, and—"

He pushed himself erect. "Her working here didn't have anything to do with anything."

"I just thought, since she's a friend as well as an employee, you might know if something was bothering her lately."

"You're an accountant. Keep your interest on business." His expression and tone approached *snarl*.

She took a surprised step backward. Where'd this temper come from?

"Ah, shit." He sagged against the desk. "Sorry."

Sorry he snapped? Sorry he told her what he really thought about her? Or sorry he tipped his hand that he might not be blameless in Marcy's death?

Holly eased behind the visitor's chair. If he made a move to hit or hug her, she wanted a sturdy object between them.

Tim's shoulders slumped. "I can't stand coming here and not seeing her." He stared at the floor as if it were purgatory. "She was too young to die."

Then again, maybe he was just drunk and upset.

"She's alive as long as we remember her," Holly said gently.

Okay, that was lame.

"Well," she said, edging toward the door. "I'll let Brea know you want to be alone."

Her gaze slid from the nearly empty bottle on Tim's desk to the console behind the conference table, where she knew he kept liquor. Should she confiscate everything inside it?

Tim didn't answer and she wondered if he'd even heard her.

"I'll be okay." His voice was flat, drained of the earlier emotion. "Life goes on. So they say."

Before she could think of a response, her cell phone rang. She dug it out of her pocket and checked the display. *Mother.* Thank God. She hit the connect button. "I'm leaving in a minute. Can you meet me at Tri-Ag?"

"Well 'hello' to you, too, darling." Her mother's voice was warm with concern and a touch of amusement.

"Hello, Mother. It's taken me months to get a foot in the door out there. We cannot be late."

"That's why I called. The Chamber meeting is still going."

Holly glanced at her watch. That meeting should've finished an hour ago. "Why?"

"They're arguing about the Point property. Some people would rather hold onto their private parking lot than see it developed productively."

"Are you going to make the Tri-Ag meeting?"

"I may be a few minutes late, but I'm more concerned about you. I tried to call earlier this morning, as soon as I heard the news. Are you okay?"

"I'm fine. A little tired, but fine." Guilt over not calling the previous evening poked her.

A thud sounded behind her. She whirled. Tim had vanished.

What the...? "Gotta go." She dropped the cell phone into her pocket.

"Tim?"

A rumbly belch broke the silence. She followed the sound and peered around the desk. Tim lay sprawled on the floor, passed out cold.

Well, that went well.

She might need to refine her interrogation technique.

Now what?

Brea rushed into the room. "Holly. Thank God. That cop's here again, wanting to talk to Tim."

"The cops?" She glanced from the receptionist to the slumbering suspect. Talk about bad timing.

"This detective—God, he's gorgeous—seemed a little PO'd when I said Tim wasn't here. I mean, Tim's Mercedes is right there in the parking lot. Where is he, anyway?"

Holly ignored the "gorgeous" comment—*have at it, honey*—and pointed behind the desk.

Brea took one look, then her face crinkled, fighting laughter. "What did you do to him?"

"Excuse me?"

Brea waved away the comment. "I knew he was hammered. He lurched in, mumbling, 'Don't tell Nicole I'm here.' "

"That would explain why she was in *our* office looking for him."

"What was she doing there? I told her to check upstairs, with the money people. As soon as she left, I tried to find one of the property guys to help." The receptionist propped her hands on her ample hips and nodded at Tim's inert form. "This is getting to be a habit."

"Really?"

"He was at Crazy Horse Casino Friday night, completely trashed."

"Are you sure it was Tim?" Surprise colored her voice.

"Oh, yeah. I see him down there all the time."

"I didn't know he gambled." Holly gave Tim another dubious inspection. "I hate to leave him on the floor, but I need to get moving."

Brea gauged the distance to the sofa. "Think we can haul him over there?"

"Worth a try." Holly kicked off her high heels.

Brea grabbed Tim's arms and tugged.

"Gee, thanks." Holly hooked her fingers under his ankles. "Give me the dirty end."

"Hey, you're farther away if he hurls."

They maneuvered the man around the desk.

"At least Nicole doesn't have to worry about him driving drunk." Holly adjusted her grip. "I've seen him have a beer or two, but I've never seen him drunk."

"That's because you only see him when Nicole's around. He doesn't drink much in front of her."

Interesting. "Why not?"

"Her parents. I'm not sure about her dad, he ran out on them, but her mom was an alcoholic." Brea's hand slipped and Tim's arm flopped to the carpet. "Damn. Gotta rest."

They stopped halfway across the office, Tim's body sprawled between them.

Wow. "To look at her, you'd think Nicole grew up a pampered princess." Holly flexed her hands, then re-gripped Tim's ankles.

"She married well," Brea said. "Ready?"

They lifted his body and shuffled forward a few steps.

"I thought today—his being drunk—might've been about Marcy," Holly ventured, probing.

"Maybe." Brea shrugged. "Her being dead totally sucks."

"Do you have any ideas about what happened to her?"

"No…which is too bad, since I wouldn't mind talking to that detective again."

Holly rolled her eyes. "Trust me, you don't want to hook up with him."

The other woman grinned. "Speak for yourself."

They tugged Tim closer to the sofa.

"Did Marcy ever talk to you about some guy named Alders?"

"Never heard of him." Brea nudged the coffee table away from the sofa. "You know, now that I think about it, Marcy was a lot of fun but she didn't talk much about herself."

"I feel bad about it now. Did anybody really know her?"

"Her sister?"

"I guess." Holly measured the distance to the cushions. "Okay, on three."

Brea nodded. "One, two, *three*."

With a heaving jerk, they lifted Tim's limp body and swung it onto the sofa.

Holly's stocking-clad feet slid as his weight shifted. She took a staggering step and dropped his legs. Arms waving, she fought for balance and lost. Her face landed in Tim's soft belly, perilously close to his belt.

Her disgusted, "Oh, yuck," was muffled by fabric and flab.

"What is going on?" demanded an outraged female voice.

Trying to find somewhere that didn't include Tim to put her hands, Holly wallowed off the couch and her client.

"What do you think you're doing?" Tim's wife arranged her baby blue eyes and pink lips into something that looked like a scowl.

Brea silently sidled out of the room.

Damn. No good deed went unpunished.

"We all know this isn't what it looks like," Holly scrambled to her feet. "The man is passed out."

Nicole crossed her arms and tapped her foot.

"Brea and I didn't want to leave him on the floor." Holly closed her mouth to stop herself from babbling.

Nicole's nose went up. "When you blew off your office, I didn't realize it was a literal concept."

Holly recoiled, as if the woman had physically slapped her. "I beg your pardon?"

"Stick to massaging the numbers. You don't have the assets"—Nicole raked a disparaging look down Holly's underdeveloped chest—"for anything else."

"Now, wait a minute."

But Nicole stalked past her and touched Tim's arm. "You can leave now."

Anger churned Holly's stomach. Anything she said would make things worse. Gritting her teeth, she retrieved her shoes and briefcase. At the door, she made one more attempt. "Hope he's okay."

"He has *me* to take care of him." Nicole repositioned Tim's arms.

Poor slob.

Chapter Nine

Monday afternoon

Holly left the 70s-era concrete building that housed Tri-Ag's business office. She managed not to strut or high-five herself on the way to her car. She'd rocked the meeting. It had taken a few minutes to get past the newspaper article which implied she was a murder suspect, but everybody had settled down and discussed ways to make use of the latest agriculture tax incentives.

She picked up Highway 240 and headed toward her office. Minutes later, she left the highway at Leslie, planning to avoid the worst of the commercial district surrounding Columbia Mall. Traffic piled up near Costco and then stopped for the traffic light at Grandridge. The Tom-Tom Casino was visible on a side street, partly hidden behind a strip mall. The scene in Tim's office ran through her mind, along with the surprise Brea had revealed.

Tim was a gambler?

His drunken night at the Crazy Horse could've been a one-off, but according to Brea, he gambled a lot.

Win or lose, gambling wasn't showing up in his financial statements.

Holly idled at the intersection and studied the casino's

sunbaked building. Brea had no reason to lie about Tim's gambling. Even if she thought gambling was a waste of time and money, it wouldn't bother her—if his financial records reflected it.

If he was only dropping a few hundred here and there, no big deal.

If it was more than a few hundred, and he was deliberately hiding it... That could wreck his credit rating.

Not to mention what would it mean if Desert Accounting had signed off on his finances.

The light turned green and the car ahead of her inched forward. She eyed the casino. Everyone connected gambling with money laundering, loan sharks, and the mob. But this was Richland, not Las Vegas. She didn't see any way Tim's gambling could be connected to Marcy's murder. But if he was hiding things from his accountant, she needed to know about it, if only to protect Desert Accounting.

Impulsively, she turned into the casino's parking lot. She *did* need to talk with the Tom-Tom's manager. After all, he was one of Desert Accounting's multiple casino clients. Besides, she had the gambling commission audit documents in her briefcase that she planned to deliver this week. So what if she hadn't called and made an appointment with him? It wasn't like she was avoiding the place.

Okay, being honest, gambling accounting was another area where she was scrambling.

Her father understood gambling accounting. Thankfully, the rest of his auditing team was still in place, because her knowledge of the industry-specific rules was...limited. The skills she'd acquired with the M&A Group—spotting risk patterns and anomalies—applied to any industry. But at times like this, she could've throttled her father with her bare hands for leaving the firm—and his clients—in the lurch.

If she knew where he and his yoga guru could be found, that

is.

Contacting the casinos about their gaming commission audits had been dumped onto Holly's To Do list. She suspected her mother didn't want any more reminders of her husband than absolutely necessary. Just coming to the office every day had to be a challenge, she realized in a flash of insight and empathy.

She could do this for her mother.

And satisfy her concerns about Tim at the same time.

~$~

Holly opened the blacked-out entry door and stepped inside the casino. Instead of a pseudo-Native American look, the Tom-Tom had gone for Vegas flash—lots of fluorescent lighting, cheesy casino-themed wallpaper and industrial-grade plaid carpeting so appalling that not even absorbing sound, dirt, and random spilled drinks redeemed it.

With a quick glance around the main room, she spotted the office cluster and headed in that direction. She could introduce herself, drop off the engagement letter, and then casually ask if Peter Ayers, the casino manager, knew Tim Stevens.

Adjusting her smile, she opened the door and stepped into a surprisingly modern office. "Hi, I'm Holly Price. I'm looking for Peter Ayers."

Two women half-hidden behind cubicle walls looked up, but it was the man at the desk in the corner who rose and came forward with an outstretched hand. He gave her suit a quick scan. A frown twitched his eyebrows, but he smiled and said, "Donna mentioned you'd be by this week."

An air of quiet confidence accompanied his firm grip. His poly-cotton shirt and giant western belt buckle were standard business attire for the area. Holly knew her designer suits were excessive for the area, but since she was only going to be in Richland for a year, she couldn't justify a new wardrobe.

Peter led the way to his desk. "Do you have a draft of the engagement letter?"

"In my briefcase." She took the closest of the visitor seats.

The casino manager eased into a swivel chair and moved a few things around on his desk, squirming a little. "Sorry to hear about your dad."

She nodded, not interested in talking about her father's desertion.

Peter gave her another doubtful inspection. "Will you be taking his place?"

Her father's vanishing act had left Desert Accounting scrambling on too many fronts. "No, it'll be the same team as last year. Amanda is our most experienced auditor and I don't want to get in her way."

His expression initially gave away his relief—her inexperience wasn't going to create a problem for him—and then showed his confidence in Desert Accounting in spite of her father's AWOL status.

They discussed the initial fieldwork for the cage accountability and listed target delivery dates. "That's all I need today," she said. "I'll stop by on Wednesday. We can wrap up the details then."

"Okay." Peter gathered the documents into a tidy pile. "I'll follow you out. It's time for my walk-through."

They angled across the casino's main floor toward the entrance. Gamblers stood and sat in front of an astonishing variety of machines, with enough lights, whirlers, and sounds to please the most jaded five-year-old. An overweight woman slumped on a stool in front of the machine at the end of a row. A cup of quarters nearly disappeared in the folds of her thighs. She dropped coins, pushed the button, and frowned at the results.

Holly tilted her head and said, "I thought everybody had converted to electronic script."

Peter gave the patron a quick glance, then scanned the remaining rows of slots. "We keep a few of the older machines. I'm not sure if it's a nostalgia thing or if some gamblers prefer the tactile sensation of handling coins."

A grin lit his face. "Personally, I think they like the coins spraying everywhere when they hit a jackpot."

He filled the remaining walk with pleasant conversation. Spillover from the local vineyards' harvest tours was filling seats in the casino. The glorious autumn weather—blue skies and moderate temperatures—was drawing droves of tourists to the Columbia River Basin.

"One of my clients mentioned how much he enjoys coming here," Holly said.

"That's the sort of feedback I like hearing. Which client, if you don't mind me asking?"

"Tim Stevens. You know him?"

"Oh, sure. Nice guy. Comes in about once a week."

With a sinking heart, she thought, *every week?* "I guess all developers are gamblers at heart."

"Good point. Stevens is a good customer. Doesn't make a scene if he loses." Peter smiled. "He brought his wife in a couple of weeks ago."

"Oh?" Nicole didn't seem like the type who'd enjoy it.

"She had a blast playing the slots. I was surprised he didn't bring her in again." He shrugged. "Maybe I just like seeing pretty women in here. I'm real partial to brunettes."

"Brunettes?" She couldn't keep the startled reaction out of her voice. Nicole was as blond as they came.

"No offense. Blondes are pretty, too."

A brunette? *Oh crap.* She scrambled, thinking furiously.

"That's okay."

Damn. Tim was gambling *and* cheating on his wife? What else was he doing?

Peter suddenly blinked and looked as if he'd love to rewind the conversation and answer a different way. "Uh, I could be thinking about a different guy."

Before she could decide how to tactfully ask if the brunette was Marcy, Holly's internal alarm sounded a warning. She glanced to the side, expecting to see one of the gamblers checking her out. Instead, she noticed a man leaning against the far wall. Deeply tanned with dark hair brushing his collar, he wore jeans, a fringe-trimmed shirt, and a cowboy hat with an intricate turquoise band. The hat-brim shaded his features, but his posture said he was watching something with fixed determination.

His body type—and the intensity of his scrutiny—reminded her of Frank. For half a second, part of her shrieked *Run!* while the rest chided, *Frank's in Seattle.*

Everything about the guy said, "law enforcement." Except here, it must be "security." But what had caught his attention? As subtly as she could, she scanned the room, looking for anything out of place. Was something about to happen? Something bad, like a robbery?

She stole another glance. He'd moved away from the wall. Hands on his hips, he blatantly stared at *her*.

A shiver of unease ran down her spine. She hadn't done anything he could consider threatening. Her briefcase looked out of place, but all it held was a bunch of papers.

Peter said something about the Basin's winter gloom holding off, and then cocked his head. "You okay? You look a little peaked. Can I offer you something from the snack bar?"

"No. Thank you, though." Holly lowered her voice. "Do you know that man? The one wearing the cowboy hat and fringed shirt?"

Peter craned his neck. "Sure, that's my security manager. Want to meet him?"

Security. She'd guessed right. She held up a hand, stop-sign style. "He just made me nervous. But that makes sense if he's security. He's scary enough to keep everyone in line."

He must have seen her as out of place—a non-gambler. The suit, the briefcase. She breathed a sigh of relief. *Over-reacting much? Of course it isn't Frank.* Just another cop-wannabe bouncer with an attitude.

"That's what we hire them for," Peter said.

Obviously the casino needed protection. She had to remember that not all law enforcement people—even the intense ones—were crazy like Frank. "I'll be careful not to attract his attention next time."

Peter smiled. "Now, that'll be hard to do."

With a wave to dismiss his compliment, she escaped through the front door.

The sense of unease followed her to the car.

Chapter Ten

Late Monday afternoon

Multiple file reviews later, Holly restacked the folders on her credenza and placed the completed ones in her out-box. She checked with the staff working on last-minute tax returns, then said, "I'm going out for a while to clear my head."

The staff probably thought she meant *clear it from taxes*, but she needed to clear her head—and her name—from Marcy's murder. She didn't know if Tim's brunette and gambling habit were connected to Marcy or if they were yet another ball to keep in the air, but she hoped Marcy's sister, Yessica, could shed some light on her sister's life—and death.

Holly crossed the Blue Bridge over the Columbia River and drove into Pasco. She knew Yessica's store was located in downtown Pasco, but Marcy had driven the one time they'd visited the place. She'd have turned on her GPS, but she couldn't remember the exact name of the boutique. She cruised the streets around the courthouse and Farmer's Market. One-story buildings lined the roads —some newly renovated with bright colors and awnings; others remained minimalist 70s-era bland. They all housed businesses catering to the area's predominantly Hispanic population.

Twenty minutes and a few wrong turns later, Holly spotted the store and pulled into an angled parking space near Celia's Confectionery. Sweet, carbohydrate-laden odors drifted through the bakery's door and permeated the air. Holly's mouth watered and her stomach growled, reminding her she'd skipped lunch.

Pastry. Afterward.

Holly bypassed the bakery and entered La Boutique. Pristine First Communion dresses and frothy *Quinceañera* and Sweet Sixteen gowns crowded the racks. Based on the displays, she thought the *Quinceañera* seemed more debutante ball than Hispanic religious ceremony and coming-of-age party.

The showcase of beaded "First Heels," gloves, and sparkly tiaras snagged her attention. A small white purse—the perfect size for summer cocktail parties—caught her eye. She twisted, trying to read the price tag.

"Holly?" Surprise colored Yessica's tone.

Holly jerked away from the purse display with a guilty start.

"You have a beautiful store." She gestured at the clothes and accessories. "Marcy had a flair with clothes, too. She always looked so put together. I guess it runs in the family."

"Maricella loved pretty things." Yessica closed the cash register. "But I don't think you came for a *quinceañera* present."

"Actually, I hoped to see you." Holly had headed to Pasco, suspecting Yessica might have sought solace in the ordinary routine of managing her boutique.

Wary surprise shifted the woman's eyebrows and narrowed her eyes. The expression drew attention to the dark shadows underneath them.

"I saw your store was open and stopped in. I didn't want to disturb your family by going by the house," Holly said.

"I needed to get away." Yessica no longer met her eyes. "People depend on me. If the store isn't open, my employees don't work."

"You don't have to explain." Work would give Yessica something besides Marcy to focus on.

"Why did you want to see me?"

How to get into this? That Holly wanted to understand what was going on in Marcy's life? That she should've known more than she did about her friend? "There are things I don't understand."

Yessica fidgeted with her rings, then looked directly into Holly's eyes. "Me, too. The newspaper said you found her body. It mentioned the strange coincidence—very convenient—that *you*, her friend, were the one who found her. Are you here about Maricella or are you really looking to clear yourself?"

Holly went still. Her mind raced to get ahead of Yessica's unexpected reaction. "Both. I really need to understand why she's dead."

"I know you two were friends, but it's not your place to figure it out. You're an accountant, not a police officer. It's up to them to find who killed her. To clear you. Or not."

How could she get past Yessica's anger and reticence? *Yes, I'm a suspect* probably wasn't a good start and *JC's ruining my business reputation*—definitely a bad follow-up. But this wasn't idle curiosity. "Marcy was my friend. I swear I didn't have anything to do with what happened to her. That reporter—"

"I know you'd never hurt her." Yessica waved her comment away. "And I know all about *that* reporter."

"It seems murder sells a lot of newspapers."

"He's using Maricella, and my family, to sell his newspaper." Yessica's mouth twisted in a grimace. Color rose on her face, two hectic red spots on her smooth olive skin. "Where was he after she disappeared? When we wanted his help?"

"I don't think he cares about Marcy at all." Holly wanted to direct Yessica's anger in another direction. JC had brought up an "ex" when she mentioned Lee, and Tim had talked about a guy named Alders who gave Marcy a lot of grief. Marcy's reappearance in Pasco, meshed with her reluctance to talk about her past, created a troublesome combination. "Did Marcy have a restraining order against Lee?"

Yessica did a classic double-take. Drawing Holly with her, she moved closer to the wall. "Maricella told you about Lee?"

Was Lee his first or last name? Holly crossed her fingers and nodded. "A little. It was why she moved back here, to get away from him."

A guess, but apparently it was right on target.

Lips pursed in silent contemplation, Yessica scanned the boutique.

Watching the woman from the corner of her eye, Holly made her own assessment of the patrons. Two girls who looked entirely too young to be planning a coming-of-age party rifled the frothy white dresses. A mother–daughter pair was engrossed in the wedding gowns.

"I'm glad she told you."

Holly refocused on Yessica. Up close, the woman had the red-rimmed eyes and tight-pinched face of angry grief.

"Maybe it meant she really was moving on. I told her to stay away from Lee from the moment she met that man. I knew he was bad news even before the bastard started hitting her. Not that she ever admitted he did it."

Lee hit Marcy? Outrage flared, but Holly forced herself to stay still, to listen and shoulder part of Yessica's pain.

"Why didn't I do more?" Yessica plucked a tissue from the box behind the counter.

Holly touched her arm, a tangible reassurance. "You did the best you could. Marcy knew you loved her."

"Love." Yessica snorted. "Maricella thought Lee loved her. I'll never forget how she was. 'He's wonderful, Yessa.'" Her hands fluttered in exaggerated gestures of rapture, the tattered tissue a ragged banner. "All he loved was his money," she added darkly.

Rich plus Seattle most likely meant Alders was in the high-tech industry and could've been the owner of a startup. Wouldn't it be horribly ironic if her Mergers and Acquisitions Group sold his company? Ugh, then she might have made the bastard even richer and more entitled.

But damn, if Marcy had confided in her, she was supposed to already know all this. Improvising, Holly said, "Marcy never told me how she met him. Was he from Pasco or did they meet when she was living in Seattle?"

Yessica's anger ebbed, replaced by weariness that bowed her shoulders and carved lines into her face. She stuffed the tissue remnant into a pocket. "They met at a coffee shop near her office. Knowing what I do now, I suspect he followed her there—made it look like an accidental meeting."

"He was stalking her?" Holly kept her tone level—Yessica was already upset—but concern and futile frustration tightened her hands into fists. She knew exactly how it felt to have someone invade her life that way.

Her first date with Frank had been at a coffee shop, too. It had all started so innocently. Was that how Marcy got sucked in? A charming guy. A pleasant setting...

But things had deteriorated from there, apparently for both of them.

"Stalking her?" Yessica's hands rose and fell. "Who knows? She seemed so happy, but when I met him, I got a bad feeling, you know?"

She *did* know. Her creep detector had saved her a few times, but it hadn't kept Frank Phalen from stalking her.

"Maybe if I'd said more..."

Holly gave Yessica a reassuring squeeze. "If Marcy was that caught up in Lee, she wouldn't have believed you. And you thought she was happy." Maybe Marcy had been happy. Maybe Lee had simply pursued her. At least, at first...

"When she stopped coming home, we thought she was too busy and too happy to make the trip." Yessica shook her head, tumbling glossy, dark hair across her shoulders. Hair so like her sister's, Holly's heart ached anew.

"Maybe she was."

"I think she was afraid Mama and Papa would see the bruises," Yessica continued as if Holly hadn't spoken. "Or maybe that bastard Lee Alders wouldn't let her out of his sight."

Her stomach wrenched. When had Marcy realized she was in a destructive relationship? Had she ever admitted it, even to herself? Holly thought about the mystery boyfriend and kicked herself for not becoming a better friend. She should've given Marcy a chance to talk about it—with someone who understood.

Another thought intruded. What if Peter's gambling brunette was someone else and Marcy had gotten mixed up with Lee again?

"The lies that man told. All 'I've changed, baby. I'll never do it again.'" Yessica's voice mocked the clichéd phrases. "He better not show his ugly face around here again, or..."

Yessica's glower warned that Lee might go home minus a body part or two if he showed up.

"Was he here? Last week?" Holly asked.

"A couple of weeks ago. Lee's such a damn charmer. Mama never believed he beat Maricella. The bastard was smart enough not to hit her face. Mama kept telling her to stay with him like a good wife should."

Mrs. Ramirez encouraged her daughter to stay with an abuser? Holly struggled to keep her dismay off her face. Her own mother had been as protective as a grizzly bear over her cubs when

Holly finally admitted Frank frightened her.

She'd moved three hundred miles across a mountain range to get away from Frank, because when she stopped and admitted it, he *still* frightened her.

"Lee got Mama to tell him where Maricella was living and working. When she disappeared last week, Mama was convinced she'd gone back to him and his fancy Westside condo."

"Do you remember where he lives? The address?"

Yessica rattled off an address, a condo in the high-rent district overlooking Lake Washington.

"Why did she attract that sort of man?" Tears of frustration filled Yessica's eyes. "Her childhood—our childhood—was sweet. Papa and Mama loved us very much. We had family. No one mistreated her. But it was like she thought she didn't deserve to be loved by a good man."

What a sad and simple statement. Everyone deserved an opportunity for love. In spite of her career aspirations, she hoped for the same chance. "You can't blame yourself. You tried, but nobody really knows what's happening in someone else's mind, or why they make the choices they do. Marcy loved being back here, close to her family. She talked about all of you, all the time."

Yessica's tears overflowed. "She spoke of you as well. She said you were a friend."

Holly grabbed another tissue, then stepped closer. "I wish there was more I could do." The only thing she could do right now was put her arms around a grieving soul and hold on tight.

A few minutes later, Yessica wiped her eyes and sniffled. "Thanks."

Holly stepped back. "Have you told the police here about Lee Alders?"

"Don't they know? Maricella got the papers, the restraining order." Yessica dabbed at her nose.

"In Seattle?"

"Yes." Confusion wrinkled Yessica's forehead. "The women's advocate took the papers to the courthouse and the judge signed them."

"I don't know exactly how it works, if there's a central database or something. The local cops might not know about the restraining order." Holly considered what JC would say if she suggested he look at Marcy's ex. "It would be better if you told the police about Lee."

JC needed to know what Lee had done. That was where he should concentrate, not on Tim and Alex.

Or her.

Chapter Eleven

Tuesday morning

Holly spread the newspaper over the files on her desk. Coverage of Marcy's murder had already moved from the front page to the second section. Today's article offered a preliminary assessment of Marcy's life, starting with, "No criminal record."

Like that should be the highlight of anyone's life.

The story mentioned Marcy's job at the real estate company, the planned memorial service, and a private interment. Holly nearly spewed coffee over the next line. "Police again questioned local accountant Holly Price and developer Tim Stevens."

WTF?

What was the reporter trying to do, force her to talk to him by otherwise ruining her business? Holly was still staring at the sentence when a masculine voice said, "You checking out the story in the *Tri-Cycle?*"

"What?" She gave Rick Stewert a startled look.

"The *Tri-City Courier.*"

Oh. Tri-Cycle. Baby reporters with training wheels. She nodded. "Yeah."

The sandy-haired man lounging in her office doorway gestured at the newspaper. "Did they manage to get any of it right?"

"The part about finding Marcy by the Snake River is right. According to this, she was already dead—shot—when she went into the water. She didn't drown." A shudder rippled over Holly's shoulders. Drowning topped her personal list of horrible ways to die.

A frown followed. Being shot probably ranked second.

"Marcy was a sweet girl. I'm gonna miss seeing her around. I feel bad for her family." Rick dropped into the visitor chair. Her senior manager squirmed and grimaced. "This chair really sucks, you know?"

She'd known the guy since high school, so she grinned. "Makes people leave faster."

"Is that a hint?" Laughter sparkled in Rick's hazel eyes.

"Not yet." She tapped a finger against the newspaper. "Of course, I'm not sure how accurate any of this is. According to the reporter, I'm still a Person of Interest."

"Really?" Rick's face mocked horror. "I'd hate to find out I worked for a felon."

"Very funny. The article says they're trying to locate the original crime scene."

"Makes sense. Wherever Marcy was shot, there'll be evidence. The cops probably talked to everyone upstream from Big Flats. Hopefully somebody will give them a lead."

JC's focus on the people around Marcy made more sense in that context. All the police had to go on was what they could learn from people who knew her. She bit her lip, uncomfortable she hadn't been more help, but really, there wasn't anything she could've added.

Then again, JC's approach, asking about Tim and Alex the way he did, didn't exactly inspire confidence. He'd seemed to start with the assumption the men were guilty. Maybe he was so used to dealing with people who casually broke the law, he'd forgotten not everybody did.

"Earth to Holly."

She blinked.

Rick's grin slowly faded. He stepped across the office and closed the door. "I need to talk to you."

Uh-oh. Closed door equaled trouble. She scanned his face, running a quick catalog of possible issues. Another job offer. Staff problems. *Please don't let it be staff problems.*

"What's on your mind?" she asked.

He flexed his fingers, making a false start. His gaze roamed the office, but there weren't many trinkets to distract him. Holly had packed up her father's stuff when she moved into the office and hadn't bothered to unpack her own belongings.

Rick leaned back and crossed an ankle over his knee. "How long are you here?"

She blinked again. How long was this conversation going to take? "I don't have anything scheduled until late this afternoon."

"No, I mean, how long are you going to stay? In Richland?"

"I don't know exactly." She couldn't see her watch, so she didn't know *exactly* when she planned to bolt for Seattle.

He drummed his fingers against his knee. "When your dad took off, I figured you came to help your mom."

She nodded.

Rick dropped his foot to the floor and leaned forward, his shoulders a rigid line. "The way I see it, you're running yourself ragged bringing in new business for one of two reasons."

Wow. She'd hoped to avoid *this* conversation entirely. She forced her expression to stay neutral.

"Have your parents filed for divorce?"

She folded the newspaper and tucked the local section into her "Marcy" file, buying time. He may be a friend, but he was an employee. A key employee she needed to keep onboard. "Between you and me?"

"Sure."

"Not yet. Mother signed separation papers."

"Good." He nodded again, apparently checking off an internal list. "Your parents probably owned the practice jointly, but he walked away."

She figured this wasn't the time to mention that both her parents had given her a small ownership stake in the practice. Of course, since they'd made her a member of the limited liability company instead of an employee, she wasn't paid a fixed salary. And since she was taking a leave of absence from her Seattle job, she wasn't drawing a salary there either. Which meant, she stayed broke.

Definitely something wrong with that picture.

Rick continued, "Washington's a community property state. Your father will likely get half the practice in the settlement, as of the time they separated. The new business should stay with your mother."

"I don't do much estate work."

"If you stay," he paused and gave her a pointed look, "you'll need to learn it. Anyway, I hope that's the reason for all the new clients—your mother needs the cash from the new business to buy him out."

"Honestly, I'm not that involved."

His skeptical look said he didn't believe her. "The other alternative is you're building up the practice to sell it."

She winced inwardly. The staff was not supposed to know that. The clients were definitely not supposed to know. "Mother asked me to help. To bring in more business. That's what I've done. She hasn't told me her longer range plans."

"Holly." He used the same cool tone. "I didn't move to

Seattle when I graduated because I wasn't interested in working for a big firm."

She pasted on her understanding smile. When she left Richland for college, she had no intention of returning to the small town. High risk, high reward; she thrived on the high-profile pressure of the mergers and acquisitions work.

"I didn't want the hours or the stress," Rick said.

Oh crap. He was going to leave. He couldn't leave. She needed him to manage the staff. To handle the project work.

And dammit, she liked him. He was one of her allies, her friends.

Rick recrossed his legs. "I talked to Bill Druise over at Wiltshire and Caruthers. He said we'd be working together soon."

Blabbermouth. Druise wouldn't last two minutes in corporate transactions.

"That was seriously jumping the gun," she assured him. "Mother told me W&C called. They've thrown out some feelers, probably hoping to pick up the practice at a bargain basement price—which isn't going to happen, by the way. She didn't say whether they made an actual offer. Or if she'd even consider a proposal."

His shoulders relaxed an inch. "That's a relief. I don't want to leave Desert Accounting."

"That's good to hear. I don't want you leaving, either." Slumping in her chair, she kneaded the muscles in the back of her neck. "Now quit worrying."

"I'll quit worrying when you quit bringing in more clients." The teasing note was back in his voice.

She made a shooing motion. "Go harass the staff or something."

"Or should I say, when you earn your 'walking money'?"

"Out." She pointed at the door and Rick left, wearing a self-satisfied smirk.

Holly stared at the mess on her desk. She might feel overwhelmed at times by everything her mother asked of her and privately bitch about it, but she'd never regret helping her.

Had she handled Rick appropriately? Although he'd seemed okay with her explanations, the boss role still felt foreign.

With a twitch of her shoulders, she set Rick and his questions aside. She was only here a few more months. Rick might end up working for a slightly larger firm, but he'd be okay. In the meantime, she had to focus on what was important.

She propped her elbows on the desk and braced her forehead against her palms.

So many things were important.

Clearing her name. Solving Marcy's murder.

Shoring up her mother. Bringing in new work. Selling the company.

Then there was her and Alex. And maybe JC.

With all of them important, it was almost overwhelming.

The biggest challenge of all might be figuring out what was *most* important.

Chapter Twelve

The necklace *had* to be a clue.

Holly leaned toward her computer monitor and studied the blown-up image she'd Photoshopped from the picture at Tim's party. She concentrated on the shiny ornament around Marcy's neck.

Nice rock.

Yessica might know where Marcy got it, but with yesterday's unexpected revelations about Lee, she hadn't thought to ask her about it. She picked up the phone and called Yessica's store.

"I'm sorry, Mrs. Herrera isn't available. May I take a message?" a woman's voice asked.

Holly left her name and cell phone number. Most likely Yessica was with her family, arranging Marcy's wake. Drumming her fingers on her desk, Holly frowned at the picture. Who else could she ask?

Her gaze drifted guiltily to the stack of files in her in-box. She ought to be preparing for her next meeting or reviewing files. Instead, she rummaged through the desk drawer for the phonebook, found the list of local jewelers, and dialed the first number.

An hour later, she dropped the handset back into the cradle. She'd gotten "We don't give out that information," a few "No comments," which probably meant that irritating reporter must have had the same idea, and a couple of "The police already asked's," which meant JC was once again BSing her about what he knew about Marcy.

Big shock.

With a discouraged sigh, she picked up the first client file and wished it would review itself.

Two hours later, Alex strode through her office door. She pushed aside the paperwork. "Are we having lunch?"

She glanced at her calendar but the noon slot was clear. "Before I forget, do you know where Marcy got that diamond heart necklace?"

"Goddammit, Holly. Will you quit playing amateur sleuth?" Alex slammed the door. "And you should've called."

She took in the flared nostrils and anger snapping in his eyes. Okay, so subtlety, self-control, and emotional support weren't Alex's strong points. "What's wrong? Did something happen at the restaurant?"

He batted her question away with an impatient gesture. "What did you tell him?"

"Tell who, about what?"

"That detective. The asshole who came to your house."

Oh, *that* detective. "I didn't tell him much. You know, I'm actually embarrassed by how little I know about Marcy."

"Not about *her*. What did you tell him about *me*?"

"You?" Holly stiffened. The way he was acting, she'd figured the health department had threatened to shut him down. "He asked how long we'd been dating. I told him not long. Why?"

Alex raked his hands through his thick, dark hair. "Would you quit acting so dense? What'd you tell him about Tim and me? Our finances?"

She narrowed her eyes. "Nothing."

He placed one deliberate foot in front of the other. Splaying his hands on her desk, he leaned over it. "Bullshit. He said you did."

Anger pumped heat from Holly's gut to her cheeks. She surged to her feet and pushed her face to within inches of Alex's. "And I just told you I didn't. Why do you believe some guy you just met over me?"

"What reason would he have to lie?"

"I can think of several. The better question is, why are you so upset? Is there something you haven't told your accountant?" *Much less the woman you're dating.*

Alex straightened, paced the narrow space in front of her desk, then dropped into the visitor chair. "God, this chair sucks," he muttered.

Damn macho pride. No way was he going to apologize. Why had she ever thought he was fun to hang out with?

Holly wrestled her temper under control. "It would've been nice if you'd asked for my side of the story instead of assuming the worst. And to be honest, I don't appreciate you making a scene at my office. I would never undermine your authority at the restaurant."

"I didn't—"

She cut him off. "What exactly did Detective Dimitrak say?"

Alex scrubbed his face with his hands. "He said he talked to you about our finances, but he wanted clarification."

She maneuvered her expression into negotiating mode, projecting a confidence she didn't necessarily feel. "He asked. I told him your finances were confidential. What did he want you to 'clarify'?"

"What Stevens Ventures owns besides the Stevens Building."

"What'd you tell him?"

Alex stuck his hands in his pockets and rattled some change.

"The shopping center in Sunnyside and the medical office park in Yakima."

Her eyebrows rose. "That's it?"

That was less than half of what the two men owned. A darker question overrode her surprise. "Why didn't you tell the police about the rest of it?"

Her client wasn't meeting her eyes.

"That's all I could think of off the top of my head." He slumped in the chair like a cornered teenager. "I didn't know what you'd told him. He acted like he thought we were dirty."

"Jeez, Alex, that's the oldest trick in the world. Make somebody think you know the whole story by telling part of it and they spill the rest. But why would the police think your finances have anything to do with Marcy's death?"

"Who knows? I don't need this cop hassling me. Sunday was bad enough. I got the third degree from how many of them?" He pushed out of the chair and paced. "That detective, Demi...whatever, wants to make Tim and me look guilty."

Alex waved his hands, working himself up again. "He acted like Marcy saw something she wasn't supposed to see. About *us*. That we killed her to shut her up. Which is totally fucked up."

"Of course you didn't have anything to do with her murder. You and Tim don't have anything to hide." Other than that gambling thing. And the brunette...

She watched Alex pace. He had a quick temper, but why was he acting so defensive about his finances? He hadn't done anything illegal...had he?

Could he be doing something else, something not connected to Marcy's death, that worried him? Desert Accounting didn't handle the restaurant's books—Alex kept it separate from the Stevens Ventures group—but she'd never questioned his integrity.

"Are you or Tim doing something we should all be concerned

about?" The accusing words were out before she knew it.

Alex whirled and slammed his hand onto the desk. The heavy wood absorbed the blow, but she still flinched. "I cannot believe you asked me that."

And yet... "That isn't an answer." She wished she could retract the question, but she also wanted to hear what he'd say.

He pulled in a deep breath, his nostrils again flaring like an angry bull. "I haven't done anything illegal. Does that make you feel better?"

The sarcasm was an added bonus.

"Not really. Your reaction seems out of proportion to JC asking a few questions."

"JC." Alex's lips thinned. He nodded as if she'd just confirmed something.

"What?"

"That cop doesn't want anyone getting next to you."

Holly picked her jaw off the desktop. "That's crazy. There is nothing between JC and me. That was over a long time ago."

"It sure explains why he's riding my ass."

"Maybe he doesn't have a better suspect yet. Come on, Alex. Don't you read mysteries? The police always look at the victim's friends and family."

Alex snorted in reply.

She gave an exaggerated roll of her eyes. "If Detective Dimitrak hangs around here, it's because he thinks I'm part of his grand conspiracy. He asked me where I was last Tuesday."

"You?" Alex barked out a laugh. "You're tough enough, but you couldn't have shot Marcy. You hate guns."

"What makes you say that?"

"I'm not totally blind and oblivious." He dropped into the chair and stretched out his legs, finally relaxing a notch. "You didn't like it when I shot the pheasant and you hated when I fired my shotgun. You jumped about two feet in the air and clamped your hands over your ears."

"Your back was turned. How could you have seen that?"

"I notice everything about you."

Whoa, where did that come from?

"Look, I shouldn't have unloaded on you just now," he said, "but I didn't like this guy's questions. He implied you'd told him a lot more than you say you did."

"You don't have anything to worry about. I told him there was no way either you or Tim were involved in Marcy's death. But if our relationship is going to work, we have to learn to talk to each other."

He didn't speak, apparently invoking the universal male reaction to the words *We have to talk.*

Freeze.

Run.

He slapped his hands against his knees. "I better get going if I want to have the restaurant open tonight."

Sure, she accepted his apology, and he was welcome for her covering his butt with JC. Anytime.

"Are you going to Marcy's wake?" she asked. They hadn't made any plans after Sunday's awkwardness.

"The viewing? Most likely. Are you sure you want to go? It'll probably upset you."

Apparently they weren't doing this together. "It'll be important to Marcy's family that people show up. I'll call Laurie. She wants to go."

Tension radiated from Alex's body. "I may stop in, but I can't stay. The dinner rush."

Ah, yes, the restaurant. His standard excuse whenever he didn't want to do something. "Maybe I'll see you there," she said.

"Maybe so." He turned to leave.

Right. *Maybe so* pretty much summed up their entire relationship.

Holly watched his retreat, not buying either his *I notice everything* or the *JC's still into you* business. She couldn't believe Alex was a murderer, and she doubted JC actually thought so. But what if the detective had picked up on...something else?

She rose and walked to the staff area. Rick had the big cubicle next to the window, a prime spot in the office pecking order.

"What's up?" he asked.

"When you get a chance, would you ask one of the staff to pull the Stevens Ventures financials? I have the quarterly meeting with them on Friday."

"With Marcy gone, we haven't gotten the latest data."

Holly never ventured into the bookkeeping side of Desert Accounting. The bread and butter of most local accounting practices, it was her mother's province. "I'll ask Tim about it, but please pull together whatever we have."

She returned to her office, doubt nipping at her heels like Alex's bird dog. Pulling the financials was a precaution, but it wasn't protection. If Alex or Tim were doing something they shouldn't, she did not want to be blindsided.

Or dragged down with them.

Chapter Thirteen

Tuesday evening

Holly powered through the yellow light at Leslie and Gage Boulevard, then hooked a right onto Keene. She glanced at her watch—only a few minutes behind schedule.

She did a quick personal inventory—dark suit, subtle makeup, Kate Spade purse. *Good to go.*

Ten minutes later, she hustled Laurie out her front door. Bentley, the psycho-beagle, hysterically threw himself against the barrier, distraught at being left alone.

"Are you sure leaving him loose is a good idea?" she asked.

Laurie patted an errant strand of hair into place. Her hair streak was still bright blue, but in deference to the solemn occasion, she'd slicked her hair into a demur bob instead of the spiky fringe she usually wore. "He'll settle down. I have to drug him if I put him in a crate."

"Maybe rescue dogs—"

Her friend gave her the evil eye. "He's just misunderstood."

"He misunderstood your sofa," Holly muttered. "And your shoes. And..."

The dog drove her nuts, but talking about the crazy animal beat obsessing about the wake. The thought of being trapped in a room with Marcy's crying relatives made her skin crawl.

Doing it for Marcy. Right thing to do. Got it. Holly pulled up behind a car waiting at the subdivision exit. The first car darted into a break in traffic and she rolled to the stop sign.

"Given the death grip you have on the steering wheel, I take it you're more than your usual end-of-the-day, wound-tight, stressed-out self," Laurie said.

"I'm not wound tight." Holly powered through a lull in traffic and headed for the Interstate.

"Right." Laurie readjusted her seatbelt. "So rather than talk about what's bothering you, let's discuss something mindless, like that lame book we're reading for the book club."

"I used it as an insomnia cure." Except the book hadn't helped the last two nights.

"The heroine spent so much time navel-gazing, I thought, jeez, no wonder your husband killed himself." Laurie's words trailed off as she seemed to remember they were headed to a wake for a woman who *hadn't* killed herself.

Holly knew she had to quit worrying about the wake, but the alternatives were even less appealing. Stress about work. Get upset about Marcy. Think about running into JC again. She didn't need the emotional whipsaw. With everything going on in her life, she was already arguing with herself on a daily basis. She glanced at Laurie. "Do you ever feel schizophrenic?"

"I assume there was a progression through that labyrinth you call your brain—you know, traffic to work to books to mental illness—but what are you talking about?" Laurie tugged her seatbelt and turned toward her. "And it better not involve my dog."

Holly moved into the right lane, letting the SUV crowding her bumper pass. "My life was already complicated. I have my screwed-up family, nine million clients, my house, pressure to bring in work. But all this stuff with Marcy, I can't get it out of my head.

One minute, I'm trying to explain cost averaging to one of the staff and the next, I'm back in that clearing. Seeing Marcy's body...those horrible birds." A shudder crawled across her shoulders and down her spine.

"It must have been awful." Laurie reached across the center console and touched her arm.

Holly blinked back tears, concentrated on the turn at Queensgate. *Focus on what you're doing. On moving forward. On what you have to work through.* She released a stabilizing breath. "I've looked at a few things, but I'm not getting very far investigating Marcy's death. JC showed up at the office again yesterday with more questions."

"Oh, really?" Laurie raised an eyebrow.

"Do not start with me. The man's ruining my business."

"What do you mean?" Concern replaced the smartass expression.

Grimacing, Holly drove across the Yakima River bridge. "You saw the newspaper, the Person of Interest thing?"

Laurie nodded.

"That's bad enough—it's worried a few clients. But the way JC keeps coming around, pushing me, he suspects something. Not necessarily me, but...something. He had the nerve to ask for Tim and Alex's financial statements—without a warrant."

"Can you do that? At the hospital we have all kinds of rules about not handing out medical records."

"Same privacy issue. JC didn't offer specifics, but if something *is* going on with Alex and Tim, and indirectly, Marcy, JC thinks I'm the link."

"You *are* sort of in the middle of the triangle."

She made a noise of frustration. "Alex is hell-bent on drawing a triangle that includes him, JC, and me. When Alex showed up today, he really and truly pissed me off."

"What did he do this time?"

If she hadn't been driving, she'd have closed her eyes and groaned. She recounted the ridiculous argument.

A thoughtful expression twisted Laurie's lips. "Alex could be one of those guys who thinks the only way to communicate is to yell, fight, and then make up."

"That is *so* not me." The car tires hummed over the Columbia River bridge. The three cities—Richland, Kennewick, and Pasco— climbed the barren hills where the Columbia, Snake, and Yakima rivers flowed together. The rivers created lovely vistas but made getting from place to place a challenge. "I don't know if there even *is* a relationship at this point. I'm seeing a side of Alex I don't like."

"If you're going to kick him to the curb, at least you have JC waiting in the wings."

"Laurie." Holly scowled at her friend.

"Just sayin'." Laurie raised her hands in surrender. "Beats sleeping alone."

"Well…I never slept with Alex."

Laurie stared at her for a long moment. "You mean, you haven't…? Hot Latin man? What is *wrong* with you?"

Holly shifted her shoulders defensively. "Casual sex… Not happening. Learned that early on from the crew I run with in Seattle."

"I thought you love Seattle and your job there."

"I do. The M&A work's exciting. I work with smart people. But that's the downside, too."

"Why?"

"They know they're smart. Some of them are complete assholes. They think they're more important than the rest of the world." She shrugged. "They're my crowd—accountants, attorneys, investment bankers, venture capitalists—but you can't get close to them. Not and survive."

"You never hooked up?"

"No way. First of all, you never know whose corner they're going to be in on the next deal. And these guys are serious about only one thing—money. Well, two things—money and themselves. They wouldn't put 'woman' and 'responsibility' in the same sentence. If I want to get laid, it won't be with someone who'll try to embarrass or manipulate me later."

"Sounds...lonely."

Holly studied the lights of Pasco and thought about Laurie's comment. "Lonely is probably why I started dating Alex in the first place."

"If it doesn't connect, it doesn't connect."

"That about covers it. He's fun." She shrugged. "We might've had a chance if it wasn't for his family."

"People come with baggage."

Didn't she know it.

The Road 66 off-ramp—the exit for Alex's restaurant—appeared on the side of the Interstate. "His family is so involved with the restaurant, I've spent more time with them than you normally would at this stage. His mother's made it real clear she hates me. The rest seem to be either in her camp or ready to plan the wedding next week."

Laurie nodded. "That's a lot of pressure when you're getting to know someone."

The next exit sign—downtown Pasco—reminded Holly of Monday's bombshell. She filled Laurie in on what Yessica had told her. "I had no idea Marcy's marriage was such a disaster. Now I feel like a bitch because I was always talking about going back to Seattle. At the same time, I understand, at least a little, what she went through. I could've helped. Or at least been there for her."

"Yet another thing Marcy was hiding," Laurie said.

Holly's defensive hackles rose. "I'm hurt she didn't trust me, but I understand why she didn't tell us. I didn't want everyone to know about the crap I went through with Frank."

Laurie was quiet for so long, Holly turned to stare at her. "What?"

"You do realize, if you go back to Seattle, Frank will still be there."

Holly digested the comment. She'd managed to effectively ignore that detail in her "Get back to Seattle" campaign.

From the corner of her eye, she saw her friend studying her and wondered what was behind all the comments.

She had a sinking feeling its initials were "J" and "C."

Chapter Fourteen

"There it is." Laurie pointed to a low-slung, red brick building. They'd gotten lost twice and cruised Lewis and Court Streets four times before they found the right cross street.

Neither ventured into downtown Pasco very often. Their usual hangouts—wineries near their houses, a few music places, a couple of favorite restaurants—were across the Columbia River in Richland.

Holly peered at the discreet, nearly impossible to read from the street, placard. "Are you sure? I sorta expected a Gothic manor."

"You've watched too many *Six Feet Under* reruns."

"Like I have time to watch TV." She entered the crowded parking lot. "It must be packed inside."

She cruised through the lanes, looking for an open slot. She paused beside a Dumpster and sized up the possibilities. "Think I'll get towed if I block it?"

Laurie eyed the big green box instead of the open space. "What do you think they throw in there?"

"Thanks for that image." Holly drove to the far side of the lot and tucked the BMW into a nonexistent space, close to a graffiti-covered building.

They studied the tags, then exchanged a glance. "The lot's

pretty well lit," Holly ventured.

"I'm sure it'll be fine." Laurie slid out into the twelve inches between the BMW and the adjacent car. "Can you imagine working in a funeral parlor?"

They both shuddered.

"I'd always halfway expect something to jump out of a coffin," Holly said.

Laurie hitched her purse over her shoulder. "Or creepy music to play, and this guy who looks like he hasn't seen the sun in twenty years to appear out of nowhere."

Holly stopped on the walkway leading to the narrow porch and stared at the funeral home. The place looked like an office building.

Ordinary. Well lit. Crowded.

Huh.

"We have to go in now, don't we?"

Laurie sighed. "Yeah."

"Do you have any idea what we're supposed to do?"

They moved toward the entrance, shoes clicking against the concrete walkway. "My grandmother died a couple of years ago," Laurie said. "Everybody signed a book."

"You mean, like at a wedding? That's disturbing."

"That way, the family knows who was there. There's usually a line of relatives near the casket you're supposed to talk to." Laurie's mouth twisted in an uncertain frown. "Although I wonder if the police released her body yet."

"Maybe there won't be a casket." Holly fervently hoped if the casket was there, it would be closed, and that some mortician hadn't tried to put Marcy's face back together.

Laurie readjusted her purse strap. "Anyway, after you talk to the relatives, you hang around a while. Pray. Meditate."

Holly's heart sank to somewhere near her toes. She was so

not ready for this. What was she supposed to say to a bunch of people she didn't know? *I'm sorry. I'm sorry. God, but I'm so sorry?*

She followed Laurie up the stairs, wishing she hadn't worn high heels. Apparently, she was going to spend the next few hours both physically *and* emotionally uncomfortable.

Laurie opened the door and they entered the crowded foyer. People Holly didn't recognize clustered in tight knots, talking in low voices. She didn't see the book Laurie mentioned, the Ramirez family, or anybody who might tell them what they were supposed to do next.

Holly searched the crowd and spotted Rick near the door to an interior room. He caught her eye and tilted his head. The women eased through the crowd toward him.

"Is that Rick Stewert? When you said he was working at DA, you didn't tell me he'd gotten so cute." Laurie smoothed her skirt and tucked her hair behind her ear. "How do I look?"

"You can't go out with him. He works for me. It'll be messy when you break up."

"What do you care? You'll be long gone before we get to that stage."

As soon as they reached Rick, he said, "Laurie Gordon? I thought you moved to Portland."

"I've been back a while. I can't believe we haven't run into each other."

Laurie gave her a look that said, *Why didn't you tell him I was back?*

Before Laurie and Rick could start flirting, Holly asked, "Have you seen Marcy's family?"

"In there." Rick hooked a thumb over his shoulder, indicating the doorway behind him.

"Where?" She craned her neck and looked past him at the throng.

"Far side of the room. Most of them are sitting down. Tim and Nicole are here somewhere."

Holly looked around the crowded room but didn't see the couple.

"Good luck finding them." Rick smiled at Laurie. "We need to get together and catch up. It was great seeing you again, but I am outta here."

He turned to Holly. "For the record"—he checked the crowd, the expression on his face somewhere between horrified and overwhelmed—"I want to be cremated when I die. And no funeral service. Just say nice things when you dump my ashes in the Columbia River."

"O-kay," Laurie said to his departing back. "That was definitely more information than I wanted to know."

Holly stifled a laugh at Laurie's appalled expression. "I don't think any of us handles death very well."

"Amen to that. Let's get this done and go home."

"Do you see where the reception line starts?" The crowd parted for a moment and Holly saw someone else she knew. Alex—with his mother.

Naturally.

Alex's full name was Alejandro Qunito Arroyo Montoya, but Holly could never remember if his mother went by Montoya or Arroyo. Given that she was normally good with names, Holly figured it was a mental block based on the old battle-axe not liking her. The *bruja* had never wanted her precious Alejandro to date a *gringa*—especially a non-Catholic blond *gringa*.

Mrs. Montoya noticed Holly at the same moment Alex did. He took a step in her direction, but his mother deftly intervened. With just a touch of her finger to his forearm, Alex turned into Alejandro. He curved a solicitous arm around his mother's shoulders and leaned closer to hear whatever she was whispering.

113

Only Holly saw the tilt of the woman's head, the triumphant movement of her mouth, and the sideways look she tossed at her rival when Alex moved, not toward Holly, but to a table set against the far wall.

So that was how it was going to be. *Mama's boy.*

Not for the first time, Holly wondered if the putdowns were aimed at any woman who had the audacity to date Alex, or if it was her, specifically, who drew his mother's wrath.

She leaned to the right, ready to share her observation with Laurie, only to discover her friend had vanished into the crowd. She swiveled her attention back to the drama across the room in time to see Alex return. He threaded past people, balancing a glass of punch. He made no move to leave his mother's side and Holly was damned if she was going to crawl over there.

Fine.

She stepped into the inner room. Begin phase one of Who Killed Marcy.

"You look so much like Marcy," she told the first person she met.

The woman offered a closed-mouth smile. "I'm her aunt."

"You're young enough to be a cousin. Were you...close?"

The woman tilted her head. Something that might've been quizzical, but could've been suspicious, narrowed her eyes. "How did you know Maricella?"

Holly froze, panic draining the blood from her head. Argh. Bad move.

The woman's lips tightened.

Answer, answer, say something. "We both lived in Seattle..."

Holly knew immediately she'd made a mistake. The look in the woman's eyes was pure suspicion now.

"Were you friends when you lived there?" she asked.

The aunt wouldn't tell her anything if she thought Holly had been friends with Marcy and Lee while they were together. "I met Marcy here. She told me about Lee. He was a real..." She caught herself before she said *dick*.

The woman shifted uncomfortably. She glanced away, her eyes focused on something over Holly's shoulder. "Don't bring him up. Nobody wants to talk about him."

"Do you know where he is?"

An arm snaked around her waist and pulled her against a male body.

Frank. Adrenaline spiked her system. She twisted, trying to break free. "Let go."

But the odor wasn't Frank's.

That detail registered as warm lips pressed her cheek.

"Thank God. A familiar face," Tim said.

Damn. All this talk about murder and stalking had her overreacting to everything.

Marcy's aunt eased away.

Tim's eyes tracked the woman as she faded into the crowd. "What are you doing, talking to her about Marcy like that? Trying to play amateur detective? Jesus, Holly, give it up. Let the police handle it before you make things worse."

What was it with him? A flush colored his face, but she didn't smell liquor on his breath. "Worse than what?"

"I never know what to say at these things." He spoke as if he hadn't just totally dissed her. "But I sure wouldn't pester the dead woman's relatives."

Okay. She'd pester him instead. The throng shifted and pressed them closer together. At this rate, she'd be intimately acquainted with him before the night was over. She pulled as far away as the crowd permitted, and said, "I wanted to ask you yesterday—"

Tim shoved his hands into his pockets. "Yeah, about that."

She waved off his discomfort. "You were upset and had too much to drink." She shrugged. "Actually, you were probably one of Marcy's closer friends. Did she tell you who she was seeing?"

He stepped back, pushing the couple behind him aside. "We weren't that close. Why would you think we were?"

"Whoa, I'm not implying anything." Talk about protesting too much. "I just hoped you might know where Marcy was before she disappeared."

He leaned forward, his voice a whispered hiss. "The police are already making assumptions. Don't add to them."

"I'm not." The small hairs on the back of her neck suddenly lifted. She peered over her shoulder, half-expecting Alex's scowl. Instead, she met Nicole's narrow-eyed gaze. The woman's expression moved to *considering*, as if working out the angles on something. Something she was rather unhappy about.

Surely Nicole wasn't still mad about the stupid sofa incident.

Holly turned her head, hoping the glare was directed at someone else. She swung back again, but Nicole's gaze had drifted. The stocky man standing next to Nicole chattered away, seemingly unaware she no longer listened. Maybe the stocky guy said something that upset her. Maybe Tim's drinking had upset her and her glare had been aimed at him.

The crowd shuffled and hid the pair from sight, but Holly was far more interested in creating some distance away from Tim. "Awkward" didn't begin to describe feeling caught between Tim and his wife. "Look, another client's here. I need to speak to him. I'll see you later."

"Sure." Tim looked rather lost and forlorn as she moved away.

She spoke to several people she knew while she worked up her nerve to approach the Ramirez family. She'd almost made it to the reception line when a hand grabbed her arm. She jumped and turned. "Jeez, Tim, will you quit doing that?"

"Sorry." He jammed his hands into his pockets. "I wanted to clear the air. It's been a couple of rough days. I shouldn't take it out on you."

She couldn't help but wonder which Tim was the real one—the one who'd unloaded on her or the likeable guy she usually saw. "It's been tough on all of us."

She still intended to find out what he knew—exactly how well he knew Marcy—but she'd ask in a less public venue.

Tim's vaguely anxious expression altered to one of pleasure. "Hello, sweetheart. I wondered where you disappeared to."

Nicole emerged from the crowd. Holly could see her dress now—a bright blue sheath.

How inappropriate. Holly frowned. The dress choice surprised her, given how socially savvy Nicole usually appeared.

"I'm making the rounds. There are so many lovely people here." Nicole's tone was sweetness and light.

For half a second, Holly wondered if she'd imagined the woman's earlier unhappiness.

A tiny frown creased Nicole's forehead. "Some people are blaming Marcy."

Holly caught the flinch that spasmed across Tim's face. Even if he wasn't having an affair with Marcy, it must be hard for him to express his grief around Nicole.

"That's really not fair," Nicole continued.

For once Holly agreed with the woman. The stocky man she'd seen with Nicole earlier that evening must have said something rude, been one of those blame-the-victim idiots.

"I spoke with Alex." Nicole turned her baby blues on Holly. "I'm surprised you're not with him. Things are so difficult for him right now."

And the détente went out the window.

What did *with him* mean? Still dating him? Supporting him? *What difficulties?* Before Holly could sort out the multiple messages in Nicole's statement, Tim smoothed a hand over his wife's shining hair. "How are you feeling, sweetheart?"

Nicole snuggled against him, melting into the circle of his arm. "I'm tired, honey. So much has happened."

Tim's fingers touched his wife's cheek in a tender gesture. She gazed up at him, adoration shining from her eyes.

Wow, Nicole had Tim's number wired—*Be the big man and protect me.* Holly felt uncomfortably like a chaperone at a teenaged party—unwelcome and ignored.

"Let's get you home," Tim said. "Should we call the doctor?"

The couple turned. Sheltering his wife under a protective arm, Tim pushed through the crowd.

Relief at escaping the couple slammed into the realization that Holly couldn't keep avoiding the reason she was there—Marcy's family.

Alrighty.

She squeezed past groups of people and found what had to be the extended Ramirez family. Assorted people who looked like Marcy stood in ranks between the visiting crowd and what Holly could only call a shrine. Photos and mementoes competed for attention with dozens of flickering candles. All of it was smothered in flowers.

At least there wasn't a casket.

She approached, more nervous than she was before presenting an analysis of a multimillion-dollar acquisition. She wished she hadn't lost Laurie in the crowd. Most likely, her friend bailed or found somebody she knew to talk to.

Long before she was ready, she reached the first members of Marcy's family. "I'm sorry for your loss," she repeated to each adult she passed. Some nodded. Others murmured, *Gracias* or Thanks for coming.

Showing up, trying to find words, was the right thing to do, but it felt woefully inadequate. As Holly made her way along the receiving line, it hit her how far the impact of Marcy's death reached. She'd been daughter, sister, cousin, and aunt as well as friend. All these people loved her and had been part of her life. Holly glanced around the crowded visitation room. She hoped they'd told Marcy often enough that she was loved while she was still alive.

Holly shook more hands and murmured words.

She dreaded the thought of a relative's death and receiving these words from strangers. The finality of Marcy's death smacked her. She knew she wasn't immortal—no longer had that childish perception. But the knowledge usually dwelt deep in her subconscious.

She was close enough now to see Mrs. Ramirez. Holly's maternal drive was still dormant, but she had friends with children and realized how lucky she was to be close to her own mother. She couldn't begin to image the horror of identifying your child's body. Of having to deal with that level of loss.

Finally, she reached Mrs. Ramirez. The older woman sat before the vestiges of her daughter's life. Her eyes were dark, shadowed pools. Suffering draped her figure with the dignity of a Madonna. The quiet grief reminded Holly of Michelangelo's *Pieta*, the grief-stricken mother cradling the broken body, not of a prophet or a saint, but of a beloved child.

Holly spoke from the heart. "I'm so sorry. Marcy was my friend and I'll miss her."

For a long moment, Holly worried she'd offended her. Then Mrs. Ramirez gravely tilted her head.

"I'm sorry for your loss," she said, feeling like a not very bright parrot.

Mrs. Ramirez looked up, her gaze drifting past Holly's shoulder.

The older woman's expression changed. Recognition flashed through her dark eyes and color flooded her cheeks. *"Usted."*

Who, me? "Yes, ma'am?"

"¿Qué estás haciendo aquí?"

What am I doing here? Holly blinked in surprise. "I wanted to say how sad—"

The older woman's eyes narrowed and anger puckered her mouth. *"Si hubiera hecho su trabajo, mi Maricella estaría viva."*

If she'd done her job, Marciella would still be alive.

Holly gaped at her. "Mrs. Ramirez?" What was she supposed to have done?

The woman rose, four and a half feet of fury.

Holly took a quick step back—straight into a solid body. Her high heels tangled with big feet and she would've fallen if arms hadn't reached around and caught her. Warm, hard hands gripped her, even after she regained her balance. They held her like they meant to hug her for the next lifetime.

They also carried the most amazing man-smell.

She knew this touch, this smell.

JC.

She forgot about the past few days, the worry and the grief, and relaxed into his protective embrace. Her body ignored her brain's *"Move!"* and instead shifted slightly, tucking perfectly into his shoulder. His warm body and subtle cologne wrapped her in a seductive blanket.

This feels so right.

About the time she was ready to purr like her mother's cat, she remembered she was at a wake, in a crowded public place, being yelled at for some reason by an irate Hispanic matron, while practically being cuddled by a man who—

Holly bolted upright and whirled around. He seemed reluctant to release her, but she could've imagined that along with the rest of the embarrassing episode. Cheeks flaming, she focused her attention on putting some space between them.

"You okay? You sorta tripped there." His warm brown eyes locked onto hers and another jolt rocked her insides.

"You changed cologne."

If possible, her cheeks burned hotter. *Great.* That statement had spoken volumes. And he knew he'd gotten to her. She could see it in the satisfied expression on his face, the arrogant jerk.

"A lot's changed. Not everything, though." The corner of his mouth turned up in a private smile. "I'd still hate to see you get hurt."

What was that supposed to mean? She'd had it with his one-liners and innuendo. She nearly snarled something choice, but her grown-up half reminded her, *Handle it later. This isn't the time or place.*

"I'm fine." Her tone could have produced ice cubes. "Thanks for catching me. Of course, you shouldn't have been standing so close."

If she'd tripped, it had been over his big feet. She ignored the immediate impish reminder correlating big hands, feet, and other body parts. Why did JC have the ability to turn her into an idiot without uttering a word? He wasn't even looking at her. His attention was focused on the furious woman behind her.

Mrs. Ramirez pushed Holly aside. Tipping her head to look at the tall detective, the diminutive matron punctuated the outpouring of angry words with fierce stabs of her finger at his chest.

Ah. She'd been yelling at JC the whole time.

"*No español.*" JC mangled even the simple phrase. He threw a beseeching glance at Holly before returning his attention to the tiny woman in front of him.

Marcy's mother continued her tirade.

"Mrs. Ramirez," he said in the calm tone of voice all cops seemed to use on hysterical people. With a flash of irritation, Holly remembered hearing it from an assortment of uniformed men on Sunday afternoon. "Let's settle down. Talk this through. What can I do for you?"

He stopped talking, letting Mrs. Ramirez rant, even as people noticed the altercation.

"*¿Por qué no detenerlo?*"

"Why didn't you stop him?" Holly automatically translated. Stop who, from doing what?

More heads turned and silence rippled away from the epicenter of Mrs. Ramirez's wrath. Holly raked a look across the crowded room. The older women surrounding Marcy's mother watched with crossed arms and pursed lips. The men appeared ready to jump in if JC so much as twitched in the wrong direction.

Holly turned back to JC. Somehow, he was lowering Mrs. Ramirez's volume, taking control of the situation, even in a language he didn't speak. Mostly he let the older woman vent, but he interjected a phrase—in English—whenever she paused for breath. It was his tone as much as his words. His body language helped. His posture said, "*I'm not a threat*," while simultaneously staying ready for any hint of violence.

He leaned in Holly's direction. "Jump in any time."

"You talking to me?" Holly tried to step back, but a solid wall of bodies blocked her retreat.

JC gripped her arm and pulled her closer. His eyes never left Mrs. Ramirez and he continued to nod occasionally. "What's she saying?"

"Most of it isn't very nice."

He turned his head at that. A smile lit his face, and her heart-rate—damn its traitorous hide—picked up. "I got that. Trust me, I've heard those phrases before."

"The rest is variations of, 'If you'd done your job, Marcy would still be alive.'"

A brief grimace clouded JC's face. "Uh-huh."

Mrs. Ramirez turned to Holly. "*Silencio. Muestre respeto.*" In rapid Spanish, she berated Holly's rudeness for interrupting.

She waited for the older woman to take a breath. "*Lo siento. Él no habla español.*" Sorry. The detective doesn't speak Spanish.

Mrs. Ramirez turned a furious glare on JC. "*Él no lo intenta.*"

He didn't try.

Holly kept her comments to herself. JC *had* tried to learn the language. Years ago, she'd helped him pass Spanish 101. She wasn't sure if Mrs. Ramirez meant his dismal language skills or whatever she thought the police should've done to prevent Marcy's death. Either way, Holly figured she was out of there. People were staring and this was *so* not her problem.

She took one step and again felt JC's warm hand circle her arm. His mouth moved close to her ear. Heat spread, turning her awareness up another notch.

"Don't leave," he whispered. "I need you."

Chapter Fifteen

Holly quirked an eyebrow at JC. *Oh, really?*

"To translate."

He held onto her arm. Imploring eyes gazed at her...

A hum of attraction started in her head and worked its way south. JC's hand on her arm, the whisper of his words across her ear, his scent, everything about him set off bottle rockets inside her. She gave her imagination the tiniest bit of free rein. *What if...*

What she was feeling must've shown in her expression, because something hot flashed through JC's eyes before he pulled on a cop-face—serious, boy scout, you-can-depend-on-me, I'm-a-professional.

Whoa, whoa, whoa. With a quick inhale, she scrambled to raise her own defenses. This was JC. *So not going there.*

"Please tell Mrs. Ramirez, on behalf of the Franklin County Sheriff's Department, I want to offer our condolences," JC recited. "We're sorry for her loss."

Biting her lip, she turned to Marcy's mother. JC's statement didn't go far enough. She embellished as she translated.

By the end of her speech, Mrs. Ramirez looked mollified. At least she wasn't still glaring at either of them. A few of the surrounding relatives even nodded approvingly. The crowd wasn't openly staring, and normal conversation sounds had resumed.

Holly was feeling rather pleased with herself when she heard JC's quiet, "Whew."

That simple release of tension sent ripples down her spine. He lifted his hand, cupped her shoulder, and pulled her close. The casual intimacy lulled her; his distinctive scent caressed her. She wanted to slide her arms around his waist and sink into his embrace. Shivers shimmied across her breasts and clenched her belly muscles in a wave of pure desire.

What the...?

She lifted shocked eyes to meet JC's gaze and saw the same physical reaction in his expression.

He released her like she'd burned him.

Reality smacked her in the face. She felt as confused as the village simpleton.

What the...? Was she still seriously attracted to him? Not the casual, if you can forget all the bad karma, we had great sex back then, but I'll never, *ever*, follow up on it fantasies she'd secretly harbored. But the *whoa, this guy totally turns me on* kind of attraction.

Was he as interested in her, or was he just trying to get her attention and realized he'd invaded her personal bubble?

Did she *want* him to be attracted to her again?

Before she could even begin to sort it out, JC asked, "What did you say to her?"

She blinked, again two beats behind. Wait a minute. She was an intelligent professional.

Take a breath and get centered.

"You still can't speak Spanish?"

Oh, that was brilliant.

One corner of his mouth curled. "I thought that was rather obvious."

She punched his chest. "Hush. You know what I meant. Let's get out of here while we can."

125

"But—"

"Now. While none of Marcy's relatives are upset with us."

JC slammed his arms into obstinate male mode. "I need to talk to Mrs. Ramirez."

"Are you crazy? This isn't the time to question the woman. Talk to her tomorrow." *Argh.* "Except the funeral's tomorrow. Can't it wait?"

"No. She wants me to figure out who killed her daughter. How am I supposed to do that if nobody will tell me anything about the woman?"

"Didn't you talk to Marcy's parents already?"

He blew out an exasperated breath. "I tried. When I got to their house on Sunday, there must've been a hundred people inside. Half of them took one look at me and vanished. The rest sat and glared. All I got was Marcy was a saint and nobody wanted to hurt her."

Of course. He'd had to tell her parents about finding Marcy's body.

A stab of blinding insight hit her. *It was Mrs. Ramirez's perfume on his coat.* "Damn, I recognize it now."

"What are you talking about?"

"When you came by my house Sunday afternoon." Double head-smack. "Never mind. Look, all you'll do tonight is make everybody mad again. Get a copy of the guest register and talk to them later."

JC was watching Mr. Ramirez practically sob on the shoulder of an older man. JC's own shoulders sagged an inch. "Finding them again will be the problem."

"How hard can—" she began, and then closed her mouth. She knew nothing about the Ramirez clan. Marcy had moved out of her parents' neat bungalow, but the extended family could be scattered across eastern Washington. Add in their friends, and the crowd really could be anywhere by tomorrow.

"What was I supposed to be doing, anyway?" JC asked, almost as if he were talking to himself.

The press of the crowd kept her uncomfortably close to him. Fatigue tightened the skin around his eyes, as though he hadn't slept since she and Alex found Marcy's body. He'd missed a small place on his jaw when he shaved. Obviously, he'd cleaned up for the wake, but the tiny patch of stubble made him human.

She wanted to run her finger over the spot. Memories tangled with the present reality. Who was this man? He'd matured into a ruggedly handsome adult. Her gaze shifted along his cheek to his mouth. He had firm, masculine lips. His neck and shoulders were nice—strong and muscular, without becoming one of those no-neck bodybuilder types. In spite of his fatigue, he exuded an aura of strength. He was also standing straighter now, as if he were aware of her inspection and maybe wanted to make a good impression.

Stop. This kept getting weirder. She turned away and locked eyes with Alex. He stood beside his mother, watching her and JC intently.

He looked seriously pissed.

What was she doing, checking out JC when the guy who was technically sorta her boyfriend was in the same room?

But Alex *wasn't* her boyfriend. They were just friends, hanging out together. Of course, JC didn't know that. And from the expression on Alex's face, he'd conveniently forgotten it too.

JC touched her arm, reclaiming her attention. The resulting tingle was entirely inappropriate.

"Thanks for your help tonight. One session of standing there taking it from Mrs. Ramirez was enough to last a lifetime. Whatever you said at the end helped settle her down."

He was just doing his job. His fingers caressing her arm didn't exactly fit with that explanation, but she wasn't sure he was even aware he was doing it. *She* was so aware of *him* she was ready to explode. In the middle of the crowd, she could isolate his unique blend of soap, citrusy aftershave, and testosterone-laden male. The combination was driving her nuts. "That was nice."

JC raised an eyebrow and smiled, turning her statement into something else.

"What you did."

His smile deepened.

"For Mrs. Ramirez." Heat climbed her cheeks. "Letting her vent."

He just watched her, his damned dimples distracting her.

Words kept tumbling from her mouth. "Sometimes guys don't understand. All women really want them to do is listen while we get it out of our systems."

JC leaned closer. She could've sworn he was smelling her hair. And liked what he smelled, because he was definitely crowding her personal space more than the surrounding people required.

"We don't want you to do anything," she continued, "fix it, explain it, or anything else." *Shut up!* She was babbling like an idiot.

"I'll keep that in mind." His voice was low and intimate.

He studied her face. She could almost see the debate going on behind his eyes.

Intensely regretting her verbal oversharing, she braced for his next maneuver.

"I didn't try to fix anything, but I did talk to a friend at the Seattle PD," he said.

She frowned, looking for the connection. "Why? Were you hoping I'd done something terrible in Seattle? That the only reason I came back was because I was running away?"

Dimples flashed again. "The possibility occurred to me."

She folded her arms, dislodging his hand, and tapped a foot.

"Why'd you really call them?"

"I found something disturbing."

She froze. Disturbing combined with the Seattle police department meant only one thing to her—Officer Frank Phalen. Even *thinking* the man's name left a bad taste in her mouth.

"I found your protective order."

"Bully for you." She felt violated all over again. First by Frank, then by the Seattle PD's refusal to take the harassment seriously, and now by JC's knowing about the whole damn mess. And she couldn't even complain about his reading the order because it was a public record and anybody who wanted to could look it up.

JC scanned the group behind her. "I thought you might want to know. Phalen was reprimanded by the department after you complained."

"Reprimanded." Phalen had flat-out stalked her. "He got his hand slapped for harassing me, camping in front of my house, following me—"

Threatening me.

"In the official report, he claims you two were dating and you didn't handle the breakup well."

Holly's mouth dropped open. Shock and outrage left her sputtering. And *naturally* JC believed the rumors, what the other cops told him. "*I* didn't handle rejection well? We went out a couple of times and he wanted to buy wedding rings. I didn't."

His gaze swung back and pinned her in place. His brown eyes carried a message she couldn't interpret.

"You think just because our relationship ended badly, I made this stuff up?" The words ground out between clenched teeth. She couldn't remember the last time she was this angry. "Screw you, JC."

She pivoted on her heel, but JC grabbed her arm. "Wait a minute." He tugged her back. "I never said I didn't believe you. I'm telling you because he pulled the same shit with another woman. She raised a bigger stink than you did. They fired him."

She jerked her arm free and gave JC her best squinty-eyed stare. "Frank Phalen reinforced every bad thing I ever heard about the 'thin blue line.' "

"There are all kinds of officers. Some are like him. Ones who don't understand that behavior isn't acceptable."

"You're avoiding the issue."

His tone went hard and flat. "I don't like the idea of some guy, especially an officer, harassing women."

She caught her breath at his intensity. Forget the theoretical. His expression said he didn't want anyone harassing *her*, Holly Price, specifically. She swallowed. "Sounds like we finally agree on something."

He glared down at her. "I want to know if Phalen contacts you."

She didn't need JC telling her how to run her life. Trying to control her life had been one of Frank's horrible habits. "I doubt that will be necessary."

God, she hoped it wasn't necessary.

"He's going to blame you for getting fired. That kind of guy won't admit it was his own screw-up that caused his problems."

Like JC or her father admitted theirs? Yeah. Got that.

"I've handled Frank all by myself this long." Even if it did include moving.

Temporarily moving.

And speaking of moving, a graceful retreat sounded like a brilliant next move.

Clearly, she wasn't getting any information from Marcy's relatives tonight. Time to find Laurie and leave. She scanned the room, but didn't see her friend's blue hair, which should've stood out in the sea of brunettes.

"Gotta go," she told JC and dodged between two people before he could say another word.

So much for graceful.

She angled across the room. She felt Alex's glare and JC's gaze following her. At the doorway, she risked a glance over her shoulder. JC wasn't just watching her, he was measuring her in that blatantly male way that made her aware of every inch of her on-fire skin. She felt as though she were wearing her sexiest piece of barely there lingerie instead of the most conservative black suit she owned. For a second, she was glad she'd worn high heels that made her legs look a mile long and lifted her butt into something that from the right angle might be considered a booty.

The next instant she wondered what she was doing—strutting for a guy she'd sworn never to think about again, much less help, talk to, flirt with, or whatever it was she was doing. A man she needed to deal with strictly on a professional basis.

She turned around and found Alex's glare had intensified to a laser of death. What was *his* problem? He was pissed because she wouldn't go over there and subject herself to his mother's snubs? Newsflash—the floor crossed two ways. Alejandro could grow a pair and come to her.

"Screw this," she muttered. She didn't ask to get caught between two competitive Neanderthals.

She moved into the foyer and looked around for Laurie. Raised voices caught her attention—along with most of the people in the room. Heads turned.

There was a commotion at the front door.

She caught the words and the voice.

That damn reporter.

Chapter Sixteen

"The police are questioning the owners of Stevens Ventures." A young man holding a mini-recorder stood just inside the door of the funeral home. He'd cornered a middle-aged woman, but he spoke loudly, as if he wanted to be overheard. "Sources inside the sheriff's department say they have questions about Tim Stevens' possible involvement in Ms. Ramirez's death."

Holly gasped. As far as she knew, the only thing Tim had done was offer Marcy a job.

And maybe have an affair.

"Were you concerned about Ms. Ramirez working there? Tim Stevens' business partner, Alex Montoya, found the body. Is there a connection?"

Holly whirled around and looked for Alex. He'd go ballistic if he heard this crap. She didn't see him or his mother. Hopefully they hadn't noticed the commotion, or were too far away to hear the guy's questions.

She turned back to the reporter. Should she say something? Defend Tim and Alex?

A group of men who looked a lot like Marcy swarmed out of the inner room. They filled the entrance hall with noise, the clatter of feet, voices speaking English and Spanish.

"¡Salga! Leave! This is a private function." An older man led the pack.

The reporter stood his ground and directed his next question to the crowd. "What about Ms. Ramirez's husband? Why isn't he here? Have the police been able to locate him?"

Holly felt like a spectator at a tennis match. Her head swiveled between the group of men and the reporter. The scene was ugly, but if somebody actually answered the guy, she'd get some answers too.

"Have the police given any indication Ms. Ramirez was involved in activities that contributed to her death?" The reporter moved closer to the older man.

"Get out!" One of the younger men stepped forward, not touching the reporter, but definitely in his face. "Now."

An angry barrier of men hid the reporter from sight. Holly turned and scanned the crowd for JC. He seemed to be good at calming yelling matches. Her gaze raked across the room. Given his height, he should've stood out in the crowd. Apparently, he was still in the inner room, probably trying to question another family member.

The woman in front of her spun around. Feverish red spots lit her cheeks and her teeth clenched around the words which seemed ready to burst from her mouth.

"Yessica?" Holly stared in astonishment at the furious woman.

"That reporter doesn't want to interview anyone for the truth. He's telling more lies."

"He's just making noise, trying to get a reaction." Based on Yessica's expression, the reporter had succeeded.

"It isn't right. Why is he dragging my sister's name through the mud?"

"He can't print stuff like that." At least she didn't think he could print blatant speculation. Although he'd had no problem printing she was a Person of Interest. Which might be factual, but it sure seemed like slander—or was it libel?

"Was Ms. Ramirez afraid of her husband?" The reporter hadn't given up.

The men pushed the reporter outside.

"Dammit!" Yessica sputtered. "Why is he doing this?"

Holly's earlier words to JC rang through her head. *Women just need someone to listen while they get it out of their systems.*

Tears overflowed Yessica's eyes—eyes that had the same tilted corners and warm brown color as Marcy's. Holly fumbled in her purse, found a battered package of tissues, stepped closer, and held Yessica while she cried.

A few minutes later, Yessica wiped her eyes and sniffled. "Thanks."

Holly stepped back. "Did you talk to the police? Have you told them about Lee Alders?"

The color on Yessica's cheeks deepened. Her gaze drifted over the remaining crowd. "My mother wouldn't like it."

"It could be important."

"You don't understand. Mama and Papa don't want to make Maricella look bad. She was a good girl." Yessica shredded the tissue. "I can't prove Lee killed her, so why bring him up?"

Holly gestured toward the front door, where there were now sounds of a scuffle. "It's going to come out. If nobody tells him anything, that reporter will print whatever he wants."

Yessica raised her eyes and stared at the doorway. She turned and glared at Holly. "How did that reporter know about Lee? Did you tell him? You said you'd keep it quiet."

She jammed the mangled tissue in her pocket and took an angry step toward the inner room.

"Wait." Holly grasped her arm. "I understand you want some privacy—believe me, I *really* understand. I didn't say anything. The restraining order is a public record. So is her marriage. That's how the reporter found out."

"We don't want to discuss it. We don't want to ruin her reputation. It's all she has left."

"Then get on top of it. Spin it in your favor."

Yessica hesitated. Uncertainty joined the anger in her eyes.

"Make people see Marcy as the victim. Tell your version of the story." Holly scanned the throng for JC.

In seconds, she found him—watching her. Their gaze met and lingered. Stifling the other messages she sensed in his eyes, she tilted her head toward Yessica and mouthed, "I need you."

Chapter Seventeen

"What's up?" JC gave the men still clustered near the funeral home's entrance a quick inspection before shifting his attention to Holly.

"Detective Dimitrak, you've met Yessica Herrera, haven't you? She's Marcy's sister."

JC didn't so much as twitch at the sudden formality—had she ever called him Detective rather than JC?—but Yessica recoiled. "I don't think this is a good idea. I told you, my mother won't like it."

"If you tell Detective Dimitrak about Lee, about what he did, the police will know to look harder at him."

"You mean, tell them *everything* that man did?"

At Yessica's stricken expression, Holly said, "It's the only way we can help Marcy."

With their backs to the crowd, the three of them created a bubble of privacy while Yessica repeated her story. After her initial hesitation, she spoke more freely than she had at the boutique. When she finished, Holly asked, "Do you think Lee had something to do with...what happened?"

How big a step was it between beating someone and killing them? Had Lee realized he couldn't control Marcy any longer and lashed out in a rage?

"I don't know. Maybe." Yessica's shoulders slumped. "He hit

her, but he always seemed to know when to quit. Maricella would lie and cover for him. I suspected, but I didn't know for sure until I stopped to see her on my way to Bellingham. She looked awful."

Yessica's fingers fluttered to her ribs, as if touching her sister's battered body.

Holly murmured a soothing phrase and laid her hand on the grieving woman's arm. As Yessica leaned toward her, JC subtly shifted positions and covered them. Holly glanced at him. Had she overstepped some boundary?

He dipped his head, a nod she interpreted as encouragement.

"I convinced her to leave with me. We went to the hospital." Yessica's lips trembled. She grasped Holly's hand, as if she needed the anchor of a human connection.

Holly suspected Yessica was reliving that day, seeing it instead of the crowded reception hall.

"Lee broke her ribs—it hurt her so much to breathe. *Ay, Dios mio*, the bruises on her body. Maricella was so ashamed, like it was her fault. That hurt me the most. He broke her spirit."

Yessica's hand dropped to her side. "We got the protection order, but I couldn't leave Maricella in Seattle. I brought her home with me."

"Did it help? Did Lee stay away after that?" she asked.

"At first, he called. When he came to see her, Maricella was very angry."

Holly could imagine what Marcy felt when her husband hunted her down. Fear. Fury. A sense of inevitability.

"Other than that," Yessica continued, "she never mentioned his name. Did she say anything to you?"

Holly shook her head. "Not specifically. She started seeing someone this fall, but she wouldn't tell anyone who."

"*Mierda*," Yessica cursed.

Mierda indeed. Holly knew the sick feeling in the pit of her stomach, the constant tension, the hyper-alertness that came with wondering when a man—a sick, twisted person—was going to appear next. The constant looking over her shoulder, worrying about what Frank would do, was nothing compared to what Marcy had faced. Had Lee re-entered Marcy's life? Refused to be forced out?

"I have a few questions." JC quietly took control, drawing out details of the protection order Holly hadn't known to ask about.

Yessica leaned into his concerned attention.

Holly watched the exchange, a silent observer. JC had been a good listener when they were in college. Police work—or maturity—had refined his skill. Was that all it was? A skill? A tool to get what he wanted? Or was he genuinely concerned?

While JC led Yessica through Marcy's ordeal, taking notes this time, Lee Alders' name cycled through Holly's head. She might not have the databases JC could access, but she knew people in Seattle. People who could find out about the bastard.

"Holly." Yessica's voice drew her back to the visitation hall. She moved close and pressed a cheek to Holly's. "Thank you. For everything."

And then Marcy's sister was gone, which left Holly alone again with JC.

While he scribbled in a small notebook, she edged away. She should find Laurie and leave. Helping with the investigation intrigued her. It was being alone with JC that was the problem.

"Hold on." JC caught her eye. He stuffed the notebook in his pocket. "That was nice."

She gave him a narrow-eyed glare. "Don't make fun of me."

"Who, me?"

His dimples erupted and Holly caught her breath. She needed to learn to deal with those silly little indentations again.

"Really." His face returned to serious mode. "Ms. Herrera

needed to talk and you listened."

"How much of that did you already know?"

One side of JC's mouth quirked, as if he were making a decision. "Some of it. I found the protection order Sunday night when I ran Ms. Ramirez's name."

"Not before then?" JC must've run her name at the same time. Dammit, she'd have told him about Frank if she thought he needed to know.

She tamped down the anger. Part of her sympathized with Yessica's desire to shield Marcy, but Lee's violent behavior could drive the murder investigation in a new direction.

"Ms. Ramirez never notified us or filed a complaint." JC rocked back on his heels. He lifted one shoulder in a shrug. "Ms. Herrera mentioned Alders when we interviewed the family and Mama Ramirez shut her down hard. Now that Ms. Herrera's opened up, if she remembers anything else, odds are she'll call me."

Holly gave JC a considering look. He was talking but he hadn't told her anything about the investigation. When they were together before, she'd known how to get him to talk. What was he like now? Was he a negotiator, willing to make a deal and trade information, or did he like to hold all the cards?

"I need to push the phone company to turn over their phone records," he said, almost as if he were thinking aloud. "See how often Alders contacted her."

Most likely JC wouldn't share those phone records with her.

Holly thought about Tim's angry rant on Monday morning. He knew about Lee Alders, so Marcy had talked to Tim, but not the local police. Why would Marcy do that? And why hadn't Tim mentioned it to the police?

Tim's knowing about the guy could be completely innocent. "Marcy might've talked to her husband on the office phone."

"I oughtta ask for those records too. If Stevens would quit canceling our interview, I could ask him about contact at the office." JC opened his cell and mashed a speed dial.

Not that JC was paying any attention, but she shrugged. She eased one foot from her shoe and flexed her squashed toes. She'd love to go home and put her feet up. More people—in addition to Tim, Nicole, Alex, and his mother—had left while they were talking with Yessica, so it wasn't as if she was being rude and bailing out early.

Contacting Tim was JC's problem, but she kept seeing the devastated expression on Tim's face and hearing the anger in his voice when he mentioned Marcy's husband. Most good guys couldn't stand the idea of a man hitting a woman. Abusers were down there with pond scum—perverts and child molesters. But was Tim's reaction too much? If Tim and Marcy were that close, why had he canceled his meeting with JC, and why didn't he tell the detective about Lee?

Holly pursed her lips and shifted her weight to her other hip, grimacing at the protest from her sore feet. Alex had jumped all over her after his interview with the cops. Why was Tim ducking the police?

And why had Alex hedged his remarks to them?

Or…was JC lying to her about what he knew and when he knew it?

There was also the too convenient to be coincidental fact JC had been directly behind her—without announcing his presence—when she'd tried to talk with Mrs. Ramirez.

She gave a disgusted snort. All this paranoia was giving her a headache.

"If I wasn't afraid you'd tell me, I'd ask what you were thinking about."

"What?" She looked into JC's amused eyes.

"Don't ever play poker. You can't hide a thing."

"You don't think I can do the expressionless face thing?"

He leaned closer, trailed a finger down her cheek, and slowly slid it across her lower lip. Instantly, her heart rate picked up and her nipples stood at attention.

A satisfied gleam lit his eyes. "I rest my case." His voice was husky, bedroom soft.

A blush warmed her cheeks. She took a step backward and crossed her arms over her traitorous chest. "Were you born a jerk or did you take special classes at cop school?"

He laughed.

The sound was so unexpected, so out of place at a wake, heads turned, and once again they were the focus of too many pairs of eyes.

"You seem to like being part of my investigation. You've got the toughness to be an officer. And the curiosity. Let's see how you do with tenacity." He winked and sauntered away.

Holly gritted her teeth.

Payback would come. Somehow, she'd get him back for that.

And payback would come before JC Dimitrak did.

Chapter Eighteen

Holly pushed through the funeral parlor's front door. She'd spent the last twenty minutes wandering through the rapidly dwindling crowd, looking for Laurie. The odds were slim Laurie had decided to wait by the car, but she was running out of places to look.

Her cell phone chirped its "new message" tone. She fished the phone from her jacket pocket and Laurie's voice came from the speaker. "My cell's about to die, so I'll make this quick. My neighbor is here. You look like you're, *ahem*, busy, so she's giving me a ride home. I'll—"

Silence.

"You've got to be kidding." Holly glared at her phone as if it were deliberately withholding information, although obviously Laurie's phone had died mid-message. "Damn cell phone company." If it would post messages more reliably, she might've caught Laurie before she left.

Well, at least she knew where her MIA friend was.

She stuffed the phone back into her pocket and limped toward the parking lot. She was never wearing heels again. She didn't care how good they made her legs look or if her suits looked stupid with flats. After wearing them all day and standing around on the tile floor at the mortuary for hours, she just wanted to get home, take off these instruments of torture, and pour a glass of wine.

A *big* glass of wine.

Naturally, she'd had to park in the back corner of the lot. She angled across the asphalt and squinted at her car. It looked like something had spilled over the hood, leaving random stripes on the paint. She moved closer and realized the streaks were huge scratches.

For several seconds, shock nailed her in place. Then anger spiked through her like Mount St. Helens blowing its top. She stalked around her vandalized car. Deep gouges marred the paint.

Her beautiful car. She *knew* she shouldn't have parked next to the graffiti-tagged building. The ripped-up fence and rubble had warned her she was asking for trouble.

She scowled at the damaged car. One more crappy thing at the end of a totally crappy day.

Damn, she didn't have time for this. Finding someone to repaint the car. Dealing with the insurance company—which would probably triple her premium. Double damn. And she'd need a police report for her insurance company. A keyed car would be so low on the Pasco cops' priority list, she'd end up waiting forever—in her stupid high heels—for an officer to arrive.

With a muttered curse, she opened her cell, ready to call in Pasco's finest, when the *Duh. JC's already here* light flashed on. Surely, he would write up the report.

She returned to the visitation room. JC stood at one side, talking to an unhappy-looking Hispanic man. The older man turned when she approached, but JC didn't even glance in her direction.

She waited at a discrete distance, shifting from one sore foot to the other, and listened to the detective's questions and the man's reluctant replies. Finally, it sounded like JC was finished. She stepped forward and touched his elbow. "When you have a minute, I need you outside."

The Hispanic man nodded once and walked away. JC's eyebrow twitched and his eyes turned a warm shade of brown. The corner of his mouth lifted toward a smile.

"My car," she said pointedly.

The smile reached grin proportions. His dimples appeared in full glory.

She fought the urge to stamp her foot. He was misunderstanding her on purpose, just to watch her squirm.

Which she refused to do.

"What are you, twelve?" She enunciated the words precisely, as if that would keep JC from turning them around on her. "Someone keyed my car. It's sorta dark in the back corner of the parking lot, but you can still see the damage. I'd appreciate it if you'd write up the incident report."

JC's smile vanished. He wrapped his hand around her arm and guided her toward the door. She started to point out she could find the parking lot and her car all by herself, but his warm fingers distracted her. Little sparks kept jolting her brain and female parts, making her far too aware of his body during the trek across the lot.

"Should've known you'd drive a Beemer." It was his cop tone, not the guy voice. He released her arm and circled the car, inspecting the long scratches on the doors, fender, and hood. "Who've you pissed off lately?" He folded his arms over his chest.

"Other than you?"

"Come on, Holly. I can think of at least one person. Your boyfriend looked unhappy earlier tonight, and I notice he isn't out here with you now."

"Why would you even go there? Like I would date some asshole who'd do this."

"Passive aggressive. All he had to do was walk by the car and extend a hand." JC waved his hand in a zigzag pattern that mimicked a cut in the Beemer's fender. He turned and made a show of scanning the parking area. "People were wandering in and out of the visitation room, but somehow nobody noticed a pissed-off boyfriend."

"One, he's not my boyfriend. Two, he doesn't have any reason to be pissed off, and three, his mother would give him an alibi anyway."

"If I saw my girlfriend flirting with another guy, I wouldn't put up with it. Not many men would."

"I told you I'm not his girlfriend. And I *wasn't* flirting with you."

His face said, *Liar, liar.*

Yeah, yeah, pants on fire. "There's no way Alex would mess up my car."

"What makes you so sure?" JC's face turned expressionless. "He led you to a dead body. Keying a car would be a no-brainer."

She forced her hands to stay still so she wouldn't slap him. "You know damned well the dog found Marcy. If you'd do your job instead of—"

Using our personal connection to—

She wasn't giving JC any more ammunition in the weird war they were waging. "Never mind."

He moved, and suddenly he was standing much too close to her. "What were you going to say?"

She retreated a step and smacked into the car. "Nothing. Just write up the report. I want to go home."

He followed her and practically pinned her against the fender. "You can't use our past to push me away forever."

"This has nothing to do with our past. And I'm really not interested in discussing that right now."

145

"I think you know something. About the car. Maybe about Marcy."

She shoved a palm against JC's chest, but that was as effective as budging five-o'clock traffic in downtown Seattle. "I don't know anything about Marcy. And how could I possibly know who messed up my car? I was inside—helping you."

Going to him had been a huge mistake. "Just forget it. Sorry I asked."

She slid sideways, but his hand again locked around her arm. "Why would your boyfriend damage your car?"

"He didn't. It was probably one of the guys who tagged that building." She gestured at the graffiti-covered wall. "Let go of me."

"Answer my question."

She stared fixedly at his hand around her arm. "Or what? You'll beat it out of me?"

He froze and she knew she'd landed a punch behind his armor.

He released her but didn't move out of her way. His voice and expression were equally cool. "I have never hit a woman. Never. Or hurt a witness or a suspect. I thought you'd remembered at least that much about me."

It had been a low blow. Guilt and regret painted a new blush over her cheeks. "JC," she began.

"*You* came looking for me. Then you had to turn it into a battle of wills. If you don't want my help, I'll be happy to call the Pasco PD."

She shouldn't have said it. She'd lashed out because he kept pushing. "Look, I—"

He jerked his chin toward the car. "Trust me. Alex had something to do with this. Either directly or indirectly."

Damn it, if he did, they were done for sure. She stared at the gouges on her car. "Why would he? Drawing attention to himself would be stupid if he has something to hide. Not that he does." She pulled in a deep breath. What a mess. "But everyone at the wake could see he was ticked I was talking to you."

JC absorbed her reluctant admission. Mr. Efficient Police Officer, he stepped over to the mobile office in his car and whipped out the report, but it was obvious his already low opinion of Alex had slipped another notch.

She wasn't far behind him on that score. Defending Alex was the right thing to do—JC had stepped over the line with the personal attack and there was no evidence Alex had vandalized her car. Still, after Alex's quasi-seduction attempt on Sunday, the yelling match at her office, and tonight's non-encounter with Alejandro and his mother, she wondered why she hadn't seen this unattractive side of him before.

JC handed her the signed report. He glared and used his stern, police officer voice. "From now on, stay out of my investigation."

Her chin lifted and *Where do you get off telling me what to do?* nearly came out of her mouth. "You said Yessica's information helped." She couldn't resist adding, "And might I point out, she talked to *me*, not you. It looks to me like you need my help."

A muscle flexed in his cheek. "I appreciate your help. But what if your car took a hit because of it?"

"Don't be—"

"And what if *you're* the next target?"

Chapter Nineteen

Wednesday morning

Holly lifted a hand from the steering wheel, tapped the Bluetooth receiver, and said, "Mother."

The system scrolled through its electronic memory, pulled the contact, and dialed.

"How's studying for the CPA exam going?" she asked a moment later.

"Eh..." Donna Price mumbled something unintelligible.

"You *are* studying, aren't you? You only have a few weeks left on your Testing Notice."

"I know."

Holly drummed an impatient finger against the steering wheel. The traffic light stayed red. "I can't stay here forever. You have to get licensed."

"I will."

Her cell phone signaled another call. "Hang on a second."

She squinted at the display.

Alex.

Grimacing, she held the buzzing phone. Did she want to talk to him?

Not really.

She switched back to her mother.

"Who was that?"

"Alex."

"Oh? What did he want?"

She really didn't care. She'd ignored his repeated calls last night—sent them to voicemail—unsure what she wanted from him, herself, or anybody else.

"Nothing."

Before her mother could ask more questions, Holly hurried to the reason for the call. "Are you going to be in the office today? We need to finish Nuclear Imaging's engagement letter. I want to get it on paper and signed before Doug stops being blinded by your new hire's cleavage."

Amusement rippled through her mother's voice. "How's she working out?"

The light changed. Holly headed up the hill to Desert Accounting. As much as their new employee irritated her, they needed all the staff they could get. "She's settling in, trying to figure out where she fits."

"How about you? Are you settling in?" Donna asked.

Holly ignored that question, too. Some things were obvious.

"You know, you could make this a permanent position, if you wanted to," her mother said.

Holly's mouth dropped open. She couldn't have been more stunned if her mother suggested that she run naked down George Washington Way, join one of the area's New Wave churches, or perform some other *completely* unacceptable action.

"You don't have to decide today. Just think about it."

Hadn't she made it infinitely clear she wasn't staying in Richland after her mother got licensed? Holly turned into the parking lot at her building. "You know, I agreed to help you sell the practice, but I'm starting to think you don't want to sell."

"I am having second thoughts," Donna admitted.

Holly absorbed this new information. She grabbed her briefcase and slammed the car door. Could her mother run the business by herself? She seemed to be handling her husband's desertion, but how much of that was a façade intended to reassure the clients?

And her daughter.

"Don't worry. I won't deliberately fail the exam."

"That thought hadn't even occurred to me."

Until that moment.

Holly tugged open the outer door of the office building. She walked into the office and stopped dead in her tracks.

"Oh. My. God."

"What? What's the matter?"

"Gotta go." Holly ended the call.

Open-mouthed, she looked first at Tracey and then the metal contraption in the center of Desert Accounting's lobby.

There was a pig.

In a cage.

In the middle of the lobby.

"We've been pigged," Tracey announced.

The porker shuffled through the litter and emitted a few grunts.

"No kidding." Giggles built in Holly's chest. The complete absurdity of the situation hit her. "Please tell me somebody didn't use him, uhm, her? to pay their bill."

The receptionist's laughter rolled across the lobby. "It's a fundraiser." She held out a bright green piece of paper.

Only in Richland.

"What's the deal?" Holly managed around her giggles. She ignored the buzzing phone in her pocket. Her mother would find out about this when she got to the office.

"A guy from FFA dropped her off. Sammy's sister is dating the FFA advisor, so they probably got Rick's name through him. Anyway, Rick has to come up with three hundred bucks to get rid of her. The pig. Not the sister."

"Is anyone not related in this town?" Holly glanced at the flyer. The pig stayed with the recipient until they raised the "purchase price." Once the money was delivered and the pig "owned," the owner chose the next target/recipient.

Thank you, Future Farmers of America.

The pig made a wet, sputtering noise.

"Ugh," Tracey and Holly groaned in unison and clamped hands over their noses.

"Are there any clients in the office?" Holly asked.

The receptionist shook her head.

Holly dropped her hand and yelled, "Rick!"

A moment later, the manager stuck his head around the corner. "You bellowed, boss?"

"You really didn't want to go to the big city." She nodded at the pig.

"Figured you needed to see where bacon came from."

"I hate bacon. Get this thing out of here."

Rick ambled into the lobby. He stopped a few feet from the crate and inspected its contents before giving her a disingenuous smile. "I hit up the staff, but I need another hundred. Open your pocketbook and pony up."

"Why is this *my* problem? The crate has *your* name on it."

"Your lobby. Enjoy the ambience of *eau-de*-pig." He turned and sauntered toward the staff area.

Dammit. Rick knew she couldn't leave the pig in the lobby *and* that she wouldn't fire his insubordinate butt. She jerked open her purse. "Lucky for you I hit the ATM on the way to work."

He re-crossed the lobby and reached for the money. "Think of all the happy future farmers."

Inspiration flashed on the one bright spot in Piggy-Gate. She whipped her hand back. "You get the cash on one condition."

His eyes narrowed. "Which is?"

"The pig goes to the police department when it leaves here."

He didn't try to hide his smile. "Any particular officer? Or should I say detective?"

She tapped a finger against her cheek, pretending to consider his question. "The Franklin County Sheriff's Department could use a laugh today."

"Done." Rick grabbed the cash. "This job's been good for you. A couple of months ago, you wouldn't have bellowed."

"I didn't bellow. Bellowing would not be an improvement in my disposition." Bellowing was a nosedive off the IQ platform.

"Sure it is. You needed to loosen up."

The pig flopped on its side. Shavings drifted through the wires and littered the carpet.

Holly turned to the amused receptionist. "Think the cleaning service has some industrial-strength deodorant?"

Tracey's laughter followed Holly down the hall. She'd love to see JC's reaction when the pig showed up. After all, she could sweetly explain it was for charity.

After dumping her briefcase on her desk, Holly made a quick pass through the office. She glanced in her mother's office—still vacant—and checked on the staff—busy. She settled at her desk with a cup of coffee, and stared at the piles of paper.

As Tim had noted, life had an annoying habit of moving on. Business withholdings still had to be calculated and filed. The end of the year would come whether she wanted it to or not. The Washington State Department of Revenue and the IRS didn't care about personal problems—they wanted their money.

Holly gave the papers another disgruntled look. Maybe they'd magically review themselves. "I need to focus."

She pulled the accident report from her briefcase—she had to call her insurance agent—and placed it on her desk. JC's bold signature scrawled across the investigating officer's line. Her finger followed the flowing ink in an idle caress. It felt as though a lifetime had passed since Sunday morning instead of a mere three days. In less than a week, JC had strolled back into her life and taken up residence.

Damn him.

Was she too close to the situation to be objective? JC thought Alex was responsible for the damage to her car. She didn't want to believe it. Alex had a hot temper, but he'd never shown signs of violence.

Did Alex not like her talking to JC because he picked up echoes of the old attraction? Or did he have something to hide? Something she might spill to the detective?

But if Alex didn't key her car, then the vandalism must be because she'd stirred up trouble. But all she'd done was talk to Yessica.

Holly pressed her hands against her forehead. No. The damage couldn't be related to Marcy's death. Some thrill-seeking kid or local gang-banger—probably the same ones who tagged the building—had keyed her car, pure and simple.

With a sigh, she dropped her hands. Her gaze landed on the newspaper. At least today's article focused on Marcy's husband. Lee Alders was the most logical murder candidate. He was violent. He'd hurt Marcy before. He had to be the killer. The police would track him down. For once, the word "closure" didn't sound like a cliché.

The case wasn't anywhere near closure. The article contained far more speculation than facts, but if there was one thing Holly knew how to do, it was background research. She turned to her computer, launched the Internet browser, and typed Marcy's name into a records search program. Within seconds, she was looking at a marriage certificate. Maricella Camelia Ramirez had married James Lee Alders in King County.

Interesting. The ceremony had been in Seattle and not in Marcy's hometown. From the size of the crowd at the wake, she'd have thought the wedding would've been held in Pasco. Maybe Lee Alders insisted on the inconvenient location. Or maybe Holly was reading too much into the information. Marcy and Lee might have had more friends in Seattle.

She opened another tab and googled "Lee Alders Seattle." Amid the links to a museum in Georgia, genealogy sites, and sports results, she found multiple references to Lee Alders' sale of his company to Telnex.

The sale made a minor splash in Seattle but the news faded quickly. Subsequent references mentioned a lawsuit filed against Alders in the state's Superior Court.

"He stole my idea and I can prove it, " Nyland, the CEO of a competing tech company, claimed in the newspaper article. "His message caching system uses elements I invented."

A female spy in Nyland's company allegedly provided Alders with key features that allowed him to quickly bring his system to market. The following paragraphs compared details of the two companies' designs.

Holly didn't understand the technical issues, but one thing was clear. Nyland felt he had a good case for patent infringement. And Alders had done the infringing.

She scrolled through the links. No court decision. Weird.

She googled Nyland's name. Dozens of hits filled the screen. She clicked the first link and rocked back against the desk chair. Nyland had died during an extreme sporting competition.

He was ice climbing with Lee Alders when he fell.

Son of a bitch.

"It was an accident," Alders asserted in a statement to the police. "I heard the crack, yelled at him to get clear, but there was nothing I could do. The first screw pulled and he was gone."

She read the rest of the article. Either Nyland lost his footing and fell off the face, or someone tampered with his equipment.

An accident or murder? Either way, the man who'd challenged Alder's success was gone.

Holly stared at the computer screen. In addition to abusing his wife, Lee Alders had evidently abused professional relationships. And possibly killed a man as a solution to his business problems.

Had he also found it a convenient way to get rid of an expensive, inconvenient ex-wife?

She returned to the computer. The patent infringement case died with Nyland, but the story didn't. Speculation about Alders's role in both the infringement and Nyland's death abounded—that kind of mud stuck to a man and never washed off.

She clicked through more links, trying to find what Alders was doing now.

No current mention of him.

The guy couldn't just vanish.

The public databases exhausted, she tried the SEC website and queried public companies without success. If Alders went private—joined or started another company—she didn't have the resources to find him.

But she had friends who did.

She picked up the phone and made a call.

Chapter Twenty

A squeaky wheel announced the arrival of the file cart. The mailroom kid stopped outside Holly's office and deposited a handful of envelopes in her in-box. "You won the jackpot today."

He reached under the hanging files, hefted a package, and dumped it on her desk. "Some woman from Stevens Ventures dropped this off."

Holly eyed the huge manila envelope. She emptied the contents onto her desk and groaned at the pile of forms and reports. The temp agency had sent someone to Stevens Ventures to fill Marcy's job. Clearly the new person had no idea how to organize and summarize the information. It looked like she'd packed everything remotely related to the company's finances.

Holly was half-tempted to send the mess back and tell Tim to organize it himself. "What's with the shoebox approach?" she grumbled. "They're a business, for heaven's sake."

"Don't shoot me. I'm just the messenger."

"Yeah, yeah." She crammed the papers back in the envelope. "Take this to Rick." If the guy had time to hustle a pig, he could clean up Tim's mess too.

The file clerk scooped up the package and moved down the hall.

The phone rang, the single beep of an internal call. "What's up, Tracey? Is the pig gone?"

Tracey's amused tone rolled over the line. "On its way to its new home with the sheriff's department." She hesitated a beat. "Crystal Blue called. She canceled."

"Canceled as in needed a different time? Or canceled as in don't call us, we'll call you?"

"Crystal didn't ask to reschedule. She mentioned the Person-of-Interest thing."

Damn. Another lost opportunity. She couldn't afford many of them if she was going to sell Desert Accounting and get out of Richland. "Thanks for letting me know."

She replaced the receiver and slumped in her chair. Great. Not only was JC messing with *her*, he was messing with her *business*. Pointing him at Lee Alders wasn't good enough. She was going to have to find more evidence. Otherwise, at this rate she wouldn't have an accounting firm to sell.

Her life was not supposed to be this complicated. Things had been simple when she arrived in Richland. Do the job. Make the deal. Sell Desert Accounting. Get back to Seattle.

Her life in Seattle was busy, interesting. The city held life's good things—theater, restaurants, and real work. The people she worked with there respected her. If it got a little lonely, well, everything had a price.

Still, Richland was getting to her. Threatening to suck her in. People recognized her at the grocery store, the dry cleaners. Clients introduced her to their families when she bumped into them at Costco. Even her house had captured a piece of her.

She straightened her shoulders.

Forget all that.

Bottom line, she'd put her life on hold for her parents. It was the right thing to do.

But she was *not* getting stuck in Richland.

She returned Crystal's marketing materials to its file in the drawer and stowed her disappointment. Why did the losses hurt more than the successes lifted? One "ah-shit" certainly wiped out a dozen "atta-girls."

Crystal might get over the gossip and reconsider. If she didn't, there were other opportunities. Holly resolutely opened another drawer and pulled out Fred Zhang's folder. She was still studying the Zhangs' financial statement when one of the staff knocked on her door an hour later. "Do you have time for a couple of questions?" Sammy asked.

"As long as it doesn't involve a pig."

He hesitated, flight written all over his posture.

Learn not to scare the staff.

She'd have to frame that rule and hang it on the wall. "Just kidding. What's up?"

Sammy edged into the office and eased a folder onto her desk. "Rick told me to handle the Stevens Ventures paperwork. I transferred most of it to bookkeeping, but there are a couple of companies I don't know what to do with."

Holly opened the folder. The uppermost paper was a property tax notice. "Walla Walla County? I didn't know Tim owned land there."

Sammy pointed at the owner block. "There's nothing in our system on TNM Ventures, either."

"I've told Tim to let me know when he starts a new company." She managed to keep irritation out of her voice. "He's probably already behind on filing something. I'll ask him about it." She made a note of the company name and frowned. "A Wyoming address?"

"Yeah. I wasn't sure it's even one of theirs."

"Tim must've gotten an incentive to incorporate there." It happened, especially if it potentially meant jobs for the state. She rifled the remaining papers and pulled one. "Creekside is part of the Yakima retrofit."

Sammy took it, nodding. "Okay. I saw a folder for Creekside Manor."

In all, there were four companies she'd never heard of. All four shared the same Yakima post office box mailing address. "Leave these with me. Do what you can with the rest."

"Will do." He reached for the folder.

Holly leaned back and crossed her arms. "Is your sister still with the sheriff's department?"

Sammy nodded.

"What'd she say about the pig?"

For a second, he froze, then gave a lopsided smile. "She cracked up. I know it was a pain—the smell and mess. But the group really needs money. I figured Rick could raise it."

Holly waved a hand, dismissing the pig and Sammy's apology. "I thought it was rather...innovative. Just tell me one thing."

Sammy's tightly curled fingers betrayed his tension. "Yes?"

"These farmer friends of yours. Do they raise llamas?"

"Um... I'm sure they don't send them to people's offices."

She narrowed her eyes. "Too bad. I hear they spit." She was still thinking about that payback.

Looking a little confused, Sammy vanished in the direction of his cubicle.

She eyed the four new Stevens folders.

Damn, she needed to get a life.

She'd barely gotten her head back into the Zhang financial statements when the devil himself appeared at her office door. That's what she got for thinking about JC. She'd gone and summoned him.

Before he could open his mouth, she raised her hand in a palm-out, "stop" sign. "No. No more questions." She gave him

159

her best evil-squint.

He smiled, a long, lazy invitation.

Her stomach did a slow flip-flop. "I've told you everything I know about Marcy. Twice. I would do anything to help find her killer, but I. Don't. Know. Anything."

"I was hoping you'd say that."

She cocked her head, letting surprise and more than a little suspicion cover her other reactions. "That I don't know anything? You know I meant about Marcy."

"That you'd help. Come on." He waved a hand and gestured her to her feet.

"Why? Where? This isn't about the pig, is it?"

His dimples appeared and her pulse kicked into a higher gear. She really had to get a handle on those dimples.

"Translating."

Damn, hung with her own words. She *had* opened her mouth and offered to help.

She reluctantly reached for her jacket. "Surely you have someone on the force who speaks Spanish."

"You won't need your coat."

Huh? She followed him out the door. He wasn't wearing a jacket, so she couldn't help but notice his nice tight butt. "How's the investigation coming? Find out anything about Lee Alders?"

"Does your lobby usually smell like a pine forest?"

"Is that your normal negotiating style? Ignore anything that doesn't fit your script?"

His head turned and his dimples reappeared. "Did you say something?"

She rolled her eyes and trailed him into the lobby. The pig cage was gone, the shavings vacuumed. The place smelled overwhelmingly piney, but it beat swine stench any day of the week.

Tracey gave them an approving smile. "Enjoy your lunch."

It wasn't worth trying to explain.

JC opened the outer door and gave every indication he was enjoying himself.

"You know, this is exactly what irritates me about you," she said. "Does it even cross your mind I have my own work to do?"

He just smiled and stepped across the atrium to Stevens Ventures' door.

The kind of interpreting JC needed suddenly occurred to her. She halted abruptly. "No. I can't."

Chapter Twenty-one

JC's hand at the small of Holly's back propelled her into the Stevens Ventures' lobby. Except for JC and her, the place was vacant—the receptionist desk empty, the phone lines blinking.

She dug her heels into the plush carpet. "I won't be part of an interrogation. These people had nothing to do with Marcy's death."

JC finally looked at her. "Lillian isn't being interrogated."

So, she was right about the kind of interpreting he needed.

"We need to ask her about Marcy. Lillian worked with the vic— the woman. She might know who Marcy was seeing."

Holly turned away. This wasn't like translating at the wake. That was spontaneous, defusing a crisis. This was...insulting. "You're using me."

"Holly." JC pulled her in front of him. "I wouldn't ask you to do this if it wasn't important. She's your friend. She'll be more comfortable with you." He slid his hands to her shoulders in a gentle caress.

Refocusing her or reassuring her, Holly wasn't sure what he was doing. For one long moment, she wanted to put her arms around his waist and lean into his shoulder. *Make all this go away.*

"Lillian's upset. I'm not using you to get to her." His tone managed to sound intimate and reasonable at the same time. "If you can talk to her. Well, sign. Help her calm down. That's all I'm asking."

"That's not all you're asking, and you know it." She broke free of his hold and moved to the receptionist's desk. He was making nice to get what he wanted, in this case an interpreter, not because he cared about either her or Lillian.

More manipulation, an area he excelled at.

"Please. I need your help."

"You need me when it's convenient." She scanned the foyer, refusing to look at him. "What happened to 'stay out of my investigation'? That's always been your problem. You bend the rules, but only when it helps you."

JC didn't say anything. Reluctantly, she glanced up. He was watching her, a curious expression in his eyes. "Is that what you think of me?"

"Yes. No. Yes." She wasn't ready to have this conversation. She certainly didn't want to have it where anyone could walk into the middle of it. "But you've always done it—made up the rules. For everybody else," she blurted.

It left her feeling she couldn't depend on him.

"Always?" His lips thinned.

She really, *really* didn't want to have this conversation.

Apparently he didn't either, because he moved in front of her and studied her. He didn't try to touch her again, but he stood between her and the exit.

"The guy who works back there, Fu…" JC hooked a thumb toward the back office area.

"Phoua. He's a property manager."

"Yeah, him." JC took a breath and plowed straight ahead. "Look. Pho said he'd seen you do that 'hand stuff' with Lillian. And I remembered you used to do it in high school, so—"

"That 'hand stuff'?"

"His words, not mine." The color on JC's cheeks darkened. "Sign. For deaf people."

"I believe the politically correct term is 'hearing-impaired.' And it's called American Sign Language."

"Right. We called the college looking for someone who, uh, speaks it. They're contacting a teacher, but it might take a while. Lillian's upset, so I took a chance you might be in your office." He trailed off with a beseeching expression.

Holly folded her arms and gave him an exasperated expression in return. He wasn't all smug because he knew she was going to cave and do what he wanted—bring Lillian down off the ledge. They both knew she was doing that for Lillian. "You are a master manipulator," she gritted out.

He didn't bother to hide his smile. "Does that mean you'll do it?"

"I have a client meeting in an hour. Marcy's funeral is after that, so I can't run late. Unless you plan to provide me with a police escort, I'm out of here in thirty minutes. Let's get this over with."

She crossed the lobby and passed Tim's office, well aware that once again JC had gotten his way. In the back of her mind, she was surprised he'd let Lillian's interview get away from him.

She strode past the smaller offices the property and project managers used. She'd planned to catch Lillian after the funeral anyway, and find out what had been bothering her on Monday. If it was related to Marcy's death, it would undoubtedly come out during this session.

Another thought occurred to her and she stumbled.

"You okay?" JC caught her arm.

She waved him off. Surely, Lillian's unease on Monday wasn't *guilt.*

A rumble of male voices spilled from the office Lillian had

shared with Marcy. Holly took in Lillian's anxious expression, and grabbed hold of her temper. Had JC done something incredibly stupid like accusing Lillian of killing Marcy?

Her gaze swept the office. A pistol-toting shrimp of a man perched his scrawny rump on the corner of Marcy's desk, swapping stories with Phoua. A woman Holly didn't know, apparently Tim's new temp, hung on the uniformed officer's words. As he spoke, the officer tossed glances in Lillian's direction, which seemed to further fluster the woman. Her gaze darted between the other three, obviously trying to follow their words. Occasionally, her eyes dropped to the pistol, handcuffs, and other menacing metal stuff attached to the patrolman's belt.

Now Holly understood how the interview had spiraled out of control. She'd bet money Shrimp was the first officer on the scene, not JC.

JC nudged Holly into the office. Four heads swiveled in their direction, but Holly focused on the relief pouring off Lillian's shoulders. The payroll clerk's hands began a ballet of words—fingers, hand shapes, gestures.

"Slow down," Holly signed. The men's attention was a distraction, making her fingers awkward. "You aren't in trouble," she said as she signed. "The police have questions about Marcy." She gestured toward Marcy's desk.

The Shrimp slid off the desk. "Why'd you say that out loud? She can't hear you."

She flashed an impatient glance at him. His slight stature was deceptive. Defined muscles bulked his shoulders under the dark blue uniform.

His attitude raised antagonistic bristles, but for Lillian's sake, she pushed them down. "She reads lips."

He gave first Lillian and then Holly a disgruntled look. "She sure acted like she couldn't understand a word we said. How's she even work here if she can't hear?"

"Dickerman." JC's voice carried a warning note. Apparently she wasn't the only one who'd caught the derogatory tone.

Shrimp's face lost all expression. "Are you the interpreter?" he asked in a polite, neutral voice.

Fed up with the crap Lillian was forced to put up with— people who couldn't be bothered with someone who was different—Holly slammed her hands onto her hips and got in Shrimp's face. "Reading lips isn't just lips. It's the mouth, the whole face. Body language. Expressions. Those things communicate as much as the words. If you pulled the cop-face routine and didn't remember to speak directly to her, no wonder she couldn't understand you."

"Cop-face?" She heard JC's amused tone from behind her.

She wasn't interested in his attempts to lighten the atmosphere. "Why didn't you just write down the questions? That's how she 'works here.' Mostly with computer data and e-mail."

Dickerman didn't even have the grace to look embarrassed. "We thought about it, but by then she was practically hyperventilating, doing head-on-a-stick. Swiveling back and forth between us."

Disgusted, she turned to Lillian and signed, *The man's an ass.*

At some silent message from JC, Deputy Shrimp left the office and returned moments later with two plastic chairs from the break room. Phoua and the new woman got the message this was their cue to leave. Holly couldn't help but notice JC had taken charge without saying a word. Unlike the Shrimp, he didn't need to throw his weight around.

The younger officer stepped toward Marcy's old desk. JC stopped him. "We don't need both of us here. See if you can find the next person on your list."

He said it in a neutral tone, but Holly knew a rebuke when

she heard one.

Shrimp did, too. With no expression on his face, but a lot of tension in his shoulders, he said, "Yes, sir. I'm on it."

The door clicked behind him.

The stress level in the office dropped ten degrees.

Holly sat in front of Lillian's metal desk, acutely aware of the man sitting beside her. He hadn't cleared the room to be nice. He didn't care about Lillian's feelings. He wasn't taking her side against the Shrimp. He was just trying to get what he wanted.

Of course, he *did* need any information Lillian could give him.

Let's get this done.

With Holly interpreting, JC asked casual, general questions about what Lillian did and how well she'd known Marcy. The interlude gave the payroll clerk time to calm down before getting to the important stuff.

"Do you know who Ms. Ramirez was dating?"

Holly dredged the gestures from her memory, finger-spelling when she couldn't remember the shapes.

"I don't know who she dated. Sometimes she talked on the phone, but she turned her back." Lillian pivoted her body and demonstrated—shielding her face from the watching pair.

"Were you aware of anyone who might have threatened Ms. Ramirez or wanted to harm her?"

Holly thought the question rather obvious, but faithfully translated it.

Lillian tapped her fingers on her desk. She toyed with the stapler, aligning it in the already organized workspace. Finally, she lifted her hands and swept them through a flow of words. "One time, a scary man came here. Marcy was upset when he arrived. I don't know what Marcy said, but he said, 'You weren't hard to find.' I stood up, to leave and give them privacy, but Marcy grabbed my arm. She pulled me back to my seat. Her hands were trembling like she was afraid."

Was the "scary man" Marcy's boyfriend or her husband?

"What happened next?" JC asked.

Holly translated the question. She noticed the subtle tension in his body. Under his relaxed body position, his muscles were taut. He held his torso forward slightly, ready for action. She could appreciate the self-control required to pull off the appearance of casual confidence. Knowing how aware of body language Lillian was and concerned his might distract her, she kept the payroll clerk focused on herself, rather than the detective.

"They argued. I tried not to watch, but Marcy became angry. Her face turned red, her gestures big." Lillian's hands mimicked the other woman's gesticulations. "The man—Marcy called him 'Lee'—never—"

"Lee?" JC touched Holly's arm. Under the circumstances, she figured she wasn't supposed to notice how warm his fingers were, or the electric effect the contact had on her. The way the warmth spread and her nerves gave off sparks in response.

"Are you certain?" His voice sounded calm and reasonable.

She turned to him. "Are you asking if I'm certain of the translation or if she's certain Marcy called him Lee?" From the corner of her eye, she noticed Lillian's tentative frown and darting glance at JC.

"The latter. Go ahead." JC gestured for her to translate the question.

Lillian raised her eyebrows, asking for clarification. Holly converted the words and Lillian nodded a definite confirmation. "Marcy called him 'Lee.' "

"What did Lee do?" JC asked.

"He stayed calm. Never wrinkled his face or—" Lillian's features hardened into an aggressive expression, neck tendons tight, jaw clenched. "He was very menacing. He scared me. Marcy must have been loud when she talked, because Tim came into the office."

Holly stiffened and she sensed JC's sudden interest. Tim had never mentioned this confrontation to her. Had he told the cops?

"Tim pointed at the door, telling him to leave. The man said something. Marcy drew back and Tim stepped between them. I only caught an occasional word, but Lee seemed to threaten them."

Holly could envision the scene—the contrast of the organized workspace and the roiling emotions, the space too small to contain the anger and fear, the aggressive intruder and the intimidated women. Lee menacing. Tim trying to be in charge and protective.

"Lee reached inside his jacket." Lillian mimicked a dive for an inner pocket. "We all cringed. I thought he had a gun. But he pulled out a thick envelope and threw it on Marcy's desk. He said she'd better sign it and he would be back later."

"Holy crap," Holly muttered. Marcy had never breathed a word about any of this.

"Go on," JC urged.

"Marcy sat down in her chair, like she'd fought a battle." Lillian slumped, demonstrating. "I went to her, but she made the 'I'm okay' sign."

"What did Stevens do?" JC asked.

Holly couldn't help but wonder if JC's real interest at that moment was in Tim or Lee. Her fingers wove through the appropriate signs, as interested in the answer as he was.

"Tim left, following Lee. I think maybe Tim wanted to make sure the man was gone."

"What was in the envelope?"

"I don't know. Marcy opened it. Whatever the papers said

made her angry. She smashed them." Lillian's hand closed into a fist around imaginary papers. "She telephoned someone, grabbed her purse, and left."

There was a moment of silence as they all processed the scene and the implications. Where had Marcy gone when she stormed out?

"When did this happen?" JC asked.

Lillian pulled out her calendar. Fingers touching the entries, she moved backward through the days. "Thursday, the week before Marcy disappeared."

"Did the man, Lee, come back to the office?" he asked.

"Not while I was here."

"Did Ms. Ramirez tell you what was in the papers that made her angry?"

"No."

JC tried several more questions, variations on the same theme of Lee and the mystery papers. Holly could sense his frustration, but his voice and expression stayed calm. His two main suspects had been in the victim's office, argued bitterly, and the only witness was deaf.

Holly signed, "Is this what you wanted to tell me? When I saw you on Monday?"

Lillian's gaze darted toward JC before returning to Holly. She shook her head.

"What did you ask her?" JC's voice intruded.

Of course he'd noticed the exchange. But apparently Lillian considered the topic unrelated to Marcy's murder. Holly gave JC a disingenuous smile. "I asked if she thought you were cute."

He leveled an exasperated glare at her that said she'd hear about that later, but she figured if Lillian wanted to talk to her about something personal, what business was it of his?

"Didn't Tim mention this when you questioned him?" Holly

asked.

JC immediately clammed up. "You know I can't tell you that."

A brisk tap sounded and a man stepped through the office doorway.

"Hello." His hands swept through the greeting gesture in sync with his words. The interpreter had arrived.

To her surprise, Holly was reluctant to leave. What else did Lillian know that JC wouldn't tell her later?

Chapter Twenty-two

Holly dashed into her office and grabbed her briefcase.

"Remind my mother about the Fred Zhang meeting, please," she asked Tracey. "I'll go straight there after Marcy's funeral."

She pushed through the front door. Two magpies exploded off the pavement in a flurry of black feathers. Instantly, she flashed back to the clearing at Big Flats and the seagulls surrounding Marcy's body.

A shudder rippled through her. She rejected the image, but her eyes tracked the birds to a Russian olive tree on the hill behind the office. When she moved to the Tri-Cities, she'd thought the black and blue birds handsome and couldn't understand why the locals hated the cheeky scavengers. She'd considered it more prejudice toward an import—until the first time she'd seen magpies eating quail babies in her backyard.

She bypassed the spot that interested the scavengers. She didn't want to know what piece of road-kill had attracted them.

A sedan entering the parking lot distracted her. Tim wheeled his Mercedes into a parking space two cars beyond her BMW. Great timing. She had a million questions for him—although *What exactly was your relationship with Marcy?* might not be the place to start—and she didn't have time to ask any of them.

Tim climbed from his car, doing his best imitation of a casual male.

Holly stifled a sigh. Like Monday's drunk and the awkwardness at the wake never happened.

"Kaylin give you the information for our meeting?" He reached into his car and pulled out a leather satchel.

"Who? Oh, the temp. She sent over a bunch of stuff. Didn't you hire a bookkeeper? It's sorta expensive having us pull the papers together."

Tim waved a dismissive hand. "Don't worry about the bill. Things were tight for a while. That's all settled."

"Glad to hear it." Holly opened her BMW's back door and dropped her briefcase on the seat. "I was surprised to see you started new companies."

"New companies?"

"There were a couple. One's TNM Ventures."

"Oh. How…?" His voice trailed off.

"I noticed a property tax bill."

Nodding, he blew out a breath. "That's not an operating company. That's land I bought on the Snake River. I thought it'd make a nice weekend place."

"It's a lot of land." Although zoned agricultural, the bill had been substantial. And according to the tax statement, there was at least one building on the property.

He stepped around the front of her car, dropped his satchel, and leaned against the fender. "Most of it's planted in grapes—the water rights came with the land."

"If it's on the river, I'm sure it's beautiful."

"Listen." Tim lowered his voice to a confidential tone. "Don't mention the land to Nicole, okay?"

Holly's internal radar pinged and questions raced through her mind. Why would he hide the land from his wife? Damn, why did any man hide assets? Preparing for a divorce? Having an affair?

Were her instincts right on track—Tim's relationship with Marcy was more than friendship?

"I bought the land as a gift. Now…" Tim stepped closer. "Nicole's spotting. We're afraid she'll miscarry again."

Miscarry? Holly's brain recalibrated. Totally missed that one. "I'm sorry, Tim. I didn't know she's pregnant."

"She just found out. We don't want to tell anybody until she gets past the first trimester."

"That makes sense." She hoped he didn't expect anything more. She didn't know the first thing about children or pregnancy.

"We both want kids." Tim continued as if she hadn't spoken. He pushed his hand through his hair. "It's just, lately Nicole's obsessed with having a baby. It's all she can talk about. I'm worried about her."

Holly made sympathetic noises. What could she say? She wasn't hearing the tick of her own biological clock.

Frustration tightened his mouth. "She's seen so many doctors. Most think her pregnancy problems are related to her childhood, but none of them can give us a reason why she keeps miscarrying."

Tim looked miserable. Holly wanted to kick herself. When she saw him on Monday, he'd probably been drunk and crying over their baby, not Marcy. Why couldn't guys ever admit what was truly bothering them? Or that they even had feelings? "I'm really sorry. I hope things work out."

With a start, she remembered Nicole's comment earlier that week about getting so "big." Was she in denial about the miscarriage? That had to make things harder on Tim.

He dropped his hands to his thighs. "Look, Holly. This is probably bad timing, but I'm glad I caught you. There's something else I wanted to talk to you about."

She glanced at her watch. "I'm on my way to a meeting. Are

you going to Marcy's funeral this afternoon? We can talk after that."

"Maybe." He studied the toes of his shoes.

She controlled the instinctive double-take. The question had been rhetorical. "She worked for you. I thought you were friends. Why wouldn't you go?"

"I don't know what I'm going to do. That isn't what I wanted to talk about." He traced one of the slashes on her car hood. "Sorry about your car."

"Yeah, I wasn't thrilled either." Could ya get to the point? She forced her leg not to jiggle with impatience.

Gaze locked on the car, he brushed away a fleck of paint. "I talked to Alex. He told me you two had a fight."

"Anything between Alex and me doesn't involve you." She reached for the car door handle.

"Come on, Holly. You know the argument was about the mess at the wake. His mother can be a royal bitch. I've seen her screw up his relationships before."

"If you knew that, why'd you introduce us?"

Tim shifted his weight against the Beemer. "Marcy said you weren't dating much. We thought it'd be fun for you to meet people, get out of the house."

Angry warmth flooded Holly's cheeks. So now she was some kind of charity case?

"Don't be mad." Tim slipped his hand around her arm. "Look, I saw how Mrs. Montoya manipulated Alex at the wake. I can help patch things up. The guy's really into you. You're good together. Don't throw something away before you give it a chance."

Why were they even having this conversation? Holly tugged her arm free and held up a warning finger. "One, I'm not the one throwing anything away. And two, like I said, this is between Alex and me."

So, butt. Out.

Tim held up his hands in male surrender mode, which meant he didn't understand a word she'd said. "Hey. I'm not interfering."

"Yes, you are, and you're out of line."

"*Me* out of line?" Tim's face flushed. "I heard about the way you were carrying on with that detective last night. *You're* the one screwing over your boyfriend. And it becomes *my* business when I wonder if that's how you handle your business affairs."

"Carrying on? Screwing over?" she sputtered. "*Affairs?* Is there something else on your mind?"

His hands flew forward, placating. "Oh, shit. I'm not handling this right. It's just...I mean—"

"I get the message. But let me make something perfectly clear. Business always comes first. You're my client. I don't even discuss client business on a cell phone in public. What you implied—that I'd blab about your business—is the equivalent of me accusing you of building an office tower with substandard materials."

"I didn't mean—"

"Yes, you did." She didn't bother to curb her impatience.

"I wasn't smearing your rep, honestly. Ah, hell." He scrubbed a hand over his face. "Alex called. Between that detective hounding both of us and his seeing you two together... The guy's got a lot of pride."

"Make up your mind. Alex is into me. He thinks I 'screwed him over.' He has so much pride he couldn't say, 'Excuse me, Mama, my friend's here all alone. It looks like she needs some help.' "

Tim's hand rocked. "Nobody's perfect."

"Including you."

"Excuse me?"

"You knew about Lee Alders. Why didn't you say anything? If you had, maybe JC wouldn't be hounding you."

Tim flinched, but didn't bother denying he knew about Lee. "What was there to say?"

"Everything. Lee came here. He *threatened* Marcy." She raised frustrated hands. "Was Marcy seeing him again?"

Surprise and what might have been anger flitted across Tim's face. "Not that I was aware of."

That wasn't much of an answer. Arms folded, she waited for more. He'd witnessed a key exchange between Marcy and Lee and still hadn't admitted it. *Why the lies?*

Tim pushed away from her Beemer and paced to the front of the vehicle and back. "I saw the newspaper this morning. The police think Alders killed her?" He raised a questioning eyebrow.

Like JC would tell her about the latest police theory. Holly shrugged. "Do you think he could've killed her?"

Tim focused his gaze on the car fender, his face a study in concentration. "Maybe."

"Maybe you should put talking to the cops on your priority list." Holly opened the driver's door to slide in.

"Hmm?" Tim glanced in her direction. "Yeah. I have to do that eventually."

Holly stopped, surprised. "You really haven't talked to them?"

"I'm supposed to meet with them today."

"Alex and I talked to them days ago."

"I had to reschedule. I have a lot on my plate."

"We *are* talking about Marcy's murder."

"What am I supposed to tell them? I don't know who killed her." Tim's expression was more irritated than concerned. "My foreman says the cops are questioning everybody at the Yakima site. The construction guys, delivery people. All the surrounding

177

businesses. Hell, they even talked to the guys in the Taco Truck."

"Can't say they aren't thorough."

"All they've done is waste a lot of time I have to pay for."

"So give them a better suspect."

"Alders could've done it." Tim shoved his hands into his pocket and rocked on his heels. "The guy's such an asshole, he probably did."

Thank you, Captain Obvious. "I need to go. I'll see you and Alex on Friday at eleven."

"Right."

She hopped in the BMW. "Unless I dump your files on one of the managers," she muttered.

Chapter Twenty-three

Holly entered the now-familiar office at the Tom-Tom Casino. In spite of Tim delaying her with that ridiculous conversation about Alex, if she hurried, she could deliver Peter's contract and still make it to the funeral on time.

Peter rose from his desk and met her halfway across the room. "Do you have the engagement letter?"

"Ready for your signature," she said. "It has everything we discussed."

Within minutes, Peter had signed the document and they'd scheduled the initial accounting fieldwork. "Let me walk you out," he said.

In contrast to Monday's easy conversation, a tense silence lay between them. Holly tried to think of something she might've said or done to upset him, but drew a blank.

"Listen, Holly." Peter rubbed his chin. "I got to thinking about Tim Stevens, what we talked about. The brunette."

Ah. So that was bothering him.

"I misspoke. She wasn't his wife."

Big surprise. "How did you know?" she asked.

He studied the floor, not meeting her eyes. "Tim threw a Texas Hold 'Em tourney a while back. Invited a bunch of his contractors and their wives."

"Oh."

"His wife ran around, talking to everybody, but you could tell she didn't like it."

"Didn't like what?"

He shrugged. "Being here. Gambling."

"I guess you must be pretty good at reading people."

"Occupational hazard."

"So the brunette wasn't his wife. She could've been a friend."

"Nope." Peter scuffed his toe along a peeling seam in the carpet. "Look, I'm not here to be the morality police. It's...my security chief started seeing her. I told him not to get involved with a woman who'd cheat with a married man, but..." He grimaced.

Part of her wanted to defend Marcy—if it was Marcy—while the rest of her was appalled. Marcy was seeing Creepy Security Guy?

Maybe she was attracted to weird guys. Look at her husband.

"Your security chief was dating her?"

Peter shrugged. "A couple of days after they were in here, he said he was seeing her."

"Hang on a minute." She propped her briefcase against the closest machine and pulled out the group picture. "Is this the woman you're talking about?"

He laid a finger on Marcy's image. "Like I said, pretty and upbeat. I can see why men are attracted to her."

"She's dead," Holly blurted.

Peter froze. "Are you sure?" He raised a hand. "Of course you're sure. Damn, what a waste."

"That's one way to put it."

She watched the other shoe drop. His head turned, his gaze darting around the room. "I'm sure my security chief didn't have anything to do with it."

"I'm sure he didn't."

Holy crap, JC needed to know about this.

Holly hurried to her car. What had Marcy been doing with Peter's chief of security? That didn't track with the Marcy she knew. Then again, did the possibility of Marcy having an affair with Tim ever register?

Movement at the casino entrance caught her eye. Creepy Security Guy was leaning against the doorframe, a familiar posture she couldn't quite place. He raised a hand, a finger-gun pointing at her.

Her mouth went dry and a band of tension made breathing difficult. Had he heard Peter tell her about Marcy? Was the finger-gun a threat? She climbed into her car and started it, then sneaked another peek. A chill sifted down her spine. *He was still staring at her.*

The exit was on the other side of the parking lot. Great. Now she had to drive past him. She eased the car forward, determined to focus straight ahead.

The figure by the door drew her gaze like hooks were anchored in her eyeballs.

He touched the brim of his hat, a casual salute, his face lifting from the shadow for a split second.

Her breathing stopped.

No. It couldn't be.

Black spots crowded the edge of her sight, left tunnel vision that obscured the pavement. Somehow, she made it out of the parking lot, then pulled to the side of the road.

She gripped the steering wheel with shaking hands.

Oh, my God. She knew the guy was freaking her out but now she knew why. Creepy Security Guy looked just like Frank Phalen.

It couldn't be him.

Could it?

Chapter Twenty-four

Wednesday, late afternoon

Three hours later, Holly drove away from a disastrous meeting with Fred Zhang. With stiff fingers, she crammed the Bluetooth into her ear, punched the office contact, and jammed the phone into her pocket.

"Desert Accounting."

"Is Mother in the office?"

Tracey hesitated a beat. "She didn't make it to the meeting?"

"Would I be asking if she did?"

Tracey cleared her throat. "Good point. She called, said something came up and to let you know she'd be late. But your phone went straight to voicemail."

"Dammit." Holly slammed her fist against the steering wheel. "Fred Zhang was so ticked off Mother didn't show up. He didn't even try to hide it."

"I'm sorry," Tracey murmured.

Holly didn't know who she was angrier with: her mother, Fred, or herself. "I spent a lot of time and energy getting this meeting arranged, coming up with good ideas for his company."

Tracey maintained a tactful silence.

Her initial snit aired, worry poked at Holly. "Should I start calling the hospitals? I mean, where is she? She isn't answering her cell."

"I'm sure she's okay."

Traffic had thickened into the evening homeward rush by the time Holly reached the center of Richland. She turned left beside the central park. The city boasted a town square, but instead of a picture-perfect historic courthouse, two butt-ugly federal buildings lined the west side of the square. Holly wasn't sure if they were built in the 50s or 70s. Neither decade produced exceptional architecture. The hulking pre-cast concrete walls and slit windows of the courthouse looked like a bunker or a fallout shelter. Given the Hanford nuclear site's proximity—and Richland's reason for existing—the resemblance was most likely deliberate.

"This town is going to drive me crazy," Holly muttered.

"What do you mean?" was Tracey's cautious response.

She turned onto George Washington Way and joined the throng crawling away from the park. Flat-topped, one-story buildings with metal awnings lined the street. Mom and Pop stores, insurance co-op, a restaurant/diner. "This place reeks of the 50s."

"It's not that bad."

Holly heard the smile in Tracey's voice. "Yes, it is. Fred Zhang's Neanderthal attitude came through loud and clear. He only agreed to the meeting because Mother and his wife are friends. He had absolutely no interest in anything I had to say. 'What could a young, unmarried woman *possibly* know about business,' should've been hung on a banner over the man's desk."

"What do you want me to do besides listen?" Tracey's sympathetic voice filled Holly's ear.

Part of her wanted to lean on Tracey's shoulder and sob. I'm so tired of being lonely. Overworked. Stressed out.

Tracey didn't need to hear her personal problems.

Let it go.

Holly slumped in her seat, propped her elbow on the window ledge, and rested her head on her curled fingers. "Sorry. I'm venting."

"I figured that out a few minutes ago."

"The meeting with Fred was just the crowning glory to a crappy day. Marcy's funeral was a major sobfest. I wanted to go to the graveyard, but no, I had to fix my makeup and show up for this stupid meeting that was a complete waste of time."

"There are always going to be close-minded men like Fred. Brooding about the wasted time won't change anything."

With a twitch of her shoulders, Holly channeled the *hakuna matata* dude, and relegated the mess to the past. "You're right. I just needed to get it out of my system."

But she was *so* going to have it out with her mother.

If she could ever find the woman.

"Are you coming back to the office?" Tracey asked.

"I'm not sure."

Holly ended the conversation and flipped over to her messages. JC still hadn't called her back. The guy had dogged her for days, but now that she actually had news—*Frank Phalen might be in town and he may have been dating Marcy*—JC had vanished.

Her fingers tapped a nervous dance across the wheel. Had it really been Frank? Would he really leave Seattle to follow her here? Why would he do that—and not try to contact her? Besides, the Frank she knew would never work as a security guard.

Had she simply tacked Frank's features onto Creepy Security Guy because she'd been upset about Marcy? Learning this stuff about Marcy had stirred up all her bad memories of Frank.

After only a few dates, Frank had called constantly, insisting on knowing her schedule, attempting to control who she saw and where she went. That was when she told him it was over.

He hadn't taken it well, to say the least. He'd threatened enough to scare the crap out of her, but he'd never beaten her like Lee hit Marcy. Frank's threats had been psychological rather than physical.

Why hadn't Marcy turned to her family? Her friends?

Frustration followed Holly down G'Way and perched on her shoulders at the red light. Small, wooden houses lined the street, resisting the encroaching business district. She stared at the newest mixed-use building as she inched toward the highway. What had the developer been thinking when he painted it that awful color? Thank goodness Stevens Ventures hadn't built it—she didn't have to pretend to like it.

She pressed the Bluetooth again and said, "Mother."

To her surprise, her mother answered.

"Are you okay?"

"I'm sorry I missed the meeting."

Was that okay or not? "What happened?"

"I'll tell you about it later," her mother said hurriedly.

And disconnected.

Like that explained anything.

Well, at least she knew her mother was alive.

Traffic stalled completely at the next intersection. Holly sat at the red light at Bradley, staring at the overhead road signs. Pasco. Kennewick. Interstate 82.

Those signs were the story of her life. Three directions. Three choices.

She could turn left to Pasco and confront Alex. He'd left a dozen messages in her voicemail. They ranged from his initial tirade after Marcy's wake to a three-o'clock-in-the-morning, plaintive, "Call me."

She could go straight and take Highway 240 back to Kennewick and work. Joy of joys.

Or she could turn right onto the interstate and go home. To her house in Hills West. To Seattle.

She sighed. Either way, she'd be alone.

Again.

The light changed.

She turned left.

~$~

Even as she looped around the interstate exit, Holly was already second-guessing her decision. She wasn't in love with Alex. She liked him. They'd had a great time together—right up until the hunting expedition and its disastrous conclusion.

Finding Marcy's body wasn't Alex's fault—and she was overreacting to the incidents at the wake. He wouldn't have keyed her car. That was too passive aggressive for him. And as for his mother, well, if she had serious designs on the guy, the witch would be a major hurdle, but really, who cared? She just wanted someone fun for a few months while she was still in Richland.

Someone who could be a buffer between JC and her.

Someone who might keep JC from getting past her defenses.

Was she about to do something incredibly stupid, like patch things up with Alex, simply because on too many levels JC scared her? She could walk away from Alex. JC? She couldn't go through that again.

Not that she'd actually consider getting involved with JC again.

Ugh. She wanted to pound her head against the steering wheel. Using Alex wouldn't be fair, but neither of them had ever expected anything more than a good time. And she wouldn't be using him, just getting things back to where they'd been *before*. She'd catch him before the restaurant opened, clear the air, and arrange to go dancing or invite him to Bookwalter Winery with Laurie and her on Saturday.

She straightened in her seat, feeling marginally better. Having at least part of her life back to normal would let her focus on straightening out the rest of the craziness.

The parking lot at Alex's restaurant held only a few cars. Alex's distinctive Z stood amid the sedans and econo-boxes clustered beside the employee entrance. Holly parked near the front door and burst out laughing. The pig crate sat at the restaurant's front entrance.

Alex would go ballistic when he saw it. What was JC thinking, sending it to the restaurant? The health department would go crazy. But oh, if anybody deserved to get a pig, it was Alex.

Did he even know it was here? Surely the FFA guys wouldn't just dump it and run. She'd missed the delivery at her own office, but there had to be a process for transferring the crate.

She approached the entrance. At least outdoors the pig didn't smell as bad. A huge tag sat on top of the crate, taped to the green instruction sheet she'd already seen. She turned the tag to the light and read:

> Holly Price had the crate.
> Paid the fee.
> Chose another's fate.
> A new address for the pig.
> Tag, you're it.

Her name was entered on the sender's line.

All of it was written in JC's bold slanting script.

Oh my God. She stared at the tag, horrified. She was screwed. JC had gotten her back—and made things even worse with Alex, all with one stroke on a form. She ripped the tag off the crate and crushed it.

She was *so* sending that llama to JC's department.

She pulled her cell from her pocket, expecting to call since the front entrance was usually locked. To her surprise, the door swung open when she tugged the handle.

She paused near the hostess stand and let her eyes adjust to the dimmer light.

The pig was a huge complication. Maybe she could get it out of here, send it to Tim, without Alex ever knowing it was there. She could call Rick, ask him to arrange for its relocation.

She rubbed her temples. Or Alex could learn to laugh and deal with it himself. But if she and Alex were going to try again, the rules were changing. There'd be *fun*. And no yelling.

She moved further into the restaurant. A clatter of silverware and Spanish chatter came from the main dining room, where several men and women were preparing tables for dinner. Salsa music pulsed from the speakers and the women swayed between the tables with an easy grace.

One of the men noticed Holly and stepped in her direction. "We're not open yet."

"I'm looking for Alex. Is he in the office?" She headed toward the hall without waiting for an answer.

"Hey! You can't go in there."

Her gaze swiveled from the office door—*closed*—to the server's face—*worried*. So, Alex wasn't alone.

"It's okay." Head held high, she strode forward. Was he carrying on with one of his staff? And he had the nerve to be angry with *her* for talking to JC?

"But—" The waiter shrugged and returned to the dining room.

Alex's raised voice came through the closed office door. She slowed her footsteps. Maybe he wasn't sweet-talking another woman. Maybe he was chewing out an employee.

The door flew open and JC strode from the office.

Oh. Crap.

Alex appeared behind the detective. Anger rippled from every pore of Alex's body, but JC was doing his impassive cop thing. Stalking toward her, his face remained expressionless, but his heels hammered sharp blows on the Mexican tile floor. His eyes swiveled in her direction, registering her presence, but his pace didn't change.

She looked from JC to Alex. The tension between the two men had passed "uncomfortable" and was headed straight for "danger zone." Her attention swung back to JC. "What's going on?"

"It's business."

Like that clarified anything. She was getting tired of everyone's non-answers.

"Why—" she began.

"Ask Montoya about his alibi," JC cut her off. He brushed past her, headed for the lobby.

Alex vanished inside his office. She followed. "What was that all about?"

He turned on her the second she cleared the door. "What in the *hell* did you tell that man?"

She rocked back on her heels. "Excuse me?"

"And what the fuck were you thinking sending that pig out here? Are you trying to ruin me?"

"No. *What* is going on?"

A string of Spanish curse words answered her. Alex leaned against his cluttered desk and slammed his arms across his chest. "What happened to your car?"

"I told him you didn't have anything to do with that." She took another step into the office, but Alex's furious expression stopped her from moving any closer. For a moment, she considered turning around and walking out, but curiosity won.

"What happened to your car?" The words squeezed past Alex's clenched teeth.

She held onto her temper. Once again, she had to be the designated grown-up. She was getting pretty sick of that. "Somebody keyed it while I was at Marcy's wake."

"And you called that detective instead of me."

Like she'd have asked Alex for anything after the way he ignored her? "He was already there."

"I noticed." Alex's lips remained stiff with anger.

Keeping her tone level took effort. "I needed a police report for my insurance company. It'll cost a fortune to repaint."

He nodded once, a short jerk of his chin, conceding her point. "That detective thought I damaged your car."

She kept her mouth firmly closed. JC clearly thought Alex *had* done it, but she wasn't going to say it.

"I told you already, Dimitrak thinks I'm guilty. That I'm involved in Marcy's murder. And that you are, too." His finger stabbed at her.

"Me?" Holly's hand flew to her chest. "I didn't have anything to do with Marcy's death." Was that what JC meant last night? When he brought up Marcy and Alex?

"First words out of his mouth were, am I trying to intimidate you?"

"Why would you—" She shook her head. That made no sense. JC should know Alex wouldn't—*couldn't*—intimidate her, even if he was somehow mixed up in Marcy's murder.

Which he wasn't, was he?

Alex pushed away from the desk. "Then it was, did I mess with your car because I was afraid you weren't backing Tim and me? Were we worried you were on his side now?"

"There aren't any sides here. We all want the truth." She leaned against the bookcase, her attention on Alex as he paced.

"I told Dimitrak he was crazy. That none of us—me, you, Tim—had anything to do with Marcy's murder. Nobody's trying to keep you from saying anything."

She spread her hands in a gesture that was simultaneously frustrated and placating. "I told him that too. I don't know what he's after. Just now, he said to ask you about your alibi."

"Jesus." Alex's hand flashed. "That's exactly what I'm talking about. Why in the hell didn't you tell him we went to the movie Tuesday night?"

She paused, thinking. "That was Monday."

"It was Tuesday." He shot a hand through his hair. "What are you trying to do to me?"

She stepped away from the bookcase. "What are you talking about?"

"Every time you talk to that asshole"—Alex's finger jerked in the direction JC had gone—"he lands on my doorstep." His finger stabbed at the floor.

Anger tightened her chest and warmed her neck. "It wasn't anything I said."

He brushed aside her statement with an irritated wave. "Dimitrak kept going on about the four of us. You. Me. Tim. Marcy. That we were all tangled up together. He hammered on, where was I, since you screwed my alibi, and who wanted Marcy dead. Like I have a goddamn clue."

Holly threw up her hands. "What am I supposed to do about it? I didn't tell him you did anything."

"Oh, sure. And then—"

He stopped, but Holly saw something darker in his mulish expression.

Arms crossed, he leaned back and adopted an I-don't-give-a-damn attitude. "How long have you been fucking him?"

His words slapped her hard. She might have a lot of faults, but screwing around wasn't one of them. "How *dare* you? I did no such thing. What is your problem?"

Alex dropped his arms and the pose. "Don't play innocent. I saw you last night."

"I tripped. He caught me. End of story. Why would you think the worst about me?"

"He had you wrapped up like…like—" He threw his hands in the air and stalked the length of the office. Throwing the curtains aside, he peered out the window. He may have been trying for aloof, but his fist crumpled the fabric in a furious tangle.

"You're being completely irrational."

He snorted. "Why'd you keep whispering in his ear?"

She slammed her hands onto her hips. "I was translating."

"Can't you do better than that? It looked *real* tight from where I stood."

Why was she putting up with this? "Get over yourself."

He stomped toward her. Anger snapped in his eyes. "That asshole had the nerve to tell me if I couldn't take care of my woman, someone else would."

"*What?*"

"I gotta give it to you. At least you didn't sneak around. You two put it right in my face."

"Wait a goddamn minute." Her temper rose along with the warmth climbing her cheeks. "I just told you nothing was going on. And you *still* don't believe me?"

"I know what I saw."

She punctuated her next words with sharp finger stabs. "If my talking to the detective bothered you so much, why didn't you come over and say something?"

Silence.

It said a hundred things, none of them good.

"Yeah. I thought so."

Alex slumped against his desk and glared at her. "All that bullshit you fed me about not having sex until we had a relationship, is that a line you big-city girls use on all your clients?"

She'd never wanted to punch someone so badly. "If you can't tell the difference, I guess you have your answer." Holly spun toward the door, fed up with Alex *and* his attitude.

"You think you're so smart. You know, you date two kinds of girls. Ones you take home and ones you don't."

She heard the rest of the unspoken slur. Eyes narrowed, she whirled. "Is that what your mother was whispering in *your* ear last night?"

"Don't talk about my mother." Alex's finger flicked a warning arc. "You never made any effort to get to know her."

"*Me?*" Holly thumped her chest. "What about *her?* She went out of her way to make sure I knew how much she disliked me. And she knew I understood every slur she muttered. Which you *also* didn't say a word about."

With an irritated snort, Alex strode toward the window. "You never tried to fit in."

"What was I supposed to do? I can't change the fact I'm not Hispanic."

He whirled to face her, his expression unreadable.

She threw up her hands. "We're done."

He opened his mouth, but she cut him off. "I tell you what. Just have your mother pick out your next girlfriend. It'll save everybody a lot of trouble."

Chapter Twenty-five

Thursday morning

Heart thumping, Holly staggered from her bedroom in the gray predawn light. She brushed away the remnants of a nightmare. Masked gunmen and Marcy's bloated corpse had stalked her dreams. Still half-asleep, she stumbled into the living room and tripped. Pain jolted from her shin to her brain. "Dammit!"

Wide-awake now, she rubbed her sore leg and glared at the offending paint can. JC was screwing up her life again. If the damn man hadn't tied up her entire Sunday, she would've finished painting the living room. Then the can wouldn't have been where she'd trip over it.

Okay, she'd burned off a little anger slapping paint on the walls last night, but the argument with Alex was at least partly JC's fault.

She shuffled into the kitchen, limping on her bruised leg.

Yeah, yeah, she should've moved the stupid can.

She offered a mumbled thanks to the person who had invented automatic timers, then poured a mug of coffee and inhaled the rich aroma. Caffeine. Nectar of the gods.

The view from the east-facing windows caught her attention. Rosy streamers flung reds and golds onto clouds like something from a Peter Maxx psychedelic painting. The colors chased across the sky and reflected off the rivers. "Wow."

Abruptly, the sun cleared the mountains on the horizon and scalded her eyeballs with unfiltered rays. When she blinked, the sky had transformed and shone a cerulean blue in a vast overhead bowl.

She loved this house.

From her counter stool, Holly savored both the view and the first rush of caffeine. The Yakima River curled below her hillside home, lazily rolled through the Chamna Nature Preserve, before looping back to join the Columbia River.

A line of geese glided across Bateman's Island, headed for the offshore sanctuary. She shuddered as the birds evoked memories of Alex's hunting. Inevitably, her thoughts turned to Marcy's murder.

She sipped more coffee. She didn't want to get all morbid and weepy about being alive when Marcy wasn't. The whole thing was just so...weird.

She danced away from the next thought. Why wasn't she more upset?

Marcy wasn't a close friend—she hadn't touched her life in a deep way—but she knew the woman.

Still uncertain what state her emotions should be in, Holly showered and dressed for work. Her grandfather had died from old age and smoking. But Marcy...?

Everybody said she was sweet and pretty and good.

Nobody was all sweetness and light. Everybody's life contained some gray areas.

Holly had the uncomfortable feeling the question everybody should be asking wasn't *who* killed Marcy, but *why*?

~$~

In one smooth move, Holly dumped her briefcase, deposited Alex's flowers on the credenza, shrugged out of her jacket, and punched "voicemail." She stared at the flowers as the phone connected. Did Alex really think he could smooth over the angry accusations with a seasonal assortment?

In his dreams.

And what was up with his so-called alibi? She knew without checking that the movie was Monday night. Where was he on Tuesday that he didn't want to admit?

She couldn't believe he'd had anything to do with Marcy's death...but why lie?

A huge envelope filled her in-basket and a stack of file folders lay on her desk with a Post-it tacked on top. She read the brief message—"Please countersign, Donna."

Donna, not Mother.

Holly still couldn't get used to calling her mother by her first name.

Apparently, her mother had put in an early morning appearance at the office. She'd cleared half a dozen projects, but a dozen more clamored for Holly's attention.

The first voicemail message played through the speakerphone. She jotted notes and wondered how many of the projects she could pass to the staff.

Several client messages finished, then Alex's baritone filled the office. "I guess you aren't in yet."

He needed to find someone else—someone who thought his fight-and-make-up cycle was acceptable.

"Look, I shouldn't have unloaded on you last night."

Ya think? She started to erase the message. She'd already

deleted the ones he'd left on her cell.

"That cop really riled me up."

Her finger hesitated over the keypad. Was Alex actually going to apologize?

"We were both upset. Said some things we shouldn't. But..."

He paused and she could nearly see him shift position to try a different approach. His vocabulary apparently didn't include the words, "I'm sorry."

"I don't want to break up..."

Like they were ever actually together?

Not.

"I like you, Holly. We were having fun..."

Yeah, they had, but was he living in Total Denial-land? Why would he want to keep dating? They were so done. Finished. Over.

"Damn, I don't want to have this conversation over the phone. I have no idea how you're reacting."

Interesting. She gave the phone a thoughtful inspection. This didn't sound like male pride. While painting last night, she'd rerun the argument, and examined both the words and the nuances. She'd decided Alex really didn't want her, but he didn't like *her* dumping *him*.

"Call me."

Why the push? She deleted Alex's message. The next recording began, but she barely noticed. She and Alex weren't a love match. They'd both known things were temporary.

She stared out the window at the traffic on Grandridge. What did Alex really want? JC had harped on Alex's and Tim's finances. Was Alex afraid she'd uncover something? He had his own bookkeeper for the restaurant. Restaurants—any cash-based business—were notorious for manipulating income. Sometimes it provided a cover for other activity—drugs, money laundering. She'd seen no evidence of either, but was Alex trying to make their relationship more serious, hoping to protect whatever he was hiding?

If he was hiding anything.

Did he really think he could convince her to look the other way? Clearly, the man didn't know her. If Alex was doing something illegal, she'd never put up with it.

With a disgusted sigh, she noticed the silence. The message system wanted something from her. Damn, was there anybody or anything that didn't?

She shelved Alex and his mystery motives and replayed the last message. She had plenty of other things to occupy her time. Notes from clients lined her legal pad.

"Call me." Laurie's voice. "Call me, call me, call me."

What had her so excited?

Holly nearly hung up to return Laurie's call, but the next message began: "Holly. Devon Edwards. I have the information you wanted. Call me around eleven."

Yes! She gave a double-fisted victory pump. Her friend from the M&A team had come through. Impatient now, she waited out the remaining messages. With a glance at her watch—plenty of time before she needed to call Devon—she picked up her cell and said, "Laurie."

The phone connected and her friend's voice bubbled from the speaker. "You are not going to believe this. Marcy was pregnant."

"Are you sure?"

"My brother-in-law's part of the investigation team."

"I forgot your sister married a cop." *Duh!* It was how Laurie had known about JC's job, marriage, and divorce.

"He told her Marcy was pregnant. She told me."

Holly shook her head. "Wow. Pregnant."

"Yet another major life moment she didn't share with us."

"She couldn't have been very far along. She wasn't showing."

"Any idea who the father is...was?"

Tim's name immediately ran through Holly's mind, followed by Frank's.

"I can't help but wonder if she really had a new boyfriend..." Laurie's voice trailed off.

"The manager at the Tom-Tom told me his security chief was dating Marcy."

"Wow, that raises a few possibilities. Does JC know?"

"Like he'd tell me. I called him after I found out, but he hasn't bothered to call me back. Peter said they started dating the week before..."

"Then his security guy couldn't be the father."

Holly drummed her fingers on her desk. "I told you what Lillian said about Lee Alders. What if he forced his way back into Marcy's life?"

"Emphasis on force."

"From what I hear, Mrs. Ramirez is the only person who'd be happy if Lee did show up. Maybe that's why Marcy didn't tell anybody. She didn't want to admit she hooked up with him again."

"Maybe." Laurie sounded doubtful. "Some women go back to an abusive spouse, but Marcy seemed to have her act together."

Holly rearranged some papers, stalling. She really couldn't see Marcy with Creepy Security Guy—but Tim? What if her instincts were right on target and Tim and Marcy had been having an affair? Whose baby was he crying over on Monday? If he was involved with Marcy, he'd lost both a lover and a child. But she had absolutely no proof of an affair, other than one night at the casino. "My vote's Lee Alders. According to the newspaper, he's missing."

"Where is the guy? Outer Siberia?"

It had been nearly a week since they'd found Marcy's body and still no word about her husband. "He has to know the police want to talk to him."

"Think he used his millions to buy a new identity?"

"He's probably someplace where he'll have an alibi, and he hired somebody to kill her."

"Yeah, he looked in the Yellow Pages under 'Killer for hire,'" Laurie said.

"There are plenty of out-of-work, desperate people in debt. He could've waved ten thousand tax-free dollars in front of some badass and shown them Marcy's picture. Bam."

"Glad to hear your imagination still works. Listen, I gotta get back to work. I'll see you tonight at book club. We can talk then."

Holly hung up and slumped in her chair. Had Marcy really, truly been pregnant? The provenance sounded good. Deputy to wife to sister.

There was one way to find out.

She hunted through her desk drawer and found JC's business card. Taking a deep breath, she punched the number into her cell phone.

"Dimitrak."

Short, clipped tones. Why did men answer the phone that way?

"Morning, JC."

His voice changed, a smile hiding in the warmth. "Miz Price. To what do I owe the honor? Or do you need another mess cleaned up?"

The sarcasm was a bonus feature, but she decided not to be insulted.

Rocking back in her chair, she tapped the business card against her desk. "I'm just looking for confirmation of a little story I heard."

"About?"

"Marcy. I hear she was pregnant."

Silence. Absolute silence.

Gotcha. She dropped the card and propped her elbow on her desk. "If you hang up on me, I'm going to be really, really mad."

"What makes you think the victim was pregnant?"

So he wasn't denying it. "Come on, was she or wasn't she?"

"Who told you about this alleged pregnancy?"

"Alleged?" She made a rude noise. "You have a leak. Deal with it."

He was too experienced to fall for her ploy. "Where'd you hear this rumor?"

"JC. Focus. If Marcy was pregnant, that opens things up. I know you're keyed on Alders, but what if he isn't the father?"

"Holly." He sounded exasperated. "I can't discuss an ongoing investigation, but strictly theoretically, that would make it more likely that Alders killed her. If he did it."

"But what if it was the other way around?" she suggested. "What if she was going back to Alders and the other guy didn't want to let her go?"

"Care to suggest a candidate? Have a suspect or, say, an actual motive?"

Yessica might know. She jotted the woman's name at the top of a fresh sheet of paper. "I don't have any proof."

About Tim or Security Guy.

"Then stay out of it." It was his cop voice again, all humor gone.

"You're the one who keeps putting me in the middle." She dropped the pen and tucked her arm over her stomach.

"Look. Do you know something you need to tell me about?"

"Not really..." All she had was instinct. Maybe a woman's intuition. JC was so obstinate. He wouldn't admit Marcy was pregnant. No way would he tell her about the rest of his session with Lillian. Of course—she suppressed a grin—Lillian would tell her if she asked.

There was also Marcy's mystery letter's contents, but Holly had her own ideas about discovering those details. She retrieved her pen and drew a rectangle above Yessica's name, then added the shallow V of an envelope's flap. "I do have a question."

"Why am I not surprised?" Amusement was back in JC's tone.

She added some warmth to her voice. "I was thinking about the necklace. The one Marcy was wearing."

"And?"

"It was a custom piece. Maybe one of the jewelry stores would remember it." She drew intertwined hearts below Yessica's name and added another question mark.

"Amazingly enough, we already thought of that. We've talked to every jeweler in Richland, Kennewick, Pasco, Benton City, Sunnyside, and Yakima."

She'd suspected as much from her earlier attempt to locate the vendor. "You don't have to be snide. What about Seattle? Alders lives there. He could—"

"Holly," JC interrupted. "We know how to conduct an investigation. Now, do you know something? Something *useful?*"

"Well…" She gave the word multiple syllables. "Maybe if you'd returned my earlier call…"

Should she tell him what she'd learned about Tim and Marcy at the casino now, or after she had more facts? That maybe they were having an affair? That maybe she'd seen Frank? That maybe Creepy Security Guy was Frank and maybe he'd been dating Marcy right before she died?

That was a lot of maybes.

"I didn't have a chance to call," he said. "And as fascinating as I find this conversation, I have actual work to do. Or was there something else you wanted?"

The man could be so infuriating. "There are lots of things I want. Not all of them are good for me."

"I'll keep that in mind." Laughter rippled through his voice. "I'm hanging up now."

She gave it one last try. "So you aren't going to deny Marcy's pregnancy."

"Good-bye, Holly."

Chapter Twenty-six

Still smiling over JC's responses, Holly punched in a Seattle number.

"Devon Edwards."

Like JC, just a name. She used to answer the phone the same way. No "hello." No "good morning." At the time she'd thought it was professional, but today it simply seemed abrupt. "I got your message."

"How's my favorite shark?"

The nickname made her smile. It carried a hundred memories of analysis, deals and late night strategy sessions, and most important, the buzz of success.

"Alive and chomping." In an instant, she was transported three hundred miles over the Cascades and into her old life. She could almost hear the hum of financial engines, the crash of multimillion-dollar deals, and the nonstop drone of the billing department. She felt a rush of pleasure, craving the adrenaline high. It was an environment she hungered after, as addictive as any drug. She shook her head to clear it. "How's William?"

"Lazy slug was still in bed when I left this morning."

"Yeah, but he'll have dinner on the table this evening."

"True."

She heard the satisfaction in Devon's voice and abruptly

wished there was someone waiting for her at her house. Brushing the wistful thought aside, she asked, "What did you find out about Lee Alders?"

"I take it your interest in the guy is personal rather than professional."

"Good boy. Never assume."

He laughed. "I saw Alders' name in the *Post* earlier this week. Dead woman, person of interest, any info, yada, yada. Should I be a concerned citizen and call the Seattle PD?"

Habit kicked in. Holly picked up the handset. Potentially sensitive information was transferred over a landline, never a cell or speakerphone.

"I know the lead investigator with the local sheriff's department. I'll pass it along." She couldn't keep the smile out of her voice. She imagined JC either getting pissy about her having information he didn't or delighting in telling her he already knew. She actually hoped it would be the former. Sparring with him could become her favorite activity.

"Is the personal interest Alders or the cop?"

"Neither." She'd called Devon because he knew everybody, but the downside was anything personal she told him might end up on the gossip circuit. "Alders was married to a friend of mine. I'm trying to understand what kind of person he is."

"Hope she got a good settlement."

Settlement? It took a second for the term to register. Devon had interpreted "was married" as *divorced* rather than *dead*.

Holly listened to Devon shuffle papers and wondered if that was what the mystery envelope contained—a proposed settlement offer. She traced a curly circle around Yessica's name. What else did Marcy's sister know?

Devon said, "Here it is. Alders made his money in the tech market. He developed a message caching system that he sold to

Telnex. The process made a splash. Telnex stock surged after the acquisition. Then Telnex was snapped up by a bigger fish."

"I read about the sale. Looks like he sold during that boomlet we had a couple of years ago." The tech market's irrational exuberance bubble burst long ago, but solid companies, products, or processes continued to attract buyers. If Alders' message system worked well, it wasn't surprising a bigger player bought it.

"The tech market's made a great comeback—it's been a crazy year with deals. Now we have to ride out this yo-yo market and see what the international markets do. "

She wanted information on Alders, not Devon's commentary on the economy. "Give me the inside scoop. What'd you find out about Alders' deal?"

Devon filled in the details. Holly recognized several of the participants. She added another doodle to her paper, doubtful the money people would—or could—answer her real question. Could Lee Alders kill his wife?

"We didn't handle the transaction, but I heard it was an outright sale. Cash, not stock."

"Whose idea was that?" Tech companies used stock whenever they could—as compensation, to pay the bills, to buy other companies. Going public, and cashing in, was still the Holy Grail.

"I heard Alders wasn't willing to hold stock in a company he didn't control. Bottom line, your friend's hubby walked away with roughly forty million."

Forty million might not make him the next Bill Gates, but it wasn't exactly chump change. "What did he do when Telnex stock took off—and he couldn't cash in on it?"

"Something disagreeable, I'm sure."

Hmm. Devon didn't like the guy. "What's Alders doing now?"

"He fancies himself a mini-mogul."

She laughed at the catty tone. "Tell me how you really feel."

"Okay, Alders knows his stuff," he said grudgingly. "You might not have found his name because he's hiding behind a holding company. No one would touch him otherwise. Did you hear about Nyland?"

"I read a couple of articles that implied Alders helped himself to Nyland's ideas."

"Nyland conveniently died. Convenient for Alders, that is. Alders would've been out millions if Nyland had won. And paid another million in legal fees. I wouldn't trust Alders with my company, but his firm's played angel—and I use that term strictly in the financial sense—to a couple of startup firms."

That surprised her. "He doesn't seem the altruistic type."

"Trust me, he's only in it for the money."

No doubt. Had Alders considered the possible financial loss from a divorce sufficient motive for murder? People had definitely killed for far less.

"What did you think about him, personally?" she asked.

"He spends a lot of time on his sailboat. Goes heli-skiing, glacier climbing. You know, compensating. You knew Alders was climbing with Nyland when the guy died, right?"

"I thought that was strange. If the guy sued Alders, why were they together?"

"They were competing in a climb. A fundraiser for that charity that arranges sporting events for disabled vets. I'm sure they weren't doing it out of the goodness of their hearts. They both wanted to win. Showing each other up added bonus points. Or it did until Nyland died."

Holly looked out the office window, idly watching the cars lined up to turn left into the mall. Alders had gotten under Devon's skin—not an easy thing to do. "I get the impression you don't like him."

There was a pause. "If I was talking to anyone else, we wouldn't be having this conversation."

Holly sat up straight. "I understand."

"We were involved in a transaction with one of his new companies earlier this year. I can't tell you any more than that."

That hurt. She wasn't sure which stung more, that Devon thought he had to explain his reluctance to discuss the deal or that he considered her one of "them" instead of "us," no longer privy to inside information. "Okay."

"A lot of tech guys don't have the world's greatest social skills. Alders… He seems like a nice enough guy at first."

"Sounds like there's a great big 'but' in there."

She visualized Devon's grimace and half-shrug and wondered which way the story would go. Yessica had said Alders was violent, but from what she'd read, psychopaths—or was the guy a sociopath?—understood how to cover their tendency to take whatever they wanted. To be successful, instead of having actual feelings or caring about society's definition of right and wrong, they learned to react to appropriate social cues.

"The deal closed right after Nyland died," Devon said. "There were serious rumors Nyland's death was deliberate. I heard Alders paid big money to 'experts' to make sure it was labeled accidental. Alders walked away—was never charged—but most people think there's blood on his hands. And the deal we worked with him? In the boardroom, he was pure charisma. Smooth. Always said the right thing. But what I initially saw as unrealistic expectations were actually demands. It was subtle, but the manipulation was definitely there. He thought he was smarter than everyone in the room. I was glad we weren't working for his firm."

Holly wound the phone cord through her fingers. "You think he killed Nyland?"

"Alders is a complete a-hole. Totally ruthless—and I don't

mean in the good business sense. You said he was married to a friend of yours?"

"I never met him." If Devon wanted gossip, she didn't have any to offer. She hadn't even known there *was* a marriage until two days ago.

"I hope your friend invested the proceeds in something besides the tech market."

Had Marcy gotten any money from Lee? She considered Lillian's description of the confrontation at the office. Alders couldn't serve divorce papers himself, but he would've enjoyed the power play of throwing a copy—the mysterious envelope?—on Marcy's desk.

"I'm not sure what she would've done with the settlement money." She jotted another note. *Check court records for marriage dissolution papers and a settlement agreement.* "Would you do one more thing for me?"

"Keep this up and I'll have to turn the meter on."

"Come on, Devon. Desert Accounting doesn't have the databases you use. And you have the best network. I knew you could find out what this guy's doing."

When all else fails, lay it on thick.

"You gotta live in the big city to know what's going on. How's life in the eastside wilds? Got a horse and buggy yet? Or should I send a haz-mat suit?"

Holly bristled. Eastern Washington wasn't exactly a technical or radiological wasteland. a"If I need either, I can probably find somebody who has one." She kept her tone cool but changed the subject. "I ran across something interesting the other day. One of my clients has four companies, all registered in Wyoming, with the same person listed as the sole officer."

"This officer isn't a Washington local?"

"No. That was the second thing that pinged my radar. The

owner, who *is* a Washington local, isn't mentioned on the registration papers at all."

"What business are the companies in?"

"I ran them through the Secretary of State's web page. They're listed as holding companies. All set up this year."

"What bothers you specifically?"

Nothing she'd said really raised a red flag. It was the combination of events and the way she'd discovered the corporations that bothered her. "They may be legitimate. I can't imagine the owner doing anything illegal. But as his accountant, it bothered me he didn't tell me he set them up. And this guy, the officer, I ran him through the Wyoming state registry database and got over a thousand hits."

"Hmm, a proxy."

She heard the note of interest in his voice. He liked a mystery as much as she did. There were legitimate reasons for a company—its owners—to use a proxy, but a proxy could also be hidden behind. "For that many companies?"

"I remember reading something about it. Give me a day or two. I have some mop-up to do on our last transaction."

"Thanks for looking into it. And for the info on Alders." Devon had confirmed her initial impression of the guy.

"When are you coming to Seattle?"

It had been ages since she'd last crossed the mountains. All too soon, snow in Snoqualmie Pass would make the trip treacherous. "I'm working my butt off trying to stage Mother's company. It doesn't leave me much free time."

"Next time you visit, you need to meet Erica."

Visit? Erica? "Oh?"

"Erica Ruda. She started about a month ago."

Started.

A month ago.

The words echoed and mocked. The partners wouldn't casually bring in additional people. There was only one possible reason they'd hire a new analyst.

A cold fist tightened around Holly's chest, squeezed the air from her lungs.

The team had replaced her.

Chapter Twenty-seven

Devon chattered away, oblivious to Holly's stunned silence. "Erica was great on our last transaction. She totally uncovered a partnership the target was using to hide losses."

Spots danced at the edge of Holly's vision. She clutched the receiver with one hand and the edge of the desk with the other. *The team filled my place?*

She took a leave of absence. She didn't quit. That was *her* spot. The position she was *going back* to.

Devon paused and she found her voice. "I'm glad to hear business is so good."

"It was off for a while with everything spooking Wall Street. When the market picks up, things will go crazy. Some players are looking to snap up companies whose stock's in the crapper. Jeez, stock values were below book for a while there."

Holly's shoulders relaxed and her breath came easier. They were busy. Of course they needed more people. Hadn't she suffered through that with the project work she was bringing in to Desert Accounting? Erica was an addition, not a replacement. "Sounds like I'll be getting back at the right time."

Devon's pause was short, but she caught it.

"It'll be great to see you," he said.

She noticed the ambiguous phrasing. It was why he wasn't a

partner. He gave away too much in his tone and his expression. "What are you not telling me?"

"Look, I heard Arashiro plans to call you. You have to make a choice."

Her stomach cramped.

She wrestled the panic and held her voice steady. "Thanks for the heads up on the boss's call. And for the info on Alders."

"Sure."

Don't babble, cut it off. "I have to run. A meeting to prep for. You know how it goes."

"I'll call if I find anything on the proxy guy," Devon said.

Don't call us, we'll call you.

She fumbled the receiver into place with a shaking hand. Trying to swallow the huge lump in her throat, she stared at the instrument. What if her boss said, "If you want to stay part of the team, you have to get back over here. Now."

He'd promised her a year.

If she didn't go back, she'd lose everything she'd worked so hard to achieve.

She'd given up friends, fun…dammit, she'd given up her *life* for that team. She'd put her career ahead of everything.

She *had* to go back.

But if she left, her mother would lose everything. The accounting firm…her livelihood.

How was she supposed to choose?

She could look for another position in Seattle later, but the team was the best. Going anywhere else would be an admission of defeat. She'd start in a hole and have to prove herself all over again. It would take dozens of deals before every attorney, broker, and peon quit thinking they could pull a fast one on her.

And for what? To make the partners richer? The team members were well paid, but it was a fraction of what the principals raked in.

She buried her face in her hands. What did she want? *Really* want? She'd always believed it was her career and everything that came with it. Challenge, respect, affluence. But it was all an illusion.

Step away and it vanished.

Remove the job and she had nothing.

Tears filled her eyes. Blindly, she grabbed a tissue.

Her independence amounted to nothing more than solitude. She'd end up an old lady at the senior center, recycling used greeting cards.

She dropped her hands and glared at the office around her. Why was she killing herself bailing out her parents, anyway? Her father deserted them. Her mother blew off an important meeting without explanation. Did they even care if Desert Accounting prospered?

Holly dragged in a deep breath and released it.

She cared about the business. She'd done solid work for the clients, trained the staff to handle the more challenging assignments, and built the firm's reputation. Other companies were noticing.

What if she stayed?

She flattened her hands on the desk and stared straight ahead, stunned she'd even considered the possibility.

After a beat, she measured the pros and cons. The bookkeeping side of the business—her mother's realm—brought in steady income, but for her, it defined boredom. It was the project work that challenged her. Working with clients, getting to know them and their business needs, added a surprisingly satisfying aspect to her professional life. With the mergers and acquisitions team, the owners had simply been interchangeable faces eager to sell for the largest pile of dollars possible.

She shot to her feet. What was she doing even *thinking* about staying in Richland? She didn't know her real job was in jeopardy. She was jumping to conclusions with no evidence to support the theory—the mark of a rank amateur.

Until her boss told her she no longer had a position with the team, she refused to worry about Erica or who did what on the latest transaction in Seattle.

Chapter Twenty-eight

The clatter of a dozen conversations filled the restaurant where Holly had arranged to meet a friend for lunch. The newest restaurant in town, Fat Olive was doing a brisk business. She bypassed the hostess stand and slid into a seat facing a rangy blond man. "I'm buying, since you're about to give me free legal advice," she declared without preamble.

Walt Chambers laughed. "Consider it payback for the client you sent me last month."

They'd gone out twice before deciding they made better friends and business colleagues than a couple. After ordering— calzones and a Coke—Walt asked, "What am I giving you free advice about?"

"Divorce."

He raised an eyebrow, questioning, since *she* clearly didn't need the advice. A moment later he said, "Ah, your parents."

Her parents. Marcy and Lee. Take your pick.

He sipped his pop, then continued, "It's called dissolution of marriage in Washington. I'm surprised your parents don't already have temporary orders in place."

"And temporary orders are...?"

"For starters, either of them could've filed a motion to keep the other from cleaning out their investment account or changing beneficiaries on insurance policies or retirement plans."

"I'm not sure Mother knows to do that."

Walt shrugged. "If she has halfway competent legal counsel, they would've taken care of it. Who's representing her?"

"I don't know." She pulled out her phone and made a note to find out.

Had Marcy put anything in place? Was that what had angered Lee? She really needed to talk to Yessica.

Their food arrived and they ate while continuing the conversation.

"As far as living expenses go," Walt said, "both your parents are capable of working."

"I don't know what my father's situation is. Job-wise. Could he really ask for alimony?"

"It's called maintenance here." He tapped his finger on the table, thinking. "He can ask. If your mother disagrees, it'll be up to the court."

"Wait a minute." Holly laid down her fork. "You mean I could be over here, busting my butt, and end up having to support him while he's playing Downward-Facing-Dog?"

He fought a smile and lost. "Never heard it described in quite those terms."

"Yoga. Instructor."

The smile changed to a grimace. "Ah."

Her mother had ducked the issue for too long. As much effort as Holly was putting into growing Desert Accounting, she wanted to know where her parents' marriage—and company— were headed. "What about their assets? Will Mother have to give him half?"

"Washington's a community property state. At least in theory, everything either spouse earns while they're married belongs to both of them."

"What about the new business I've brought in?"

He rocked his hand in a *maybe* motion. "Ultimately, the division's up to the courts. Your mother could claim it's separate property. But both of them worked there and it sounds like the company grew while they were married. She might have a hard time making that stick."

"But he cheated on her and walked out. That doesn't seem fair."

"'Fair' doesn't matter. The court doesn't have to divide things fifty-fifty. The judge tries to be equitable."

Holly wanted the information about her parents, but Marcy and Lee faced the same challenge. Devon said Lee had sold his company for forty million. Could a guy like Lee really fork over twenty million? "It doesn't matter who actually did the work?"

He shook his head. "It's all community property."

"What if one of them wasn't working while they were married?"

"If one spouse stays home and takes care of that side of the couple's life instead of holding an outside job, the courts take that into consideration."

She had to talk with Yessica. If Marcy had a good attorney, most likely Lee would've had to pay her alimony or maintenance and a substantial settlement. Both would've been next to impossible for a wife-beating, control-freak to agree to.

With Marcy dead, he wouldn't have to give up anything.

"How are *you* doing?" Walt asked. "Doesn't matter how old we are, parents splitting up is hard."

She was tempted to unload her worries, but innate caution held her back. Instead, she escaped the personal questioning with a woman's all-time favorite excuse. "Excuse me a minute. I need to use the restroom."

The restrooms were located down a short hall behind the

reception area. As she angled across the seating area, a woman called, "Holly."

She scanned the restaurant, then zeroed in on a well-dressed blonde. Nicole sat with several of her friends—polished women who looked as though their only job was the care and feeding of their husbands' careers. She'd been vaguely surprised to find the type on the east side of the Cascades, but then again, it did tend to be conservative territory. Although the way Nicole blew through money—and given the way they were dressed, apparently her friends did too—she could hardly be called fiscally conservative.

Holly approached the table. One of the women looked familiar, but she couldn't place the other two. Tim's wife wore wool slacks and a cashmere turtleneck, but under-eye shadows marred her usually flawless complexion.

Should she offer congratulations? Tim said they hadn't told anyone yet about the pregnancy. If Nicole had previously confided in her, Holly would've mentioned it, but she didn't feel close enough to the woman to bring it up.

Nicole didn't bother to introduce the other women. Instead, she asked, "Are you seeing Walt Chambers? I thought you and Alex were exclusive."

"Walt and I are discussing business." Not that it was any of Nicole's business.

"Ah, your parents' divorce. How are you handling that?"

This conversation—even if Nicole were a friend, which she wasn't—wasn't one Holly would ever have at a restaurant in front of strangers. "It won't affect business."

"Wow. You need to stop obsessing about work." Nicole smiled at her friends. A smile that added, *Can you believe this?*

"When it's something you enjoy, it hardly seems like an obsession."

"Is that why you give your clients

such…personal…attention?" Nicole again glanced at the other women. "Aren't your husbands her clients?"

She turned back to Holly. "Do they get the same kind of 'handling' you give Tim?"

Bitch.

Even Nicole's friends looked startled. The brunette Holly sort of recognized gave her an appraising look.

Damn if she'd let Nicole run off business she'd worked so hard to bring in.

"My clients respect my business ability." Holly walked away with her head held high, but the restroom mirror confirmed a deep blush colored her cheeks.

When she returned to the table, Walt asked, "What was that about?"

"I'm not entirely sure. Nicole seems to like rubbing my nose in the fact that I'm not married or part of the pampered crowd."

Walt gave Nicole an assessing inspection. "She'll be singing a different tune when she gets served."

"Served with what? Wait, you mean divorce, er, dissolution papers?" Holly's mouth dropped open. She turned and stared at Nicole before remembering she should be discreet. "Tim's divorcing her? Are you allowed to tell me that?"

"Tim isn't my client." Walt shrugged. "Another attorney delivered the papers to the service at the same time I dropped off a notice. I don't know if he's served them yet."

"If he has, Nicole has balls of steel. So does Tim, for that matter." She glanced at the women's table and found Nicole watching intently, as if trying to figure out what they were discussing. "They were doing their lovebird routine at Marcy's wake."

Walt shrugged. "Appearance and reality. Did you know your parents were having problems?"

She raised her hand, palm up. "I live in Seattle. Other than holidays, we talked on the phone."

Walt shot another glance at Nicole. "She's either taking it incredibly well or else she hasn't been served."

Holly picked at her calzone. "What if Tim changed his mind? Decided not to divorce her?"

"It happens. Counseling, whatever. People work things out. Sometimes it's more convenient to stay together."

She peeked at Nicole, rather disconcerted to find Nicole was *still* watching them.

What if Tim had decided to stay with Nicole because of the pregnancy?

But if he did, where had that left Marcy and *her* baby?

Chapter Twenty-nine

Tracey handed Holly a stack of pink message slips when she returned from lunch. "You had a visitor."

Still wondering about Tim and Nicole, Holly flipped through the slips of paper. "And?"

"He was...intense."

She shifted her attention to Tracey. "Client?"

"No. He wouldn't leave his name, just said he'd be in touch."

"He didn't say what it was about? What did he look like?"

Tracey shuddered. "I'd say tall, dark, and handsome, but there was something about him that made me nervous."

Holly lowered her hand, her fingers tightening around the message slips. She ran the Rolodex in her head. What scary guy did she know that Tracey didn't? Creepy Security Guy? Frank? Lee Alders? "If he shows up again, call the police."

Tracey blinked. "The police?"

Closing her eyes, Holly shook her head. "Okay, that sounded nuts. Or paranoid. Use your judgment. You read people well."

Still clutching the messages, she wandered down the hall to her office. A messy stack of papers sat in the center of her desk. The attached message, written on Stevens Ventures letterhead, read, "I found these papers when I cleaned out Marcy's desk. I didn't know what to do with them."

Holly gave the pile a disgruntled glare. What exactly was Tim paying this woman to do? Make her life miserable?

After tucking her purse—a vintage Gucci—into her desk, Holly went through the stack of papers, sorting them into company piles. Several documents concerned the four new LLCs, and others connected to yet another new company.

Why all the new companies?

She placed the operating company information aside for Sammy. Staring at the unknown entities, she tapped her nails against her desktop. She had some time before the meeting with Bruce Fairchild—assuming her mother showed up. Yesterday's vague, "I got a phone call" didn't begin to explain why her mother had ducked the Zhang meeting.

Holly crossed the atrium to Stevens Ventures. An attractive brunette, the woman she'd last seen cozying up to Phoua and the Shrimp, sat at the reception desk filing her nails. A new, triangular brass nameplate sat on the desk. It said, "Kaylin."

"May I help you?" Kaylin asked.

Holly introduced herself. "I have a few questions, if you have a minute."

"I'm so glad you're here." The woman dropped the nail file in the drawer. "I found another stack of financial stuff. Do you want to take it with you, or should I drop it off?"

Was she serious? "Usually the documents are more organized," Holly hinted.

Kaylin held up crossed index fingers, as though warding off a fate worse than death. "Tim hired me for property management. He mentioned some bookkeeping, but I made sure he only meant records related to the actual property." She waved a manicured hand. "Rents, regime fees, the usual. I don't mind helping out. I mean, see? I'll sit up here when Brea goes to lunch, but I don't do bookkeeping."

"I'm confused." Holly propped a hand on her hip and wrinkled her brow. "Tim told me he'd hired someone to fill Marcy's position."

"Marcy? Was she the woman who died?" Kaylin quirked her mouth to the side. "Poor thing. Men sure used her."

"Used? You mean, took advantage?" Men? Or did Kaylin mean Tim specifically? "I don't understand."

Kaylin leaned forward. Her voice dropped to a confidential level. "Tim dumped some project management responsibility on her for the retrofit in Yakima. I hate to say bad things about someone who died, but it's clear she didn't know what she was doing."

"Really?" That was strange. Holly was surprised Tim let Marcy get in over her head.

Kaylin straightened, taking on an aggrieved expression. "Half the permitting and inspection requests got rejected because the paperwork was wrong."

Surely, Tim wouldn't knowingly jeopardize his buildings. Why would he let Marcy take on the remodeling project if she couldn't handle it?

"I had to redo the PERT charts, figure out what should've been done, and rework what *was* done."

Kaylin rattled off a litany of woes. Holly made sympathetic noises while her mind churned. Why was Tim burying Marcy in work? Could something be happening with the Yakima project a more experienced property manager would recognize? Or was he hoping to keep her so busy she wouldn't have time to notice any financial discrepancies? And what about the new companies?

Marcy might not have picked up on weirdness with the Yakima project, but she definitely would've noticed the new companies.

And asked about them.

"Even if I was remotely interested in bookkeeping," Kaylin continued, "I wouldn't have time to touch it. God, I hope it isn't as screwed up as *my* paperwork is."

"It isn't messed up. There's just a lot to go through before I meet with Alex and Tim tomorrow."

Think positive. Maybe Tim wanted to help Marcy move into a new field.

Or maybe it was simply cover for all the trips she made to Yakima.

With a sinking heart, Holly wondered if Marcy actually handled the Yakima retrofit or if the trips were just an excuse to spend time with Tim.

"If you'll pack up the papers you found, I'll take them with me," Holly said. "We can get the QuickBooks download and pull the trial balance, but I need a starting point for the new entities."

"I know the financial stuff is important, but you might as well be speaking Chinese. I don't have a clue what that means."

A superb idea occurred to her. "How about I pull the records in Marcy's, I mean, *your* office? I can get the information on the new companies and see what needs to be filed before the end of the year." *There. Brilliant.*

Kaylin shrugged. "Sure. Let me set the phone to auto." She mashed a few buttons on the console and rose to her feet.

Holly followed the woman through the familiar hallway. Developers started new entities all the time. Typically there was a separate corporation for each development project. Separate legal entities shielded the rest of the business if anything went wrong. Problems at one development didn't create a liability for the others. Maybe Tim started the new companies, planning ahead to when pent-up demand for housing and office space returned with the improving economy.

With a lighter heart, Holly entered Marcy's former office with

Kaylin trailing behind. There wasn't anything ominous about the messed-up paperwork or the volume of unfiled and disorganized documents. Marcy had simply been buried in learning a new job and got behind with the bookkeeping part.

Twenty minutes later, Holly closed the last file cabinet. "Nothing."

Damn.

The metal drawers contained only the normal information related to the existing operating companies. "Tim started five new companies. Where's the paperwork?" she asked the temp. "Not the current statements you sent over. The permanent files. Incorporation. Property. That stuff."

She glanced at Lillian's file cabinets but didn't bother opening the payroll records. Drumming her fingers, Holly studied the desk Marcy had used. "Those papers you found, they were in the desk?"

"The envelopes were crammed in the top drawer. I guess she didn't have time to file them."

"Maybe Marcy planned to take the records to the satellite office. She used that office a lot." Holly leaned against the file cabinet, thinking through the missing paperwork. Bits and pieces of misfiled paperwork she could understand, but entire files? For all the new companies? The part of her that used to dig into financial statements for the M&A team smelled something that stank as bad as a dead skunk in the middle of Columbia Parkway.

Holly stepped away from the cabinets, heading for the door. "It sorta makes sense that the files are at the other office."

If Tim—and by proxy, Marcy—was hiding something, the small, unstaffed Yakima office offered a good starting point to discover what it was. "I have to go by there anyway. If you'll give me Marcy's keys, I can pick up everything while I'm there."

Kaylin hesitated. "Tim didn't say anything about that."

Holly shrugged and kept walking, the other woman at her

heels. "You can drive over there yourself if you want. You'll have to go by the post office and then pull everything I need from the files."

Reaching the lobby, she half-turned and hoped the woman would take the bait.

Kaylin dropped into her chair behind the reception desk, her expression a combination of curiosity, caution, and dismay. "Where is the other office? What kind of stuff would you need?"

Holly placed a hand on the front door and spoke over her shoulder. "Yakima. I need incorporation documents, everything that was filed with the Secretary of State. Then there's property records, loans, any operational activity. I'm not sure how file Marcy filed them, but worst case, it shouldn't take more than a couple of hours." She frowned. "Maybe a little longer."

"I don't know what that stuff looks like." Kaylin opened the center drawer and removed a ring of keys. "I found these in Marcy's desk. Are they what you're talking about?"

Holly took the keys and shuffled though them. She recognized three of the distinctive flat post office box keys. One box here, one in Yakima. Where was the third box? "These are the ones. Thanks. I'll drop them off later."

Tim opened the door to the building's atrium as Holly left his office.

"Were you looking for me?" he asked.

Not really.

She didn't want to talk to him, much less accuse him of anything, until she knew more about the new companies. It could be innocent, if somewhat messy. She glanced over her shoulder at his office. Kaylin would tell him she'd asked about the new companies.

Come on. Think of something. She blurted out the first question that came to mind. "Who is Alan Bowen?"

Tim looked blank. "No idea."

He moved past her. "I don't want to be rude, but Nicole and I have a meeting with the bankers about Southridge Park. I need to prep for it."

Holly's "due diligence" radar pinged with his answer. Tim should've recognized the man's name. "Bowen's listed as the managing director on TNM Ventures."

Tim pivoted toward her. A flush started at his chest and climbed his neck. "What are you doing looking at TNM? I told you that isn't an operating company."

Holly blinked, surprised by his anger. "Whoa, slow down. I'm confused. Kaylin sent over the bank statement. It looked like there was substantial activity."

"Well, there isn't. I set up TNM for future activity. I'm considering a development in Spokane."

Hadn't he said it was to buy land for Nicole on the Snake River? Having trouble keeping his stories straight? And none of that explained the bank activity. "Spokane? Then why is the company registered in Wyoming?"

Tim sighed, looking impatient. "The business climate in Wyoming is more favorable. The restrictions and regulations in Washington are out of control. The liability insurance alone is eating me alive."

A knot of worry loosened in her stomach. She was reading something into the situation that didn't exist. "I noticed the premium increase."

His explanation didn't line up with the facts, the tiny voice in her head nagged. Insurance followed business operations, not the incorporation location. "Tim, that doesn't make sense."

A look close to panic slid across Tim's face, then vanished. "Maybe we should talk about this."

"No hurry." Holly moved toward Desert Accounting's door,

already regretting asking the questions. "I'm sure it's just a mixup. And I can't talk right now. I have a meeting. In fact, I was just leaving."

"You can't." Tim grabbed her arm. "We need to talk. Now. Not tomorrow."

He swung her around. Clutching her arms, he pulled her close. His face hovered inches away from hers. "You're getting the wrong idea."

She turned her head and strained backward in the too intimate grip. "Tim—"

He tightened his hold, grasping both her arms, nearly shaking her. "I can explain."

"Am I interrupting?" Nicole stood in the outer doorway, a stunned expression on her perfect features.

Tim released Holly's arms as if they were radioactive.

Nicole's eyes flicked from Tim to Holly and back. "What's going on?"

"Nothing." Tim and Holly answered simultaneously.

She spun away from Tim and headed for the safety of her own office. "Don't be late for our meeting tomorrow," she called over her shoulder.

~$~

Holly's fingers drummed a pattern on Bruce Fairchild's conference table. Catching herself, she stilled the nervous gesture and offered the gray-haired man a smile while her gaze slid to the clock on the credenza. 2:34. "I'm sure Mrs. Price will be here any minute."

Making excuses made everyone look bad—Holly, her mother, Desert Accounting. She had to pin down her mother—*Donna*—about why she'd been so uncharacteristically distracted this week.

Groping for a topic—any topic—Holly tried to remember if the morning news offered more than the continued hunt for Marcy's ex. Where was the guy? Outer Mongolia? The longer Lee Alders stayed hidden, the guiltier he looked.

She glanced around the conference room. Dark leather chairs surrounded the highly polished mahogany table. Slatted shades behind heavy drapes filtered the afternoon sun. Her attention landed on a pair of mounted pheasants. "Do you hunt?"

Bruce followed her gaze. With a smile, he relaxed, slowly rocking his chair. "I got that pair of roosters on the same day. I was out at Schoolhouse. You know where that is?"

"Off Highway 12, near the McNeary Refuge?"

"That's right." He looked a little surprised and a little pleased. He launched into one of those step-by-step reenactments that men gloried in. She pasted an interested expression on her face and silently cursed her mother. Where was she this time?

Selling Desert Accounting's services was different than her other job. It had taken her a while to figure out how to approach people. With the Seattle-based M&A team, clients came to them, drawn by the firm's aggressive reputation. In a smaller town like Richland, business depended on relationships. Once she had the right project and the right opportunity to get inside the company and up-sell, her mother was supposed to pave the way through her network. Every time she bailed, Holly was left scrambling to cover.

As if she'd read Holly's mind, Bruce's secretary appeared at the door. "Excuse me. Donna Price just called. She said she was running late and to start without her."

Holly pasted a fresh smile on her face. Her mother was a dead woman.

The secretary directed her next comments at her boss. "Donna said to tell Cynthia 'Hello' and that she's enjoying working with her on the Holiday gala. The chefs lined up for this year sound fabulous."

Major employers like Bruce sponsored the event—a primary fundraiser for area charities and one of the few dress-up affairs in the area.

Bruce beamed after his secretary left. "Your mother is a wonderful woman. Terrific organizer. You must be happy to be here, working with her."

"It's been a real adventure." Holly kept the ironic note out of her voice.

She opened her folio and pulled out the analysis Rick had produced.

Why wasn't Rick here, delivering this? If her mother kept pushing responsibility for the practice onto her shoulders, Holly intended to make some changes, starting with Rick's role.

Forty minutes later, she wrapped up her assessment of the company's tax position. The company had overlooked several opportunities in the latest legislation. By Holly's—make that Rick's—assessment, they'd receive a healthy income tax refund.

Bruce watched her over steepled fingers. "Do you intend to stay in Richland?"

Holly smoothed the startled expression off her face. Not many clients asked this bluntly. She couldn't—wouldn't—lie outright. "We'll see how things play out."

He accepted the veiled reference to her father and she didn't amplify. Her comment had been vague enough to imply whatever Bruce wanted it to mean.

"I hear good things about you and your mother's firm. Fresh ideas." He gave an approving nod.

People talked about Desert Accounting? Called it "her" firm? "Thanks. I've met some terrific people here."

She reached for her briefcase, but stopped midway as she realized two things. She had more friends here than in

Seattle…and she liked what she did at Desert Accounting. The little voice in her head muttered, *No shit, Sherlock. You just figuring that out?*

Bruce made polite chitchat while she stowed her papers. After the requisite handshake, she left his office and climbed into her Beemer, armed with a follow-up meeting to discuss succession planning. Once she cleared the parking lot, she tapped the Bluetooth. "Mother."

The phone connected, but she wasn't surprised when the call went straight to voicemail.

"The meeting went well." Holly gave her mother the one-minute version. The corners of her mouth turned up. "Did you know people refer to Desert Accounting as 'our' firm—as in yours and mine, rather than Dad's? We should talk about that."

Chapter Thirty

Thursday evening

Holly parked in front of La Boutique, triumphant she'd found the store without making any wrong turns, and hurried inside.

"Holly?" Yessica stepped away from the cash register.

"My book club meeting starts in a few minutes—we meet at the library—but I have another question."

She'd already decided not to mention the pregnancy. If Yessica didn't know, she wasn't going to be the one to tell her. The woman didn't need another reason to grieve. "Lillian told me about Lee coming to see Marcy at the office. About him giving her a letter. Did she talk to you about that?"

Yessica fidgeted with her rings, then looked directly into Holly's eyes. "I realize you're trying to help, but why are you doing this?"

Holly went still, wondering what she'd done wrong. Yessica had talked to her before. "What do you mean?"

"The more I think about it, the stranger it seems. Why are you looking into Maricella's death?"

Holly pursed her lips and considered how to answer. At last she said, "I want to know *why*."

At first, it had been to clear her name and Desert Accounting's reputation—plus some curiosity—but the more she learned about Marcy, the more she needed to know how and why Marcy's relationship had spiraled out of control.

Yessica tilted her head and waited. Her expression said, *Not good enough.*

Holly straightened the brochures heaped on the counter. If she expected Yessica to open up, she had to meet her at least halfway.

Painful admissions didn't come easily.

"I knew a man in Seattle…with the same…dominance issues. He tried to…" How could she describe it? *Rearrange? Control?* "Take over my life."

"And?" Yessica demanded.

"You mentioned earlier about Marcy and Lee meeting at a coffee shop. That caught my attention…I started seeing a guy that way too…"

How to explain? Holly sighed. "It sounds so *ordinary.* Like anyone else meeting a new guy. We had coffee. I mentioned to Frank I loved mocha lattes. A few days later, he brought a mocha latte to my office. I thought it was nice. I was working crazy hours and it gave me a break and us a chance to talk. He did it again the next week, and again, it seemed sweet."

Yessica shifted. "I don't understand. How is this connected to Maricella?"

"Frank started coming by *every* day. He expected me to stop whatever I was doing and talk to him. He never considered the fact that I was working sixteen-hour days on a transaction or that I had a demanding job. It was all about him. And he always brought the damned mocha latte. It turned creepy and controlling, like he was making decisions about what I could drink. I mean, what if I didn't want a mocha? What if I wanted a double-shot or a decaf?"

She forced her mouth to close. She sounded crazy.

"Why?" Yessica asked. "You and Maricella. You're smart. Pretty. Why would you get involved with men like that?"

Holly fiddled with the stack of brochures. "It's insidious. At the beginning, Frank was charming. Attractive. Charismatic." Devon's comment smacked her. *In the boardroom, Alders was pure charisma.*

Damn. She raked a hand through her hair. "Bottom line? I got away, but it's made me more sensitive to women trapped in a bad relationship. In Marcy's case, I think the police are asking the wrong questions. That they're going about this the wrong way."

Yessica's lips thinned. After a long moment, she said, "Maricella was very angry after Lee came to see her. He had no right to come to her office. She had the paper to make him stay away."

Yeah, yeah. *He walked right through that restraining order and put her in intensive care.* The line from the old song rolled through Holly's head and she nearly gagged. No. *No country music.* She had to get back to Seattle, home of Nirvana and grunge music. "Did she mention other papers? Lillian said Lee gave your sister an envelope. Whatever was in it upset Marcy."

"Lee made a divorce settlement offer. It was an insult."

Gee, what a surprise. Lee tried to stiff Marcy at the end of their marriage. "You didn't mention the settlement offer the other day."

Yessica's hands lifted and fell. "What was there to say? It was another example of what a *cabrón* he is. Lee wasn't just a bastard, he was a cheap bastard. Maricella didn't sign the divorce papers. Are they important?"

"They might be. One last question. Did Marcy sign a prenup?"

"A what?"

"A prenuptial agreement. Papers signed before they got married that said what would happen if they divorced."

Yessica shook her head in baffled silence. "Maricella never mentioned anything like that."

Holly wrestled for a nanosecond over who should tell JC. He might not listen if she tried to explain it. His brusque "Stay out of it" carried the day. "You should tell Detective Dimitrak about the separation agreement."

"Why?"

"Money's a huge motive for murder."

And Lee Alders had at least twenty million reasons to kill his estranged wife.

Chapter Thirty-one

Thursday night

Along with a few book club members, Holly and Laurie waited outside the library's community room while the leader cleared the room. Stragglers from the meeting filtered through the lobby and headed to their cars. Finally, Gwen turned off the light and closed the door. With her messy bun and horn-rimmed glasses, the woman looked more like a stereotypical librarian than the women who worked in the library.

The book club meeting had been the usual mix of analyzing the novel while dishing on kids, husbands, and friends. Marcy had been mentioned, but the club members weren't personally involved. They'd already moved on, relegating Marcy's murder to the past.

Holly couldn't let the investigation go. In addition to the unhealthy relationship issue—pick the bastard du jour: Lee Alders, Frank Phalen, Creepy Security Guy, or anyone else screwing up a woman's life—Tim was tangled up in something and Marcy seemed to have been right there with him.

Maybe Laurie could help unravel a few threads. "Want to grab a cup of coffee?"

"Holly, don't forget to send out the reading selections for next quarter." Gwen tucked her novel into her tote bag.

"Don't pick any more of these dreary ones off the Book Club List," Brittney, the perpetual class clown, said. "If I want to be depressed, I'll call my mother."

"Well, I don't want any of those vampire ones you like." Gwen locked and tested the door.

"What about something just for fun," Laurie suggested. "Like romantic suspense. We could compare love scenes and decide if it's anatomically possible."

All four of them laughed.

"Guess you single women actually get to have a love life." Brittney lifted a significant eyebrow. "Do share."

"What are you complaining about?" Holly asked. "You obviously have one. You've got two kids."

"And your point is? Trust me, those critters put a serious crimp in your love life. So." Brittney turned back to Laurie. "Inquiring minds want to know. Creative love scenes? Details, please."

"Herman and I have made a serious commitment," Laurie replied, straight-faced. "He'll love me as long as his battery lasts."

"You named your vibrator 'Herman'?"

"Herman is not a vibrator." Laurie folded her hands in an imitation of a prim schoolteacher, an image totally at odds with her blue-streaked, spiked hair. "He's an anatomically correct, inflatable companion."

Brittney burst out laughing. "They make male blowup dolls?"

Laurie feigned a moue. "Don't hurt his feelings. He was a special order."

"Oh, bullshit. I've known you for fifteen years. There is no way—"

Gwen's face flamed a brilliant red. "You two are embarrassing me."

Holly figured that was probably their intention.

Gwen slid her tote bag over her shoulder. "I think we should read something significant."

"Everybody send me a suggestion and I'll route it to the group," Holly offered. "We'll read whatever gets the most votes."

Laurie cut off Gwen's protest. "It's the democratic approach."

Laurie and Holly waved to the two women and strolled toward their cars. The narrow parking lot beside the library stayed full, the building crowded with after-work browsers and teenagers who spent more time flirting than doing homework.

"You're not serious about the blowup doll, are you?" Holly asked.

"Of course, I am. Herman's always willing to indulge any fantasy and he doesn't hog the covers or snore."

Gwen's ancient brown Toyota passed and they waved again.

"Don't try to convince me you don't have a 'friend'," Laurie said. "Anybody who watched *Sex and the City* learned the joys of a Rabbit."

"I'd rather have the real deal. Can Herman keep you warm on a long, winter night?"

"The optional, auxiliary battery pack powers a mini-heater."

Holly stepped off the sidewalk, snickering. "Okay, stop. I surrender."

"Does that 'real deal' comment mean you decided to go out with JC?"

"Oh, please."

An engine cranked in the parking lot across the street. Holly glanced at the darkened building. Someone must've worked late. She was glad for once it wasn't her.

"Why are you being so defensive? JC's single, employed, sexy, and he's into you."

"You can't be serious. He's cocky, arrogant, manipulative, and, and…"

"He pushed your buttons, didn't he?"

Holly laughed as the ridiculousness of the situation hit her. "All the wrong ones. You know how I feel about egomaniacs."

"Now there's a leap. Arrogant to egomaniac. Me thinks she doth protest too much."

Why was she putting up such a battle? She didn't need a man to make her life complete, but she wanted one eventually. Wanted a family, a life partner. She didn't see Alex in that role, but JC had already had his shot and blown it. "Maybe I attract the wrong kind of guy."

Laurie hitched her tote bag and resettled the load. "Well, if JC doesn't turn your crank—which I totally don't believe—there's a guy in radiology."

She groaned. "Not another one." The endless stream of incompatible men her friends pushed at her was probably why she'd started dating Alex in the first place.

"Ron's cute and he broke up with his girlfriend a month ago. That's long enough he's ready to go out without doing the ex-bashing thing. How about I ask him to go to Bookwalter's with us on Saturday?"

Holly cleared her throat. "I'd rather talk about Nicole." She'd already told Laurie about the scene at lunch. "Do you think Tim's really going to dump her?"

"Based on what I saw Tuesday night, it would surprise me."

"Women like her make me feel inadequate," Holly admitted. "Like I was absent the day they handed out the secret to female wiles and how to twist men around your little finger."

"She wasn't always like that." Laurie considered. "Or maybe she was. But anyway, she completely reinvented herself."

"What do you mean?"

The truck across the street reversed with a clash of gears, then idled, its engine thumping.

"Find it, don't grind it," Laurie called, rolling her eyes at the truck. "Don't you remember middle school?"

"I was in California then."

"Oh, yeah. Anyway, Nicole transferred in as this stringy-haired blonde kid. I think her dad worked construction and came to Richland looking for work. He took off and left them here. Her mom stayed drunk and they lived on welfare."

Holly stared at Laurie. "Brea said Nicole's mother was an alcoholic. But that and destitute... How'd Nicole pull off the transformation?"

"Forget that dumb as a doornail routine. She's smart as they come."

"I remember now. She acted like an airhead in high school but got straight A's."

Laurie made a face. "Of course, she was screwing a couple of teachers and had most of the jocks buying her clothes and jewelry."

"I guess Tim's enough older he didn't know about all that."

Headlights illuminated the parking lot as the truck eased toward the cross street. Holly squinted at the sudden brightness. "Why isn't she working? She'd be perfect in management at more companies than I can name."

"I think she likes being Tim's wife and doing the charity organizing."

"She sure likes spending his money, but it seems like a waste of talent. If Walt was serious about Tim divorcing her, she might need to rethink that."

The truck bumped across the road and entered the library's parking lot, accelerating as it cleared the entrance.

"What an asshole," Laurie said, watching it. "Don't you hate people who cut the corner at red lights?"

"Seriously." The women edged closer to a parked Chevy SUV, giving the older truck room to pass.

"That truck's going too fast." Laurie glared at the oncoming driver.

And coming straight for them. *Holy*—

"Look out!"

Chapter Thirty-two

Something warm trickled into Holly's eyes. A wide band of pain settled around her temples and tightened, throbbing into a headache. It pounded in time with the shriek of a car alarm.

Laurie huddled against the bulk of the SUV. "My ankle," she moaned.

Holly rose on her hands and knees, and winced at the chorus of pain. She crawled gingerly across the narrow gap between the cars and peered at her friend's foot.

Oh, no.

Two women appeared at the rear of the vehicles. "Are you okay?" one asked anxiously.

"Call 911," Holly said, her attention fixed on Laurie's ankle. The Chevy's rear tire had her foot pinned.

Damn, what should she do now? Her first-aid course hadn't covered anything this serious. "We can try to shift the car and get your foot out, but maybe we should wait for the ambulance."

Holly glanced at the older of the two women. Clad in elastic-waist jeans and a sweatshirt, she looked like somebody's mom. Cell phone pressed to her ear, the woman was focused on whatever the 911 operator was saying.

"Tell them to hurry," Holly said.

"They said don't try to move the car." The woman lowered

her phone. "You're bleeding, by the way."

Holly touched her forehead and came away with shaky, bloody fingers.

"He could've killed you," the other woman, the younger of the pair, sputtered. "He must have been drunk or something."

Holly looked at her blood-splattered sweater and wondered if she could use it as a bandage. A warm rivulet trickled down her cheek. She dabbed at it with her forearm.

The pulsing wail of a siren began. She figured a Pasco cop was blasting up Lewis Street. The cavalry to the rescue. The two women had vanished, probably headed to the parking lot entrance to flag him down. "Another minute," she told Laurie. "Hang in there."

"You don't think he meant to hit us, do you? The guy driving the truck."

"Of course not." Denial immediately kicked in.

Holly stared at Laurie's foot, unable to completely deny the obvious. What had she stirred up? Or rather *who* had she stirred up? Marcy's killer? Frank? Lee Alders? Creepy Security Guy?

Laurie grimaced and maneuvered onto her back. Her leg twisted at an awkward angle. "He probably meant to bump you off. You *are* the only witness to Marcy's murder."

"Nice try, but I didn't witness anything. No, this is one of your multiple admirers, desperate for your attention." Laurie *couldn't* have gotten hurt because of her.

"I can think of better ways to attract me," Laurie mumbled. "Chocolate. Jewelry. Signal flags."

The older woman came back, arms laden. "I had some paper towels in my car. And a blanket. We should keep your friend warm."

"Thanks." Holly gave her a grateful smile. Definitely someone's mom. In a good way.

She tucked the blanket around Laurie, and then pressed a paper towel to her own aching head. Now that the immediate crisis was past, her headache was growing to titanic portions.

More people crowded around the damaged cars. The entire library must've emptied into the parking lot, the patrons drawn like coyotes to the carnage.

"Did anybody see which way the truck went?" Holly called.

A babble of voices answered. She grimaced, wishing she'd stayed quiet.

Spinning blue lights splashed across the crowd and a patrol car bumped into the parking lot. The siren drilled into her skull. About the time she thought she might lose it, the officer killed the racket. Moments later, the policeman approached the wrecked cars. He swiveled his head between her and Laurie, then stooped to check on Laurie's foot. "An ambulance is on its way, ma'am."

Holly sagged against the Pathfinder adjacent to the Chevy SUV. Of all the people on the police force, why did the responding officer have to be the Shrimp? She fervently hoped he didn't remember her—or the grief she'd given him about Lillian.

Why was a Franklin County deputy even there instead of a Pasco city cop?

His assessment of Laurie complete, he turned and gave Holly a calculating look, clearly trying to place her. A moment later he rose, pivoting on his heel without a word to her. Shrimp—*what was his name?*—turned to the circle of curious bystanders. "Hit and run. Anybody get a description of the vehicle or the driver?"

The woman who'd called 911 stepped forward. "That truck tried to hit them." Indignation fizzed around her like a Fourth of July sparkler. "He drove right at them."

"Can you tell me the license plate? The kind of truck?"

"It was old and dirty. The light over the tag was burned out, but it had a Washington tag. It looked like A-2-4-something."

"The truck has a huge dent in the front fender," her friend added. "How hard could it be to find?"

"Did you see the driver?"

The younger woman shook her head, then pointed at the adjacent row of cars. "I was over there. I heard it going too fast and turned around just in time to see him aim at those two women. Are you sure they're okay?" She peered around the officer.

Slumped against the Nissan's door, Holly watched Shrimp try to extract anything useful from the witness. Several Pasco patrol cars had arrived by then, and other officers talked with various people around the parking lot, but they were too far away for Holly to hear the conversations.

She wished the ambulance would hurry. Laurie had given up any pretense at banter. Eyes closed, moaning periodically, she clutched Holly's hand.

Holly hoped Laurie had only twisted her ankle instead of crushing it. The gash on her own head burned. She eased the paper towels aside and felt another trickle roll down her cheek.

Damn.

Everything hurt. Her head pounded with a crashing headache. Her left hand and knee had a major case of road rash. She was going to have some nasty bruises, and to add insult to injury her favorite jeans now sported a huge tear, and blood splattered her sweater.

Another car, a Crown Vic that screamed *I'm-an-Unmarked-Police-Car*, stopped beside the Pasco cruisers. She recognized the figure behind the wheel.

Terrific.

The car incident was now *officially* a complete disaster.

~$~

JC strolled over to join the group assembled beside the damaged cars. "Hello, Holly."

"What are you doing here?" she asked. *Gimme-a-break, no-verbal-warfare-tonight* threaded her resigned question.

Without answering, he studied the bashed-in fenders, clicked his tongue, and shook his head.

Why did he take such a perverse pleasure in making her feel guilty? "I'm the *victim* here, not the driver. Vic-tim."

He crouched beside her. His lips twitched into a smile. He leaned close and whispered in her ear, "You know, you look real sexy with your hair all messed up and your eyes kinda droopy."

Outrage warred with confusion. "You can't say stuff like that when you're working. It's sexual harassment."

He sat back on his heels. "Who says I'm working?"

"What, you show up at every hit-and-run accident scene?"

"Only when there's a pretty woman involved." His smile deepened into a full-on grin and those blasted dimples popped into view. Damn, most people looked cute with dimples. JC's appeared and the temperature rose ten degrees.

Trying to slow her pitty-pat heartbeat, which *wasn't* helping the pounding in her head, she gathered her tattered dignity. She ignored his sexist remarks and demanded, "If you're not working, why are you here?"

"I guess that worked," he said.

And damned if he didn't stand up, turn around, and stroll over to where the squad sergeant talked with a guy in street clothes that she hadn't even seen arrive.

She stared after him. Was that supposed to be a distraction? A come-on? Or was he trying to make her mad? Whatever it was supposed to be, she sorta wished he'd come back.

"Forget about the blind date," Laurie said. "Admit it. You should start seeing JC."

"Hush. You're delirious."

Shrimp squatted in front of her. His nametag read Dickerman, the name she now remembered hearing JC call the smaller man. "I'll take your preliminary statement. Detective Patton will talk to you at the hospital."

Her head throbbed and she wished Dickerman would speak more quietly. "I don't think I need to go to the hospital, but Laurie should. Do you know when the ambulance will get here?"

Laurie's face was white and if her grip got any tighter, Holly was going to have to go to the hospital for a mangled hand.

Dickerman studied Laurie's pale, sweating face. "I'll check."

He crossed to a patrol car and toggled his radio.

Holly scanned the other groups, looking for JC. He stood beside the patrol sergeant, watching her. He didn't break the contact when their eyes met. The intimacy of his gaze flustered her, and she turned back to Laurie. "Any minute now."

Dickerman returned. "Ambulance is inbound. Can you tell me what happened?"

Maybe he didn't remember her. She felt a flash of relief. She hadn't been a total bitch, but she hadn't been very nice to him. "We were walking to our cars and heard the truck start. It was parked beside that building."

She pointed across the street. "Do you think he'd been drinking?" Maybe that was why the vehicle had been parked behind the darkened business.

He ignored her question in that irritating way all cops apparently did. "What happened after you heard it start up?"

"When it came into this parking lot, it was going too fast. We turned around and saw he was drifting across the aisle—that's why I thought maybe he'd been drinking—and I realized he was going to hit us if we didn't move."

"Where were you, exactly?"

"Behind this car." She pointed at the bashed-in Chevy SUV. "I pushed Laurie between the cars and dove after her."

The officer looked at the bloody mass of paper towels Holly was holding to her temple. "Did he hit you?"

"I think I hit the Pathfinder's mirror." She waived a hand at the adjacent vehicle.

Dickerman stood and played his flashlight over the mirror. "Yeah. There's blood here."

An ambulance rolled into the parking lot and added its flashing lights to the chaos. A competent-looking man and woman jumped out. The EMTs quickly examined Holly and Laurie, then concentrated on Laurie's ankle.

Holly shifted her position, trying to move out of their way. Her scraped hands protested, and her knee announced it was most unhappy with the one-point landing she'd made on it. None of it was fatal, she reminded herself. Just damned uncomfortable. She pushed; the pavement ground into her raw palm. "Ouch. *Shit.*"

Warm hands grasped her arms and lifted her to her feet.

JC stood in front of her. He drew her away from the cars, giving the paramedics room to deal with Laurie and maneuver a stretcher. They'd connected some kind of jack to the SUV, probably to lift it off Laurie's foot.

JC stared at Holly's forehead and then made a slow assessment of the rest of her injuries, ending by raising her hands for inspection. "You were lucky."

She tried to think of something to say that didn't sound idiotic. He was standing too close to her, but his warm bulk felt comforting. Nearly getting run over apparently threw intelligence and common sense to the wind. Her hands trembled and the *what-ifs* were lining up in her head, clamoring for attention. What if she'd been slower to react? What if the SUV had shifted a few more inches and landed on Laurie's body instead of her foot?

What if—

JC slid a hand up her arm to her shoulder and then back down to her elbow. He left it there, gently tugging her nearer. The urge to snuggle into his chest was nearly irresistible. His presence made her feel safe and protected. To her surprise, just his being there made her feel better.

With a sigh, she gave in to temptation and leaned into his shoulder.

Just for a second.

His arms wrapped around her. She didn't pull away. His fingers traced a reassuring pattern against her back. Neither spoke.

Some of the tension seeped away. Standing clasped in JC's arms felt like the most natural thing in the world. Her head fit precisely into the hollow of his shoulder. He knew just how to touch her, his hands confident and comforting. Eye closed, she shifted and buried her nose in the fold of his jacket. His scent triggered memories and instincts. Of their own accord, her hands rose and slid around his waist. His arms tightened and his chin touched the crown of her head in a gesture that was achingly familiar.

Behind them, the EMTs lifted Laurie onto a stretcher and wheeled it to the ambulance, then the female medic returned. JC's arms retracted and he moved away. Holly immediately missed the warmth and security.

The EMT ran practiced hands over Holly, checking for injuries. She flashed a penlight into her eyes and her headache exploded. Eyes closed, she collapsed against the Pathfinder and let the impersonal metal support her instead of JC's warm arms.

"You need stitches for that cut, and you should be checked for concussion." The medic pressed a bandage to Holly's temple.

Her eyes cracked open. "It's not going to scar, is it?" Warmth immediately climbed her face and she hoped JC hadn't heard her question.

The woman smiled, showing the strained teeth of a smoker. She nodded in JC's direction. "Don't worry. He'll still think you're pretty."

Holly started to protest, "It isn't like that," but the EMT was urging her to the ambulance.

JC stepped over. "Just a second," he told the medic.

The woman moved to the vehicle and helped her partner load their gear.

JC clasped Holly's arm. She wasn't sure what to make of him constantly touching her. On the outside, she thought she was doing a pretty good job of faking calm and collected. He was watching her like he was afraid she might start screaming or doing something hysterical and really hoped she wouldn't.

Inside, she *was* screaming. All she wanted to do was curl up in his arms again and let him protect her, but *hello*, the world didn't work that way. She sighed and rubbed small circles into her uninjured temple. "I do not need this right now," she muttered.

JC smiled, dimples and all. "When exactly is it a good time to get run over?"

She dropped her hand, ready to glare at him, but realized how crazy her comment sounded.

"Did you get a look at the driver?" he asked, back in detective mode.

"I only caught a glimpse of a floppy hat and clenched hands on the wheel."

"We have a description of the truck, an old, white half-ton. Like there aren't a million of those around here. At least this one has a brand-new dent in the front fender. But the driver—" JC blew out a disgusted breath. "Hell, we've heard everything from a Mexican farmworker to a middle-aged woman. The only thing everyone agrees on is long hair and a hat."

"Sorry. It all happened so fast. The lights were shining right in our eyes."

"It's okay." His fingers squeezed her arm. "We'll find the truck."

One of the Pasco police cruisers pulled out of the parking lot. JC's hand moved to her shoulder and gripped it. "They want to know"—he nodded at the remaining Pasco cops—"if you're aware of anybody who'd want to hurt you."

"Wait a minute. I know there's a murderer running around." And all the other creepy bad guys. "But before you assume this was my fault, can we at least consider the possibility it was some drunk. A hit and run." She stepped back and shook off his hand.

He sighed, as though she was being unreasonable. "Holly…"

He reached for her, but she held up a hand. "That's what Shr—Dickerman said it was. A hit and run." Her head pounded in time with her words.

"I understand. It's scary. And it's personal. I want to help you figure out why. Denial isn't helping."

She brought her fingers to her forehead, testing the growing lump. Her hand trembled. She dropped it to her side. "I didn't 'provoke' this. I'm so normal and law-abiding I bore myself."

"So I'm supposed to think someone's after Laurie?" JC's tone dripped skepticism.

Their heads turned toward the ambulance. "Of course not. Don't let the spiky blue hair fool you. Laurie is the sweetest person I know. Her life is even more boring than mine. She doesn't even have a boyfriend. She has—"

"She has what?"

Warmth climbed her cheeks. Okay, maybe not so boring. "Fantasies," she substituted for "an inflatable friend."

The look on JC's face would've been priceless in any other circumstances. "I see."

She seriously doubted that. "Look, I get that this could've been somebody like Creepy Security Guy."

"Who?"

"The security guy at the Tom-Tom. He looks like Frank and he pointed at me. He made his fingers like a gun," She held out an index finger and cocked thumb, demonstrating. "And he might have been dating Marcy before she—"

JC's face tightened with every word she babbled. "And you planned to tell me this, when?"

She snapped her mouth closed and examined his stony expression. *Oops.* "Um, when I knew if there was anything to it?"

"*Holly.*" His tone was pure frustration and exasperation.

One of the patrol officers appeared beside them. For once she didn't mind the interruption. "We need you to get in the ambulance, ma'am. We'll meet you at the ER and take your statement. We may need you to come to the station afterward."

"But my car—"

"We'll make arrangements," the officer said, and returned to his cruiser.

"C'mon." The skin crinkled around JC's eyes. He tipped his chin toward the ambulance. "Or do you need me to drive you to the hospital?"

"No, thanks. I can take care of myself."

He picked up her left hand and examined the abraded palm. "And doing a terrific job, I might add."

Doors on patrol cars slammed. An officer revved an engine and fired up his siren. Holly grimaced in pain.

"Between your hand and head, if you think I'm letting you behind the wheel, you're nuts. Get in the damn ambulance." JC dropped an arm around her shoulders. "And Holly, there better not be more to this security guy story, because if you mess in my investigation again, I will personally arrest your pretty little ass."

Chapter Thirty-three

Friday morning

Using only the unabraded tips of her fingers, Holly shifted her BMW into drive. She'd managed only a few hours of restless sleep after getting home from the hospital the night before. Tired, cranky and sore, she'd called Tracey and asked her to reschedule most of the day's appointments.

Showing up at the office—maintaining her routine—would be therapeutic. Even if JC was right about some maniac gunning for her, no way would she let him bring her life to a crashing halt. She'd sworn after the miserable experience with Frank she'd never again let a man dictate her choices. Either the maniac *or* JC.

And if there was any merit to JC's notion the truck incident might be a warning about poking into Marcy's death, that meant she had to work harder to figure out who or what was behind it. She wasn't exactly sure how to go about that, other than to keep asking questions.

Of course, that was what JC insisted had gotten her into this predicament in the first place.

But he had to be wrong about the truck incident as a warning. Because if he was right, Laurie had gotten hurt because of her.

"Dammit," she muttered as she approached the next red

light. The good part about coming into the office so late in the morning was the lack of traffic.

The downside was she'd noticed the black 350Z right away.

With dark-tinted windows and a distinctive profile, the Z was hard to miss. Any car following her would have made her nervous after the truck incident, but this particular vehicle packed emotional baggage.

The Z followed her up the long hill on Grandridge and into the office's parking lot.

Damn it, Alex.

She pulled into her usual spot and cut the Beemer's engine. Her emotions were already all twisted up, trying to figure out what to do about JC and his apparent interest in her. She didn't need Alex getting his ego out of joint too. For a second, she considered peeling out of the lot and avoiding whatever Alex wanted, but that childish maneuver would only postpone the inevitable confrontation.

She climbed from her car, stiff and sore in places she didn't know could be stiff and sore. Her hair was a wreck. They'd shaved part of it off at the hospital when they'd stitched the cut on her temple. Bruises peeked out of her blouse, leaving her looking as though she'd been on the losing end of a World Wide Wrestling event.

With a groan, she opened the car's back door and removed a folded suitcase trolley. Alex parked his Z in the slot beside her, but she kept her attention firmly on her briefcase. Tugging the handles, she maneuvered the satchel off the backseat and onto the trolley.

"Hi." Alex stepped from the sleek two-seater.

Holly headed toward the office building. "Whatever it is, it can wait until eleven."

The meeting with the Stevens Ventures owners was the one appointment she hadn't rescheduled.

"Holly, wait."

"Not now." She kept walking.

"This isn't about the company. If you'd answer your phone or return my calls I wouldn't have to show up like this."

She looked over her shoulder, impatient. "There's nothing to talk about. Your mother—"

"This has nothing to do with my mother," he interrupted.

Actually, nearly everything about their screwed-up relationship had to do with his mother. She turned and faced him. "Fine. What is it?"

Alex closed the Z's door and eyed the trolley. He gave her a quick inspection, a question puckering his forehead. "This is about you and me."

He had to be wondering about the Dockers and sweater she was wearing instead of her usual business suit. "There is no you and me," she said. "There never was. You've known all along I planned to go back to Seattle."

"You could stay if you wanted to."

"Why should I stay? What's here for me?" She wondered if her questions—and the answers—would be different if she were having this conversation with JC.

"What's in Seattle besides a job? You know, I happen to like you. I like that you're smart and pretty. I even like that you aren't afraid to get in my face and stand up for yourself. There could be a 'you and me' if you'd give us half a chance." Alex narrowed the distance between them.

"Alex." She raised and dropped her free hand in a frustrated gesture. "We want different things out of life."

"How would you know?"

"Excuse me?"

"How would you know what I want from life?" He stopped a few feet away. Feet flat, hands resting on his hips, he looked more like a grown-up than she'd ever seen him before. It was rather disconcerting.

She stared at him, then sputtered, "Of course, I know. The restaurant. Your family."

"Those are outside things." He made a brushing wave of his hand. "I'm talking about what's in here." His curved fingers tapped his chest. "You don't have a clue because you never stopped and opened up long enough to let me in. You're so busy running around being important, you've lost sight of what really is important."

"You're wrong." Warmth scalded her cheeks, as if she'd been slapped, but she held up her chin in defiance. "Trust me, I know what's important. I'm figuring out where and how I want to live my life and who I want in it."

And one thing had become clear. She wasn't interested in spending her life with him.

"Where is this coming from?" she asked him. "Why are you here? We broke up. Remember?"

"We *argued*." His fingers flicked in a dismissive gesture. "I'm over being mad. I'm ready to make up."

Seriously? She wanted to smack her forehead, except that would hurt. She thought about smacking *him* instead. *You said some pretty hideous things. And what did you do with the pig, by the way? Yeah, so not going there.* "This is exactly what I'm talking about."

"What?" Alex's expression grew a little pissy. "People don't fight in the perfect world you live in?"

"Let me get this straight. You came here and threw it in my face that I don't know anything about you, right? Well, you're doing exactly the same thing, making assumptions about me. If I'm so important to you—" She raised her left hand, palm out, wiggling her fingers for emphasis, and then gestured at the bandage on her temple. "Hello? When you decided to come play

Mr. Sensitivity and Self-Awareness, did you happen to notice the bandages?"

"What happened?" Alex frowned for a second, then stepped forward as if he intended to hug her.

"It doesn't matter." She waved a hand to fend him off. "I'm tired. I'm sore. This is pointless. All you've ever seen of me is the outside. When you drove up just now, all you noticed was I was here and I wasn't wearing a business suit."

"That's not true," he protested.

"Admit it, Alex. You're not upset about breaking up."

Alex's cheeks darkened as a flush rose along with his temper. "I don't know why I bothered."

He took two steps toward his car, then stopped and pivoted on his heel. Fixing her with a glare, he said, "When you're all alone this weekend and want to know why, don't lay it at my doorstep. Just look in the mirror."

He climbed into his car, slammed the door, and drove away.

She stared after him. Did he actually think they could patch things up? Or was the canned speech supposed to make him feel better by painting her as the villain?

She couldn't help but compare Alex's actions to JC's. Last night she'd seen yet another facet of JC's personality.

One she liked.

A lot.

She could still feel the solid strength of his arms and chest, the gentleness of his touch as he examined her injuries. He'd maneuvered her past most of the red tape at the hospital and waited patiently while bureaucracy ground through the rest.

Her face creased with a wry expression. Of course, he'd also had a great time pushing her buttons, including that shot about looking sexy with her hair messed up—but the comments had served a purpose. They'd kept her distracted, preventing her from obsessing about the accident.

She turned toward her office building. She'd saved obsessing for after she'd gotten home. JC had offered to take or follow her home, but she wasn't ready to make that leap. Now that she thought about it, he'd looked kinda relieved too, when she'd said, "No, thanks."

The rest of the night had crawled past with a lot of tossing and turning. Glaring lights, the truck roaring toward Laurie and her. The screech of metal, crash of breaking glass, and Laurie's scream. It was all jumbled up with "Who?" and "Why?" in a crazy tumble of images and impressions.

Holly tugged her briefcase trolley onto the entry walkway. She wasn't stupid. Even as she'd insisted at the hospital, the police station, *It could be an accident*, she'd tried to figure out what she'd done, who she'd made nervous enough for someone to lash out at her.

The name that kept surfacing wasn't Alex, Frank, Creepy Security Guy, or even Lee Alders.

It was Tim.

She didn't want to believe Tim would deliberately hurt her.

Maybe it really had been a drunk driver. The reporter who'd shown up at the library while she wasn't paying attention had said so on television last night. The news snippet had generated a flood of calls—to her and, according to JC, to the police. So far, none of the tips had led anywhere, but it was simply a matter of time before the police found the truck and its driver.

The outpouring of concern proved one thing. Alex was wrong. She *did* let people into her life. She had friends. Lots of them.

She tugged the door handle with her fingertips.

His cruel comments still hurt.

259

Chapter Thirty-four

Back pressed against the building's glass door, Holly struggled through the entrance. She eyed Desert Accounting's office, then turned toward Stevens Ventures. As she wrestled the cart past the door, Brea jumped to her feet and hurried around her desk. "My God, what happened?"

"It looks worse than it is."

Brea elbowed her out of the way and tugged the trolley inside. "In that case, are you lost? Tim and Alex are supposed to meet you at your office."

"I know. I need to talk to Lillian for a minute. Okay if I leave this here?"

"Sure, I'll keep an eye on it."

Holly nodded her thanks and crossed the lobby. Without the impediment of the cart, movement was easier. She rolled her shoulders, shrugging off residual stiffness. Midway across the room, she stopped and turned. "I meant to ask you earlier. Did a dark haired guy—tall and sorta scary looking—ever come in here asking for Marcy?"

Brea shook her head. "Who is he?"

"I'm not sure but the manager at the Tom-Tom Casino said his security manager had started dating Marcy. If it's who I think it is, and if he really was dating her, he'd have shown up here."

Repeatedly.

"If someone like that came here, especially if he asked about Marcy, we'd have all heard about it. I can ask around though."

"If anybody remembers it, please let me know."

"I'd rather tell that hunky detective. We *are* talking about a possible suspect for Marcy's killer." Brea twitched an eyebrow and smiled.

Her brain/mouth filter trapped, *He's mine.*

Whoa. No he isn't.

Instead she said, "Okay."

She headed toward the payroll clerk's office. If Creepy Security Guy was Frank and he really was seeing Marcy, he'd have made a nuisance of himself at her workplace. Someone would've noticed—and mentioned—him hanging around. Then again, the casino manager could've gotten their dating wrong.

Lillian lifted her head when Holly stepped into the office, apparently catching her motion at the doorway. With furrowed eyebrows, her fingers rolled through "What happened?" She pointed at Holly's bandaged hands and temple.

"I fell." She didn't want to dredge up the details. Dodging those explanations was one of the reasons she'd ditched her clients today.

Lillian watched her with worried eyes. "If you want to talk about..." Her hands finished in a vague, encompassing gesture.

"Really. I fell in a parking lot." Holly briefly held up her bandaged palm, then continued. "Road rash."

The payroll clerk nodded, as if she still believed an evil boyfriend had taken his fists to her.

"Earlier this week, you said you wanted to talk to me." Holly's hands were stiff and the bandages across her palms made her gestures awkward.

Lillian glanced at the doorway, as if she didn't want anyone to see them together.

Holly took a seat with a dismissive wave. As if anyone in the office could handle more than basic signs. They certainly weren't going to be overheard, especially if she simply signed and didn't speak aloud. "Is it something about Marcy? Tim?"

Lillian's gestures looked tentative. "The Southridge building. Tim hired a lot more people than he usually does."

Holly waited for Lillian to continue. "And," she prompted.

"We've never used this many people before."

"It's a big project." Holly didn't want to jump to conclusions, even with her internal monitor screaming warnings about all of Tim's business. "Is there something specific making you uncomfortable?"

Lillian chewed on her lip for a moment, then signed, "Marcy filled out all the paperwork."

Holly fidgeted with the stapler, trying to think of a reasonable explanation. Finally, she forced her hands through the gestures. "Maybe the workers needed help with the forms. Or didn't speak English. Or..."

Lillian again glanced at the door. "A lot of them used the same post office box for an address."

"Damn." Holly's shoulders sagged as she considered the implications. Marcy, honey, what did you get yourself into?

The next thought was equally unsettling. If hiring the excess workers was fraud, was Marcy the instigator or merely a co-conspirator? Had she invented employees, looking to steal money, or had Tim put her up to padding the payroll to remove excess cash from the company accounts?

Lillian's expression probably mirrored hers. Worry. Concern. Hoping somehow there was another reason.

Alrighty. Holly squared her shoulders, even though it hurt in more than the physical sense. If something illegal was going on, she needed proof. Pasting on what she hoped was a reassuring smile, she signed, "Do you have a list of the extra employees? And a copy of the paperwork?"

"I'll get it to you," Lillian promised.

"One more question. Did Marcy and Tim ever…" She couldn't remember the sign for "flirt" so she finger-spelled it.

Lillian gestured, not understanding.

She was running out of time to be circumspect. If Tim was responsible for last night's truck incident, she wanted to know where—and how—to watch her back. "Did you ever see them act like they were more than friends?"

"They never hugged or kissed, but there were signs." The expression on Lillian's face might've been dismay or disappointment. "Looks, smiles, comfort in each other's personal space."

Of course, Lillian had noticed the body language. More than most people, she was attuned to that layer of communication. "You didn't mention it to the detective."

"He didn't ask about them, only if someone would hurt Marcy. Tim would never hurt her."

Holly wasn't so sure about that. Lillian's hands moved slowly. "I miss Marcy. I still expect to look up and see her."

"Me, too." Holly let her expression say the silent part. That she hoped they were both wrong about Marcy's involvement in whatever was happening at Southridge.

~$~

"Well, aren't you Ms. Popular this week?" Tracey beamed at Holly once she managed to wrestle the trolley into Desert Accounting's office. A vase of roses graced the corner of the receptionist's desk.

"For me?" Surely Alex wouldn't spring for flowers two days in a row. The first bouquet had surprised her. Two seemed excessive, even for him.

"They came this morning. Open the card. Who are they from?" Tracey extended a white florist's envelope.

Holly fumbled with the small card until Tracey grabbed it and extracted the note.

"To second chances." Tracey peered over her reading glasses. "What does that mean?"

She gave the receptionist a perplexed look. "I'm not sure."

A second chance with who? Alex? Her heart skipped a beat. JC?

She cautiously peeked into her college memory file. Had JC ever sent her flowers? She couldn't remember, and she had no idea what kind of dating moves he currently used.

"There's no name." Tracey flipped the card front to back. "Alex? Or someone new?"

The receptionist's eyes held an avid gleam as she sensed the possibility of juicy details.

"I don't know."

Was JC really looking for a second chance? Showing up at the library last night, that hadn't been police work.

Or manipulation.

Was it?

Could he have faked the way he'd held her? She'd felt not just safe, but cherished.

"Let me see the card." She studied the words. It wasn't JC's distinctive handwriting, but he could've called in the order. And the cryptic message sounded like something a guy would say when he didn't want to commit himself.

Unfortunately, she couldn't exactly call up JC and ask if the flowers came from him.

She sighed with frustration. She really didn't need another mystery right now.

~$~

Holly had maneuvered the trolley and flowers into her office when she heard her mother's voice.

Donna Price burst through the door in a flurry of maternal concern. "I heard about the accident on the news this morning. Are you okay? Why didn't you call me?"

"It wasn't that big a deal," she began.

Her mother stared at Holly's forehead before shifting her attention to her daughter's hands. "Not that big a deal?"

"It looks worse than it is."

Donna stepped closer, then brushed back Holly's hair. "I was worried sick when I heard. I called, but your phone went straight to voicemail."

"I was exhausted. I didn't get home until late last night. I needed to sleep, so I turned it off. I let Tracey know I'd be late."

Her mother's lips narrowed just a tiny bit and Holly realized calling Tracey and not her mother was probably a strategic error.

"Well, I hope there is a special spot in hell reserved for drunk drivers." Her mother crossed her arms in universal parental disapproval mode. "Especially ones who hit and run."

Holly did a double-take. She could count the number of times she'd heard her mother curse on one hand.

"I nearly dropped my coffee cup when the news anchor mentioned it this morning."

Holly blessed the cameraman, the film editor, and everyone else at the television station involved in the decision to feature Laurie on the stretcher and the smashed-in cars, rather than Holly curled up in JC's arms. The thought of explaining that little encounter to her friends and mother made her head hurt nearly as much as the blow to her temple.

"Do the police have any idea who did it?"

Holly shook her head. JC hadn't told her much. Fortunately, Shrimp—*why couldn't she remember the guy's name?*—had vanished at some point during the evening, but the Pasco cops had been even less forthcoming than JC. "I'm not sure how much they have to go on."

"Maybe they'll find the car." Donna's expression softened. She again stroked Holly's hair, then cupped her undamaged cheek. "You didn't have to come in today. We'll manage."

Since when? Holly shook off the grumpy reaction. "It's sweet of you to be concerned, but really, I'm fine."

She moved to her desk and struggled to unstrap her briefcase from the trolley.

"Let me get that." Her mother bustled across the office. She removed the satchel from the cart, placed it on the desk, and opened the leather case. The phone rang and she reached across the wooden surface toward the receiver.

Holly glanced at the caller ID. Tom-Tom Casino. "Let it go to voicemail."

Her mother's surprised expression asked, *Are you sure?*

Okay, so it wasn't her normal operating style, but whatever the caller wanted could wait until Monday. She didn't want to deal with the casino audit, Peter's remorse over outing Tim, or Creepy Security Guy today.

Holly pressed the power button on her computer and logged in. "I'm tired. My hands and knees are scraped and sore. If I get caught up on some paperwork today, I'll have the weekend to rest and recover. I'll be good to go on Monday."

"Okay." Feet dragging, her mother headed for the door. "I'm right down the hall if you need anything."

"Mom? I mean, Donna?" It felt really weird to call her mother by her first name, even if she was the one who suggested it for "in the office."

"Yes?" Donna glanced over her shoulder.

"What's going on with you this week? Missing meetings, being so distracted. You're acting more like yourself today, but...I've been concerned."

Her mother stepped back into the office and closed the door.

Holly eyed the closed door and wondered if she was ready to hear whatever her mother planned to say.

Hands clasped in front of her, Donna seemed to be struggling for words or the right place to start. Finally, she said, "Your father called. Apparently he likes sitting on his behind in the sun."

Holly blinked at the tart expression. "And?"

Donna perched on the edge of the visitor chair. "I had to come to terms with it. Actually face it. Our marriage is over..." She shook her head.

Holly didn't know what to say. "Maybe Dad isn't cut out for monogamy...I mean, this isn't the first time he's done this."

"Oh, Honey. Don't blame your father. Well...I do blame him, but his first marriage...they were so young. I'm surprised that one lasted a year. We've been married thirty years and as far as I know, this is the first time he's strayed."

"Well, he went big when he did it." She couldn't keep the acerbic tone out of her voice.

"Straight off the deep end." Donna brushed a hand over the smooth leather of Holly's briefcase. "Now I'm trying to handling the emotional fallout and deal with calls from the attorneys. Proposals, counterproposals, temporary arrangements. Unraveling a lifetime is rough. Untangling it from a business is a bitch."

My God, cursing twice in one day. Is this the "new" Donna Price? Still, at a deeper level, Holly didn't want to know more about her parents' marriage. "I'm here if you want to talk." *Please don't talk to me about Dad.* "And Mom, I'm part of this business now."

Holly waved a bandaged hand at the office. "I need to know where you're headed with Desert Accounting. What your plans are, period."

"I know. I've already dumped so much on you. You're doing a wonderful job, but if you're leaving, I have to figure out how to manage on my own. Unless, of course, you want to stay."

She traced a finger across the computer keyboard. "I'm thinking about it. Let's sit down this weekend and brainstorm. My head's not up to it right this minute."

"Of course. Let me know if you need anything today." Donna rose and hurried out of the office.

In the vacuum of silence following her mother's overwhelming energy, Holly dropped the stoic pretense. Shoulders slumped, hands limp, she sat at her desk, ignoring the blinking message light and the prompts from Outlook. Instead, she wondered about Tim and Marcy. Tim was building layers of companies to hide something. Marcy knew about it. Beyond the irregularities in the business, what was happening to the pair on a personal level?

Whatever they were doing, did Tim have it in him to kill the woman?

Had Tim been behind the wheel of the old truck at the library?

She hated feeling this way about a guy she liked. At the beginning of the week—just a few short days ago—she'd told JC everybody liked Tim. He was a fun-loving extrovert.

The police were keyed on Lee Alders as the prime suspect. Allegedly, he'd killed once to protect a fortune. Nothing would stop him from doing it again.

She'd never met Alders, but she did *not* like him. Even if the police couldn't prove he killed Marcy, another idea occurred to her about getting justice for Marcy and her family. She tapped in the number for La Boutique.

"Yessica? Hi, it's Holly. Do you have time for another question about the day Lee surprised Marcy at work?"

Anger rippled through Yessica's voice. "You have more ideas about why that man killed my sister?"

"It's more legal stuff. Paperwork."

"If you're wondering about the papers, I think Lee wanted to see her reaction that day, to see her get angry or upset. Or maybe he just wanted to intimidate her like he used to. Or—"

"Yessica." She leaned closer to the speaker, as if that would somehow get the woman's attention. "I want to make sure I understand the situation correctly. Marcy and Lee were separated and not divorced."

Holly could envision Yessica puffing up like an angry hen. "That's right. She hired the attorney to divorce him because he was so cruel to her."

"And the papers in the envelope he gave her, the ones that upset her, that was a property settlement offer."

"The offer was an insult. He should've given her half." Marcy's sister sputtered with fury. "He'd calculated what a housekeeper would've charged him for all the years they were married." Yessica's voice grew louder. "He didn't even add in what a prostitute would charge."

Holly cringed at the mental image the bitter comment evoked.

"He said the company was his, that Maricella hadn't done anything to deserve part of the profit. Who did he think managed the rest of his life when he was working? Who kept the other workers from quitting when that man was so awful? She gave everything to him and their marriage, and what did he do? Treated her like…like…"

She didn't want Yessica wrapped up in the domestic violence that probably followed Marcy's benevolent interference in Lee's business. "Did—"

"She never had a chance—a life." Tears thickened Yessica's voice. "He killed my sister."

For a long moment, the only sound was the woman's sobs.

Holly's fingers twisted the phone cord. "I'm sorry. I didn't mean to upset you."

There was a long sniffle, then silence. "Some days everything gets to me."

"I know. Something will remind me of Marcy and it'll hit me all over again."

A muffled sniff came from the speaker.

They talked for a few more minutes, reminiscing, until Yessica sounded calm again. "One last question," Holly said. "Do you know if Marcy made a will?"

"I doubt it. Who thinks about death when you're so young?"

In Holly's circles, wills weren't about death. They were about power. Passing wealth to the next generation. A subtle form of immortality. "It won't bring Marcy back, but this might make things, well, different for your family."

"What do you mean?"

"If Marcy wrote a will when she got married, it was probably reciprocal. She and Lee most likely left everything to each other. But if she didn't or if she made out a new will when she came back here…"

Understanding strengthened Yessica's voice. "Then part of what that *cabrón* owns goes to my family."

"Right. But like I said, I don't have any idea where any of this stands—the will, a separation agreement, anything."

"Maricella's attorney will know." Determination added power to Yessica's words.

Yessica had a new mission now—hit Lee Alders where it hurt the most.

In his wallet.

Chapter Thirty-five

Holly reached out to knock on Rick's cubicle frame, remembered her injured hand, and instead stuck her head around the corner.

Rick and Sammy looked up from the file they were discussing.

"I hate to interrupt, Rick, but can I see you in the conference room when you get a second?" she asked.

"We're at a good stopping point." Rick set the file aside. "What's up?"

There was a limit on how much she wanted to say about Tim, even within the walls of Desert Accounting. "We need to perform some long overdue due diligence."

"I know you used to work for a transaction group," Sammy said. "What does 'due diligence' mean?"

She considered how to answer in guy terms. "Before you bought a used car, you'd want to know it ran, right?"

Sammy gave her a look that said, *Well, duh.*

"So you'd check for Bondo, rust. Get a Carfax report to see if it'd been wrecked or trashed by a flood. Maybe have a mechanic run tests."

"Got the picture."

"Buying a 'used' company is the same thing. Is the asset

272

labeled 'building' an office tower in Pasadena or a burnt-out shell in Watts? Are there liabilities hidden somewhere that are going to come back and bite you?"

"And you want to look at one of our clients?" Rick's surprise showed in his voice.

She nodded.

"Anything I can do?" Sammy asked.

"Thanks, but not right now."

Sammy headed to his cubicle and Rick followed her down the hall. As soon as they entered the conference room, he said, "You're better with the staff than you realize."

A faint blush warmed her face. "Thanks."

She closed the conference room door while Rick picked up the financial statement she'd prepared for her meeting with Tim and Alex. "Stevens Ventures. What's bothering you?"

"I'd like to get your take on the financials first."

She sat down and pointed at the chair beside her. They opened the report for the holding company—the parent company that owned all the operating subsidiaries—and for a moment examined the figures. On paper, Stevens Ventures appeared to be in good financial shape.

Rick pulled more folders from the stack. Opening them sequentially, he studied the report for the first operating company, then moved to a second and third entity. "The individual company increases aren't that big, but in the aggregate, the increase—sales, profits—is impressive."

"Business looks like it's improving. That may be an illusion."

"The numbers are right there. Numbers don't lie."

But people do. "Does the increase over last year make sense in this area, in this economy?"

He returned to the reports, studied them. Finally he said, "You're worried the entire report is bogus."

"Basically. I'm trying to keep an open mind, not jump to conclusions, until I see the underlying documentation." Tim hadn't hired them to perform an audit. Looking at the detail might include stepping into some murky, gray areas—something she wouldn't involve anyone else in.

Rick folded his arms and looked at her, a thoughtful expression on his face. "The source documents on those construction projects will be with the project managers or filed at Tim's office."

"We usually don't see them."

"If we're just doing a compilation, bookkeeping gets the downloads, filters the information to the right company, plasters 'unaudited' all over it, and prints the financial statement."

"Just so happens, I printed the registers." She retrieved a stack of papers from the credenza.

They spread the printouts across the conference table. The schedules revealed an interlocking grid of payments. Dollars moved from company to company. Companies Tim apparently owned. Companies she'd never heard of. Companies that paid each other, borrowed cash, passed money back and forth to everyone but the banks.

She frowned at the numbers, willing them to change to something reasonable.

They stayed in nice, neat black-and-white columns, telling the same story they had earlier. Her experience was mergers and acquisitions, not forensic accounting. If she'd found this kind of mess during due diligence, she'd file a three-word report. *Walk away. Fast.*

"Last year, we audited the company developing Southridge," Rick said. "It was clean. But these others..." He shook his head. "We don't have enough information to say, one way or another."

She remembered the new Southridge hires Lillian had

mentioned. "Have we started on this year's audit?"

Rick shook his head. "I don't think Tim's signed the engagement letter yet."

She wondered if Tim would sign—or if she'd accept the engagement with everything she'd found so far. "All we have right now is screaming instinct. It could be sloppy bookkeeping and correcting miss-postings for all we know. But those new companies…" She ran her fingers through her hair, tested the bandage at her temple. "That stack of Stevens Ventures material I gave Sammy earlier this week, we need to look at it."

Rick reached for the phone. "Should be in the file room."

Moments later, the file clerk delivered the large envelopes. "Can't get enough of this, huh?"

"Detail is my middle name," she said with a smile.

She waited until the clerk left. "There's one company we can analyze. The laundromat."

She sorted through the envelopes and found several bank statements. An amazing amount of cash flowed into the account. Several large checks had sucked most of it back out. "There's no way the laundry generated that much cash."

Rick picked up the statement and whistled. "What in the hell is Stevens doing?"

She rose and paced across the conference room. She wasn't sure she wanted to know the answer and even less sure she wanted to learn Marcy's role in the mess. "Do the math. Even if every machine in the place ran around the clock, it couldn't produce that cash flow."

"I know you like the people over at Stevens. But we both know what this looks like." Rick dropped the bank statement.

"There's one more thing we can check before we call it a day."

Rick raised a questioning eyebrow.

"There's a property tax notice."

"For which property?"

"It's TNM Ventures or Properties or something like that. I hate to ask, but would you see if you can find it?"

"Sure." Rick reached for the pile of documents. "Have you thought about how it impacts Desert Accounting if Stevens is doing something wrong?"

"*If* Tim's doing something wrong? This *reeks* of fraud."

A sharp intake of breath turned their heads. Nicole stood framed in the doorway, clutching the doorknob. A kaleidoscope of emotions fluttered across her face—surprise, hurt, anger.

Oh, crap. How much had she heard? Embarrassment warmed Holly's face. "Nicole. I wasn't expecting you."

Nicole's fingers whitened around the door handle. "Obviously."

"Listen..." Holly didn't know what to say. She wanted to hear Tim's explanations first.

"I get the picture. You can't have Tim, so you're out to ruin him. I've had it with your lies." Nicole whirled and stormed down the hall.

"Dammit." Holly's sore knees made running impossible, but she hurried into the lobby.

Tracey was alone. She peered over her reading glasses. "What was that all about?"

"Nicole took something the wrong way." It was pointless to go after her and talk. She'd need to calm down first. Holly's shoulders slumped. "The timing on this is awful. I feel bad enough for Nicole right now. Maybe losing the baby and all."

Not to mention that Tim was planning to leave her.

"She's pregnant?" Tracey glanced at the door Nicole had stormed through.

"Apparently."

Confusion wrinkled Tracey's face. "I saw her at the pharmacy a couple of weeks ago buying Plan B."

The morning-after pill.

Holly returned her puzzled look. "Tim told me Nicole's been trying to get pregnant. That she's miscarried a bunch of times."

He'd flat-out lied.

Or Nicole had lied to him...

Tracey raised her eyebrows and shook her head. "Plan B's only used for one thing."

To prevent a pregnancy.

The two women exchange glances. "What a mess," Holly muttered.

She returned to the conference room and found Rick sorting documents. "Did you get her straightened out?" he asked.

"She was already gone. I'll find her after I have a talk with Tim."

A long, *long* talk.

"Going back to your question, you're right." She gestured toward the documents. "This could be bad news for Desert Accounting. I won't sign off on anything, even a compilation, without figuring out what's behind this."

"I'll bring the tax notice to your office," Rick said.

"Thanks." She glanced at her watch. "I need to make a few phone calls. It looks like Tim and Alex aren't going to show up for our meeting."

She moved to her office. She wasn't surprised Alex ditched the meeting after their confrontation in the parking lot, but Tim's failure to arrive concerned her. He might've seen her in his office that morning, talking with Lillian, and guessed what they were discussing.

Holly dropped the financial statement on her desk. Should she tell JC about Stevens Ventures' financial problems—or lack of them? Things didn't look good, but she didn't have anything concrete.

Rick hurried through her office doorway, a property tax notice in his hand. "This is a lot of land."

Tim had mentioned water rights for the land he'd purchased. Nobody bought blocks of land on the eastside without access to water. "Let's see where it's located."

Turning to her computer, Holly opened a property tax website and typed in the plot's coordinates. Within seconds a map of Walla Walla County appeared, the relevant parcel shaded a soft gray.

Shit.

Icy fingers trailed down her spine.

The land bordered the Snake River.

Upstream from Big Flats.

Where they'd found Marcy's body.

Chapter Thirty-six

Friday evening

With a groan, Holly looked at the living room walls, the paint cans, and finally, the ladder-scaffold thing. A pair of boards rested between upside-down V-shaped metal supports. It looked like a giant caterpillar had swallowed an oversized tongue depressor. The guy at Home Depot insisted it was the greatest for overhead painting—*You don't have to constantly move it like a regular ladder*, he'd said. She could walk down the narrow platform while she painted around the windows and next to the ceiling.

Home Depot guy had carried the package to her car and, with an inviting smile, offered to set it up. Figuring she had enough complications in her life, Holly had thanked him and driven home alone.

Her neighbor had helped wrestle the package into the house, but she'd set it up herself, following directions that could've been written in Sanskrit. She gave the contraption another doubtful inspection and hoped it wouldn't collapse when she climbed onto it.

Why had she taken on this project?

Because it had to be done and she couldn't afford to hire

someone else to do it.

Moving right along.

She dropped an angled paintbrush onto the platform.

You can do it. It's just the edges.

If she finished the detail work tonight, she could use the roller to paint the walls tomorrow, and be done with the living room. The carpet guy would come on Monday and then she could think about furniture for the room.

With a loud "Ouch, dammit," she wrestled the paint bucket onto the platform and then climbed the scaffold. Upbeat 80s-era music pulsed from her iPod.

Consider it exercise. *Bend and dip. Reach and paint.*

Ignore the bruises. Ignore the stiffness.

She'd plastered Band-Aids on her less-damaged right hand. After a little experimentation, she found a way to hold the brush that didn't pinch her scraped palm.

She concentrated on painting and tried to ignore the buzzing questions about Tim and Stevens Ventures. She still couldn't believe Tim and Alex had blown off their meeting that morning. Alex letting their personal conflict interfere with business didn't really surprise her, but was Tim suffering from a guilty conscience?

She reached up and glided the brush across the wall. Would Alex's restaurant show the same level of inflated cash flow as the laundromat?

Did she really want to know?

And then there were Tim's phantom companies. What was that all about?

Part of her wanted to call JC, but she could envision the way the conversation would go.

Holly: There are these companies, lots of them.

JC: And?

Holly: They're incorporated in Wyoming.

JC: And?

Holly: Okay, so you can incorporate anywhere, but there's something that's not right. The companies don't do anything except move money around.

She could hear JC's derisive snort, his snide comments about civilians and investigations. *Stay out of my investigation unless you have something tangible to add.*

All she had was suspicions and theories.

If she was going to talk to JC, she'd better have something real to tell him. Unless and until she had conclusive proof Tim was doing something illegal or illicit—or even that he might be having an affair—she wasn't going to say a word about any of it to Detective JC Dimitrak.

She'd painted a wide strip next to the ceiling and had almost finished the wall around the windows when the doorbell sputtered. *Thank God.* Gwen and Laurie. Reinforcements to help her move the blasted contraption.

She hesitated at the edge of the scaffold. She knew she ought to go peek through the side window and personally open the door, but it was her friends, right on schedule. "Come in."

The bell *britzed* again.

She rested the brush against the scaffold crossbeam. *Dammit, don't make me climb down.* "It's open."

The front door flew open. JC's leather-clad shoulders did an excellent job of filling the doorframe. Faded jeans clung to muscular thighs and lean hips. He stepped into her foyer. The overhead light danced across the subtle highlights in his hair and accentuated the planes of his face.

Yummy.

Her mouth went dry while other parts had a different reaction.

He propped his hands on his hips. The movement revealed a

pistol-free waistline.

She unstuck her tongue long enough to lick her lips. She ought to smack herself upside the head to get her brain functioning, but given the paintbrush, that could get messy. "I take it this isn't an official visit."

He clenched his teeth so tightly she was afraid she might have to call for the jaws of life to reopen them—which would be a real waste of that infinitely kissable mouth.

"Let me get this straight."

Uh-oh. It was his cop voice. Completely cool and detached.

"Not only did you not lock your door, but without knowing who it was, you yelled 'Come on in'?"

Oh, yeah. *This* was why she shouldn't start dating him again.

Right, snickered her inner teenager.

"And your point is?"

He pushed the door closed, then twisted the deadbolt. "It's a simple process called Locking The Door. I know you aren't stupid. What is it that you don't get about this whole situation?"

Holly gaped at the furious man. "Which 'situation' are you referring to? The investigation? The unfortunate incident in the parking lot?"

Their quasi-reunion?

"You know damn well what I'm talking about," he ground out.

Good thing the pistol had been optional tonight, given how pissed off he was.

Her hand tightened around the paintbrush. For a long second, she considered winging the brush at him, but then she'd have to climb down to retrieve the damn thing, which meant she might get close enough to touch him. That could get even messier, and she had more than enough paint on her already.

He dragged a hand down his face. "Goddamn it, you couldn't

keep your pretty little nose out of my investigation and now some nutcase is gunning for you. So I'll make it real simple. Lock your doors. Check to see who it is before you unlock one, much less open it."

Typical. One weak moment on her part—she *knew* she'd regret leaning on him in that parking lot—and he thought he could order her around. She shook the paintbrush at him, although she really, really wanted to throw it. "Who do you think you are? What makes you think for even one *tiny* little minute you can tell me what to do?"

"You know exactly who I am." He advanced on her like a purposeful panther, all barely restrained power and gliding athleticism. "I'm the cop who can't keep his mind on his work because he's worried about what some pain in the ass CPA is going to do next."

"And this is *my* fault?" She glared at him. "No one asked you to worry."

"That's one of the things I worry about most."

She straightened, stunned. His face was saying a lot more than that. It said he was totally into her. Every female part of her jumped up and down in response, going "Ooh, ooh!"

"This isn't a game of Clue." His tone approached *growl*. "Stay out of my investigation."

"Need I remind you, you're the one who dragged me into it? *You're* the one who found my language skills so convenient."

"Damn it, Holly. That's not the point. Did you blank out the part where someone tried to run over you last night?"

"That was an accident."

"An *accident?*" His hands swept through an exasperated motion. "What is it going to take to get through to you?"

"There's nothing to *get through*." She stabbed the air with her paintbrush for emphasis, which JC completely ignored.

283

"Someone tried to *kill* you. And what do you do? Do you take any precautions?" He threw out his hands. "Hell, no. Not only do you leave the damned door unlocked, you yell at the fucking thing for any maniac in the world to just 'come on in.'"

"Yeah, and look at what maniac walked in."

His eyes narrowed. "Lose the paintbrush and get down here." He jabbed a finger at the floor. "Now."

"No." Her pulse pounded in her temples and her fingernails dug into her already sore palms. "I have stuff I need to do and it doesn't involve you."

"Like hell. You're gonna tell me exactly what you're up to."

"I'm not *up to* anything. I don't know why anyone would want to hurt me. I'm not convinced someone is."

"This is exactly what I'm talking about." He looked as though he was ready to pull her off the platform and shake her. "And if you halfway figure something out, would you tell me? Of course not."

"If I told you, you wouldn't believe me." She glared at him through the charged atmosphere. "And for the record, I am *not* messing in your investigation."

"Well, you're sure as hell making *someone* nervous."

"Sounds to me like that person is you. What's the matter? Frustrated I won't let you make up the rules anymore?"

"You've thrown that line in my face one time too many." His chest rose and fell on sharp inhalations. His muscles bunched under his jacket, reminding her how powerful he was. "You may not like it, but I have rules for a reason, and it's usually a good one."

"Really." She slammed her hands onto her hips and winced at the protest from her sore palm. "How frickin' convenient. You have rules until they get in the way of something *you* want."

"What's that supposed to mean?"

"Figure it out. You're the hotshot detective."

He stalked across the floor, wrapped his hands around her waist and lifted her off the scaffold.

"Get your hands off me." She wiggled free, and shook the paintbrush at him.

He threw up his hands and headed wordlessly for the door.

"That's right. Walk out. You're good at that." The words were out before she could swallow them.

He spun. "Wait. Are you saying *I* walked out on us? That it was *my* fault?" He gave her an incredulous stare. "That's rich. Since you've conveniently forgotten, let me remind you. *You* dumped *me*. *You* left."

She threw the paintbrush on the floor. Paint splattered, ignored. "*Me?* You have the nerve to stand there and blame our breakup on *me?*"

"I asked you to *marry* me. I wanted to build a life, a family, but all you could see was the big city and the bright lights."

"And like a fool, I said yes to marriage, but *after college*. I asked you to come with me to Seattle, but, no, you always had to be the one in charge. It always had to be *your* way. And in case *you've* forgotten, I may have left, but I came back."

She stopped, afraid angry tears might overwhelm her. She'd come home that night to talk to him, to surprise him. Well, she'd surprised him all right. She'd walked into his apartment and found him on the sofa with Meredith.

If he'd hoped to make her jealous, it hadn't worked.

If he'd wanted to break her heart, it was an Oscar-winning performance.

"It didn't mean anything." He'd clearly followed her thoughts down memory lane.

She squeezed her eyes shut. "Don't you realize that makes it even worse?" She opened them to stinging pain. "You *cheated* on me. How was I supposed to trust you? And in case you've forgotten, you *married* her. I hope it meant *something*."

"I screwed up! Is that what you want to hear?" With two quick steps, he towered over her. Anger radiated around him. "And yeah, when you dumped me, I got shit-faced drunk and turned to someone else. It was the biggest mistake of my life, and I've paid for it in more ways than you'll ever know. But aren't you forgetting something?"

"I remember every detail of that night." *Every heartbreaking, gut-wrenching second.*

"No, you don't. You remember what you wanted to see—me with someone else. That way you can lay all the blame on me."

"You're saying it was *my* fault you ran around behind my back?"

"I was with her because— You. Walked. *Out.*" His voice rose with each word until he was shouting.

"Did you come after me? Did you even try to call?" she yelled back. "Hell, no. I came home because like an *idiot* I thought we still had a chance to make things work. I'd been gone one goddamn day, and I found you screwing another woman!"

"You told me we were *over*. You threw the fucking ring at my head. I was angry. Hell, I was furious."

"I asked for time to think and you said no."

"Think about *what*? We were crazy in love."

"That was never the question. At least *I* thought it wasn't a question."

"No," he overrode her. "The question was, I asked you to marry me and you didn't love me enough to say yes."

"That's not true. I've always loved you."

Oh, shit. Had she said that out loud?

The expression on his face—shock, satisfaction, and—*oh God*, was that a smidge of hope?—said far too much.

Her throat tightened with a strangling squeeze. She swallowed past the painful lump. "The issue wasn't love. It was you and your damn rules."

Just like that, the spark in his eyes vanished.

She plowed ahead. She'd waited six long years to say this, and she was going to get it all out. "You wanted to decide everything. Where we lived. Where we worked. *If* I worked. Everything! You never listened to my dreams. Never cared what I wanted."

They glared at each other, bristling like a pair of junkyard dogs.

Slowly his expression changed from furious to grim, a look of raw pain in his eyes.

She didn't know what to say. In spite of everything he'd put her through—the tears, the hurt, the loneliness, all of it—she still loved him.

"I'm sorry I hurt you. Sorry it ended like that. But you hurt me too. I don't think you've ever admitted you weren't blameless. You broke my heart. I've never loved anyone the way I love you. I was too angry at the time to see that. And then it was too late."

His words tore at her defenses. How had they managed to screw up so completely? Thrown away something so precious? "Why? Why was it too late? If you'd come after me. If you'd talked to me the way you are now…"

"I did come after you."

Her hands covered her mouth. He *had* followed her that night. Stumbling. Half-naked. Zipping his jeans. At the time, it had only made her more furious. She'd run away, so hurt, so angry. Nothing he could have said then would've made it any better.

"When you wouldn't talk to me…" He shook his head. "I was young and stupid. My pride wanted *you* to come back, to make the first move. By the time I'd cooled down enough to realize I was making the biggest mistake of my life, Meredith presented me with a bigger one."

Her gaze snapped up to meet his. "What?"

"She told me she was pregnant."

Hormones she didn't know she possessed flooded her senses. With a creaking, groaning lurch, her long-dormant baby clock started a countdown. Jealousy burned through her veins.

Meredith the home wrecker—had his child?

Chapter Thirty-seven

"She was pregnant?" Holly swallowed the watermelon-sized lump lodged in her throat. Even saying the words was torture.

What was wrong with her? She'd never wanted children.

Never *admitted* she wanted children.

"You have a child?"

JC's head twitched. A spasm rather than a shake. "No."

Relief roared through her, followed by a spark of insight. "That's why you married her."

"It was the right thing to do." He slumped against the scaffold, looking defeated. "She miscarried the next month. The marriage was a disaster from day one. I wanted an annulment. She wanted to hang in there, with me as her meal ticket."

"Is that how—?"

"That's not how I see all women. Just her."

It sure explained some of his attitude toward women, though. "You never remarried?"

"I..." His face shut down. His expression shouted he'd already revealed too much.

The doorbell sputtered.

Holly ignored it. She'd rather hear what JC would say next.

"Are you expecting someone?"

"Yeah, I am." *Dammit, Laurie, have I told you lately your timing sucks?*

JC released another deep breath. He crossed the room and jerked open the front door.

She really, really wanted to remind him to look to see who it was. But she couldn't bring herself to say the words.

Laurie stood on the porch. She rocked back on her crutches with a startled, "Oh. Am I interrupting?"

"No," JC said at the same time Holly said, "Yes."

"Glad we cleared that up." Laurie rolled her eyes.

JC brushed past Laurie and shot one last, indecipherable look over his shoulder. "I'll see you later. Lock the door after me."

Frustration roared inside her. *This conversation is* so *not over.*

Laurie stared at his departing back, then turned to Holly with assessing eyes. "Well, well. This has the potential to be very interesting."

"Don't start with me. I don't want to talk about it."

"You never do." Laurie awkwardly poled her way into the living room. "Too bad I didn't get here sooner. Apparently, I missed an enlightening show."

Holly stormed across the room and turned the latch on the deadbolt. There. Dammit, JC, I hope you're happy. "I didn't know he planned to stop by. I don't know what's up with him."

She retrieved her brush, noticed her hands were shaking, and dropped the brush into the paint can.

"You have any place to sit beside the floor?" Laurie glanced around.

Holly squinted her face and eyes into a *Really?* expression. "Picky, picky. How did you get here? I thought Gwen was bringing you."

"She had other plans."

"Gwen had plans?" She waved her hands around, blowing off her own question. "And you drove? With that cast?"

"It wasn't that hard. Now quit stalling. Break out the pizza and tell me what was going on in here with JC."

"I thought you were bringing the pizza."

"Round Table delivers. Start talking."

"Nothing is going on." Holly grabbed her cell and called the pizza shop.

"Bull," Laurie said the minute she finished placing the order. "The tension in here was off the Richter scale. Tell me, is this huge wall you put up to keep JC away related to him personally or is it because he's a cop? 'Cause if it's just the cop thing, you're the dumbest smart woman I ever met."

Holly stomped into the laundry room and returned with a folding chair and a handful of magazines. "Here. Improve your mind while I finish painting. But you know I have a completely valid reason not to like cops, so get off my case."

"That asshole in Seattle? That guy just pissed you off."

"Yeah, well. JC pisses me off too."

"I'd say he turns you on. In a major way. In fact, I'd say if I got here thirty seconds later, you two would've been doing the nasty right here on the floorboards."

Holly ignored her, and instead concentrated on climbing back onto the scaffold. She'd already cycled through angry and hurt before ending up completely confused about everything related to JC.

Laurie propped her crutches against the wall, squirmed around on the folding chair and thumbed through a magazine. "Oh, look. A dating guide. Should we take some quizzes and figure out what your problem is?"

"I'm not the problem." Holly picked up the brush and smoothed paint onto the wall.

Long silent minutes followed.

"This is ridiculous." Laurie tossed the magazine on the floor.

"Okay, how's this for a relationship assessment? You and JC were both young back then. *Too* young. You were completely in love, but you screwed up and it fell apart."

"He screwed up," Holly muttered. But did JC have a point? Had her actions pushed him into Meredith's arms? Okay. Maybe. Yeah, they had a huge fight. But would he have gone there if he really loved her?

"Sweetie, it's time to deal with whatever that asshole in Seattle did to you. And we definitely need to talk about your feelings for JC." Laurie smiled, a Cheshire cat grin. "Those could be quite interesting."

"Well, Ms. Sigmund Freud-ette. You're wrong. I'm not interested in JC."

Liar, liar, pants on fire.

Shut up, she grumped at the nagging voice in her head. It wasn't her friggin' pants that were on fire.

"Could've fooled me. There was some seriously interesting chemistry in the air."

"Yeah, it's called fury."

"I really don't understand you sometimes."

Holly glanced over her shoulder, then turned.

Lips pursed, Laurie regarded her seriously. "You've got a second chance with the man who turns you on mentally as well as physically, but son of a bitch, he's a cop." She brushed her hands in a dismissive move. "So you're going to use that excuse to ignore him. Instead of dealing with what broke you apart the first time, you're going to walk away from him. Again."

Holly stared at her best friend. "I cannot believe you said that."

The doorbell sputtered.

Talk about *saved by the bell*. Holly dropped the brush into the paint can and awkwardly climbed off the scaffold.

"We aren't finished," Laurie warned.

"Hush." Holly grabbed her wallet, crossed the foyer and peeked out the side window. Rather than a deranged assailant, a teenager holding a pizza box stood on the porch.

She opened the door. On the street, behind the teenager, a car slowed to a crawl. Not just any car—a Richland police cruiser.

"Everything okay here?" the officer called.

"I'm going to fucking kill him," Holly blurted. Fury clenched her fists, squinted her eyes, and sent blood surging through her face to her head.

"What?" The pizza kid took a step back. His head swiveled between Holly and the cop, flight written all over his face.

"Not you," Holly waved the hand clutching the cash. "Here."

The kid grabbed the money and bolted for his car. The police officer threw a casual salute and continued up the road.

Holly slammed the door, stormed into the kitchen, and threw the pizza box onto the counter.

"What's the matter?" Laurie trailed behind her.

"I cannot believe he did that without telling me. He had *no right*."

"Who did what?"

"JC. That's *exactly* where things went to hell with Frank." She stomped a circuit around the kitchen.

"Slow down. Start at the beginning." Laurie propped her crutches against the wall and sat on one of the counter stools.

"The beginning..." Holly opened the refrigerator and grabbed a couple of beers. "Which beginning? Frank? What happened in Seattle?"

"Either one. Both."

A cascade of memories swamped her anger.

"Frank."

The name was still bitter in her mouth. She opened the

bottles and pulled glasses from the cabinet. With a sigh, she rounded the counter, plopped onto the seat beside Laurie, and handed her a beer. "The beginning with Frank was pretty normal. He seemed fun, intelligent. I was working a lot, so for the first few months, we only went out occasionally. But gradually he started getting possessive and making comments like he was planning our future. I told him to slow down and claimed I was busy the next time he called. The coffee thing was already creeping me out—"

"The coffee thing?" Laurie asked.

Holly slumped against the counter stool and explained about the controlling coffee breaks. "He was already trying to make decisions for me—for both of us—in too many areas."

"I'm hearing annoying, but not scary." Laurie poured her beer into her glass.

"There's more. I went to the drugstore late one night. He called while I was *in the store*. What was I doing shopping so late?" Holly mimed staring at a cell phone clutched in her upturned hand. "I thought WTF? How did he even know I was out?"

"Okay, that's stepping over the line. What did you do?" Laurie asked.

Holly's hand waved in a brushing motion. "He had an excuse, said he'd had a call for service in the area and swung by to see if I was awake and wanted to get coffee or food and saw me leave. He did this whole 'I'm concerned' thing. There'd been some 'incidents' in the area, yada yada, so I didn't yell at him about it then, even though it really bothered me. Seeing me leave is different than following me to the store. And it kept getting worse. Every time I went somewhere other than the office, he'd call. What was I doing? Where was I going? With who? I don't like that person. I'd rather you didn't hang out with them. He pushed and pushed to put me in a box. Control what I did and who I saw."

"You did the right thing, breaking up with him."

Holly fiddled with her beer, slowly turning the glass. "I tried. I told him in no uncertain terms that I would go wherever I wanted. That no one told me what to do." She dropped her gaze to the pizza box, hating to even remember those days in Seattle. "It was the first time he really scared me. I honestly thought he might hit me. I backed away and he got it under control, but instead of leaving me alone, it got worse. Every time I turned around, he was right there. I changed grocery stores, coffee shops."

She shook her head. "I'd round a corner and there he'd be. Or he'd walk up behind me...He'd follow me if I went on a date, sit at the next table, and glare. He got his cop buddies to drive by my house and check for my car. I'd stand at my window and watch patrol cars slow down or stop in front of my building. They'd pull me over if I was driving and tell me to 'get my act together.' "

"Sweetie." Laurie reached over and hugged her.

"I've never felt so trapped. Who was I going to go to? The police?" She made a bitter noise. "I got the restraining order when I showed the judge the call log. Hundreds of call and texts every friggin' day. And that was after I told Frank to leave me alone. Some of those messages... God, he had me so freaked out."

"I remember you said the other police weren't helpful." Laurie shook her head. "I can't imagine...That sucks."

"I kept telling myself most of the officers were good guys. But when Mom asked for help, I was actually grateful for the excuse to leave town for a while. So what happens?" She threw up her hands. "This insane week."

"It has been nuts. But what happened tonight, just now?" Laurie gestured toward the front door.

Holly closed her eyes, took a deep breath, and opened her eyes, hoping she'd see things differently. "A Richland cop stopped outside my house because there was a pizza guy on my doorstep and a second car in the driveway. Without talking to me, JC apparently called them and asked them to do that."

"Holly...yesterday was pretty scary."

"You're missing the point. It's JC wanting to control me. Just like Frank did. Were you not listening?"

Laurie shook her head. "No, you're missing the point. Frank and JC are completely different. They're doing things for different reasons. Someone tried to hit us in a parking lot. We both know it wasn't an accident. JC knows it too. He cares about you and wants you safe."

Holly raised frustrated hands. "But on *his* terms. He's deciding for me."

"This works in your favor. If it was me and someone I used to be involved with recruits his friends to protect me...Tell me something Holly." Laurie swiveled toward her, a serious expression on her face. "If something else happened, would you trust JC— the man who was here tonight, not the kid you used to know— would you trust him to take care of you?"

Part of her wanted to blow off Laurie's question because it wasn't what was bothering her, but she couldn't help remembering how much better she felt when JC showed up Thursday night. She crossed her arms, wrestling with too many issues. She'd always been a Bottom Line women and whether she wanted to deal with the repercussions or not, the Bottom Line was she *did* trust JC to take care of her. Maybe Laurie was right. JC and Frank's motives were completely different.

"Maybe the issue isn't control," she said slowly. "Maybe it's more about communication and trust."

"Progress." Laurie smiled her Cheshire grin. "Keep working on that. Now open the pizza box. I'm starving."

Chapter Thirty-eight

Saturday morning

The central console pinged a warning when Holly started the BMW. *Low air pressure.*

Holly moved the gearshift to park, climbed out and examined the tires. The right front tire did look a little bulgy at the bottom. *Great.*

Her first stop was the gas station. A car vacuum and an air pressure machine stood side by side at one edge of the lot. She pulled the manual from the glove box and finally found the tire setting. Okay, thirty five pounds.

She studied the air machine. There was no regulator. No dial to set. How much was she supposed to put in?

Hmm.

As long as she didn't blow up the tire, she was good.

She connected the hose, squirted air into the tire, and added "Visit Tire Store" to her long To-Do list.

Minutes later, she cleared the Interstate 182/82 interchange and set the BMW's cruise control at seventy-two miles per hour. *Tire underinflated, reduce speed*, warned the console. As if in response, the front end shimmied.

She lowered her speed. Damn. Spend the morning at the tire store or drive?

It might take a few minutes longer, but the car could make it to Yakima, as long as she watched her speed. She reset the cruise control. Slow, but no warnings or weirdness from the tires.

Elbow propped on the window ledge, she gave her left hand an experimental flex. Annoyed rumbles came from under the bandage, but her fingers weren't as stiff as they'd been the day before. She squirmed into a comfortable position and watched the countryside stream past her window. Farms, orchards, and vineyards lined the Yakima River—a crazy quilt of yellows and reds that stitched together a series of small towns.

Hopefully, the extra key in her tote bag fit a mailbox in one of the towns' post offices.

The tire seemed to holding its own. She settled in for the drive and tapped her Bluetooth. "Voicemail."

Most of Friday's ignored calls were friends expressing concern over the incident in the library parking lot. Then, "Holly? Devon Edwards."

She straightened.

"I checked that Wyoming proxy. Nothing definite, but the feds are sniffing around. You sure you want this guy as a client?"

She'd asked herself the same question.

The next voicemail began and the bottom fell out of her stomach.

"Hello, Holly."

Blood drained from her face, leaving her cold and sweaty. She knew that voice.

Frank Phalen.

She'd moved three hundred miles to get away from him. But somehow, she'd known he would find her again.

"I'm glad you came to see me at the casino. We were meant to be together. To have a second chance."

Second chance? Oh God, the flowers were from him.

"Call me."

This could not be happening.

The pavement before her started a slow, swaying dance. She made it to the side of the road. The car shuddered as trucks rushed past, the buffeting air forming a counterpoint to her chorus of wails.

~$~

Holly wasn't sure how long she sat on the shoulder of the highway. Gradually, reason returned. Okay. The long hair, the clothes, the hat. Working security. Not what she expected, but she still should've figured it out immediately. Creepy Security Guy was Frank. No more rationalizing or explaining it away.

Part of her wanted to shriek, *How could you not recognize him?*

The rest went, *Oh shit, oh shit, oh shit.*

He'd seen her when she met with Peter Ayers. No wonder he'd sent the flowers to the office. *Oh crap, he knows where I work.* Sending flowers might be a gray area, but calling her violated the restraining order.

Was the order still in effect? It had been nearly a year. How long did a protective order last?

JC's words from the wake resonated in her mind. *Tell me if Phalen contacts you.*

She raised her hand to tap the Bluetooth and call JC, but the previous evening's confrontation made her pause. JC might think calling about Frank was just a pretense to contact him. Was she even remotely ready to talk to him?

Not just no, but *hell*, no.

They needed to finish that conversation, and she wasn't doing

299

it over the phone.

Five minutes after she pulled back onto the highway, she noticed a black SUV seemed to be keeping pace with her car. One thing the ordeal with Frank had taught her was to watch her back.

Her gaze drifted back to the rearview mirror. Even at her reduced speed, the vehicle hung behind her. Her thumb hovered over the cruise-control lever. She couldn't speed up with the shaky tire. After a momentary hesitation, she tapped the control to decelerate and slowed the BMW.

The sedan behind her swung into the passing lane. The SUV stayed back. A tendril of concern eased up her spine.

Damn. It was official. JC and Frank Phalen had made her totally paranoid.

You aren't being paranoid if someone really is after you.

She nipped the invasive thought. Her exit was coming up. It'd be easy enough to prove the black vehicle wasn't following her.

The Prosser exit arrived. She watched the SUV as she eased into the turn lane. It slowed, as if its driver might also exit. Eyes riveted to the rearview mirror, she coasted down the off-ramp. The black vehicle accelerated and continued on the Interstate.

She gave a small sigh of relief. Paranoia was so tiring.

Within minutes, she reached the Prosser post office and found the short row of mailboxes. Maybe the extra key belonged to Marcy's personal box. Maybe it didn't have anything to do with Stevens Ventures. She poked the key into the lock and twisted.

The lock didn't turn.

Wrong box.

Damn.

Same results in Moxee, Grandview, and Sunnyside.

She struck pay dirt in Granger. The mailbox was packed with late notices, some forwarded from another box in Ellensburg, others mailed directly to the overstuffed Granger box.

Rather than stand in the post office and shuffle through envelopes branded with bright red last-notice and past-due warnings, she pushed the stack back into the mailbox.

Okay, now she knew where the box was and that apparently nobody was cleaning it out.

Pocketing the keys, she walked to her car as though she knew what she was doing.

Now she had to figure out a way to make JC trip over the information, so the police could actually use it.

Chapter Thirty-nine

Holly's conscience walked on the legal side of the law. Breaking into Tim's office was a bad idea.

But she *wasn't* breaking in.

Tim didn't say she could have the keys, her conscience argued.

But his employee had given them to her, fully understanding she intended to go through the files, because Kaylin didn't want to do it herself.

Slippery slope.

Perfectly legal. She had keys. She had permission.

So why was she sitting in her car arguing with herself?

She climbed from the BMW and strode toward the small house Tim used as a satellite office. *Eyes front. Act like you're supposed to be here.*

This side street held a mixture of small businesses and residences. The yards were empty and traffic was light, but who knew if nosy neighbors were already reporting a prowler…

She stood in front of the locked entrance. Her heart thumped in her ears. What if Tim had an alarm system? Hesitating made her look suspicious, so she swiftly unlocked the door and stepped inside.

No loud claxon clamored. She scanned the small room. No keypad beside the entrance. No metal box in the corner with a blinking red light. She drew in a ragged breath. *Good.* No obvious alarm.

Light filtered through the dusty, open-weave curtains. What looked like a cheap dinette set stood on the right—oak-toned chairs around a spindle table—with a closed door beyond it. Sofa on the left. Desk in the corner. An open doorway opposite her.

"Hello?"

No answer.

The silence felt not so much empty as…waiting.

Halfway across the room she realized she was doing the burglar creep—one silent foot in front of the other, with the cartoonish body-lurch in time with the steps.

"This is ridiculous," she said aloud.

The door behind the table revealed a kitchen converted to a break room. It smelled of burnt coffee and microwave popcorn. No surprise there. She stepped through the rear opening and found three closed doors lining a narrow corridor. The middle door opened to an old-fashioned bathroom. She opened the door on the right and stared in horrified surprise. A queen-sized mattress on a platform frame centered the space. Rumpled pillows and tangled sheets swathed the bed. Candles in various stages of disintegration covered ledges and windowsills.

Ooh. Ick.

Apparently, she'd found Tim's love nest.

Gross.

She closed the door, not wanting to know more. If anyone ever needed evidence of Tim's infidelity, an anonymous tip could suggest a prime location to look for it.

With a shudder, she moved to the other end of the hall and wondered what lay behind door number three. If this were a Gothic haunted house, a soundtrack would be playing creepy music and a voice would shout, "Don't open the door, idiot!"

She turned the knob and again felt the bottom fall from her stomach. An industrial-scale shredder stood in the middle of the room. Several trash bags that held thousands of tiny paper chips slouched against a row of file cabinets.

Maybe the shredding was routine housecleaning—Tim getting rid of old files, unneeded project specs.

Nothing unusual. Nothing damning.

She crossed to the desk and picked up a handful of documents from the pile closest to the shredder. Thumbing through them, she felt no pleasure in being right. If this had been a due diligence with her Seattle M&A team, she'd be congratulating herself. Instead, she stared at documents that represented an $830,000 loan to one of the mystery companies. The stack contained the complete loan package, detailing a series of loans for a project that didn't exist, as far as she knew.

The papers fell from her hands, joining the blizzard of documents.

If it had really been a project that went south, the bank would've attached any assets inside the corporation, collected whatever it could on the loan, and written off the rest. Tim's credit rating would've taken a hit but business would go on as usual.

Instead…he was gambling on a shell game. Trying to cover his tracks…

She picked through the papers. More loans. More late notices.

At the height of the housing boom, Tim had borrowed money for projects he never planned to build. He'd sucked out the money to other operating companies and sent it—where?

To cover gambling losses? An expensive wife and mistress? Both?

How could you, Tim?

She looked from the papers to the shredder. Clearly the documents were being destroyed, but she couldn't tell how recently anyone had been in the office. She cast a troubled glance over her shoulder, feeling the quiet as an uneasy presence.

"Screw it." She was already in trouble if someone walked in and found her there.

She poked through the document piles, found key pages and stepped over to the copier. The groan and thump of the paper handler sounded unnaturally loud in the silence of the office. She shot another anxious look at the door.

"Shaky ground" barely covered where she stood.

Do what you came for.

She opened the first file cabinet drawer. Haphazard folders contained documents for loans, incorporations. It would take days, weeks, to process it all.

A phone shrilled.

She shrieked, jumped, and dropped the incorporation filing she'd been examining. Her injured palm slammed against the drawer. "Ouch, dammit."

Clutching her sore hand, she spun around. Adrenaline flooded her bloodstream. Her gaze darted around the room, searching for the phone. It gave a second blast, then a fax-tone chirped, and another machine spat out a page.

She'd already stayed too long. The sensation of hidden, watching eyes grew stronger. Her heart hammered, preparing to run. Maybe JC wasn't Just Crazy. Maybe he was right and the parking lot incident really wasn't an accident. Maybe Frank was driving that SUV. He could be waiting for her right outside.

Get moving and get out.

With a shudder, she scanned the room. What should she salvage?

She zeroed in on the shredder. Her sore knees complained when she knelt and retrieved the papers scattered around the machine. More default notices. Demands for payment. Intentions to foreclose.

Sorting though the mess, she found papers from eight banks and several subprime lenders. She made copies and added the duplicates to her growing pile. The originals drifted back into the snow-bank of deceit. Through it all, the creepy feeling of a stalking presence grew stronger, until tension churned her stomach.

Enough.

Even if the rest of the papers disappeared into the maw of the shredder, she had the lenders' names. The lenders would have originals too.

She stuffed her motley collection into her tote bag and reexamined the office. It looked no more disorganized than when she'd arrived. She hoped no one would notice her fleeting presence.

In the front room, she peered through the curtains, then reached for the doorknob. On the plus side, no police cars outside with guys ready to arrest her ass. No black SUV lurked down the street. The downside? Her car was parked at the curb right out front.

Smooth move. She'd never make it as a PI.

Anybody looking for her would know exactly where she was, if not what she was doing. Her gaze dropped to her fingers, wrapped around the doorknob.

Fingerprints.

She'd left them everywhere.

Her hand jerked away from the door. Oh, crap. Fear squeezed her throat, stifled her breathing. What if the banks—*the cops*—found them? Thought she was part of it?

She ran her fingers through her hair, took a deep breath. Panic solved nothing. Be reasonable. Think logically.

Okay, she'd left prints. The lines and curlicues didn't have a time stamp on them. It would've been possible or even reasonable for her to be in the satellite office. Especially after Kaylin had given her keys and permission. *Not* finding fingerprints would be even more suspicious. Then again, given the documents she'd handled, she was glad she'd created a timeline, even if it was a tenuous one. She'd much rather be accused of a quasi-legal entry than collusion in the fraud.

Alrighty. Deal with it and get moving.

She pasted on a confident smile and stepped through the front door. Once inside her car, she resisted the overwhelming urge to collapse in the driver's seat. Instead, she placed the tote bag on the floor, cranked the engine, and eased away from the curb.

Long, nerve-wracking minutes later, she powered onto the Interstate and headed back to Richland. She checked her rearview mirror. Nothing behind her but pickup trucks and sport utilities. They all looked the same to her. In eastern Washington, there were thousands of the vehicles. Most were either black or used-to-be-white. The only way to tell them apart was to count the number of soccer kids in the third row, or dogs in the back.

Her thoughts returned to the office she'd just left. No wonder Stevens Ventures' financial statements looked so good. Tim—or maybe Tim and Alex—was borrowing money and inflating income with bogus activity, flushing thousands through the operating companies.

The extra employees Lillian had mentioned created compensation expense—and removed the cash. The bank statement for the laundromat—the huge cash flow—shouted at her. There were entries for new equipment, painting, and landscaping, but those could also be bogus expenses to siphon off the excess cash.

The credit crunch had ruined the scheme. Inability to obtain new funds must've made Tim miss payments on the older loans.

One defaulted loan had apparently led to another, a crumbling house of cards. Tim's numerous companies—both real and bogus—had isolated each other from the deceit and the defaults. With no assets in the borrowing company, the lender would've been forced to write off the defaulted note. So far, there had been no pressure on the other operating companies—at least none Tim had admitted. How long would that continue?

Tracing the transactions would take weeks, maybe months. Forms. Documents. Deposits. Wire transfers. Checks. And someone had already destroyed huge sections of the paper trail, making it even harder.

How deeply was Alex involved? It would be so easy for him to flush cash through the restaurant. Had the whole thing—his personal interest in her, the dates—simply been a ruse? Had he intended to sweep her off her feet to keep her from looking too closely at the company's finances? Was that why he'd pushed so hard to keep seeing her, even after she'd broken up with him?

And what about Marcy? She must have known about the scheme. In addition to the fictitious employees Marcy had signed up, clearly she'd been the one picking up the mail and helping Tim cover his tracks. Had she been picking up and depositing the sham payroll checks, too? Holly had no idea how involved Marcy had been or her exact role in the fraud. The knowledge still squeezed her heart.

Could Tim or Alex have killed Marcy? JC's comment about the men saving their asses reverberated in her mind. The detective was the one person she could talk to about this—but the last one she should tell.

She still had nothing that directly connected either man to Marcy's murder.

As for the loans, it wasn't illegal to borrow money. Or to use the proceeds to pay off other debt. But the web of deceit the men had constructed—she shook her head. If not out and out fraud, it was certainly the height of bad management. Then there was the loan package for the nonexistent development. That couldn't be explained away by incompetence.

Holly glanced at the tote bag that concealed the document copies she'd made. She'd have to wait until Monday to contact the lenders. Tim would fire Desert Accounting after he found out what she'd done, but she'd beat him to that punch. She'd type up a resignation letter and hand it to him right after she called the banks.

Another realization jolted her. Desert Accounting did the bookkeeping and tax work for Stevens Ventures—compilations, quarterly filings, federal and state taxes, and withholdings. How had she overlooked the obvious? In order to obtain the loans, the lenders would have required audited financial statements. With the bogus companies, she hadn't done the work, but Tim could've used Desert Accounting's unaudited reports as a starting point.

Photoshopped her signature onto an audit opinion.

Implicated her in the whole illegal business.

If she were a guy, she'd be sweating. Instead, her stomach hurt. How much of the fraud had Tim and Alex tried to hide behind Desert Accounting's skirts?

The men could ruin her family.

It didn't matter that they'd hidden whatever scheme they were running from her. If Desert Accounting signed returns for the fraudulent companies, she and her mother were toast. IRS penalties at a minimum. Possible criminal charges. God help them if somehow the lenders had relied on anything her firm prepared.

When had it started? As far as she knew, Desert Accounting had audited only one Stevens Ventures operating company last year. Her auditors would've found fraud if it had occurred there. She'd found it in the bogus ones without really wanting to.

A portion of the tension she carried slid off her shoulders. Tim and maybe Alex could go to hell, but at least they wouldn't take Desert Accounting with them.

She looked in the mirror again. A black SUV closed on her BMW. As far as she could tell, this SUV was both childless and dogless. Dark tinted windows obscured her view of the driver.

The SUV's black-and-chrome grill loomed large in her mirror. Her Beemer jumped as the larger vehicle jammed her bumper. Her head snapped through a whiplash crack.

"What the hell?" She slapped both hands onto the wheel, ignoring the spike of pain from her injured palm. The BMW fishtailed, then straightened.

With a quick location check on the SUV—still behind her—she released the wheel long enough to tap the Bluetooth. "Emergency."

Silence.

"Dammit!" She'd never programmed the emergency operator into her voice contact list.

No way could she take her hands off the wheel to punch in the emergency code.

She floored the accelerator, begging every horse under the BMW's hood to run like hellhounds were after them. She'd kiss any highway patrolman who stopped her for speeding. "Go, car!"

Her gaze darted between the road and the mirror. The exit for the Port of Benton was just ahead. Other than the closed Desert Wind tasting room, there was no obvious sanctuary near the off-ramp. If she could make it to Gibbons, the busy truck stop there offered people and buildings.

The front end of the Beemer shimmed. She eased up on the accelerator and fought for control.

Where was the SUV?

She checked the mirrors.

There.

Gaining on her.

Beside her.

Another neck-cracking, heart-stopping, slam.

The BMW jumped sideways. She torqued the wheel, turned into the spin, and resisted the urge to stomp her brakes.

The front end shook, the damaged tire unforgiving. The car straightened, then slid in the opposite direction.

Time slowed. Discrete images appeared in her window. A road sign flashed past. A car horn blared.

Frightened faces at a window.

Squeal of brakes. Rocks. Sagebrush.

Snapshots of disaster.

The car spun across the median and into oncoming traffic.

An air horn blasted.

Holly closed her eyes, braced for a losing battle with the oncoming 18-wheeler.

Chapter Forty

Holly opened her eyes, intensely aware of the quiet.

She stared straight ahead, afraid to move. Barren brown hills, wrinkled by erosion, filled the visible horizon. This wasn't how she'd envisioned heaven.

Small noises intruded. Creak and tick of metal. Traffic that sounded far, far away. She squinted against the afternoon light. Her sunglasses were gone and her nose throbbed. The Beemer's air bags dangled from the doorframe and flopped across her steering wheel like a spent condom. Tiny squares of blue-tinted safety glass littered her lap.

"Holly."

She turned her head and recoiled. Frank Phalen stood beside her door. It wasn't heaven, it was hell.

He reached through the empty window frame. "You're bleeding."

She screamed and jerked away. "Don't touch me." She fumbled with her seatbelt, dislodging glass and airbag powder.

She scrambled across the console to the passenger seat. "Get away. You tried to kill me."

"I didn't try...I'd never hurt you."

Since when? Her panicked brain ping-ponged between options. Stay? Run? Safer in the car?

"I'm trying to protect you—don't go to that house again."

"What? You're following me?" How long has *that* been going on? "You can't do that."

His hand slashed sideways, impatient. "You can't get involved with that guy."

"Which guy?"

"The one with the place in Yakima. I've seen you with him in the parking lot at your office. He's scum. He's married."

"I'm not involved with Tim."

"Marcy was. Women make stupid choices."

"And you know that how?" Ignoring the stupid comment—who cared what he thought?—the only way he'd know about Marcy, Tim, and the Yakima office would be if he'd followed Marcy. "Holy crap. You killed Marcy?" She fumbled with the door handle. Farther away from him sounded like a great idea. Several cars had stopped on the highway, trapped behind the wrecked 18-wheeler. There'd be people... He wouldn't kill her in front of witnesses.

"Of course I didn't kill her." Frank looked back at the highway, worry wrinkling his forehead. "I thought maybe Marcy and I could start something, but then I found out about Stevens. When you came looking for me at the casino, I knew she'd just been a distraction."

Stupid door—it wouldn't open. She jerked the handle and shoved with her shoulder. "I didn't look for you."

If she'd had any idea he worked at the Tom Tom she'd have forced Rick to take over the project.

He cocked his head, listening. Sirens sounded in the distance.

Thank you, God.

"I can't be here when Patrol arrives." He shoved a paper through the window opening.

"What—?"

"Black vehicle." He dropped the note onto the driver's seat, turned and sprinted toward a black Jeep parked on the shoulder. He roared away as a highway patrol cruiser slewed to a stop.

Mouth open, Holly looked from the disappearing Jeep to the officer who was talking on his radio and finally at the paper. A series of letters and numbers were scrawled across it. Like she needed another mystery.

A moment later, the driver's door wrenched open. "Are you all right?"

She looked into the concerned eyes of a state patrolman. "No, I'm not all right. He tried to kill me!"

"Who?" The officer's hand dropped to his pistol. He spun, apparently checking for threats.

"Frank Phalen."

The officer turned back to her. "There's no one here."

"Frank was right here." She pointed at the spot the cop now occupied. She wasn't delusional.

He studied her bandaged face and blood-smeared nose. "Did you hit your head?"

"The air bag punched me, but I know what I saw."

She looked past the officer to the collection of cars, trucks, and vans stacked up behind the jackknifed 18-wheeler. "Didn't you see him leave? The black Jeep?"

"Why don't you tell me what you think you saw?" the officer began,

Holly sighed. Some things never changed. Policemen always answered a question with a question. "Frank gave me that paper."

The officer studied the page. "What is this?"

Like she knew? "He said, 'black vehicle.' I don't know if he meant his black Jeep or another car or something else entirely, like his contact information, or God knows what." She edged back over the console, ready to climb from the car. Tiny demons jumped up and down, jabbing their pitchforks into her neck and shoulders. She winced.

The officer stopped her. "Wait here for the EMTs. Go ahead with your story."

She sank into the driver's seat. "One minute, everything was fine. The next, a black SUV, at least I think it was an SUV"—*Could it have been a Jeep?*—"was right on top of me. It hit my car, twice. The last thing I remember was the front end of a big truck coming at me."

She swallowed and considered the possible outcomes of a truck versus BMW encounter. She glanced again at the highway and grimaced at the twinge in her neck. Most likely the truck jackknifed when the driver tried to avoid her spinning car. "Is the trucker okay?"

"He's fine. Now about this SUV. Did you get the license plate? Can you describe the driver?"

Like she'd had a chance to see any of that?

~$~

A tow truck had hauled her battered car back to the highway and the worst of the traffic had cleared by the time the officers were satisfied with her statement. After a quick but thorough exam in the Beemer's front seat, the EMT deposited Holly on the back step of the medical van. He'd finished his examination and was suggesting follow-up care when the state patrolman, the one named Nunez, returned. "I have a call for you."

"For me?" She'd have scrunched her forehead if it didn't hurt so much.

She trailed the officer to his cruiser.

"Go ahead, put him through," Nunez said into the car's radio. He handed the microphone to her and showed her how to toggle the switch to talk.

"Hello?" she asked, feeling rather foolish.

There was a burst of static. "Are you okay?" Concern colored JC's tone a warm shade.

She nearly dropped the microphone.

Wondering if every policeman on duty could hear them, she said, "I've been better."

"What happened this time?"

"It wasn't my fault."

"What happened?" Exaggerated patience from JC.

"A car hit me. And Frank was here."

"You told me on Thursday you thought you saw him."

"No, I mean now."

"Is he the one who hit you?" JC's tone sharpened.

"I don't know. I don't think so."

"Go straight home and stay there. I'll be there as soon as I can."

Prickles rose all over her. The guy was a tyrant, but she was not going to argue with him over a police radio. "Call first, Julius Caesar Dimitrak."

She dropped the microphone on the driver's seat. The other cops didn't know his name wasn't Julius Caesar.

He could have fun living that one down.

Chapter Forty-one

Holly slapped the paint roller against the living room wall and concentrated on covering another section. At least she'd finished the tedious part—cutting in the trim—yesterday. Rolling the walls was mindless, which was about all she could handle at the moment. Ibuprofen had blunted the headache and sore muscles. And if her hot water heater cooperated, she could take a long hot bath when she finished.

She was at home because she wanted to be—because she had to finish painting the frickin' wall before the carpet guy showed up—*not* because JC had told her to be there.

She wasn't stupid. Two unprovoked, potentially fatal car incidents in three days defied all possible coincidences. But the SUV ramming her on the way home from Yakima didn't make sense. With all the stops she'd made on the way to the Stevens Ventures satellite office, no one could've followed her without her noticing, and she hadn't been challenged at the Yakima site.

She smoothed the blotch of paint, considering possibilities. Frank had known about the Yakima office.

So did Tim.

And Alex.

For all she knew, Lee Alders had found out about the place too.

Any one of them could've seen her car parked in front of it.

On autopilot, she rolled paint over the wall. Did Marcy's murderer think she knew his identity? Sure, she had bits and pieces, but nothing that added up to a cohesive whole. She couldn't expose the killer.

So use your intellect and analytical skills.

Who might come after her? Tim? She wasn't sure where he stood on the Who Killed Marcy list, but was he the one creating all the "accidents" she'd had that week?

She'd worried from the beginning about Marcy and Tim. The jerk was cheating on his wife. Thinking about leaving Nicole when she might be pregnant. And stealing from banks. Why was money so damned important to him in the first place?

Holly reloaded the roller and decided she didn't care why he was stealing. Her question was whether Tim suspected that she suspected him of fraud.

And what would he do if he did?

Would he try to kill her? All he had to do was fire her and it would cut off her access to his records. He'd never struck her as having enough intestinal fortitude to kill someone. It took a certain amount of grit to deliberately run over somebody. And since he'd skipped their meeting, he wouldn't know about her concerns in the first place.

Would he?

She adjusted her grip on the roller handle and tried to focus on painting, but her mind kept churning. For a long time she painted and thought about Alex. He had a temper and liked to yell, but as far as she knew, he was all talk. He seemed to enjoy challenging her up front and personally. If he thought she was getting too close to facts he wanted covered, he'd get in her face about it.

Unless his mama told him not to.

She poured more paint into the pan and tackled the final wall section.

Okay, she really wanted the villain to be Lee Alders. The bastard beat both his wife and the court system in the Nyland lawsuit. She wanted him to pay for something.

She didn't know what Lee would do if he thought she was a threat, but the sneak attack today sounded like something he'd orchestrate. She might've registered on the man's radar since she'd stirred up Yessica over the divorce and the will. But wasn't he still missing, with how many policemen looking for him?

Frank was the wild card. She remembered his verbal threats when she'd tried to break up with him. JC had warned her that Frank might come after her about losing his job in Seattle. His call and the flowers made it seem like he thought he was still in love with her though. Frank didn't know about Alex or JC, so he wouldn't have lashed out in a jealous rage. Although he'd mentioned seeing her with Tim in the parking lot...

If he was following her, would he have seen Thursday's session with JC? Or Alex's showdown on Friday morning?

Frank wouldn't have reacted well to seeing her with either man.

And what was up with that weird conversation after the wreck? He'd scared the crap out of her, but he seemed to think he was looking out for her. That had been his excuse in Seattle for following her around. Damn, why did he have to show up in Richland? Was it a coincidence or had he followed her from Seattle? And why had he run away instead of telling the police what he saw?

She stopped, roller frozen in place. What if the assorted vehicle incidents were completely unrelated to Marcy's death? Had she pissed off another client?

No. Desert Accounting's clients—other than maybe Tim—

were happy.

She moved ahead, swinging the roller in a long W. Everything—all the weirdness of the week—was tangled together. If she could pull the right thread, maybe the mess would unravel and she could see it clearly.

Names and motives churned as she painted her way across the wall, but she didn't have any clearer idea who'd attacked her than she did when she'd started. She made the last pass with the roller, then turned and surveyed the room. Creamy white walls reflected the sunlight streaming through the oversized windows and lit the interior, making the space look bigger.

Not bad.

Her phone chirped. She fished it from her pocket and checked the screen. Blocked number.

No way.

She stuffed it back into her jeans and reached for the roller. Cleanup sucked, but it was part of the process.

The phone chirped again. The screen again announced, "Blocked number."

Wrong number? Reporter? Sales pitch? Frank Phalen?

Irritated—and determined to be strong—she opened the connection. "Who is this?"

"Are you okay? Why didn't you answer before?" JC's rapid questions didn't disguise his concerned tone.

"The number was blocked."

A pause. "Good point. Sorry. I forgot to override it."

Part of her was still pissed he'd tried to give her an order that morning, but she actually liked that he was worried, which was rather disturbing. And damn, had he really said the word "sorry"?

"How's your head?"

Her fingers touched her nose and the bandage from Thursday's gash. Today's close encounter with the air bag hadn't helped either one. She channeled her best airhead. "There are these voices..."

"That's a relief. Now you have somebody else to call up and pester."

"Don't you have somewhere you're supposed to be?" she said dryly. "Like, I don't know, catching criminals?"

"I needed to check on you."

Needed to? "Check on, or check *up* on? Admit it, you wanted to make sure I was at home."

"C'mon, Holly. Be reasonable. I can't do my job if I'm worried about you."

"So, is half the police force in two counties listening to this conversation?"

She felt JC's silent count to ten. "I tried your cell, but no one answered. Using the radio was the fastest way to get in touch with you. Nunez is a friend. He patched the call through."

Damn. Her cell *had* been in the car after the EMT moved her to the ambulance. "Having helpful friends is nice, but why would a highway patrol officer know to contact you in the first place, when I had a wreck? I didn't ask him to."

"Ah...yeah. About that. I put a code in your file."

"I have a file? As in, the police have a file on me?"

"More like a flag."

She ground her teeth. "A flag."

"On your license."

"Let me get this straight. You coded my driver's license with your contact information?" She didn't know whether to be flattered or furious. "When did you plan to share that little detail?"

"Now sounds like a great time." From his tone, if he were standing in front of her, both of his dimples would be on display.

She laughed in spite of herself. "Uh-huh."

"The state patrol turned your latest incident over to us. We'll consolidate the cases."

That took her aback. "You really think they're related?" She could almost see JC trying not to make a smartass remark and said, "I'm not that dense. I realize they're probably related, but the cars were different. I seem to be the common element."

"I wish today's incident was a coincidence, rather than because you disobeyed my direct order to stay out of my investigation."

"Excuse me? Direct order? I don't think so. And for the last time, I am *not* running around asking people where they were the day Marcy was killed."

Someone spoke in the background and JC muffled the phone. "I have to go. I'll come by and check on you later. If that's okay with you," he added in a tone that could be polite or smartass, depending on the way she interpreted it.

"Yeah. About that. I have plans for this evening."

"Cancel them."

"I'll be with friends. Being with them is better than being here alone if that asshole comes after me."

"Holly." Exasperation morphed into cop mode. "Which asshole are you referring to?"

"Frank Phalen."

There was a beat of silence. "And?"

"You did tell me to let you know if Frank contacted me. I told you he was at the wreck, but he sent flowers too."

"When? Where?"

"To the office yesterday, but I didn't figure it out until today."

"Trust me, I intend to interview him."

From JC's grim tone, she almost wished she could be there to see the confrontation. There was no question who'd win that battle.

"Phalen might've sent the flowers to the office because he

doesn't know where you live. You're not listed in the phone directory."

And JC knew that how? She let that one pass.

"If he's out there looking to make trouble, I want you to stay home."

"I hear what you're saying, but I'm going to Bookwalter with my friends. I'll be safer there with people around me."

"How are you getting there? Your car's totaled." JC clearly realized he wasn't going to win this battle.

"They have this amazing invention called a rental car. They even bring it to you. Of course, my insurance company would only spring for an econobox."

"At least it isn't as distinctive as your BMW. It'll be harder for the next maniac to spot."

"Especially since it'll be sitting in my driveway. Gwen and Laurie are picking me up."

"If you insist on going, wait for me at the winery. I'll meet you there as soon as we finish here and give you a ride home."

"That isn't necessary."

"Yes, it is. You're necessary."

Before she could respond to *that* cryptic remark, he said, "We need to finish the conversation we started Friday night."

Her heart stopped beating and she stood there with her mouth hanging open. A guy who actually wanted to talk?

Wow. Hell really *could* freeze over.

Chapter Forty-two

Saturday night

Holly watched the flickering flames in Bookwalter's fire pit. Propane heaters hissed discreetly from the terrace edges. Vines climbed the latticed windbreak. The remaining leaves shifted in the faint breeze, a soft rustling counterpart to the patter of conversations and light jazz piped through the outside speakers.

The size of their group ebbed and flowed as friends stopped to chat and then moved on. Someone on the other side of the fire pit called, "Holly, I heard you had a wreck today. What happened?"

She remembered not to shake her head. "Ugh, let's talk about something else."

Laurie elbowed her in the ribs.

"What?" Holly would've poked her back if Laurie's foot weren't propped on a bench, making her look especially vulnerable. Her friend's crutches leaned against the windbreak and a heavy cast encased her elevated ankle. "There's a difference between bottling everything up and not talking about something because it was terrifying and you'd rather not re-experience it."

"Ooh. An unsolicited admission of feelings. I feel like Yoda, or was it the old guy in *The Karate Kid*? 'My work here is done.' "

She leaned closer and whispered, "One more thing. Quit feeling guilty. It's working for me." Looking like a blue-haired elfin sprite, Laurie smiled at a cute blond guy who handed her a glass of white wine and pulled a chair close beside her.

Conversation moved to the upcoming Wine Harvest celebration, the artists' open gallery tour, and whether the area could support the proposed water park and how to pay for it. Holly let the voices move past her, punctuated by pops from the fire and bursts of music when the wine-bar door opened.

"Since you're giving all this up, you must really miss it," Laurie remarked quietly.

Holly turned to her best friend. "Miss what?"

Laurie gave her a *Well, duh?* expression. "Ever since you got here, you've been saying you couldn't wait to get back to Seattle."

"I do miss the restaurants and shopping."

"I meant to your job. It always sounded so impressive. Megadollar wheeling and dealing. Hanging out with the movers and shakers."

Holly shrugged. "I really don't miss the pressure or the hours."

"What about the challenge? I mean, a local practice has to be a step down by comparison."

"Maybe what I do here isn't glamorous, but I like getting to know the clients, helping them with their business. I'm having fun working on my house. And I have time for stuff like the book club. When people don't try to run over us." There were good things here. World-class vineyards. Live jazz. Friends who weren't ready to cut her throat on the next deal.

"That rather sucked, but is that why I caught you staring into the fire like Little Orphan Annie? Could it possibly be you'll miss what you found here when you leave?"

Holly shifted in her chair. JC's words echoed. *We didn't finish our conversation.* "I thought working all the time was the reason I hadn't found anybody special. I figured there'd be plenty of time, that eventually…"

"You'd meet Mr. Right?"

"I know it's stupid. But…" She sighed. "I'm almost thirty and I'm going home alone to my mother's cat. How pathetic is that?"

"Totally. Especially since your mother took the cat home when she brought over chicken soup. You don't even have the fur ball."

Holly rolled her eyes and picked up her wine glass. "Smartass."

"Seriously, don't settle for just anyone. We both know it's always been JC."

She nearly choked on her sip of wine. "You're imagining things again."

"JC was doing some major hovering action Thursday night."

"If he was hovering, it's because he wants to catch me doing something wrong."

Laurie leaned close. Her eyes gleamed with conspiratorial fun. "It looked to me like he wanted to catch you doing something naughty, but it's only illegal in certain states."

Holly laughed. "That part I might not mind."

"Let's not forget what I interrupted last night."

She quit laughing. It would be all or nothing with JC. There'd be no half-assed dating, marking time as she'd done with Alex. If she planned to go back to Seattle, JC was out of the picture. Permanently.

Probably.

Maybe.

And if she stayed? She'd seen things this week to admire in the man. Could they figure out a way to make a relationship work?

Laurie was looking at her expectantly. "Well?"

Unilateral decisions had landed her in this position to begin with. She still had no idea what to tell JC when they resumed their conversation. Communication and trust. Identifying the core issues was one thing. Doing something about them was the real challenge.

"I'm going to the ladies' room. Don't do anything with Blond Guy you'll regret while I'm gone."

"Who's going to regret anything?"

~$~

Holly stepped out of the restroom stall, crossed to the sink, and checked her image in the mirror. Color brightened her cheeks and a spark lit her eyes. Refusing to cower at home felt as though she were making a statement. She wouldn't be intimidated or made a prisoner by fear. Tonight was all about enjoying life. No obsessing over Tim and Marcy or the fraud. Not even any worries about Frank.

She had to admit Laurie was right about one thing. Having JC and the Richland cops watching out for Frank—and her—meant she didn't have to constantly watch her own back. In spite of the ongoing murder investigation, which she would happily leave to the cops for the next few days, she felt more relaxed than she'd been in months.

The outer door opened behind her. The chilly blast had nothing to do with the air temperature. Nicole appeared in the mirror behind her, her eyes narrowed. "Leave my husband alone."

Holly reached for a paper towel. Nicole was not going to ruin her evening. This misunderstanding had to end. Remembering how angry she'd been at Meredith—okay, that bitch really *had* snaked her man—she could understand Nicole's fury. But the woman had reached the wrong conclusion about what she thought she'd seen.

Since she planned to dump Tim as a client, she could approach Nicole woman-to-woman. "I don't have any designs on Tim. He doesn't interest me in the least."

"I'm not stupid. You're ruining everything." The petite blonde spun on her pretty little heel, stalked into a stall, and slammed the door.

Well, that worked just wonderfully.

"Don't worry," Holly called, feeling ridiculous and more than a little eager to leave the room. "I'll stay as far away from Tim as possible."

She jerked open the outside door and stepped into the discretely lit breezeway. Music, firelight, and laughter drifted around the corner of the building.

A man's form detached itself from the deep shadows of the terrace. Her heart leapt at the possibility it might be JC. But the reptile-fearing remnant of her brain screamed, *Run away!*

"I need to talk to you."

A different set of warning bells rang. She glanced over her shoulder toward the restroom. She had no interest in feeding Nicole's delusion. "Call Tracey and make an appointment."

She stepped toward the back patio. Tim's hand shot out, capturing her elbow. "No, now. You have to stop."

"Let go of me."

She tugged her arm, but he pulled her closer. His voice dropped to a hoarse whisper. "I'll fix it, but you have to stop digging into everything."

Holly froze. Why had she thought she could do the cloak and dagger thing? How many times had she complained she couldn't make a move without half the town commenting? Of course he'd noticed she was asking too many questions about him.

Did he know about her visit to Yakima?

Had *Tim* been driving the SUV?

"I did not kill Marcy, but all the noise you're making could bring the cops down on my head."

She pried his fingers off her arm. "Then do the right thing."

"I will. I promise. Just give me some time."

"Everything okay?" A man, one of the group from the fire pit, stepped onto the terrace.

She could've kissed him, except the way her luck was running, his girlfriend would pick that moment to visit the restroom.

"It's fine. He's leaving." She pulled her arm free as the door to the women's restroom banged closed. *Crap*. How much of *this* conversation had Nicole heard?

Before she could say more, Nicole stepped beside her husband and threaded her arm through Tim's. "I'm so tired, honey. I need to go home."

Both men turned their attention to the petite woman, who looked fragile and beautiful in the dim light. Holly took another step away from the couple.

"Negative people ruin the evening." She shot a glance at Holly before nestling her head on her husband's shoulder.

"Whatever you want, Honey." Tim wound his arm around her shoulders and the pair headed toward the parking lot.

"What was that about?" Her rescuer gave her a curious glance.

For a second, she wanted to tell him everything, Tim and the fraud, whether Marcy was involved, and how much Nicole knew or suspected, but she bit her tongue. The guy was a complete stranger. "Damned if I know."

They watched Tim bundle Nicole into the front seat of his Mercedes. "That is one weird woman." He shrugged and grinned. "I never went for the helpless waif routine."

Finally, someone else saw through Nicole's act. Not that it helped Holly deal with the deluded woman. She gave him a grateful smile before she turned back to the fire pit. "Thanks for the rescue."

Chapter Forty-three

The jazz trio playing inside the wine bar finished their last set.

"Are you ready to go?" Laurie asked Holly.

Gwen hovered on the other side of the chair, purse slung over her shoulder.

Holly glanced around the back patio. Several other people drained their glasses and rose, preparing to leave as well. "Well...I'm supposed to meet somebody here."

"Who?" Laurie's eyebrows rose as understanding dawned. "JC. Why didn't you say something earlier?"

"Because I didn't want to have this conversation? It isn't like that. It's business."

Laurie's mouth twitched into a three-pointed smile. "Sure, Sweetie. Anything you say."

"Really."

"We can wait a little longer," Gwen said.

"That isn't necessary."

You're necessary, rang in her memory. What did he mean by that? "You two go home. He'll be here soon. He probably got tied up with cop stuff."

Twenty minutes later, the crowd had thinned to a few clusters that bubbled with boisterous laughter and a couple who appeared oblivious to everyone else. Holly glanced at her watch again and sighed. Now what? Keep waiting for JC, call a cab, or walk? She pulled her phone from her pocket and scrolled through her contacts to JC's name. She added his cell number to her voice contacts, quietly said his name, and waited for him to answer.

His voicemail greeted her instead.

Great. Talking? Or was his phone turned off?

"Hi, JC. It's Holly. It's getting late and it looks like you were held up somewhere. I'm going to walk home. I'll talk to you tomorrow."

~$~

"You sure you don't want me to call a cab?" The waiter's eyebrow rose.

"It's only a mile. I'll be home before the cab gets here."

Holly strode away from Bookwalter. She picked up the bike path at the intersection of Queensgate and Keene, and headed toward Badger Mountain Park. Traffic on Keene was light, an occasional car whisking past, headlights bright. She angled her head, shielding her eyes, and appreciated the wide berm which separated the paved trail from the road.

The myriad stars and a full moon made a flashlight unnecessary. Hands thrust in her jacket pockets, she threw back her head and pulled the crisp air deep into her lungs. The sharp scent of sage drifted across the field and an owl called from a tree near the creek. The bird sounded poignant rather than spooky, the darkness enveloping rather than scary.

Content to relax in the moment, she strode along the path toward the park. She could cut through it to her neighborhood or keep walking on the bike path and catch the cross street. Her cramped muscles loosened and she wondered why she didn't find time to walk more often. The neighborhood walking trails lay just outside her door, simply waiting for her to notice them.

Footsteps sounded behind her.

She jumped, turned in alarm, and registered a man on the trail. Jeans, leather jacket, bare head. Her hand pressed her thumping heart as she sighed with relief and anticipation. She knew this man's build and silhouette.

JC broke into an easy jog. "Wait up."

She braced for the safety lecture about not waiting at Bookwalter. But if he planned to finish their earlier conversation, she was willing to take a stab at the trust and control issues.

Part of her brain noted that a hundred yards behind her, a car pulled from the park's lot and accelerated toward them. The rest focused on JC. He was close enough for her to appreciate the moonlight that danced through his hair and highlighted his strong facial planes.

The car slowed. Curious—and cautious—she squinted at the harsh glare of the headlights. At least she didn't have to worry about it jumping the curb and hitting them.

The night erupted—a confusion of explosions and streaking flashes of light.

"Get down!" JC tackled her.

She slammed onto the pavement. His weight crushed the breath from her lungs. Thursday's bruises shrieked with outrage.

"Stay down."

No argument there.

The car engine roared and faded as the driver sped away. For a moment, it was completely silent, as if even the insects were astonished.

JC lifted his head and stared into her eyes. "Good Lord, woman. Who'd you piss off?"

Chapter Forty-four

JC had his cell phone out. Without waiting for her answer, he mashed a speed dial and said, "Shots fired. Shooter northbound on Keene in a dark-colored SUV. It looked like a Suburban. I didn't get the full tag, just Washington ANR24 something."

Holly gaped at him. How in the hell did he get all that? All she'd noticed was a big car and really loud noises before JC body-slammed her to the ground. Speaking of which, he was still sprawled all over her on the *really* hard pavement. And—

Oh. My. God. Did he say a dark Suburban?

"We're on the bike path, just past the new construction before you get to Badger Park."

She squirmed, trying to wiggle out from under him. He frowned at her while he listened. He shifted and settled more firmly on top. She nearly groaned aloud. Under the circumstances, she probably wasn't supposed to notice, but his body heat and intoxicating man-smell set off a different kind of lights and explosions inside her.

"Sounded like he jumped on the Interstate. See if Patrol has anybody up there." He listened a moment longer. "The intended victim was our favorite accountant."

Whatever the person on the other end said made him smile grimly. "I already asked her that."

She narrowed her eyes. He was making this *her* fault? Suddenly, she could feel every rock digging into her back and the enormous bruise that was undoubtedly forming on her butt.

He closed his cell phone, but made no effort to move.

"Get off me." She swatted his shoulder.

He blocked her arm, then pinned both of her hands to the ground. "Not until backup gets here."

She struggled, but he weighed at least sixty pounds more than she did—most of it solid muscle—and he knew all that cop stuff about subduing bad guys. "You said the shooter left. That he was on the Interstate."

"He could come back."

Mm,

"You're enjoying this way too much." She could feel entirely too much of him. And parts of her were starting to really like parts of him.

"What are you complaining about? I'm putting my life on the line here, protecting you with my body."

"Protecting me? You don't even have your gun out." She glared at him. "That better be your gun that's poking me."

"What else would it be?" He gave her the innocent-as-a-choirboy smile, with a dimple thrown in for good measure.

His face was inches from hers. She studied his expression. He wanted to kiss her. It was all over his face. But after yesterday's revelations, he might be holding back, afraid to commit. Or waiting, forcing her to make a decision.

No way was he going to make the first move.

So, she did the sensible thing.

She kissed him.

It was a simple kiss, a soft pressing of lips, but he reacted as if she'd shot him. His body jerked, then froze, and she could've sworn he quit breathing. He stared at her long enough that she worried she'd completely misread him. Then he lowered his head and kissed the fool out of her.

He let go of her arms and wrapped her up in a full-body hug that sent her hormones into overdrive and left no doubt about his interest. His fingers wove into her hair and his tongue did the tango with hers.

Holly stopped caring about the hard ground when his warm fingers worked their way under her shirt. Her hands slid under his jacket and explored the wonderful muscles in his shoulders. Just about the time she wondered if the texture of his skin was as fantastic as it had been in college, she heard the unmistakable scream of an approaching siren.

JC heard it, too. He turned his head, listened for a heartbeat which, given the way both of their hearts were pounding, lasted a nanosecond. "Shit."

He scrambled to his feet, then reached down and hauled her upright. They were still straightening clothes and brushing off road grit when the first patrol car swooped to the curb.

Blue lights dancing from the rooftop flashers nearly blinded her night-sensitized eyes, but she did a quick personal inventory. All their clothes were intact. Well, mostly intact. JC had managed to unfasten half her shirt's buttons. She tugged her jacket's zipper higher, and glanced at him. He had an impressive bulge in his personal region, but maybe whoever was in the police car wouldn't notice. An uncomfortable expression crossed his face, like he'd love to adjust something, and she wondered if he was still a boxer guy.

Before she could consider the possibilities, his face transformed—it took maybe two seconds—and he turned into Detective Dimitrak.

Okay, fine. Let's all pretend nothing happened.

She crossed her arms, then brushed more road grit off her

elbow.

Wait a minute. What *did* just happen?

She gave JC an appalled look. She'd actually kissed him. On purpose. And wow. He was an even better kisser than she remembered. After all her don't-want-to-get-involved-with-him insistence, what had she been thinking? She *hadn't* been thinking. That always got her in trouble. Kissing him was complete insanity, no doubt sparked by the fact that, oh, dear God, somebody just shot at her.

That obvious fact, which she'd effectively ignored until that moment, slammed into her with the same stop-your-breath impact as JC knocking her onto the bike path.

Another patrol car slewed to a stop, closely followed by a big black Ford 4x4. After Thursday night, she knew what its arrival meant. She grabbed onto the irrelevant distraction, refusing to think about the other…things.

The 4x4 was the squad leader's vehicle. The sergeant had arrived to take charge. If this was going to turn into the same kind of circus as the incidents at the library parking lot and beside the Interstate—with a sinking heart, she saw it headed straight down that path—the captain and the press were about five minutes behind the sergeant. Shootings were still rare enough in Richland that *everybody* showed up at the scene of one.

JC was talking cop stuff with the sergeant. Two patrol officers bracketed her, their attention focused outward, alert for another attack.

She stood at the edge of their circle of activity, trying to simultaneously not think about the bullets and figure out what had happened on the bike path. The unbelievable kiss simply had to wait its turn. She didn't want to think about it, analyze it, blush over it, regret it, do it again really soon, or any of the other hundred possibilities clamoring for her attention. For at least a few minutes, she had to focus on the other part. The part where some psycho in an SUV had shot at her.

Shot, as in bullets.

As in bang, bang, you're dead.

Dead. *Like Marcy.*

The fine trembling began. She really had to learn to deal with the adrenaline rush and the corresponding whole-body-shut-down-in-shock-because-it-didn't-want-to-deal-with-reality thing. By now, she should be getting a handle on that.

She had good reflexes. Thursday night in the parking lot she'd jumped out of the truck's way and leapt sideways between two vehicles, in a move her Zumba instructor would've applauded. But nobody dodged bullets. Whoever was in that SUV tonight was simply a lousy shot.

"Holly?" JC's voice intruded.

She blinked and discovered the cops were all staring at her. An eerie calm settled over her, even as her body continued to shake with reaction.

"What do you remember?" he asked.

She sucked in a deep breath and tried to keep her voice steady. She was not going to let them treat her like an hysterical female. "I was waiting for you to catch up with me. The car pulled over to the side of the road. It didn't stop, just slowed down. The lights were bright—my eyes were adjusted to the dark—so I put up my hand to shield them. I noticed the passenger window was down, because who drives around this time of year with the window open?"

"Are you sure?" another patrol officer asked. He looked at JC for confirmation.

JC nodded and lifted his arm, miming the shooter's probable actions. "That's why there were only three shots. The driver shot through the open window."

He pointed his arm. "Bang."

He moved halfway through the shallow arc. "Bang."

He swept through the rest of the turn. "Bang. If it had been someone sitting in the passenger seat, they'd have had their arm out the window. They'd have kept shooting even after they passed us. The driver couldn't risk putting a bullet hole in his own car. It's hell to explain those later."

She ran the movie in her head. Two converging figures on the bike path. The moving vehicle approaching. It was a math problem. She stifled the urge to giggle. If a car leaves the park and travels north at forty miles per hour and the walkers go south at three miles per hour, how many bullets can the driver shoot as he passes?

Three.

Her hands shook as the reality of the situation met up with her imagination.

"We're never going to find the slugs," one of the patrol officers said. He swung a flashlight over the tumbled heaps of cracked basalt and granite, sage clumps and tumbleweeds that littered the acreage beyond the bike path. "Not without a metal detector."

"Could be worse." A sudden smile quirked JC's lips. His dimples flashed and Holly's heart did an irreverent pitty-pat. "Another five minutes and we'd have been by the irrigation canal. When you're crawling all over that field, remind yourself you could be up to your ass in duck crap and rotting cattails."

The cop looked as though he would've said something if the sergeant weren't standing right there. One of the other guys coughed, as if covering a laugh. The captain—when had he finally shown up? —said, "Let's remember we're dealing with an attempted homicide here."

Holly's breath stopped. Attempted homicide.

Attempted murder.

Her stomach felt sick and her knees seemed wobbly all of a sudden. The reality she was trying to avoid hit her upside of the head with the subtlety of a baseball bat. *She could be dead right now.*

She was alive only because someone hadn't wanted to shoot holes in their car.

"Holly?" JC had hold of her arm. "Let's go to the car and sit down."

She meant to shake her head—she wasn't sure she could walk—but he practically lifted her off her feet. The next thing she knew, she was in the backseat of the 4x4. The sergeant had left it running with the heat going full blast. At least that's what she told herself when she felt sweat bead along her hairline. It was too warm in the car. She couldn't catch her breath.

"Put your head between your knees." JC sat beside her, gripping her neck. He nudged her forward. "The windows are tinted. No one can see."

Her body folded over and she sucked in air until the spinning stopped. His hand stroked her back. She'd just started to relax when she heard the front-door latch click. JC's hand retracted and the door opened. Bright light flooded the interior.

Holly squinched her eyes closed.

"She okay?" The captain peered over the front seat.

If there was one thing she hated—almost as much as being shot at—it was people talking about her as if she weren't present. She sat up. "I'm fine."

Captain Blake—he'd introduced himself at some point— studied her a moment, then nodded. "This is what we're going to do. Officer Mittemayer is going to take Detective Dimitrak's statement, then he'll drop the detective at Bookwalter so he can get his car."

Holly could already foresee the guy's first question: Why were you walking instead of in JC's car?

"You'll go to the station, where we'll take your statement. Detective Dimitrak said he'd make sure you get home safely. We'll increase the patrol through Hills West tonight, move the floater to that sector to double the coverage, but if you'd prefer to stay with a friend, I'm sure the detective will take you there."

The lengthy session Thursday night with the Pasco police scrolled through Holly's memory. If she went to the station, it would be hours before they'd let her go. "Can't I give you my statement here?"

The captain twisted his mouth, as if he were actually thinking about it, then shook his head. "There'll be things we need to check."

"I can't tell you much." A brilliant idea occurred to her. "JC was probably the target. Some bad guy he arrested looking for revenge."

JC shifted on the seat beside her, but she ignored him.

Captain Blake looked grim, the way only a policeman can. "We've already considered that possibility."

"And dismissed it," Holly finished the sentence for him. With the week she was having, *of course* she was the automatic suspect.

Victim suspect.

At least it wasn't *suspect*, suspect.

Captain Blake turned his head, responding to one of the officers outside the car.

Damn. She sank against the seatback. A wildly irrational impression of skanky criminals occupying the seat rocketed her away from the vinyl. A shudder shimmied across her shoulders.

"This vehicle isn't used for transporting people in custody," JC said, reading her mind.

Another patrol officer approached the 4x4.

"That's my ride," JC told her.

341

She nodded. "I'll be fine," she said, reading his. Maybe if she kept saying it, she could make it be true.

"It'll be okay," he said softly. With his back to the other officers, his eyes caressed her the way he obviously felt he couldn't physically. "I'll be right behind you. I know you're exhausted. I won't let them keep you all night."

She wanted to touch him, to stroke his cheek and thank him for his thoughtfulness, for protecting her. Captain Blake clearly wasn't going to give them that kind of personal time.

"A word of advice."

At his dry tone, she gave JC a startled glance. "What?"

"Don't hit anybody if they ask a question you don't like." He winked, breaking the spell. He popped open his door as the sergeant took his position behind the wheel. "Cops hate it when you hit them."

"I'll keep that in mind," she said before both doors clicked shut. The dome light extinguished, leaving only the flashing lights of the crime scene vehicles. With a sigh, Holly collapsed against the still-suspect backseat.

Criminal cooties were the least of her worries right now.

Chapter Forty-five

Hours later, Holly trailed JC out of the police station, so tired she could barely put one foot in front of the other. Captain Blake, a patrol officer, and some guy who looked like he'd been dragged out of bed and wasn't happy about it, had made her go over her story about fifty times. They'd asked her the same question about a dozen ways.

Any idea who might want to shoot you? *No.*

Any idea who might be upset with you? *No.*

As if asking a different way might make her give them a different answer.

Have you done anything to get someone upset? *Well, duh? Apparently.*

Any idea who that might be? *No.*

Of course, she'd told them about Frank, although she couldn't quite believe he'd shoot at her. She'd asked about the paper Frank had given her, pointing out the mention of two dark-colored SUVs. To her surprise, they'd actually told her that the enigmatic scribble on the paper was a license plate number, for a vehicle registered to Stevens Ventures. A truck Tim Stevens had reported missing several days ago.

The "Tim" connection had stunned her, but...

Tim and Alex, she'd tap-danced a little there, not sure how

much she could or should say about the fraud. But she told the policemen she suspected the pair might be doing something illegal. They could get a warrant and look at the records themselves. She'd even brought up Lee Alders and the ice-climbing episode.

JC walked beside her now. If she had the energy, she'd glare at him. He looked entirely too wide awake, which meant he probably took a nap while she answered endless questions.

He opened the passenger door to his car for her, grasped her elbow while she heaved herself into the seat, then walked around to the driver's side. Somehow she wasn't surprised by the car—a Bronco—or the color—bright red. Still, she wasn't so tired she didn't notice the courtesy. When was the last time she'd seen someone open the passenger door for a woman? And why had she let him? She was capable of getting into the car under her own power.

Still, having someone take care of her was kinda nice. Not that she *needed* anyone taking care of her.

JC started the car. "You okay?"

"Let's see." She ticked the items off on her fingers. "In the past week, I've found a dead person, who turned out to be someone I knew, been trampled at a wake, nearly run over in a parking lot, practically flattened by an 18-wheeler, shot at, tackled by a cute cop, and questioned for more hours than I can count by various guys in assorted uniforms. Yeah, overall, I'd say I was great."

"A cute cop tackled you, huh?"

"I knew you'd focus on the critical element."

His dimples showed in the light from the dash, but she was too tired to react.

"Detectives notice details like that."

Her answer was a jaw-popping yawn.

The gate for the restricted parking area behind the police

station opened. He turned left onto Jadwin, then made a quick right. Figuring his car was probably free of criminal cooties, she sagged against the headrest and wondered if a five-minute nap would make her feel better or worse.

A few silent blocks later, JC pulled to the side of the road.

She tensed. *Oh, no.* She didn't want to discuss the kiss or anything else that might require more than three brain cells.

"I know this isn't the best time or place, but I need to tell you a few things."

She fought the urge to lie down on the seat and howl. He wanted to Talk About It. Which "it" didn't matter—the lecture about personal safety, questions about the psycho who apparently was stalking her, or the meaningless nature of that earth-shattering kiss.

Should she look at him or stare out the windshield? What if he wanted to apologize? What if he regretting kissing her? How embarrassing would that be? Especially after she'd slipped up and called him "cute"? She stifled a groan. "Okay."

He took a deep breath, and flexed his hands over the steering wheel. "The Richland officers think we're dating. It looked like I was walking you home and we were a little…rumpled…when they showed up. I told them we were just friends, but them thinking you're my girlfriend actually might be to your advantage."

This wasn't what she was expecting. In fact, this wasn't so bad. She turned her head and cocked an eyebrow. "Why's that?"

He smiled and his dimples did their thing. Man, she liked those little dents even when she was dead tired.

"Cops tend to take care of each other. And Holly?"

"Yeah?"

He turned to face her. "I'd like it if you'd think about that."

She gave him a puzzled look. Okay, the local police would look out for her more vigilantly if they thought she was involved with him. She could handle that. Especially since he was actually telling her about it up front.

Wait a minute. The mental light blinked on. *Was he asking her to be his girlfriend?* That sounded like a middle-school kid, not the confident detective she kept tripping over. Although right now, he didn't look especially confident.

He reached across the console and took her hand. Gently, he stroked the bandage covering her palm, slowly drew his fingers to the tips of hers. The contact cut through her fatigue and confusion and shot sparks up her arm. He took a deep breath. "I screwed up the first time we were together. We've both grown up and changed since then. Seeing you this week..."

He brought her hand to his lips and kissed the small patch of bare skin.

Her heart did a stutter-step. Was he...serious?

"That kiss tonight." He toyed with her fingers. "You're the first woman I've *really* wanted to kiss since...since I got divorced. I don't know how you feel about it, and I wasn't sure how I felt to tell you the truth, except I was thinking about it while I was waiting for you to finish your statement and I'd love to do it again. If you want to, that is."

Huh?

Her gaze moved from their intertwined hands—interesting that her brain hadn't sent "retract" signals down her arm—to his face. She couldn't be sure since the only light in the car came from the dashboard instruments, but she could've sworn he was blushing.

Who are you and what have you done with arrogant, cocky JC Dimitrak?

"Are you asking me out? Or just asking if I want to have sex?"

His mouth opened, but no words emerged. He swallowed

and tried again. "It sounded a lot better when I was practicing."

"You rehearsed that?" She had a mental flash of him trying out various phrases, but couldn't see it.

"I haven't had much—shit, this is humiliating." He snatched back his hand, jerked the car into drive, and with a chirp of tires, accelerated away from the curb.

"JC." She reached across the console and laid her hand on his arm. "I can't believe you aren't fighting off women every day, but I think I'm okay with being your girlfriend. We could try that. And we might end up having sex, but when we do, I want it to be making love. So tonight's probably not a good idea."

He turned left beside the high school, then clasped her hand and pulled it to rest on his thigh. He smiled and cut his eyes toward her. She could read the expression in them. Forget that college stuff. If the current preliminaries were any indication, they were going to really, *really* enjoy it when they did. His fingers caressed her hand and the tingling spread to other sensitive body parts. Apparently, her body wasn't as tired as her brain insisted.

JC powered onto the interstate, crossed the Yakima River, and took the Queensgate exit.

She turned over his oblique offer. It was far more interesting than the other things she could be obsessing over. She didn't want to deal with the shooting right now. Peeking at him from the corner of her eye, she found his attention on the road. His gaze alternated between the mirrors and the pavement ahead.

Just because she was scared and JC rescued her wasn't a good reason to jump into bed with him. But if he could make her melt from the things he was doing to her hand, imagine what he could do with the rest of her body.

She sat up straight. *Whoa, woman. Get a grip.*

JC rotated his hand and wrist against the steering wheel, glanced at his watch. "I'm only going to get a couple hours' sleep.

It's barely worth going to bed."

Who was going to sleep? Between the gunshots, his girlfriend offer, and that kiss, she didn't foresee peaceful slumber. But if his comment was fishing for an invitation to spend the night, she still wasn't sure it was a great idea. "Turn right here."

He flicked on the turn signal. "What are you going to do tomorrow...later today?"

Who bothered with turn signals when there wasn't another moving car in the whole neighborhood? "You mean you aren't going to tell me to stay home?"

"I've learned the futility of issuing that stellar bit of advice."

"Glad to see you're so flexible." Another yawn nearly split her face in two. "I have to go to the office for a while. You going to show up there too?"

"Too?"

"Well, you have made it kind of a habit this week."

"Oh, really?" He drove up the hill in front of her house. "What have I made a habit of doing?" He parked in her driveway.

"Following me." She opened her door and stepped out.

He got out and rounded the hood. "You make me sound like a stalker."

She dug in her purse for her keys. "So your turning up everywhere I went this week was mere coincidence?"

He dropped his arm around her shoulders. They moved up the path to her porch. His scent and warmth bypassed her brain and detonated her female parts. She wanted to wrap her arms— and legs—around him.

"I hate to pop your bubble, sweet cheeks, but Monday was work. Tuesday—the wake—was work, and so was Wednesday at Stevens' office. Thursday, the Pasco guys called me."

"Sweet cheeks?" She noticed he'd left Friday's argument— and revelations—out of the summary. "Let's not forget that flag you put on my driver's license."

She unlocked the door and turned to face him. Silently, she argued with her conscience about inviting him inside.

He pulled her close. "Are you going to be okay staying here on your own?"

"It's three o'clock in the morning. Where else am I going to go? I refuse to wake up my friends at this hour, and a hotel seems pointless."

"If you decide to stay here, I'll ask both the Benton County deputies and the Richland guys to keep an eye on you," he began.

She tensed. *Don't get mad. Talk to him.* "You know that Frank making those kinds of decisions was part of my problem with him." She looked up into his eyes and quickly added, "I know you're not like him. You're trying to protect me, which I really appreciate. Frank used his badge to try and control me."

"What are you saying?"

"Talk to me—ask me—before you decide to go do whatever you think is best."

He nodded, processing her statement. "Fair enough. Ball's in your court. I'll call them if you want me to. There is a third option, though. You could come home with me."

Her mouth dropped open. *Should've seen that coming.*

He leaned closer and his lips met hers.

It was as good as the first time. Some parts sparkled, other parts melted. Fizzy things in her brain suggested asking him into the house would be a nice idea after all. Her fingers played with his neck and hair. Apparently he liked that, because his arms tightened and he upped the voltage on the kissing until she couldn't breathe or think.

Just as she started exploring his chest, he raised his head. His eyes were dark and hooded. His heart banged against her super-sensitive breasts and another body part nudged her belly. "If we keep doing that, we're going inside. And if we go inside, I'm not leaving until tomorrow."

She blinked up at him. *Speak*, encouraged her brain. *Kiss*, urged her body. He saw it in her expression. He lowered his head again. His hands caressed her. She arched with pleasure and he groaned.

"Damn, woman. You're gonna kill me." He stepped back, releasing her. "I'll see you tomorrow. Later today. You know what I mean."

He was pointing like a bird dog, she noticed with some part of her brain. The rest of her watched with astonishment as he turned and walked to his car. What? Wait. *You can't...*

"I'll call you."

Terrific. That pretty much guaranteed neither of them would sleep tonight.

Chapter Forty-six

JC stopped at the end of her walkway, hand on his hips, staring at who knew what.

He turned.

Okay. More like it. Her smile lit a spark that ignored all that common sense stuff.

He walked toward her—and right past her. "Wait here."

"Huh?" Holly stood still for about a second, then followed him through her front door into the foyer.

He turned and pointed a finger at her. "Do not move unless I tell you to. This is a unilateral protection police decision."

Good sense warred with instinctive irritation. If there was someone in the house, she'd be both in danger and in JC's way if she followed him. Except, *wait a minute.* "This is my house, my home. Nobody has a reason to be hiding in the dark waiting for me."

JC heaved a long-suffering sigh. "Yeah, and no one had a reason to shoot at you, either. But that happened, remember?"

Like she could forget. She crossed her arms. "They could've been shooting at you. Cops have more enemies than accountants."

He rolled his eyes, turned around, and walked into the black void of her living room.

She heard him moving through the house checking rooms for

intruders, looking in closets and behind shower curtains.

Long minutes later, footsteps sounded in the living room. She swallowed, suddenly nervous. All kinds of reality had intruded while he combed through her house, including, *What in the hell was she doing with JC Dimitrak?*

What if he wanted to start up again where they'd left off? Things between them were happening too fast. She pulled the front door open. "Thanks for clearing the monsters from under the bed."

With just a few more steps, he stood in front of her. He pushed the door closed. His other hand rose and flattened against it, effectively pinning her between his arms. "Neither one of us is walking away this time."

His voice was low and deep. Heat from his body flowed over her. Her defenses crumbled faster than she could raise them.

I surrender. I'm yours.

She didn't need to say the words. They must've been written all over her. Desire flared in his eyes. He leaned closer—*oh, but he smelled good*—and his lips touched hers. It wasn't a wimpy, kissy move. It was a full-out, lust-inspiring, you're-gonna-remember-this-for-a-while kiss. Her arms wrapped around him and she gave him everything she had in response.

He groaned. His arms closed tighter around her.

Nothing had changed—and everything had changed.

Six years had passed. She'd had other lovers, but with his arms around her, his mind-blowing kisses, all her old feelings flooded back.

His hands slid down her back, cupped her butt, pressed her hips into his. His erection throbbed, hot and hard.

Oh God, but she'd missed him. Missed this.

He kissed her neck, her throat. "I've wanted you since the moment I saw you at Big Flats," he murmured against her skin.

"Hell, I've never stopped wanting you."

"Is that all this is? Wanting?"

He lifted his head and looked into her eyes. "You know there's more to it than that."

His lips claimed hers again.

Fire and need, passion and heat.

Their jackets hit the floor. He pulled her shirt free, his fingers warm against her belly. They rose, trailing ribbons of fire. His thumbs found her sensitive nipples. "I love your skin. Your breasts."

His mouth moved, suckled her through the lacy bra. Pleasure shot through her. He gave her other breast equal time before working his way back to her throat. He raised his head. His face was the picture of male gratification as he cupped her breasts. "I've dreamed about this. In my dreams, we took our time."

"Mmm."

He leaned in and kissed her again before whispering, "I don't think I can wait."

Thank God.

"Waiting's overrated." She slid her hands under his shirt, explored the length of his back. "You have on too many clothes."

In one fluid move, he jerked the shirt over his head. He had a wonderful body, hard muscle and smooth skin. Then somehow her slacks were on the floor and he stood between her legs—legs she'd wrapped around him—shifting her hips so he was exactly where she wanted him.

"Oh, God," he groaned. "Holly."

Her back pressed against the door. His warm hands caressed her. It wasn't enough.

"More, more." It came out as a muffled moan. His tongue was in her mouth again.

He made a sound that could've been her name, but she wasn't

353

sure because she'd quit thinking, quit listening, quit breathing. He shifted her weight and fumbled between them. She heard his belt jingle, the rasp of his zipper. Then his hands were on her, sweeping her panties aside.

Rational thought dragged her back from the edge of insanity. Incapable of speech, she dug her fingers into his shoulders to get his attention. *Wait.*

He thrust, and her body matched the movement, and then he was inside her, hot, hard, and oh, so male. It felt so damn good she nearly screamed with pleasure. He thrust again. Lights flashed behind her eyes and she could've orgasmed on the spot. She wanted him to keep moving so badly it was all she could do to make her mouth form the word. "Condom."

He froze.

She watched comprehension register.

"I swear I'm clean."

"That's not it."

"Oh, shit. You aren't on the pill."

She didn't need to answer.

They stared at each other.

He groaned. "Don't move. If you move, I swear I'll come. My body thinks it's eighteen again." He shifted backward with agonizing slowness.

The slow withdrawal pressed against sensitive spots and her eyes nearly rolled up in her head. "I'm going to lose it in about two seconds," she whispered.

His penis sprang free and stood between them, hot and wet. "Please tell me you have a condom." Desperation made his voice ragged.

"Don't you? I thought all guys carried them."

"I stopped years ago." He lowered her body so she stood on her feet. "Don't you have *something?*"

354

Maybe if I'd had sex in the last year. She shook her head. "Sorry." *Really* sorry.

"If I go to the store, will you promise not to move?" He jerked up his jeans, and his phone chirped. With a curse, he snatched the phone off his belt. "Dimitrak."

She was glad that growl wasn't aimed at her.

His face transformed and just like that he turned into Detective Dimitrak.

Wordlessly, he closed the phone and studied her. He might still look like the sexist man she'd ever met—dark, hooded eyes, rumpled hair, enormous erection, testosterone to his eyeballs—but she knew both of them were about to end up alone and frustrated.

"Lee Alders just surfaced."

Chapter Forty-seven

Sunday morning

Holly opened her front door and peeked outside. On the upside, no one was lurking on her front steps. In the not-so-much category, it was one of those gray mornings with fog blanketing the rivers that reminded her winter was coming. It was shaping up as a day she'd ordinarily laze in bed, except today she couldn't sleep. In the few short hours since JC had left, she'd climbed in and out of bed a dozen times, checked the locks, and watched the Richland cops cruise past.

Unlike Friday night, she'd been relieved by their presence.

She locked her front door and headed for the rental car. With a quick twist, she stuffed the Bluetooth device into her ear and dropped her phone in her pocket. She settled behind the wheel and stared at the unfamiliar controls. Where were the lights and seat adjustments?

As soon as she pulled out of the driveway, she tapped the Bluetooth. "Mother."

At her mother's groggy, "Hello," Holly glanced at the clock and winced. It was earlier than she'd realized. "Can you meet me at the office later this morning? We need to talk about Stevens

Ventures."

"Sure." Her mother sounded more awake. "Anything I need to know right now?"

She rolled the stop sign at Leslie, headed toward Gage. "It's a mess, but it'll be better if I show you. Oh, and in case there's anything on the news, there was another, um, incident last night, but I'm fine."

"*What?*" Wide-awake now.

Like her mother would let *that* slide past. "I'll tell you about it at the office."

She disconnected before her mother could ask questions.

Holly tested phrases for reassuring her mother until she reached her favorite espresso shop. "Double-shot latte, skinny, please."

She'd just climbed back into the car when a tap at her window sent her heart rate into the stratosphere and her hands into the air. Coffee surged over the rim of the cup and landed with a scalding splash on her jeans-clad knee. "Ow! Dammit!"

Nicole Stevens stood beside the passenger door. She tapped on the window again.

Holly sucked in a deep breath, and put the coffee into the cupholder. Damn. She should've gone for Spudnuts.

She poked at the buttons on the console, figuring one of them controlled the windows. The central lock clicked and released. Nicole opened the door, slid into the passenger seat, placed her Kate Spade bag on her lap, and said, "Let's go."

Holly did a complete double-take. "Damn, you scared me." Not to mention burned the crap out of her knee. "Go where? What's going on?"

Nicole's Jaguar was parked two slots away. Holly couldn't remember if it had been there when she arrived. "Do you have car trouble?"

"I need to talk to you—privately—about Tim." Nicole's fingers tightened around her huge purse, but her face remained expressionless.

Good Lord, had Nicole just found out about the fraud? About Marcy? "Do you want to sit here? Or go inside?"

"We need privacy."

It was an A or B question, but whatever.

"Just drive."

"I need to go to the office. We can talk there." Holly put the rental in reverse, backed out and headed down Steptoe. She'd hand Tim the resignation letter when he came to get his wife. "Tim can give you a ride back to your car."

"I don't want to see him right now."

Wow, Nicole must be seriously pissed at him. "What's on your mind?"

"I warned you. You didn't listen."

With a keep-your-temper-under-control sigh, Holly turned onto Columbia Trail, headed toward Highway 240. "I don't know what your problem is, but can we skip the mysterious routine? I really don't feel that great today."

"Morning sickness?" Nicole snorted derisively.

It took a second for the words to register. "I'm not pregnant. I've just had a couple of...accidents in the past few days."

"They weren't accidents."

A finger of concern ran up her spine. She gave Nicole a sharp look, but the woman was again staring straight ahead. How did Nicole know they were or weren't accidents...unless Tim was responsible and he'd told his wife.

Or...was Nicole part of it? Was she having second thoughts, bothered by the violence? "You said you wanted to talk about Tim. What's wrong? You look a little..." *Weirded out* probably wasn't the best thing to say under the circumstances. "Tired."

"Nothing's wrong. I have the perfect life. The perfect marriage."

Okay, then.

Nicole had always been a little out there, but somebody needed some serious medication. Holly wanted this whack job out of her car. Now. She stopped at the entrance to the roundabout and thought about saying, "Get out."

But if Nicole wasn't part of the fraud, that made her a victim, too. Finding out about it, or having Tim tell her he planned to divorce her, could've driven her over the edge.

Holly took a deep breath and made a decision. She'd play along, at least until they got to the office. "You're right. You're beautiful and you do indeed have a perfect life."

Hopefully, Nicole missed the sarcasm.

She watched a car enter the traffic circle and waited for it to pass. Waiting offered no insights. She had no idea how to handle the loony tunes woman. "I can tell you're upset. Do you want me to call one of your girlfriends? Tim?"

"Stay away from him." Nicole reared up in the seat. Her eyes were the kind that came with fangs and violence. "You couldn't leave things along. At first I actually thought you were like that tramp—making a play for him. I've seen you. Every time I turn around, you're all over him."

"I'm not interested in Tim. I swear. You can ask JC. That's who—"

"I should've known he'd never be interested in someone like you."

Holly let the insult slide without comment.

"Then I realized you weren't trying to ruin my marriage. You're trying to ruin Tim." Nicole opened the designer purse and pulled out a pistol. Neither the gun nor her hands were shaking.

Oh shit oh shit oh shit.

The diminutive woman lifted the pistol and pointed it directly at Holly's chest.

She'd read the thrillers, seen the movies. When the too-stupid-to-live heroine climbed into the villain's car, she always wanted to yell, "Run for it. Don't get in the car!"

Yet here she sat, already strapped into the driver's seat, while Nicole flipped a lever on the gun.

The pistol looked huge in the petite blonde's fingers, but even if she was the world's worst shot, from two feet away she'd hit a critical body part if she pulled the trigger.

A car horn sounded behind them. Holly's gaze darted from the gun to the mirror and back. Could the driver see it? Could she signal them?

Could she make a run for it?

"Uh, uh, uh." Nicole poked the pistol against Holly's ribs. "I will shoot you if you even try to open your door. Drive."

Holly actually felt the slide, the mental disconnect. Just as with her M&A analysis, distance from the scene let her assess odds. She considered and rejected options. *Jump from the car? Risk a wreck? Nicole shooting her in the close confines of the car?*

Anyway she looked at it, the cold glare of reality said she wasn't coming out of this alive.

That wasn't acceptable, so she searched for a better reality.

She pulled into the dumb-as-hell roundabout some idiot traffic planner had plopped into the busiest intersection in the city. She passed the Highway 240 connector, looping around the circle for a second pass.

"What are you doing?" Nicole shoved the pistol into her face. "Get on the highway."

Holly said a quick prayer that the gun didn't accidentally go off while Nicole was waving it around. "We need to talk about this. You know Tim loves you. He isn't having an affair with me."

She had to make Nicole see reason. She made another loop around the roundabout. "This is a big mistake. Tim loves you. He cried about your baby. He was distraught about losing it."

"I didn't lose my baby." Red, angry blotches mottled Nicole's porcelain skin.

Way to make things worse.

Panic pushed forward and Holly gave a wild look around. Why hadn't one of the other drivers noticed the crazy woman with the gun? Where was the highway patrol when you needed them? Maybe as long as she kept driving, spinning around the circle, Nicole might not notice they weren't going anywhere.

"Marcy was pregnant." Nicole spat out. She shifted in her seat, and leaned closer. "The whore."

Holly fumbled for the right words to diffuse her. "Um…"

"Why were you at that house where Tim takes his whores?"

She *knew* someone had been outside the Yakima office. "It was for work. I had to get papers from the office. Tim wasn't there."

Something flickered in the depths of those china doll eyes. Maybe Nicole believed her, but in the alternative reality she currently inhabited, it didn't compute. "Don't lie to me."

"I swear, I didn't do anything. I don't want him."

"No, you're a vindictive bitch."

The pistol pressed into her temple. She was afraid to breathe. If Nicole's finger jumped just a fraction, if they hit a pothole, she was a goner.

"I heard you claim Tim's committing fraud. He rejected you, so you're trying to ruin him."

Holly's voice emerged in a croak. "I'm not going to ruin him."

Tim did that all by himself.

"I won't let you take away everything I've worked for. I am

361

never going to be poor again." Nicole's hand didn't move. Neither did the gun. "Get on the highway." Her voice had that dead calm quality again.

There was a long silence while Holly's brain scrambled, trying to catch up and get ahead of the psycho in the next seat. With stunning, belated clarity she realized she'd been looking at the wrong Stevens. Tim may be a thief, but Nicole had killed Marcy.

Holly lifted her left hand from the wheel and pushed back her hair. As nonchalantly as she could, she tapped the Bluetooth device, activated it, and murmured, "JC."

"What did you say?"

The phone made the connection and rang. "JC Dimitrak. You should talk to him."

"Why would I talk to him?"

"Because he could lock up your crazy ass" probably wasn't the right answer. "He'll tell you I'm seeing him. We're dating."

After last night that was sorta true—it *better* be true—but who cared at this point what she said as long as they kept talking?

And breathing.

And not shooting.

She heard the rings through the earpiece. *Come on, JC. Answer the phone. Don't go to voicemail.*

The phone rang again and then JC's voice said, "I'm busy right now. I'll call you."

"Nicole, put the gun down. Please."

The voice in her ear shut up.

Nicole's expression said she wasn't paying the least bit of attention. Which would have been a good thing if it weren't for the damn pistol. She'd prefer the woman be in this time zone as long as her finger was on the trigger. "Nicole, could you at least move the gun? It's hard to drive with it in my face."

"You're doing great, Holly. I understand. You're in a car. Tell me where you are."

JC's calm voice reassured her. She was terrified if she blurted out, "Come get me," Nicole would shoot her before the cops could even turn their patrol cars in the right direction.

"Take the Kahlotus highway," Nicole said.

"The Kahlotus highway? Why do you want to go there?" she asked.

The small sigh of relief gave JC away.

Oh God, don't be worried. Be calm and strong for me, JC. Please.

"I'm notifying Washington Patrol," he said. "I'll see if Pasco has anybody near the highway."

Nicole gave her an irritated look. "You know where we're going."

"Why don't we get off here at 20th? We can get some coffee and talk this over."

"Good job, Holly. I got it. You're passing the college. Patrol is on the way." She could hear him puffing, like he was running. "Franklin County's heading in. Pasco's sending units, too. I'm getting in my car right now."

Nicole ignored her, but at least she'd lowered the pistol.

It still pointed at Holly's ribs.

Maybe Nicole's arm was getting tired. If Holly could just hold on until the police caught up...

They blew past the railroad yard on the outskirts of town. The Kahlotus exit was just ahead and she still didn't see a single police car. For one crazy moment, she thought about crashing into the underpass. The seatbelt and airbag—*did the rental have an airbag?*—would protect her, but as long as Nicole had her finger on the trigger, she wasn't going to risk a bullet to the heart.

The off-ramp looped back over the freeway. She craned her neck, hoping to see the cavalry roaring to the rescue, but all she saw were a few more econoboxes like the one she was driving plus several of the ubiquitous trucks and sport utility vehicles.

Farmland stretched to the horizon on either side of the Kahlotus highway, flat and fallow for the winter, unrelieved by a building or people. Irrigation equipment like giant fallen Tinker Toys lay atop the brown stubble of harvested crops and along the ridges of plowed fields. Nothing for even a pheasant to hide behind, much less a desperate woman.

"What's happening, Holly? Figure out a way to tell me. You can do it." JC's voice was an anchor. *A lifeline.*

She recognized the growing blue-and-white shrink-wrapped rolls of hay piled on the side of the highway, the modern version of haystacks. "Have you ever visited a dairy?" she asked Nicole. "Silverstone Dairy is a client. I'm not much into cows, but I've always thought those rolls of hay would be fun to play on."

Nicole didn't respond, but JC said, "Got it. I'm a few miles behind you."

"*How many miles?*" she wanted to scream.

The crazy blonde stared out the window, focused on something, probably the voices in her head telling her to shoot the interloper—*that would be me*—who was after her man. But if Nicole planned to shoot her, there were a few loose ends Holly wanted cleared up. "Do you know a guy named Lee Alders?"

Nicole remained silent, apparently still communicating with her internal chorus, but JC said, "Alders didn't kill Marcy. He was skiing on a glacier in northern Canada this week. He didn't know we were looking for him."

Add ruining the best sex she'd had in years to the list of reasons she didn't like Lee Alders.

But she already knew Alders wasn't the killer. The killer was sitting right beside her.

"As long as we're clearing things up," JC said. "Frank Phalen won't be bothering you again."

He won't if Nicole shoots me.

"I had a conversation with him. Didn't even need to mention the restraining order. He knows not to mess with you."

Frank is so not my problem right now. Except if she got out of this alive, Frank would still be in Richland. Was JC saying he'd reinstated the restraining order? Or gotten in Frank's face? Or…or… What could JC possibly do if Frank starting obsessing about her again? She glanced at Nicole from the corner of her eye. *Oh, God.* Talk about obsessing. The woman's lips were moving.

She had to do something. Stalling would only go so far in letting the cops catch up.

Think…prioritize…get away…the gun…

"Talk to me, Holly." JC's warm voice wasn't helping.

And say what?

Eyes straight ahead, Holly eased her hand off the steering wheel. If Nicole stayed lost in La-La Land, maybe she could grab the pistol or at least aim it in another direction. If it wasn't pointed at her ribs, she could slam on the brakes. JC couldn't be more than a few minutes away.

"Keep both hands on the wheel. It's so much safer." Nicole's blue eyes looked baby doll innocent—and china doll vacant.

They passed a stand of paper company trees, arrow straight and planted in neat rows. Holly gave them a wistful glance. Even if she made a break for their cover, Nicole would shoot her before she unbuckled her seatbelt.

Holly watched the trees dwindle in her mirror and suddenly realized where they were headed. She'd traveled this road with Alex when they went to Big Flats. "Uh, Nicole? Where exactly do you want to go?" She had no desire to hike across the fields at Big Flats, but at least there were trees and bushes to hide behind if she managed to get away.

"Don't play innocent. You know. You've been there. And I

heard you talking about the land to that guy."

Land? What guy? She searched her memory for who Nicole could have overheard her speaking with about property. There was only one possibility. Rick.

If possible, her blood ran even colder as Nicole's meaning sank in. Tim, or rather TNM Ventures, owned land upstream from Big Flats. The land where Marcy had probably been shot. She cleared the enormous lump in her throat. "Actually, I haven't been to your property on the Snake River. That is where you want to go, right?"

"They own property on the Snake?" JC's voice.

The three-sided conversation made her feel as though she had too many voices in her own head.

His calm voice continued. "Help me narrow it d—"

Silence.

The weird silence of dead air.

Her heart stopped.

She'd lost JC.

Chapter Forty-eight

JC was gone.

Holly had been dreading the inevitable call drop, praying it wouldn't happen. Coverage was spotty away from town and the Interstate. But the finality of the silent, dead air in her ear pressed a constricting band around her chest that made it almost impossible to breathe.

She was on her own.

"That's where you went with my husband. When you were sneaking around behind my back."

She snapped her attention back to her kidnapper. "How many times do I have to tell you I am *not* having an affair with Tim?"

Nicole's voice rose, shrill with agitation. "I know what you're doing."

"Calm down, Nicole. It'll be okay."

"Don't tell me what to do."

Holly shifted her gaze from the delusional woman to the business end of the pistol and back. She finally understood courage wasn't about not being scared. It was about not letting fear stop her from doing what needed to be done. Her hands clenched the steering wheel.

But what was the right thing to do when a crazy woman

locked her in a car and pointed a gun?

She had to think clearly, keep her wits, and talk her way past Nicole.

Past her gun.

Past her insanity.

Only after she survived could she give in to the need to tremble and cry.

She had too much to live for. JC's words—*You're necessary to me*—came back to her. She wanted to find out what that was all about. She wanted a chance to finish what they'd started at her front door. A chance with a man who wasn't afraid to tell her up front what he wanted.

Her.

In his life.

"Turn here." Nicole pointed at a dirt road that looked just like the dozen other dirt roads they'd passed.

No! Holly's instincts shrieked. *Keep going!*

As long as she kept driving, there would still be time. Time for the police to catch up. Time to figure out a plan. Time for JC to find her.

Nicole raised the pistol.

Holly turned onto the dirt road.

A long plume of dust followed them down the rutted lane. She hoped it would hang in the air long enough to show the police which road they'd taken. A few minutes later, the car jolted into an open area in front of a metal farm building.

She peered through the windshield. A vineyard marched down the slope to the river. Wires strung in an intricate pattern supported drooping leaves and grape clusters. Orchards climbed the hills behind the vineyard. How could any of it help her get out of this alive?

She cast a longing look at the building. The sliding doors of the barn were closed, probably locked tight.

For a nanosecond she thought about the action sequence from *Witness*—lure Nicole into the outbuilding and dump a silo's worth of grapes on her head—but she didn't think they stored grapes in silos, and Nicole wasn't dumb enough to follow her into one.

Several vehicles were parked under the attached lean-to. She ignored the tractor and focused on the white Kia. Any chance the keys were tucked above the visor? Under the floor mat?

Wait.

Marcy drove a Kia.

"Turn off the car."

End of the road. She stopped the car and turned off the engine.

Now what?

Nicole grabbed the keys. The pistol never wavered.

Holly released the seatbelt and watched it retract. For a second she thought about lunging for the gun. Then reality overrode the movie moment as she visualized Nicole's finger tightening on the trigger when she fought for control of the weapon. There wasn't much doubt where the bullet would end up.

"Get out." Nicole opened the passenger door and waved the pistol at her.

Out of the car would be better than in the car. Distance from Nicole—and her gun— improved the odds.

Nicole backed out of the car.

Should she try to reason with her? Jump out and run for it? *And go where?*

Nicole stood by the open car door, pistol at the ready. "I'm waiting."

She sounded halfway rational, but the whole scenario was insane.

Think of something, anything to distract her.

"This is a beautiful spot. I can see why you like it." On shaking legs, Holly strolled around the hood of the car, narrowing the distance to the vineyard and orchard. If she could keep the woman talking, she could buy some time until JC figured out where she was.

"I hate it. It's where Tim brings his whores. But you already know that."

"I'm sorry if Tim had a relationship with Marcy, but he's just a client to me." *Ouch, poor word choice.* "An accounting client," she amended.

Nicole laughed, a mirthless chuckle that matched the emptiness in her eyes. "At least Marcy admitted it."

"What happened with Marcy, anyway?"

"Tim's had affairs before—most men do. But Marcy actually thought she could take my husband. I couldn't let that happen. I refuse to be poor again." Nicole waved the pistol. "Move. Down to the river."

Holly stared at the gun. She didn't have to ask if the woman knew how to use it. She'd seen the results up close and personal.

How long could she stall her? Arguing with a sociopath holding a lethal weapon seemed like a bad move.

Holly's knees shook even harder. She really, really did not want to die. "Think about your baby. If you kill me, you'll go to jail. Who'll be around to raise it?"

"You think I want this kid? I only kept it this long because Tim was screwing around. The baby's my insurance policy. He'll never leave if he knows I'm knocked up."

"Then why were you buying Plan B?" she blurted out.

"Just in case." Nicole shrugged. "I'm already spotting. Tim will buy me a new Mercedes when I miscarry this one." Her face shifted to her fragile female mode. "I'll be so sad."

Holly took a step closer to the rows of grapevines, wondering how Nicole could be so cold and heartless. "You really don't want the baby?"

"Oh, please. Babies ruin your figure. All they do is scream and crap."

"But...Tim said—"

Nicole snorted. "He heard what he wanted to hear. The doctors say I probably can't carry one to term, but it's a useful way to keep Tim in line. As long as it doesn't go too far."

Holly edged closer to the vineyard. "You might want to rethink that decision." If she could really rattle her, maybe...

"Why?" Her tone carried derision rather than curiosity.

"Remember that day at the restaurant? When I met with Walt?"

Skin twitched around Nicole's eyes as the memory of the lunch meeting with the attorney registered. "So what?"

"Walt told me Tim filed divorce papers."

Nicole's porcelain skin flamed with fury. She shook the pistol at Holly. "You're such a liar. How can you stand yourself? You make up shit about everyone."

"Get out your cell phone. Call him. Ask him."

Nicole glanced at her purse, as if she were actually thinking about it.

Holly didn't need a second invitation. She turned on her heels and ran. She bypassed the grapevines. The long rows were a death trap. The narrow aisles would make her an easy target.

She'd almost made it to the orchard when a pistol blast shattered the silence. A tree limb exploded above her head. She dove under the sheltering branches of an apple tree. On hands and knees, she scrambled to get away. Another bullet tore the bark off a nearby tree.

She jumped to her feet and ran.

371

Nicole screamed at her, but the words made no sense.

Holly circled through the orchard, peering desperately through the trees as she went. *Where was Nicole?* She didn't hear any yells or gunfire, only a steady thump in the distance.

Back pressed against an apple tree, she whipped her cell from her pocket. Damn. No bars. No JC. No calling in the cops to rescue her.

If the cops weren't coming to her, she'd go to them. If she found the road, she could flag down one of the police cars that surely were prowling around out there, searching for them.

Where in the hell was the road?

The unmistakable *crunch* and *ding* of rocks pinging against a car's undercarriage came from her left.

JC! The police!

She sprinted toward the approaching vehicle and burst from the screening trees right in front of a beige Tahoe.

The SUV slid to a halt in a cloud of dust. Tim rolled down the window. Loud rock and roll poured out to greet her.

She ran toward it. "Thank God, you're here."

He turned off the ignition, killing the music, opened the door, and stepped out. "Holly? What are you doing here?"

"You have to stop her." A desperate glance revealed an empty clearing, but she heard a shout in the distance.

"What are you talking about? Stop who from doing what?"

"You honestly don't know?" She collapsed against the side of the Tahoe, trying to catch her breath. She pressed a hand to her chest, as if that would keep her heart from bursting through. "Then why are you here?"

"I came up to test the grapes. I need to check the sugar level. Why? What's going on?"

"Your wife has lost it. She thinks we're having an affair."

His jaw dropped. "What?"

"She knows about Marcy. And now she's using me for target practice."

Nicole's shouts grew louder. A bullet ricocheted off the hood of Tim's car. He flinched and spun around. "What the *hell*?"

He ducked behind the Tahoe, pulling Holly with him. "Where'd Nicole get a pistol?"

"How should I know? Talk to her. She won't shoot you."

He peered around the back fender, then turned back to her. "Wait. Are you saying—"

She watched emotions flicker as he fought to catch up.

"Oh, my God." Blood drained from his face.

"Yeah," she said. "Nicole probably shot Marcy. And that black SUV you're missing? Your wife probably borrowed it. Look, I don't care if you were having an affair. Nicole obviously had a problem with that, but you have to convince her there is nothing going on between you and me."

He stared at her. "Let me think about this."

"Are you *kidding* me?"

Turning, he jammed his fingers through his hair. "Nicole killed Marcy?"

"It sure looks that way."

"Oh, fuck." He paced the length of the car.

She risked a glance around the corner of the car. Nicole stood at the far side of the clearing, apparently consulting the committee in her head about her next move.

"You realize what this means." Tim was suddenly right behind Holly, his voice an octave higher than normal.

"Yeah. It means we need to climb in your car and get the hell out of here."

Nicole pointed the pistol at the Tahoe and fired. Window glass exploded.

"Shit," Tim yelped. They ducked, pressing in close to the rear tire.

"Come on. Let's go while we still can." Holly reached for the passenger door handle.

"Not a chance. You'll ruin everything." Tim's voice screeched in her ear.

"What's that supposed to mean?" She cut him an incredulous look.

"I know you know about the loans. First thing Monday morning, you're probably going to call the banks and tell them about the extra companies."

Well, yeah, but she certainly wasn't going to admit it right now. "What are you talking about?"

"It wasn't my fault. The banks made it too easy. Everything was fine until credit just dried up. I'll figure it out, but if you walk out of here alive, I'm screwed. You'll send my wife to prison for murder and me to jail for a couple of bad business decisions."

Holly scrambled backward. The dirt lane suddenly looked a lot safer than the Tahoe's shadow. "You can't be serious."

He stalked after her. "You realize this isn't personal, right?"

Chapter Forty-nine

"Tim." Holly backed away from the Tahoe. "You're talking about *murder*. The premeditated kind."

"You don't give me much choice."

The man was as nuts as his wife. "Of course you have a choice. Do it and you'll fry." She sprinted up the dirt road.

Tim lunged and caught her wrist. He dragged her backward, then shoved.

She skidded across the driveway, adding a new layer of scrapes and bruises. Sprawled on the ground beside the SUV, she lay directly in Nicole's line of sight.

Oh, crap.

Nicole pointed, yelled, and a bullet pinged off the Tahoe's fender.

Holly scrambled to her feet and dove behind the metal barrier.

"Everything was going great. Why couldn't you just go along?" Tim locked onto her arm again.

"Who me? With what?" Holly ping-ponged her attention between Nicole and Tim. "Wait a minute. Are you talking about Alex?"

"You're divorcing me?" Nicole yelled, redirecting her rage at Tim.

"Was Alex part of it?" If she was going to die, she wanted a few answers first.

"What the hell has Alex got to do with anything?" Tim peeked over the fender at his wife. "Of course I'm not divorcing you, honey. I love you."

"With the fraud. Your stealing." Holly jerked against Tim's hold. Where could she go if she broke free? "Did you use Alex to flush money back into the system? Was that why you pushed so hard to get us together?"

Tim scowled. "You screwed up things with Alex all by yourself. That boy's going places and you dumped him for some two-bit cop."

"Money isn't everything."

"Since when?"

The rhythmic thump Holly had noticed earlier grew louder, and a helicopter buzzed over the tree line. An amplified voice called, "This is the police. Drop your weapon."

That command only works on sane people, competed with, *Thank you, God.*

Her relief was short-lived. Tim shoved her again. She grabbed the fender and hung on.

"Let go." He jerked at her arms.

Hell no. She kicked him, but her sneakers didn't make a dent in his determination. His fingers tightened around her wrist and wrestled her injured hand from the fender. She shrieked in pain and slammed her shoe into his groin.

He yelped and staggered back, hunched around his pain, but he didn't release her wrist. "Goddamn you."

The chopper swooped lower, raising a cloud of dirt and fine pebbles. A man shouted through the loudspeaker. "Drop it *now!*"

"You *bastard.*" Nicole's shrill voice cut through the bedlam.

Tim halted warily, one hand still clutching the family jewels.

"She's yelling at *you*, asshole," Holly said. "Maybe you should rethink your throw-me-to-the-wolves plan."

"Me?" His head turned toward Nicole. "Why's she yelling at me?"

"You'd leave me for that *whore?*" Nicole was already halfway across the clearing. She squeezed off another round. More parts of the Tahoe shattered.

Tim dropped to the ground, jerking Holly with him.

"Do something! Say something," she urged.

Tim looked like a deer caught in the headlights. Finally, he rose to his knees and peeked through the mangled rear window. "Honey?"

"Why?" Nicole stood less than ten feet away. Tears streamed down her face.

The plaintive question tore at Holly's heart, but she wasn't waiting around for the next act. She took a step toward the orchard but Tim whipped out a hand and grabbed her again. He locked an arm around her waist.

"We had a good life—a perfect life. I made it perfect for you." Anguish twisted Nicole's features.

Tim dragged Holly back to the car and held her clamped against his chest, a human shield. "Sweetheart, I know that."

"You coward." Holly writhed in his grip, a helpless hostage. "Be a man for once in your life."

The cops in the helicopter were still yelling over the loudspeaker, but no one paid any attention to them.

Tim's wife advanced on him. Judging from the expression on Nicole's face, Holly didn't even exist anymore.

Tim had her arms pinned. She stomped on his foot again, but her sneakers didn't stand a chance against his work boots. In desperation, she tucked her chin and slammed her head backward into his face.

"God*dammit.*"

She heard his roar through a haze of stars and pain. He clamped down on her body until she could barely breathe.

Nicole braced a hand against the Tahoe's hood, the pistol pointing at Tim. The only problem with that arrangement was Holly was in front of him, right in the line of fire.

The helicopter changed position and hovered behind Tim and her. "Drop your weapon *now*," a male voice thundered.

Like that worked the first time?

A rifle blast split the air.

A pistol shot echoed it.

Holly screamed. Tim dodged away from the flying bullets, dragging her down with him. When she opened her eyes, Nicole no longer stood on the other side of the car.

"Nicole." Tim threw Holly aside and raced around the Tahoe.

Holly took off in the other direction, straight toward the police cars barreling down the dirt road.

Cops were everywhere.

Uniformed officers spread out, swarming the grounds. Several disappeared inside the farm building, while others examined a damaged white truck. Another group focused on the Kia. Two cops deposited a handcuffed Tim into the back seat of a cruiser. More officers surrounded Nicole. Her plaintive calls for Tim rose above the noise of auto engines, men's voices, and the whump of helicopter blades.

Holly turned, trying to see everything at once. *Where was he?* He'd said he was coming.

Strong hands grabbed her by the shoulders and whirled her around. JC stood face to face with her. Relief surged through her entire body. She didn't know whether to laugh or cry.

"About time you got here." Her voice quavered too much for the words to pack much punch.

He shook her. "I don't know whether to throttle you or...or..."

"Getting shot at by the crazy lady wasn't my idea." She reached out, curling her fingers to clutch his jacket, wanting very badly to reach under it, to feel his flesh, warm and alive and real against her own. But anything more would probably embarrass him and make her feel like a fool and—

His arms closed around her and he pulled her close. "You scared the crap out of me," he whispered into her hair. "All I wanted was to know you were safe."

"Safe? Is that all?"

"Jesus, Holly. I don't want to think about a world without you in it."

Much better. She slid her arms around his waist and rested her head on his shoulder. He didn't seem to mind in the least. Instead, his arms tightened and she felt...protected.

And cherished.

A few synapses fired in her brain. Hope poked up its inquisitive head and announced, *This is the behavior of a man worried about his woman.*

For the first time, *his woman* had a nice ring to it. She raised her head and studied his expression. It had moved past furious to something that sped up her heart rate.

"When I realized what was going on in that car—ah, hell." He brought his mouth down on hers in a crushing kiss. Neither cared that a dozen uniformed officers stood and watched them.

A long time later he came up for air. "Don't you ever, ever, do that to me again." He punctuated his words with gentle shakes.

"I promise to never again go joyriding with the psycho wife

of a sleazeball client."

His eyebrows clashed. "Holly."

Arms wrapped around his waist, she smiled at him until at least part of the tension left his body. "We need some new rules in this relationship. But don't think you can decide all of them."

A slow smile turned up the corners of his mouth. "How about in our vows we make it fifty-fifty?"

Vows? Her mouth fell open but no words emerged. She swallowed and tried again. "How about we start with dating?"

Both dimples appeared. "As a negotiator, you should know to go for the moon with your first position." He dropped a kiss on her lips. "You just have to know what you *really* want. And how to ask for it."

She smiled back, seeing the moon and the stars in his eyes. Oh, yeah. First position sounded good.

For starters.

Her phone rang.

Her gaze moved from his face to her jacket pocket. "*Now* it works?"

The Bluetooth device was somewhere in the orchard. She pulled out the phone and clicked it on. "Your maternal instinct's working sorta slow this morning," she told her mother.

"What are you talking about? I thought you were meeting me at the office."

She glanced at JC and smiled wider, thinking of all the negotiating positions she wanted to try out with him. "Yeah, about that. I may be a little late."

The End

Thank you for reading So About the Money.

If you enjoyed Holly and JC's story:

Review it. Tell other readers why you liked this book by reviewing it at Amazon, Barnes & Noble, iBooks, or Kobo. Goodreads is another excellent review site.

Read another one of my books. For more information, please go here http://cperkinswrites.com

Want advance notice for my next release? Stop by and sign up for the new release announcement newsletter on my website or Facebook page.

Thanks for reading!
Cathy

Coming soon:

The Rockcrawler Book, second in the Holly Price Mystery series

Malbec Mayhem, a novella linked to the Holly Price Mystery series

About the Author

An award-winning author, Cathy Perkins works in the financial industry, where she's observed the hide-in-plain-sight skills employed by her villains. She writes predominantly financial-based mysteries but enjoys exploring the relationship aspect of her characters' lives. A member of Sisters in Crime, Romance Writers of America (Kiss of Death chapter) and International Thriller Writers, she is a contributing editor for The Big Thrill, handles the blog and social media for the ITW Debut Authors, and coordinates the prestigious Daphne du Maurier Award for Excellence in Mystery/Suspense.

When not writing, she can be found doing battle with the beavers over the pond height or setting off on another travel adventure. Born and raised in South Carolina, the setting for HONOR CODE, THE PROFESSOR and CYPHER, she now lives in Washington with her husband, children, several dogs and the resident deer herd.

You can find her on the web at www.cperkinswrites.com or catch her hanging out at Facebook and Twitter.